Jesse McMinn is a Canadian writer, programmer and fantasy enthusiast who is drawn to creativity in all of its forms. After spending much of 2015 travelling Europe and Asia, he moved back to his home province of Ontario, Canada, where he currently lives and works.

Book 2 of the *Tower* Series

Trials

by

Jesse McMinn

Trials

ISBN-13: 978-1-925496-17-8

V1.1

Melbourne, Australia
IFWG Publishing International
www.ifwgpublishing.com

To mom and Nanny, for being my biggest fans; to dad and Emily, for surrounding me with books; and to Nicole, who's stood by me all these years.

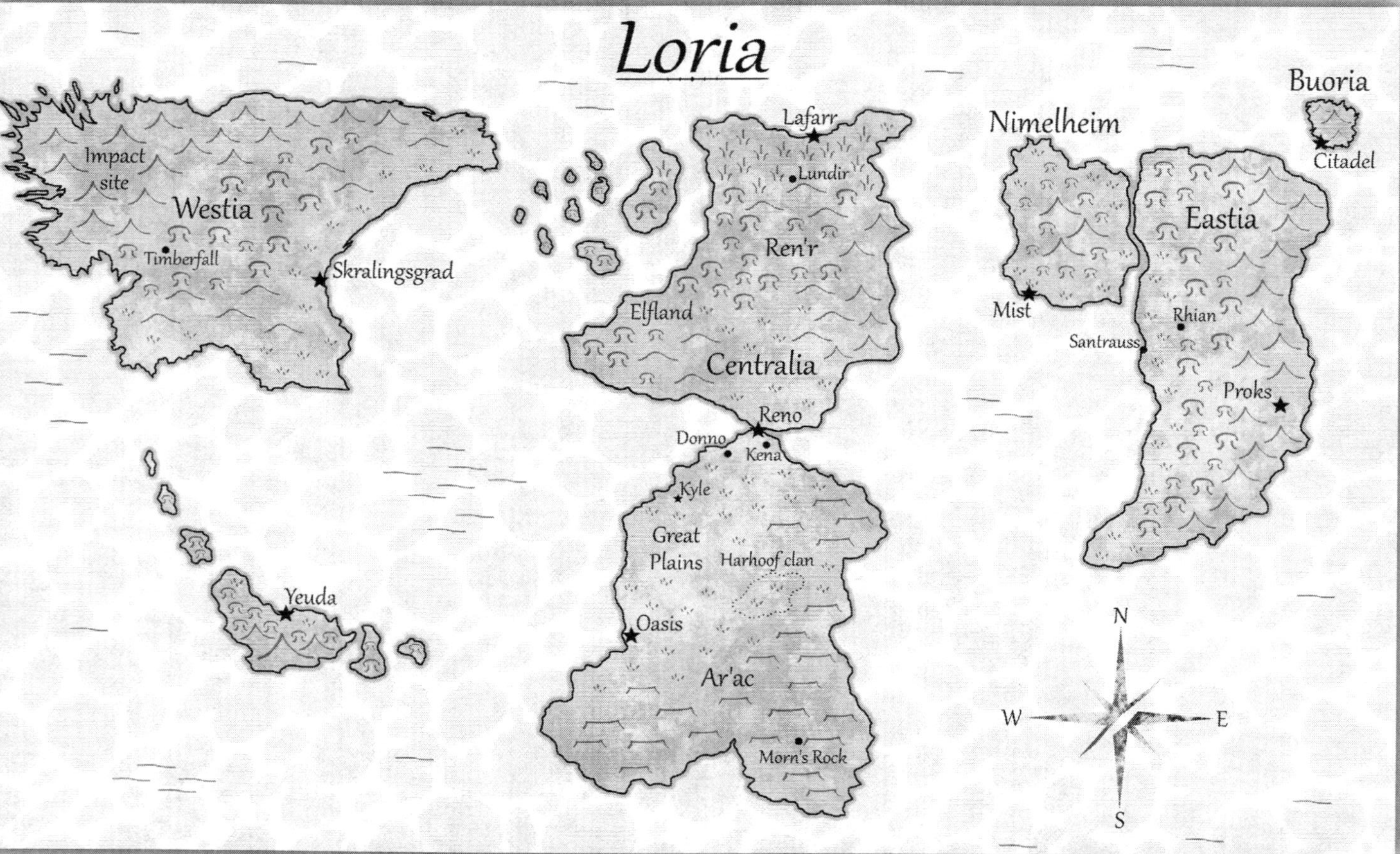
Loria
Impact site
Westia
Timberfall
Skralingsgrad
Yeuda
Lafarr
Lundir
Ren'r
Elfland
Centralia
Reno
Donno
Kena
Kyle
Great Plains
Harhoof clan
Oasis
Ar'ac
Mørn's Rock
Nimelheim
Mist
Buoria
Citadel
Eastia
Rhian
Santrauss
Proks
N
W
E
S

Kyle Campbell, twenty-six-year-old former database developer and current adventurer-in-training, slid out of bed as quietly as possible and began to dress.

Next to him, his companion Lughenor MacAlden was doing the same. Lugh was a fairly normal person, if one considered him in terms of what was thought of as normal where he was from. He could even have passed for human on a dark day, albeit one who was unnaturally tall and possessed an extra set of ears.

On Kyle's other side was Nihs Ken Dal Proks. Two feet tall, one hundred and six years old, bald, and green, Nihs was rather more difficult to confuse with a human. He was already dressed, and was watching his companions' progress with mingled smugness and impatience. From the sides of his head sprung two odd growths, a pair of curled green tentacles tapered towards the tip. Anyone who was familiar with Nihs or his folk knew that these were a special set of ears that allowed him to speak with the others of his race no matter where they might be.

Finally, at the far end of the room, taking up as much space as the previous three combined, was Rogan Harhoof. Rogan was a Minotaur, one of the furred, horned and hooved denizens of the southern plains. He was a wise, grave creature whose quietness belied an unbelievable strength. Today, his morning ritual was tinged with sadness. Only yesterday had he learned of the death of his father, Ravigan. It was not just a personal loss, but a political one: Ravigan Harhoof had been the chieftain of his clan, and his death had left his people leaderless. It was up to his son to settle the disputes that had arisen in the plains because of this, and so it was that Rogan would soon be parting ways with his companions.

The plains were not the destination of Kyle, Lugh, and Nihs. They would be traveling east, across the ocean, to meet with the elders of Nihs' race and to see if Kyle's unique situation could be better understood.

Kyle paused in reflection. *My unique situation.* That was certainly a way of putting it. Only a week ago had he been aboard the *SS Caribia*, a cruise ship on an Atlantic voyage to nowhere. Now, he was as far away from his hometown of Cleveland, Ohio as was physically possible. He was in Reno, the biggest city in the world of Loria, the strange new land he had found himself in after falling off the *Caribia.* Since he had arrived in Loria, he had learned swordplay and magic, had suffered a goblin-inflicted wound, and had flown through the air in a golden ship named the *Ayger.*

And now someone was after him. Yesterday, he and Lugh had been captured by a group of men who had known about Kyle's origins. They had escaped, narrowly, and it was the opinion of his companions that they were all still in danger.

And that was why they were now leaving the city—quickly, quietly, and before the sun rose. If all went well, they would be aboard the *Ayger* and off to Eastia before their enemies knew they were gone.

Once they had all dressed, they crept downstairs to meet with their new employers. Meya was a cleric of the church of Saint Iila, a human woman with piercing red eyes and hair to match. Her companion, Phundasa, was an Orcish wrestler. Kyle knew little about them. They had only just met the night before, and all things considered, the introductions had been somewhat rushed.

Against Lugh's protests, the group decided to eat a brief breakfast before they left the city, and Kyle had the chance to study the newcomers more closely. Meya was slight, and about his height. She wore a flowing, dress-like suit of white that identified her as a healer. She was quiet and polite, a small pocket of femininity in the rougher atmosphere of the adventurer's hideout. Phundasa could not have appeared more different. His garb was simple: a pair of serviceable short pants and a sleeveless black shirt. His arms were heavily muscled, and his hair, jet-black, was tied in a ponytail behind his head. His eyes glittered like a wildcat's, and the short tusks that jutted up from his lower jaw lent him a fearsome cast.

Meya and Phundasa did not know Kyle's story. They were only traveling with the group as far as Rhian, a city near the coast of Eastia, and Kyle and his companions had agreed that the fewer people who knew about him, the better.

They ate quickly, and left the hideout for the streets of Reno. It was a chilly morning for early summer, and a light mist took the edge off of the morning sun. The world as a whole was muffled as they made their way down to the airdocks. Kyle was tense and excited. He was eager to be back aboard the *Ayger*, on his way to the Kol's homeland. Reno had been interesting, but something inside of him was urging him on, telling him to keep moving.

He found himself walking alongside Lugh at the front of the group.

"Nice day to be out, huh?" Lugh said in a low voice.

"M-hm."

"Reno's a cool place," he continued, looking around and nodding, "but I wouldn't want to live here. Then again, I really wouldn't want to live anywhere. Keep moving, sleep in a different bed every night, that's the way I like it. The world never gets boring that way."

Kyle nodded his agreement. "Have you ever been to Proks?"

Lugh shook his head. "When I met Nihs, he'd already left the city, and the truth is there's no reason for a guy like me to be there. No one lives there but the Kol…it's not like here, where you can see all ten races walking down the same street."

"Nihs said it was underground."

"That's right. Most of the Kol cities are. Remember how I said Loria's full of caves? Well, some of the biggest are under the mountains in Eastia. Apparently, the first Kol learned the secret of magic by listening to echoes of the gods' voices down in the caves."

"Is that true?"

Lugh laughed shortly. "Not even the Kol know that."

They walked down to the waterfront and climbed the massive scaffold that led into the airdocks. Despite the time of day, they were buzzing with activity. Workers moved about on the catwalks that lined the insides of the docks, and ships arriving and departing filled the empty space with the sound of roaring engines.

The *Ayger* came into view as they made their way along the catwalk. The ship made for a rather fantastic sight, even compared to the thousands of others, with which it shared the hangar. Two massive, folded golden wings framed the teardrop-shaped hull, and the entire ship gleamed gold in the gloom of the airdocks. At times like these, Kyle could understand why Lugh was so proud of it.

They stopped to bid farewell to Rogan, who would be making his own way out of the city. Meya shook his massive hand; Phundasa bowed and said, "Though I may not be as skilled a sailor as you, I promise to take good care of the *Ayger*."

Rogan nodded in acknowledgment and ruffled the hair that Nihs did not have. Nihs hissed and swatted at Rogan's hand, though he did wish Rogan good-bye once the offending arm had been withdrawn.

Lugh held out his hand. "Good luck on the plains, friend," he said. He winced as Rogan gripped it. "It's been a pleasure adventuring with you."

"That it has," Rogan agreed. "Perhaps we'll meet again someday. The world is not so vast that a Minotaur and Selk who were once friends may never see each other again."

"Too true," Lugh said.

Rogan then turned to Kyle. "Little one," he said gravely, "I wish you the best of luck. I see great potential in you. Do not waste it." He held out a massive hand.

"Thanks," Kyle said, taking it. He was sad to see Rogan go. He had come to rely on the Minotaur's reassuring presence in the group.

Rogan backed away from them, cupping one hand in the other and touching them to his forelock in an exotic bow. Then he turned and left.

They boarded the *Ayger*, and Lugh immediately took the opportunity to show it off to Meya and Phundasa. After a brief tour, Phundasa departed to oversee the engine, while Meya followed the others onto the bridge. Kyle couldn't help but feel uneasy around her. He found her red coloring intimidating—particularly her eyes, which were bright and piercing. It didn't help that up until now, Lugh, Nihs and Rogan had been the only Lorians Kyle had dealt with. Now, he was faced with the prospect of sharing a voyage with a couple of strangers.

Meya looked around the bridge once they had arrived. "This is quite the ship," she said.

Lugh grinned from ear to ear. "Isn't it?"

"We weren't expecting anything like this when we posted the job. I feel like we're robbing you."

"No worries—we were headed to Eastia anyway."

Kyle felt a tugging at his pant leg. He peered down and saw Nihs looking back up at him.

"Lugh's at the wheel," he said, "mind giving me a boost?"

"Uh. Sure."

Nihs immediately latched onto his arm and shimmied up his body, coming to rest on his shoulder. Kyle grit his teeth and had to resist a very strong urge to throw Nihs off; his clawed fingers and toes dug into Kyle's skin on his way up. Once Nihs had settled on his shoulder, however, Kyle was oddly happy to serve as a vehicle—he felt as though he'd been entrusted with an important duty that usually fell to Lugh or Rogan.

They all gathered around the control panel as Lugh prepared to launch the *Ayger*. He set his hand on the communicator and called down to Phundasa.

"Hey Foombasa, we ready to take off?"

"At your order."

Lugh nodded and set his hand on the throttle. "All right, let's make this clean and mean."

They lifted off. Kyle was exhilarated; he had already come to love the moment when the *Ayger* rose into the sky and left the earth behind. They were moving again, heading off to adventure and—hopefully—answers. As they left the airdock colloquially known as the honeycomb, Kyle walked down to the observation deck to watch Centralia bay scroll by beneath them.

After a short while, the ship's movement slowed, and Kyle frowned.

"What's going on?" he said.

"Lugh's going to put us on a flight path that will take us to Eastia," Nihs said. "It'll make our trip shorter, and Lugh won't have to steer."

"Oh, right."

He heard Lugh talking into the communication crystal on the control panel; he couldn't make out what Lugh was saying, but the voice that answered, amplified by the crystal, was clear.

"This is the Buorish Travel Company. Your airship has been cleared to follow flight path number six-eighty-seven to Rhian, Eastia. Please disengage any autopilot and refrain from touching the airship controls while the flight path is being activated. Thank you."

A moment later, the *Ayger*'s engine hummed into greater life and the ship turned about smartly, heading eastwards on its own.

"How long will it take us to get to Proks?" Kyle asked Nihs.

"About four days, with the help of the flight path. Of course we'll have to drop Meya and Phundasa off first, but that won't take long."

"Who'll watch the engine once Phundasa's gone?"

"You don't actually need someone down in the engine room while the ship is running—it's merely useful. Lugh can spend some time down there when necessary, and I'll handle the helm. We used to do it that way all the time before we met Rogan."

"When *did* you meet Rogan?" Kyle asked.

Nihs tapped his chin. "It was in northern Ar'ac, about a year ago. He was traveling north, out of his homeland. He never did get around to telling us the story of why he left, come to think of it. Apparently he had learned something about being a sailor from a friend, so we took him on. It turned out to be one of the best decisions we ever made. I do believe I'll miss him now that he's gone."

There was a movement to Kyle's left. He jumped slightly when he saw Meya approach from his periphery. Nihs yelped, claws digging in to keep balance.

"Oh, I'm sorry," she said.

"No problem," Kyle said, feeling foolish. He went back to staring out of the window.

"Quite the view, isn't it," Meya said. "I haven't had the opportunity to fly very often in my travels…and never in a ship like this. If I were Lugh I'd be very proud of it."

Nihs' voice was dry. "Oh, that he is."

"I heard that you were traveling to Proks afterwards?"

"Yes, that's right," Nihs said.

Kyle said nothing. He was unnerved. Meya's red eyes were piercing, and even though he knew she couldn't have any involvement with the people who were after him, he didn't like where her questions might go.

"I've been to a few Kol cities before," she said, "but never Proks. What's it like? Anything like Sirkan or Kisset?"

"Hardly," Nihs said. "To begin with, it's many times larger than either. And it's much older—or at least, the city core in eastern Proks is. That is where the five great council chambers are, and the dwelling places of our elders. The west is where the less traditional Kol live. The caves there are filled with giant mushrooms, and most of the dwellings are built upon or around them."

"I'd love to see that," Meya said. "Is that where you're from?"

"Yes, my family is from eastern Proks," Nihs replied. Kyle, because he was prepared for it, heard the tension in Nihs' voice. He wondered what it was about Nihs' family that caused him to act that way every time it was mentioned.

"How about you?" Meya asked Kyle politely. "Where are you from?"

Damn, Kyle thought. He should have been ready for this.

"Kena, originally," he said, naming one of the boroughs that surrounded Reno city. "I don't go back to visit very often."

Meya smiled thinly. "I've heard that before. Didn't like the city?"

For some reason, Kyle found himself thinking about his hometown of Cleveland. "Couldn't wait to leave," he said.

Meya left the observation deck a few moments later. Nihs kept his face blank until she was out of sight, at which point he said,

"Let's hope her curiosity is sated, or the next couple of days are going to be very tense."

"Agreed."

The *Ayger* turned in a lazy circle, rising over the forest of steel and glass that was Reno city. Even half-obscured by the early morning fog, Reno was a fantastic sight. The buildings grew thicker and taller as they flew over the city's core. Then, a sight came into view that put all the rest of Reno to shame.

"That's Sky Tower," Nihs said softly.

The tower was simply too big to be allowed, too big to be real. Its base was a massive oblong dome of glass and steel, a complex that was in itself the size of a small town. Although it was currently empty, it was designed to accommodate over a thousand stores and hundreds of thousands of people—a construction that would rival Reno's current market district when complete. The tower rose stories and stories above the rest of Reno's skyline. Buildings that had looked massive before were dwarfed by the skyscraper's appearance. It was a beautiful building, perfectly symmetrical, soaring effortlessly into the open air. The sun reflected off the thousands of windows that lined its exterior. Sky Tower, the top of its spire lost in the clouds above, gleamed.

Kyle felt a thrill of fear in his gut as they passed under the structure's shadow. This was where he and Lugh had been held prisoner just a few hours before—though they were unsure who had ordered the assault, the owner of the building, James Livaldi, was a prime suspect. Kyle had the strange feeling that the building was watching them as they passed by, and he was tremendously relieved once it was out of sight.

A multitude of bridges connected Reno's core to the rest of the city on the coast nearby. Kyle couldn't believe how much of it they had yet to see. Finally, they left the city behind and flew out over Centralia's countryside. Hundreds of feet below them was a wide, complex canal system designed to let ships pass between the continents of Ren'r and Ar'ac on their way to the Eastern Ocean.

Kyle and Nihs left the observation deck shortly after, to keep Lugh's company at the helm. He was standing behind the wheel, arms folded, watching it turn on its own.

"Autopilot always gives me the creeps," he told them. "I hate feeling like I should be doing something. Hey, Kyle, why don't we get some training done?"

"Sure," Kyle said.

"Oh, and I'll just watch the helm," Nihs said, his tone scathing.

"Good man. Come on, Kyle, time to toughen you up some more."

The *Ayger's* ballroom had some time ago been converted to suit the adventurer's lifestyle. It now served as both a training room and as a storage space for the hoard of equipment that Lugh and his friends had accumulated over the years. Weapons, armor, and training equipment were all piled haphazardly in the huge space, with an area left in the center for sparring. Lugh fetched his golden retrasword from a corner and faced Kyle across the room.

"All right," he said. "Today I teach you some of the fighter's tricks of the trade. It's going to get a little complicated, so forgive me if I start sounding like Nihs.

"You already know how gaiden strikes work—the energy builds up as you fight, then you release it all at once. Well, the truth is, gaiden's just one of the energies that we fighters use. There's others—force and strike, and keen and reflex. They all build up in different ways. After all, they're a kind of magic, and different types of magic all behave their own way. Right?"

"All right," Kyle said, though without much confidence. He never would have believed that fighting could be so complicated.

Lugh laughed. "Don't think about it too hard. Just remember that you won't be able to use all your techniques as soon as a fight starts. You have to give the energy time to gather, and then release it when the time comes. Let's fight a bit and I'll show you what I mean."

They did just that, drilling all of the techniques that Kyle had been taught before. Though combat was already coming easier to him, he had a long way to go before he'd be anywhere near as powerful as the others.

Lugh stopped them after a couple of minutes.

"All right," he said, "first kind of energy I'll show you is called strike. You hit something with your weapon, strike builds up. That can be an enemy's weapon, their armor, whatever. Once strike builds up, you can release it as pure force. Like this."

Lugh swung his leg backwards, then forwards and up, letting the momentum bring him into a jump. As he rose, one knee in the air, Kyle felt the atmosphere in the room change. The air grew thick, Lugh's movement slowed, and a faint creaking noise, like the groan of an ancient tree, reached Kyle's ears. When Lugh's foot came down, a huge impact shook the equipment on the walls and knocked Kyle off his feet. He landed hard on his back while the floor underneath him trembled in the aftershock.

"Whoa," he said.

Lugh grinned, and walked over to help him up. "That's called a stomp," he said. "Shakes people off balance, makes your enemy drop their guard, and scares the hell out of monsters. Now you try one."

"How do you do it?" Kyle asked.

"Same way you saw me do it. Feel the energy, and will it to happen. It's like magic in that way. No trick to making it work; just will."

Kyle, dubious, swung his leg back as he had seen Lugh do, but his friend stopped him immediately.

"No, no, no. You need to *feel* heavy when you do it. Know you're going into a stomp before you even start moving. Take your time. Think heavy thoughts."

Kyle nodded vaguely, trying to juggle everything that Lugh had told him. He recalled what it had felt like when Lugh had stomped—the ponderous swing of the leg, the creaking, groaning sound…

He swung his leg back, around and up. He knew it had worked from the moment he started to rise. He *did* feel heavy, as though the foot he was bringing into the air was far denser than it should be. He thrust it downwards as he fell, and it struck the floor with a satisfying crash. It wasn't as powerful as Lugh's stomp had been, but it was enough to make the room shake with the impact.

"Ha!" he said, pleased.

Lugh smiled and gave him a thumbs-up.

A second later, the communicator crystal on the wall nearby crackled to life, and Nihs' angry voice rang throughout the room.

"Tesh*ur!* What are you two doing down there? You're making the whole ship shake!"

"Oops," Lugh said, not sounding particularly mortified. He put his hand on the crystal. "It's all right, Nihs, we're learning how to stomp."

"Would you like to *learn* how to give the rest of us a heart attack while you're at it? How about *learning* to pay for repairs to the ship?"

"All right, all right, keep your pants on, we'll practice something else." He let his hand fall, and the crystal's glow faded. "Well done, Kyle. You made Nihs angry, which is always a sign that you're doing it right. Let's move on to something else—but first, try stomping again."

"But Nihs said—"

"I know. Just try it."

Kyle did, and immediately understood the lesson that Lugh had intended. The force that had built up during his last stomp was simply no longer there. It was like trying to drink from a glass that he knew was empty.

"That's why you won't see fighters using the same technique over and over again," Lugh told him. "Even if you have enough energy built up for a second go, it won't be as powerful as it was the first time. Cycle through what you know, keep your moves fresh, and you won't run into that problem. Now let's teach you some more."

They sparred for quite a long while. Because Lugh kept stopping them to show Kyle new techniques, Kyle did not tire as quickly as he usually did. Lugh taught him how to lend his blows extra strength, how to sense and dodge attacks using an energy called reflex, and how to perform parries that would violently knock an opponent's weapon aside.

As Lugh taught him more and more, Kyle began to understand what he had been seeing when watching the others fight. In a duel between adventurers, the act of exchanging normal blows was merely filler, a background to the true core of combat—the constant accumulation and strategic release of combat energy. Kyle's brain hurt almost as much as his arm as he tried to recall and apply everything he had learned. It was exhausting, but when they finally called it a day and returned to the bridge, Kyle was satisfied. He was excited to improve, and almost wished that he would get the opportunity to try out his newfound techniques.

By the time they returned to the bridge a vast expanse of water was dominating the view from the *Ayger*'s starboard side. It must have been the ocean, as Kyle could not see land on the far horizon. The ship was hugging the coast to its left, still following the route that the Buorish Travel Company had mapped out for it.

Nihs, sitting on the stool that he used when piloting the *Ayger*, was chatting with Meya. Phundasa was also contributing to the conversation, his voice occasionally coming through the communicator.

"Anything to report?" Lugh asked, striding forward to gaze out the picture window.

"Nothing much," Nihs replied. "It's been rather peaceful, despite your efforts to the contrary."

"We had to practice," Lugh said. He appealed to Meya, "You don't learn anything by standing around and talking, do you?"

Meya smiled at him. "Of course not."

Nihs harrumphed.

"By the way," Meya said, "what do you do for fun while you're traveling? It's a long way to Rhian."

"This and that," Lugh said. "Did you have something in mind?"

"What do you think about a game of cards? Das loves them, so we play quite a bit."

"Sounds good to me. Call him up, I'll grab my deck. What are we playing—Siege?"

Meya nodded. "That's a good one for five people." She touched her hand to the crystal on the control panel. "Das! We're going to play cards. Why don't you come up?"

"Will do!" came the hasty reply.

Meya laughed. "He's excellent and I'm terrible, so it's always fun when I manage to win."

"You've never played Siege before, have you, Kyle?" Lugh asked him.

"No, I haven't."

"Well, I'll have to teach you, then."

"Yes," Nihs said sourly, "Lugh will teach you how to sabotage me at every possible turn."

"It wouldn't be any fun if I couldn't annoy you."

Later, in Lugh's massive master bedroom, they were playing Siege. The game, as Kyle understood it, went like this:

First, you were dealt a hand of cards from a deck of sixty. Every card in the deck was unique, and featured a picture of some character or profession—familiar cards such as the queen and king were accompanied by the wizard, the mason, the wanderer, and the knight. Each card had its own unique effect, though Kyle had no chance of remembering them all and couldn't fathom how the others managed.

Second, you sat in a circle and took turns playing cards either into your, or an opponent's, cache, which was a fancy way of saying the table in front of them. As for which cards should go where if one intended to win, Kyle had no idea. He tried to follow Lugh's lead, but most of his plays resulted in Nihs swearing in Kollic and making an obscene gesture in his direction—and Kyle had the sneaking suspicion that this was not the primary goal of the game.

As they continued to play, however, Kyle slowly began to understand what was going on, and even started to enjoy himself. The object of the game was to capture the deck's single king, which was dealt into the center of the table at the beginning of the round. One had to build their own cache in such a way that this became possible, while sabotaging the efforts of the other players. Phundasa was clearly very enthusiastic and very skilled, although the game's element of chance kept him from winning every round. Kyle surmised that Lugh was also quite good, but given the choice would always choose irritating Nihs over victory. Meya, Kyle suspected, was only slightly more skilled than he, although she seemed to achieve victory quite often for the way she played. He also learned the hard way that she could be just as ruthless as the others when it came to sabotaging each other's plays.

All in all, it was a good day. Lugh left at one point to prepare some adventurer-style cooking for the party, which they ate in complete informality sprawled here and there in his room. Kyle was amazed at how quickly it had grown dark; he was still unused to Loria's shorter days and nights. They played cards for a while longer, and then sat and talked once the game fell apart. Meya, Phundasa, Lugh and Nihs swapped old adventuring stories, while Kyle ate and listened. It sounded like a fascinating life—moving from place to place, working contract after contract, each one different from the last. Soon there was almost no light coming in from the window above Lugh's bed.

Kyle had warmed up to the newcomers considerably. He had gotten more used to Meya's presence, and had discovered under Phundasa's fearsome exterior an Orc with a great sense of humor.

Nihs was the first to bid them all goodnight, followed soon after by Meya. Lugh and Phundasa got into a conversation about politics and news from around the world; Kyle had little to contribute, though he listened with interest. Finally it was agreed that everyone was tired, and that they should call it a night.

Kyle was exhausted once he finally flopped down in his bed. He wondered if it was still because of his reursis, the magic deprivation he had suffered when coming to Loria. He wasn't complaining. He had always had problems falling asleep back on Earth, but here, sleep was always upon him before he even realized it…

Kyle's first crush had begun somewhere in the midst of grade seven. Her name was Jennifer, and she was a tall, pretty, and smart brunette in Kyle's grade. He was completely unprepared for any forays into romance; none of his classmates were the least bit capable in that respect, and Kyle wouldn't have gone to his mother for help even if he believed her capable of providing it. As such, for some time Kyle's relationship with Jennifer did not progress beyond his infatuation.

After all, Kyle reasoned, it wasn't as though there was anything attractive about him. He had no special talents, unlike the many students who acted, played music, excelled in sports, or got extremely high grades at school. It never occurred to Kyle to examine the fact that Jennifer herself was quite the same in that respect, except, of course, for her beauty, which many of the other boys in Kyle's grade had noticed.

It was difficult to listen to the other boys—Kyle had long since stopped referring to them as his friends—talk about Jennifer. He had told none of them about how he felt, of course, but it irritated him nonetheless to hear them list off all of the girls in the grade, rating them, and throwing Jennifer's name somewhere in halfway as though she were no more important than the rest. For a while, Kyle saw her as little less than a goddess, a kind of golden, untouchable figure that floated miles above him. Whenever she happened to speak with him, whether about some inane subject that Kyle had brought up or a school-related problem, it left Kyle with a euphoric feeling that stayed with him for the rest of the day. But he was never bold enough to go farther; more than anything else, he wanted to spare himself the embarrassment of being turned down.

Frustrated by the situation, Kyle began examining ways of making himself more desirable to women. Sports were instantly out. Kyle hated them, as well as the people who played them. He was no good at them, or at least had never bothered to be. Second to be discarded were arts of any kind. Kyle was not interested in music and realized that as cool as being able to play an instrument would be, he did not own any and his mother didn't have money for lessons.

Kyle's mental train slowed down. What about money itself? Money would help with everything. It would buy him presents, better clothing, the latest gadgets, even a car, once he was old enough to drive one. Why hadn't he thought of it before?

Of course, there was a problem. Kyle was only thirteen, and wouldn't be able to work legally until the following summer. But he knew that if he searched hard enough, he would find an employer willing to pay him under the table. After only a couple weeks of searching, he was proven right.

And so it was that during the summer of grade seven, Kyle worked. His first job was at a local fast food store. It was as far down the ladder as possible to be, but Kyle didn't care. He enjoyed work immensely. He worked full-time hours and took on every possible extra shift. To him, it was ideal. He was out of the house, away from the depressing presence that was his mother, and had something to do during the long, boring summer hours. He was also making money; not much by adult standards, but much more than he had ever had access to before in his life. It was indescribably empowering.

Though he hated the actual work his job entailed—feeding terrible food to annoying customers in the back of a sweltering store—he loved the results. The thought of his bank account filling up slightly with every hour allowed him to smile at the legions of customers he dealt with every day. He was also very good at his job. By the end of the summer, thirteen-year-old Kyle was already one of the most capable employees in the store. This made his boss, a sour old skinflint of a man, extremely happy; he was paying less than minimum wage for a performance that he had to struggle to get out of his older, better-paid employees. At the end of the summer, he waved Kyle off with a smile on his face, saying,

"Be sure to come back next summer! Special welcome-back rate for you!"

Damn right there is, Kyle thought. He might have been a submissive employee at work, but this did not mean that he liked or respected his boss. He hated the old man, and looked forward to the day that he would be the one on top, looking down on all the small people around him.

It was early morning when Kyle awoke, and he made his way to the bridge in sleepy silence. He had expected Nihs and Lugh to be there, and so was surprised to find it empty, the *Ayger's* wheel spinning gently on its own. He passed by the helm to stare out the picture window, and was shocked to see clear blue ocean stretching to every horizon. The sight was surreal. Though Kyle knew they had been over land only a few hours ago, the sameness of the waves and the sky made it feel as though they were suspended in space, flying nowhere in a world filled with nothing. It was calming, but Kyle could tell that it would quickly get to him if they did not see land again soon.

He waited on the bridge for a few minutes, then, as no-one was forthcoming, decided to walk out onto the deck. Here, the blue ocean was dazzling. The horizons were wide, and the air was clear and bright. Clouds dotted here and there and lent a form of perspective to the scene. It struck Kyle just how colorful Loria was when compared to Earth. The ocean had never looked this way to him while he was on the deck of the *Caribia.*

After a short while, the communication crystal on the wall of the deck started to crackle. Lugh's voice came through: "Hey! Anyone out there?"

Kyle walked away from the bannister and put his hand on the crystal, realizing that it was his first time using it. "Yeah, I am. What's up?"

"We're making breakfast, if you're interested."

"Sure, I'll be in in a second."

Lugh and Nihs were up when he returned to the bridge. Lugh was handling breakfast while Nihs studied one of his books, perched on the bannister between the control panel and the observation deck.

"Morning," Lugh said. "Enjoying the weather?"

"Yeah," Kyle said, "it's nice out there."

Lugh nodded. "The sea's usually calm just off the coast of Ren'r. We might hit some interesting weather once we get closer to Eastia, though."

Phundasa came up from the engine room to join them in a quick breakfast. Once they were done, Kyle and Lugh decided to get back to training.

"All right," Lugh said, once they were squaring off, "the next energy I'll teach you is called force. You could think of it as a fighter's relationship with his weapon. Sounds a little strange, I know. I'll show you what I mean. Let's fight for a while and then watch me."

They did so, and finally stopped at Lugh's command.

"This one's called a repulse," he said. "Might want to back up a bit."

He swung his sword in front of him, the flat of the blade set against his left hand. He brought both arms up while dropping into a wide stance, and threw his sword at the floor. As it struck the ground, a dome of force exploded out from it. Kyle saw its approach, too late to think of getting out of the way. The wave struck, and he flew backwards, landing hard on his rump a full ten feet away from where he had been standing. It was like being swatted by a giant hand.

Kyle, winded, was going to say something to Lugh when he got up, but all he managed was, "Ouch."

"Sorry, got a little carried away with that one," Lugh said. "Didn't realize how much I'd built up. Anyway, that's what a repulse can do. Use it if you get crowded—there's nothing your enemy can do to avoid it but back up or force block it, so even if it doesn't hit them you get a breather."

"But you have to drop your sword," Kyle pointed out, rising to his feet. Lugh shook his head.

"If you do it properly, your weapon bounces back into your hand once it's over. That's what force lets you do; it gives you control over your weapon even when you're not touching it. Make your sword like you, and it's harder for you to fumble your weapon or get disarmed. That's why it can be better to let force build up instead of using it." He tossed his retrasword in the air and caught it again, then pointed it at Kyle. "Make your sword like you, Kyle!"

Kyle laughed and shook his head, collecting his weapon from the floor. "Yeah, I'll get right on that."

Kyle and Lugh, both exhausted from their training session, returned to the bridge for lunch. Phundasa had come up from the engine room, and was staring out of the picture window. Nihs and Meya were at the helm, chatting intermittently.

Phundasa came up to greet them as Lugh started throwing together lunch.

"Afternoon," he said, his huge arms folded across his chest. "We've reached low ocean, if you care to take a look."

"Huh, already!" Lugh sounded pleased. He craned his neck to peer at the window. "Kyle, you should check it out, it's something to see!"

"What's 'low ocean'?" Kyle asked Phundasa, as they went down the stairs. He realized the mistake he'd made a fraction of a second later. He was so used to talking with Lugh and the others, he'd forgotten that no one else knew about where he was from. But Phundasa clearly didn't find the question strange. He pointed at the expanse of water ahead of them.

"Take a look for yourself."

It took Kyle a moment to realize what he was seeing. There was a patch of a different kind of water ahead of them: it was lighter, and Kyle thought he could hear the sound of water falling. But that didn't make sense—*a waterfall in the middle of the ocean?*

They flew closer, and Kyle's mouth fell open. It *was* a waterfall in the middle of the ocean! The *Ayger* was soaring over a huge cliff, miles across, over which an unfathomable amount of water spilled constantly. It looked as though an entire island had simply sunk down into the earth, creating a giant hole. A few small outcroppings of rock were visible around the rim of the chasm, and Kyle could even see trees growing on some of them. The sight, and the noise, was unbelievable.

Questions immediately started queuing in Kyle's mind, as they had done so many times since his fall into Loria.

"How does that work?" he asked.

Phundasa peered down at the massive waterfall. "No one really knows. It's one of the mysteries of the world—where all the water that pours into low ocean goes, and where it all comes from. But they say that low ocean has always been there, and always will be."

"What's down there?" Kyle asked. They had passed over the waterfall itself, and were now flying over the huge chasm it fed. It was possible to see walls of water for several hundred feet down, before they disappeared into mist and darkness.

Meya, with Nihs riding on her shoulder, came down to the observation deck and settled at Kyle's other side.

"That's as much a mystery as low ocean itself," Phundasa said. "No one's ever been down there, you see—the water and the magic in the chasms throws off Ephicer engines. Airships crash if they fly too far inside."

"There's more than one of these?"

"Oh, yes," Nihs said. "They're dotted around every ocean there is. There are some that you could throw a stone across, and some that could fit a country inside of them."

Kyle stared down into the pit. *There's got to be something down there*, he thought. All the water pouring over the edge couldn't just disappear. Perhaps a platform could be built on the lip of the waterfall, and someone could be lowered down into the depths…It was an exciting thought, but not one that he was willing to share. He said instead,

"I guess boats have to be pretty careful around these falls, huh?"

Phundasa laughed. "You got that right."

Kyle noticed something else, but it was on the far horizon rather than in the sea below them.

"Hey…what's that up ahead?"

Phundasa leaned forward, squinting in the direction of Kyle's outstretched arm. Thick, ugly clouds were clustered far in the distance, a patch of darkness in an otherwise pristine sky.

"Hmm," Phundasa said, "looks like a storm."

"Is that a problem?"

"Hah! I don't think anything could harm this ship of Lugh's. In any case, chances are we'll pass right by it—the wind likes to play jokes this far out to sea."

Lugh came down, eating a sandwich. "Whatcha talkin' about?"

Phundasa pointed. "A storm."

"Brilliant, we could use a wash. Sandwich, anyone?"

Captain Aarne of the *Daufin* surveyed the ocean around him and smiled: the sky was clear as far as the eye could see. He loved it when the weather behaved. He'd battled his fair share of rough seas over the years, but Aarne wasn't as young as he used to be, and these days would much rather his cargo arrive unmolested.

His ship veered to the left as it approached a section of low ocean ahead. Many ships would have gone miles out of their way to stay as far as possible from the chasms, but Aarne was an experienced sailor. He had traversed the route from Centralia to Eastia and back time and time again, and knew just how close to get to each patch without getting swept up by the current.

Someone drew up beside him, peering beyond the prow of his ship. Surprised, he turned to see who it was. *Oh,* he thought. *One of you.*

The two men had paid him for passage to Eastia, which was odd in and of itself; these days few people bothered to travel any great distance in water-bound ships. It was cheaper, but many times slower than flying.

This was only a part of the problem. Aarne was not usually a suspicious man, but there was something *off* about these men. They did almost everything together, which somehow made it worse when you saw one of them by himself—you immediately started to wonder what the other could be up to. They looked like men, but they acted like children, whispering and giggling to each other all the time. He understood that they were adventurers, which most of the time suited him fine; they were a handy bunch of people to have on your side when a fight broke out. But he knew that these two were not on his side.

Aarne preferred to avoid the gaze of the magic user in particular. There was something deep in his eye that glimmered and spun; a tiny vortex, within which your own eyes could become lost. This was the one who had just drawn up beside him, and the one who now spoke.

"It's a beautiful day, isn't it," he said.

Aarne grunted.

The man peered forwards, as though seeing something that Aarne could not.

"Is it safe to be this close to low ocean?" he asked, with apparently genuine concern. Aarne shifted uncomfortably. Though he was staring straight ahead, he could still feel the man's eyes watching him.

"We'll be fine. The falls don't pull nearly as much as people think."

"Could you get much closer than this?"

Aarne frowned. "I wouldn't. Any closer would be pushing it."

"Ah."

Silence, then: "Thank you very much for letting us ride your ship."

Aarne said nothing. *What kind of a thing to say is that?*

"We needed a ship."

Suddenly, a scream erupted behind them. Aarne wheeled around just in time to see the sorcerer's outstretched arm grow incandescent with magic. Realization struck, and he felt a flood of anger engulf him. But there was no time to do anything but stand and watch, frozen in shock, as sparks of magical electricity gathered and danced between the man's fingers. The thunderbolt burst forth, and suddenly Aarne's chest had burst open, engulfed in fire, stabbed through with a million needles of pain.

He died an instant later, as his body flew over the ship's railing and into the waves below.

Lian lowered his hood as the sailors behind him shouted and swore and drew their weapons. A smile played about his lips as he listened to the din that Lacaster was raising below. As the man closest to him ran forward with his sword drawn to strike, Lian whirled around, his arms crackling with lightning.

The sailors had been good, strong men, but Lian and Lacaster were experienced killers. Soon, there was not a one left alive aboard the *Daufin.*

Lacaster, his swords red with blood, strode up beside his twin.

"Can you see them, brother?" he asked.

Lian pointed. To Lacaster, it was as though his eyes had been fired in the direction of his brother's finger. They flew into the sky, up through the clouds, and settled on the shape of the *Ayger* in the distance.

Lacaster's expression grew hungry. "Are they close enough?"

Lian's eyes were glowing with magic. "As a matter of fact, they are. Would you be so kind as to take the helm? We're awfully close to low ocean, after all."

They gathered again in Lugh's room that night, playing cards and swapping stories. Kyle learned much of Meya and Phundasa during their conversation. Apparently, there had been a period of unrest among the Orcish tribes of Eastia some years back. Before then, Meya had been nothing more than an apprentice cleric at a local church and Phundasa had been working in a nearby village for his father. Once the fighting had broken out, Meya had been forced to evacuate her town and had eventually met up with Phundasa. The two had survived the turmoil together, Phundasa acting as Meya's bodyguard as she worked to heal those wounded in the fighting. Ever since then, the two had stuck together, flying to Centralia and starting new lives as adventurers.

The storm hit while they were talking, starting out as an intermittent tapping, then growing to a steady drone that forced them to raise their voices in order to be heard. It made Kyle think of the storm that had struck the *Caribia*, though there was no doubt that this storm was child's play compared to the one responsible for bringing him to Loria. Though the *Ayger* pitched slightly in the wind and rain, the movement was minute. Clearly, Lugh's large and expensive ship wasn't about to take any lip from the inclement weather.

The storm worsened as Meya and Phundasa's story wound to a close. The rain battered at the window, making conversation almost impossible. Lugh got up and peered out of the window.

"Listen to that!"

"Quite the storm," Phundasa agreed. "If it were snow we'd be in Westia."

Lugh turned around with a grin on his face. "I wonder what it's like out on deck?"

"Oh, *Lugh*," Nihs said.

"Come on, it'll be a blast! You coming, Kyle?"

"Sure," he said. *Maybe if I fall overboard this time, I'll end up back on Earth.*

The storm was howling when they got outside. The sky was pitch black, and the rain was driving. Kyle couldn't even see the far end of the deck from where he stood. Lugh ventured out for only a moment before giving up and dancing his way back to the shelter of the overhang.

"This is nuts, huh?" he shouted above the storm.

Kyle opened his mouth to answer, but at that moment, something flickered in his vision, appearing behind Lugh and then disappearing into the darkness. It was only there for a fraction of a second, but Kyle immediately knew that something was very, very wrong. His lungs turned to ice.

"What is it?" Lugh said.

But Kyle was running forward, his soul sword leaping into his hands. He shouldered Lugh out of the way and swung at the same time.

Something was split cleanly into two, landing with a squelch on the deck before disappearing with a *crack*.

"What the hell was that?" Lugh shouted.

The crystal on the wall crackled into life, and Nihs' panicked voice came through.

"Lugh, Kyle, get inside! We need you, *now!*"

They dashed into the hallway, the storm chasing them indoors. They started for the bridge, but hadn't gotten two steps before something burst in from one of the side rooms, coming straight through the thin wooden door. It was the same kind of creature that Kyle had slain on the deck: a single, gruesome, fleshy eye, floating eerily at head height. It looked as though it had been ripped from the face of a large creature, as dark, blue, veiny tentacles flowed from its back in a bizarre hairdo.

Disgusting as it was, it did not appear very threatening—that was, until it caught sight of Lugh and instantly flew at him, screeching. A small, many-toothed mouth opened in the flesh below the eye.

Kyle jumped forward, but too late. The creature rammed into Lugh and closed its jaw around his outstretched arm. Cursing, he dashed sideways and slammed his arm against the wall. When the creature didn't let go, he drew his dagger and stabbed at it until it broke free and sunk to the floor, disappearing in a puff of smoke as had the last. He cursed again and clutched at his bleeding arm.

"You go ahead!" he shouted to Kyle. "Use your soul sword! The others are probably still in my room!"

Kyle nodded, taking the lead as they ran down the corridor. More of the creatures burst into the hallway ahead. He swung with his soularm, tearing each one to shreds as it charged him. He was fearful that one of them would slip past him, but his training with Lugh had paid off, and they reached the bridge without incident.

The sight out of the picture window was a terrifying one. Dozens of the small creatures were clustered at the window, battering it, trying to get inside.

"*Damn*," Lugh said.

"Can we do anything about them?" Kyle asked.

"Not now! Get to my room!"

As they passed into the small hallway that led to Lugh's room, they saw his door swing open. One of the creatures, floating lazily through the air, turned to head inside. It was met by a giant green fist that punched it across the hall and into the far wall with a *splat.*

"And *stay* out," Phundasa said, striding out of the room. He caught sight of Lugh and Kyle and nodded mildly. "Evening."

"Hey," Lugh said. "See you've met our guests. The others okay?"

"For now. We had about half a dozen of the things in there. Some cursed storm that we flew into!"

The window in Lugh's room had been broken, and the storm was blowing inside. Meya and Nihs were there, looking haggard but unhurt. Meya ran to them as Nihs hopped down from the bed.

"I'm glad you're safe," Meya said. "Are you hurt?"

"Not badly," Lugh said, showing her his bitten arm.

"Ah. Here, let me." She took hold of it with both hands, and there was a flash of white. Lugh twisted his arm around to look at the wound that was no longer there.

"Great, thanks! Now, who knows what's happening?"

"I've read about these creatures," Nihs said, scuttling up to Lugh's shoulder. "They're *eyrioda*—wind demons. Storms brew wherever they gather. We must have flown right into a swarm of them."

"Brilliant," Lugh said bitterly. "All right. The flight path will take us out of the storm. We just need to keep them off the ship until it does. Let's split up—if they've been breaking windows they must have gotten in elsewhere. Kyle and I need our weapons from downstairs, so we'll head down and clear the things out. The rest of you can take upstairs. Meya, there's a bunch of them trying to get through the window out front. Do you know any hurting magic?"

Meya nodded. "I know enough. Come on, Das!"

By the time they reached the bridge, creatures had started to swarm in from the opposite hallway. Nihs jumped to Phundasa's shoulder while the huge Orc bowled into them, laying about him with his huge armored fists. Meya ran to the picture window and fired magic at the creatures clustered against it. Kyle had no idea what kind of magic she was using—the spells she cast looked like orbs of red light, and passed right through the window to strike the monsters outside.

Kyle and Lugh, meanwhile, ran down to the training room. They met no resistance on the stairs going down, but the lower hallways were filled with demons. Kyle separated himself from Lugh so he could use his soul sword without fear of striking him; Lugh brandished his dagger, heading off in the opposite direction. It was an awkward, ugly battle. Individually the eyes were easy to strike down, but when several of them struck at once they were almost impossible to keep away. After a large swing that felled two of the creatures, a third seized the opportunity to bite at Kyle's shoulder. He yelped, trying to twist his sword around to strike it. By the time he had fought it off, two more had seized hold of his right leg. The pain was brutal. Though the eyes were content to simply latch on and do nothing else, their teeth were razor sharp.

Lugh was not without trouble, either. By the time they had cleared the corridor of the dozen-odd demons that had infested it, both he and Kyle were bleeding from multiple wounds.

"Damn things," Lugh panted, looking around at all the shattered glass. "Who's going to pay for all this?"

Kyle wanted to laugh, but the pain lancing up his leg won out. He grit his teeth, and fought through it.

The ballroom, being windowless, was mercifully deserted. Kyle and Lugh donned their armor, and Lugh buckled on his retrasword.

Lugh smiled as his sword hissed into life. "That's better. Let's go get those little bastards. We'll clear out downstairs and then get back to the bridge so Meya can heal us."

"Right."

They ran outside and were immediately accosted by more of the floating eyes. Kyle and Lugh fought side by side, Kyle using the changesword he had won from the goblin chieftain. They each suffered a couple more bites, but the armor they wore prevented them from getting seriously hurt.

They chopped their way around the lower chambers then, when it was only the odd eye that they encountered, ran back up the stairs to the bridge. The battle here was ferocious. The eyes had been swarming in from the deck, and Phundasa and Nihs were each holding a hallway, while Meya struggled to keep the creatures from the front window.

"Oi!" Lugh got their attention.

"Excellent timing!" Nihs shouted. "One of you cover for me!"

"You go," Lugh said to Kyle. "I'll take the other side. Use your soul sword!"

They made a hasty swap with Nihs and Phundasa, who stepped into the middle of the room to catch their breath. Meya turned from her battle to lay on hands: Phundasa, who was forced to expose his fists in order to fight, had suffered many cuts along his arms.

Kyle fought to keep the demons back as best he could. They were thicker here than anywhere else, their bodies bumping into one another as they jostled to attack. He flailed with his soul sword, no longer bothering with technique. The *cracks* of the creatures dying soon filled the air.

"The ones with red tentacles can sting!" Phundasa bellowed. He ran back into the fray to keep Lugh from being forced back by the creatures' onslaught. Soon after, Kyle himself was forced to give ground to the eyes; not even his soul sword could hold back their immense numbers.

Kyle caught sight of one of the red-tentacled eyes that Phundasa had mentioned. He struck it down quickly, but another caught him coming from the other direction. He gasped in pain as the tentacles slapped against his arm, rasping across a patch of bare skin and leaving an angry red sting.

He fought it off, but in the time it took to do this, he was overrun. Before he knew what was going on, he was being bitten and stung from every direction, and couldn't even see where to strike to fight back. He cursed, struggling to win back control of the situation, but there was nothing he could do.

Suddenly, a red light washed over him. It grew in intensity, obscuring his entire vision and caressing his skin like a warm wind. When the light faded, all of the eyes surrounding him were dead.

Kyle, bewildered, struggled to regain his concentration. The creatures had started to flee, shooting back down the hallway to the deck. Ten seconds later, the bridge was silent.

He turned back to the others. They all looked as confused as he, but relieved as well. Meya, who'd been standing a couple of feet behind him, caught his eye.

"Was that you?" he asked her.

She nodded, stepping forward.

"Thank you," he said earnestly.

She smiled as she started to touch his chest, mending the numerous bite and sting marks that crisscrossed it. "You're welcome. Just save *my* life the next time I'm in trouble." She ran her hands along his arms, and his skin tingled, his wounds knitting themselves shut. "There you go. That should serve for now."

"Thanks," he said again.

Meya patted his arm and moved on to heal Lugh.

"So is that it?" Phundasa said to no one in particular.

"Sky's still dark," Lugh pointed out, nodding his head to the window. "Though maybe we're hitting the edge of the storm now."

At that moment, a massive concussion rocked the entire ship, and an ear-splitting crash came from the deck. Kyle almost lost his footing as the floor beneath him pitched and swayed.

A bellow that sounded like the war cry of a giant came from outside. They all looked at each other in stunned silence.

"Let's go!" Lugh's sword sprung into his hand as he led the way to deck.

Lian stood at the prow of the *Dauphin*, his glowing hands outstretched. His expression was strange. Part of him was paying attention to the water ahead, while another was far away, detached. This dichotomy was reflected perfectly in his eyes: one glowed blue with magic, while the other was normal and dark.

"How's it going?" Lacaster asked him from the wheel.

"Fine, brother," Lian replied. "I'll have them soon."

"Oh, good. And then we can go home."

"Yes."

Kyle and the others ran into the driving rain of the storm. It was still dark, though some light was cast by the near-constant sparks of lightning that jumped between the clouds. The wind howled, changing direction every second. The deck was deserted.

"Well," Lugh said, "looks like—"

A shape materialized out of the gloom. Lugh shouted a warning, and they all fell backwards as it hurtled towards the deck, slamming into it with a crash that shook the entire body of the *Ayger*.

Kyle didn't need Nihs' knowledge of monsters to know what the creature before them was. It was obviously one of the eye demons, but a kind of alpha or mature form. The single eye that dominated its face was as wide across as Kyle was tall. Its mouth, unlike the smaller creatures', was not a small, fleshy gash, but a protruding snout lined with row upon row of teeth. Tentacles that were dozens of feet in length whipped out behind it. It had wrapped several of these around various parts of the deck for purchase.

As they all watched in shocked silence, the creature tightened its grip on the deck, pulling itself toward them. Its lone eye rolled to and fro, settling on each of them in turn. Then it roared.

The din was unbelievable. The noise it made was not just loud but keen and grating, as though sheets of metal were being torn and ground together somewhere in the beast's maw. Its tongue shot out, a long, fleshy organ like that of a frog's. It was lined with dozens of the smaller eye demons, stuck to it like flies.

"Son of a *bitch,*" Lugh said.

The creature lashed out, a tentacle scything across the deck. Lugh blocked it, and immediately engaged the creature, barking instructions at the others.

"Hit it when its attention is on someone else! If a tentacle gets within range, cut it! Nihs, Meya, keep enough magic to rescue one of us if we get grabbed! If any one of those little buggers gets loose, kill it first and get it out of the way! Kyle, use your soul sword!"

Kyle needed no further instruction. He drew his glowing sword and held it in front of him, letting it act as a barrier between him and the horrific beast that had appeared before them. He was terrified. Goblins and imps had been one thing, but now *this*? He had no idea how they were going to fight back against a threat like this, and was quite convinced that they were all going to die.

The creature attacked, tentacles flying through the air and striking at every member of the party at the same time. It was trying to pull itself further and further up on the deck, bringing its huge jaws closer to its prey.

It stuck its tongue out and swung it back and forth; three or four of the smaller demons came loose and immediately dashed for the closest target.

A tentacle lashed out at Kyle. He swung at it instinctively, and missed. It caught him around the torso and yanked him forwards; he swung again, and this time the tentacle was sliced in two. As he scrambled to get away from the huge creature, which had turned its snapping mouth towards him, one of the smaller eyeballs bit him on the shoulder. He ignored it, rising to his feet and dashing backwards. Once he was out of range he slew the shoulder-biter and tried to calm his panicking body.

He noticed that the wind was picking up. But it wasn't just random gusts as before; now it was a solid wall of wind that was blowing against them, forcing them backwards and compromising their balance. In the gloom, Kyle could just make out several of the creature's tentacles that were behaving differently from the others. Their ends tapered into wide webs of flesh, and were rapidly whipping in circles. It was no coincidence that the wind was blowing against them: the creature was creating it.

Meya, to Kyle's right, was staying well away from the creature. She was launching the occasional spell at its side, but these had little effect—mostly, she was keeping a watchful eye on the rest of the battle, and Kyle knew she was saving her magic in case one of them got seriously hurt.

Nihs was using fire to keep the tentacles at bay while he attacked the creature's eye with magic. However, the demon would shut its eye defensively whenever it was in danger, and whatever spell Nihs had used would dissipate harmlessly against it.

Lugh and Phundasa were fighting their best, trying to keep their heads above the sea of tentacles and biting monsters. Lugh's sword arm got trapped in a fleshy bind; he drew his dagger and stabbed at it, forcing it to withdraw. When Phundasa's torso got similarly wrapped and the monster tried to pull him closer, he held his ground in an amazing feat of strength. He grabbed the tentacle in both hands and tried to rip it in two.

Kyle dashed forwards. A tentacle lashed out at him, and he swung at it wildly. Nothing struck him, so he ran on and brought his sword down hard on the tentacle that was trapping Phundasa. Severed, it went limp, and the Orc shrugged his way out of the coils that had been binding him.

"Thanks!" he shouted, then: "Look out!"

Kyle was too slow to react; a blow caught him in the stomach and he rose into the air, flying backwards the full length of the deck and landing hard on his back.

With an enraged bellow, Phundasa swept up the tentacle that had struck Kyle and began pulling on it, trying to rip it from the monster's back. The monster shrieked and sent another after him, but Lugh jumped in and cut it before it reached its target.

Kyle, dazed, watched the progress of the battle with bemusement. He was completely winded, and was floating in a warm puddle of near-unconsciousness. Meya ran over to him and put her hands on his temples.

"Come on!" she shouted at him. "No time for that! Up you get!"

Kyle' senses returned to him painfully as her magic worked. He was just about to sit up when Meya screamed; a feeler had reached all the way along the deck and wrapped around her leg. It lifted her right off the ground as Kyle sprang to his feet, heart pounding.

Meya, her body turning to face the demon, was being carried closer and closer to its maw. The great mouth opened. Kyle ran forward, sword out, ready to cut her loose. But as he did, the air darkened, and he sensed a massive build-up of power coming from Meya's form. An inner instinct made him duck and cover his head with his arms.

Meya, screaming, thrust both palms toward the creature. A blast of red magic flew from her fingertips, striking the monster squarely in the eye. The light of the spell burned into Kyle's retinas, and a wave of energy rocked his body. When he stood up again, Meya had been dropped onto the deck, and the creature was roaring in agony. Its single eyelid fluttered and its tentacles lashed at its own eye, trying to rub away whatever pain Meya's spell had caused.

Lacaster's brow furrowed as his twin whimpered.

"Are you all right?" he said.

Lian rubbed at his glowing eye. "Yes. I'm all right."

"How's the fight going, brother?"

"I'll get them!" Lian snapped. He redoubled his concentration, gritting his teeth.

"I'll get them…"

"All right!" Lugh shouted, "now's our chance!"

He and Phundasa dashed forward, taking advantage of the creature's bewilderment. Lugh's sword cut left and right, severing tentacles. Phundasa ran straight in next to the creature's body, and pummeled it with his huge fists. Nihs ducked and wove, trying to get in front of the demon. As soon as he was lined up, he shot a massive fireball directly into the beast's mouth.

It screamed further, and suddenly became even more dangerous as its tentacles flailed to and fro. One of them caught Lugh, who was flung backwards; the same happened to Nihs.

As Meya ran along the deck to assist them, the creature roared again. No fewer than twenty of the smaller eyes burst from its mouth in a huge swarm, and they all immediately went for the target that was presented to them: Kyle.

It was the same as the first time he had been swarmed; Kyle fought as best he could, but was soon overwhelmed. Being bitten, shoved and stung from every direction, he tried to figure out a way that he could make it out of this alive. He caught sight of a section of the deck and a solution came to him. Ignoring the pain that threatened to overwhelm him, he grabbed his soul sword in both hands and threw it at the floor.

A huge dome of blue electricity erupted from the impact point, sweeping over the deck and incinerating the eyes that had been assaulting him. It was definitely a repulse, but was far more powerful than those he and Lugh had used before. It even reached the demon itself, which shrieked again as the bolts earthed themselves in its soft flesh.

Kyle caught sight of Phundasa standing between him and the monster. The Orc turned away from the demon and crouched low, cupping his hands at knee height like someone about to give a boost.

"Kyle!" he said and jerked his head back toward the demon, motioning at his hands.

He's crazy, Kyle thought. *Does he want me to do what I think he does?*

"I'll throw you!" Phundasa shouted urgently.

Oh my god, he does.

Kyle was amazed at how naturally the movement came. He ran forward, and jumped as he reached Phundasa. The Orc, muscles bulging, threw him up over his head.

Kyle saw the great eye turn upwards to face him as he flew. As he fell, he turned his soul sword in his hands, ready to stab downwards. The creature's mouth started to open.

He collided, thrusting his sword as hard as he could. The creature screamed in agony as his soularm bit deeply into the jelly of its eye. The detonations from his nuclear weapon tore at its flesh even as it struggled to dislodge him. He pulled his sword out and stabbed again, then again. He felt a gaiden strike build up inside him, and drew his changesword with his free hand, lifting both swords over his head. He reversed his grip and thrust down, stabbing with both blades at once. His swords, wreathed in blue lightning, opened up a gash the size of a manhole in the creature's flesh.

"Kyle!" he heard someone yell, "jump off!"

He obeyed, pulling his swords out and kicking backwards off the creature. The din it was making was horrific. It was writhing in wrath and pain, and its head was whipping back and forth.

Kyle landed hard, falling on his feet but overbalancing and tumbling backwards; he was far too distracted to worry about sticking the landing. He fell right next to Nihs and Meya, who had clasped hands and were facing the monster directly. An aura of magic built up around the two of them. They pulled their free hands back together, and thrust them toward the demon. The spell that resulted was a huge ball of energy that seemed to be a combination of Nihs' fire and Meya's hurting magic. It struck the creature dead-on, shattering the remains of its eye and cracking its jaw in two. Its last cry cut short, the monster lost its grip on the *Ayger*'s deck and tumbled off into the darkness below.

Lian screamed.

"*Brother!*" Lacaster abandoned the ship's wheel, leaving it to veer as it may. He ran forward to console his sobbing brother, who was curled up at the prow clutching his eye.

"Brother! Did they *kill* it? Are you hurt?"

"*Yes!*" Lian wailed through his hands.

Lacaster grit his teeth. "They'll pay for that!"

Lian sniffed and looked at his twin in dismay.

"We can't fight them *now*. We have to escape."

Lacaster looked up at the horizon, eyes blazing. He ground his teeth in frustration. "All right," he agreed finally. "We'll escape for now. But we'll get them later, I swear we will!"

Lian nodded sadly and held out his hand for his brother to take. Lacaster grabbed it, and the two instantly disappeared in a swirl of magic.

Hours later, the *Dauphin*, completely abandoned, drifted into a patch of low ocean and tumbled over the edge, lost in the roiling waves.

There was a stunned silence on the deck of the *Ayger*. The wind, which had been howling only moments before, started to die down. Of the rest of the air demons, there was no sign.

Lugh jumped and punched the air with his fist. "Woohoo! We got it, guys, we got it!"

His outcry freed the others from their silence, and soon the air was full of relieved laughter, congratulations, and hands slapping on backs.

"That was *awesome*!" Lugh shouted at Phundasa and Kyle, grabbing them both by the shoulder. "I haven't seen a stunt like that in years! And you two!" he pointed at Nihs and Meya. "That was one hell of a spell back there! I didn't know you were *that* good at hurting magic!"

"It was a gaiden spell," Meya said humbly, brushing the hair out of her face. "I got very lucky. Now, who's hurt?"

Once everyone had been healed, they returned to the bridge, and Kyle was pleased to see that the *Ayger* had reached the edge of the unnatural storm. The skies ahead were clear, albeit getting darker as the sun began to set.

"I guess we should go cover up all the windows those little stinkers came through," Lugh said. He sighed. "Getting them all refitted is going to cost a *fortune*."

"If you're going to keep a ship like this, you have to be prepared to pay for it," Nihs said.

"Oh, come on, you saw the size of that thing. It would've *eaten* a ship smaller than this one."

"You said you've read about such monsters before," Phundasa said. "Are we safe now that the storm is over?"

Nihs nodded. "Eyrioda fly in huge swarms, which look like natural thunderstorms from a distance. I suppose we were just unlucky, and flew into them—but now that the alpha is dead, the swarm should dissipate."

"Great!" said Lugh. "Let's celebrate!"

Nihs rolled his eyes. "Windows first, Lugh," he said. "And I'm not entirely sure if this calls for a celebration. All we managed to do was *not* get ourselves killed after flying into a nest of demons."

Lugh waved a hand at him. "Don't be such a downer. Taking out a huge demon by stabbing it in the face and then blowing it up with magic is what adventuring is all about!"

Meya laughed and Kyle shook his head, smiling. Lugh's enthusiasm was catching, and besides, Kyle was thinking back to the battle on the deck and couldn't help but feel proud of himself.

They spent a while weatherproofing the broken windows as best they could, pinning the curtains tight over them and sweeping away the worst of the shards. Kyle was forced to move into a different room, as his window had been smashed and his bed covered with water and glass.

They prepared food and gathered on the bridge, while Lugh salvaged a couple bottles of wine from a cabinet in his room. They took the rest of the night off, eating, drinking, and talking about the day's events.

Once again, it was Nihs who was the first to retire. The others stayed up quite late. Lugh and Phundasa had grown very talkative thanks to Lugh's stash of wine, so Kyle and Meya spent most of their time listening to the two of them.

"That was an impressive feat back there, friend," Phundasa said loudly at one point, slapping Kyle on the back. "You should have been born an Orc! Hah!"

"Thanks," Kyle said, a little breathlessly.

"You're training as a fighter?" Phundasa went on.

"Yeah."

"What do you say to learning a bit of *thortnir*? You never know when you might find yourself without a weapon! It'll bulk you up, make your fists as deadly as your sword!"

"That," Lugh said, "is not a bad idea. Why don't you two start training together? It'll do you good to learn a different fighting style."

"Why not?" Kyle said, although he found the prospect of wrestling with Phundasa rather terrifying.

As the night wore on, Kyle found himself growing more and more withdrawn. He stared into his glass, wondering why he felt no desire to empty it.

"I think I'm going to go out on deck," he announced.

"Sure thing," Lugh said. "Let us know if any more of those eyeballs show up, huh?"

He left behind the sound of Lugh and Phundasa laughing and made his way outside. The night air was cool, and the wind on his face was refreshing. He looked out at the endless expanse of water, wondering when they would next see land.

He'd only been outside the United States a few times before now—he'd made the trip north into Canada a handful of times. He'd always found travel pointless, such a huge waste of money and time. Funny how he was now exploring a whole new world without ever really getting to know his own.

"Kyle?"

Meya was making her way towards him. She leaned on the railing next to him as she had done before on the observation deck.

"I didn't want to scare you like last time," she said.

"I appreciate it," Kyle said.

Meya just laughed.

After a moment, she said, "I'm sorry about what happened today. Das and I didn't think we'd have to include killing a giant demon in the job description."

"It's all right," Kyle said. "You didn't know we were going to run into those things. Besides, we made it through alive, so no harm done."

"You handled yourself well," Meya complimented him.

"Thanks. Your healing skills are amazing."

Meya nodded humbly. "I've had a lot of practice. You'll be paying for it in the morning, though. I can heal you, but your body is going to need time to recover."

"Right," Kyle said. Something else occurred to him. "The magic you used against those demons…Lugh called it hurting magic?" He realized he may have been asking a stupid question, and felt it necessary to add, "Sorry, I don't know a lot about magic."

"That's all right. Hurting is hard to describe. You could say it takes apart whatever healing puts together. In some ways it's more powerful than what mages do, since it doesn't have to travel through a medium like the elements to work. Some people think it's a cruel way to fight, or a corruption of what healing magic should be. But there are times I've been very glad I know how to do it."

"Yeah, me too," Kyle said. Meya laughed, and Kyle found himself saying,

"Could you teach me some of your magic?"

She smiled. "I'd be happy to," she said. "It's only a couple more days until we reach Rhian, but I could show you the basics."

It was Kyle's turn to smile. "Thanks!" he said.

They stayed out on deck for a little while longer, until Meya touched Kyle's arm and told him she was going back inside. He followed suit a few minutes after; the night was getting dark and the air was cold. Besides, Kyle was extremely tired.

He navigated his way to his new room and flopped down on the bed, thinking about the day's events. As interesting as they had been, he hoped that the rest of their journey to Eastia was not *quite* so exciting.

Grade eight had gone by in a flash for Kyle. He had returned to school full of newfound confidence, convinced that he finally stood a chance of attracting Jennifer, the girl of his dreams. But as he soon found out, there was more to taking a girl out for a date than being able to pay for it.

The first problem was that Kyle still had no idea how to approach her. He had not grown any wiser in this regard throughout the summer, and was still flat-out refusing to seek the advice of anyone else. September came and went, and still no advance had been made. Kyle kept telling himself that he was not being a coward, but waiting for the opportune moment. Clearly, he said to himself, such a large undertaking must be met with some preparation.

The social life at Kyle's school remained volatile and dramatic. Rumors flew to and fro constantly, couples came together and then split up two weeks later. Alliances were formed and emotions ran high. Kyle found the entire ordeal depressing, and he reacted to each scandalous new headline in the same way: by ignoring it completely. Unfortunately, Kyle was dimly aware that if he ended up getting involved with Jennifer, he himself would be contributing to the drama that he so hated. Just as with everything else, he dealt with this by not thinking about it.

It was November when Kyle finally decided enough was enough. Everywhere he went, he was seeing Jennifer: if not her herself, then one of her friends, or something or someone that was somehow related to her. It was maddening, and as frightening as the prospect was, Kyle knew that he would have to ask her out or it would never end.

Just go for it, came a voice from a small part of his mind. *Do it, and get it over with. Who knows, she might even say yes. Look around you—you're better than anyone else here. She could do much worse than you.*

He ran into her walking down the hallway the next day. Or rather, he saw her at her locker from a distance, and started to panic. *I should do it now!* There were still a few minutes left before class, enough time to ask her out to a movie and then leave before he had the chance to make a fool of himself.

Do it, do it, do it, said the small part of his mind.

Legs trembling and heart beating from fear, Kyle approached her. Though it seemed to take forever, it somehow took him by surprise when he finally did reach her.

"Hey! Er—hi! Jennifer!" he said.

Jennifer, surprised, turned around to see who it was. Her perfect eyes settled on him. In a movement that nearly blanked out Kyle's mind, she smiled.

"Oh—hey, Kyle!"

Crap, crap, what am I going to say next?

"Hey! Umm, I was just wondering, are you doing anything on Friday?"

"Umm, no," she said.

"Great! Ok! Uh, I was just wondering if you wanted to go to the movies with me!"

Jennifer blinked a couple times. Her eyes flickered over Kyle's face, as though she were taking him in for the first time.

"Sure," she said, then louder, "sure, ok! I'd like that."

At the last moment, Kyle stopped himself from asking, 'really?' Suddenly, he was flying. He let out a breath he hadn't realized he was holding, and a wave of relief swept over him.

"Great!" he managed to say. "Great! Umm…so…"

They made plans, and then Jennifer waved him goodbye and left for class. Kyle was elated. He couldn't believe his good luck. She had said yes! She had actually said yes!

He nearly skipped to his next class. Suddenly, everything seemed so much better, so much funnier, so much easier. He had asked Jennifer Vasquez out on a date. He could do *anything*.

Kyle woke with a bitter taste in his mouth. Jennifer Vasquez; that was a name that hadn't crossed his mind for years. They had never really become a couple: after only a handful of dates, Jennifer had let him go, claiming that she only liked him as a friend—as if they had been friends before or after their relationship. It had been a kind breakup, but Kyle had been devastated nonetheless. He had spent the rest of the year working feverishly at his schoolwork, shunning his friends and everything else. As a result, he had graduated near the top of his grade.

Huh. Jennifer. Kyle spent a moment wondering where she might have ended up. But only a moment—after all, it had been a long time ago, and Kyle would rather forget the past than dwell on it.

He swung out of bed and made his way to the deck. He was the last one up; Nihs, Meya, and Lugh were all there when he arrived.

"Hey, look who's up!" Lugh said. "The eye-stabber himself! Breakfast?"

"Sure, thanks," Kyle said, leaning on the control panel to stare out the picture window. There was still nothing in sight—no land, not even any of the low ocean.

"Sleep well?" Meya asked him.

"Well enough. Kept thinking an eyeball was going to come through my window. Are we going to reach Eastia soon?"

Lugh laughed. "Still a day and a half to go, friend."

Oh, of course, every 'day' in Loria had two periods of light and dark to it—half as much time had passed as he had thought.

"Oh, right. So what do we do for the rest of the trip?"

"Let's spar some more once you're done eating. Might as well make use of the time we have, right? I talked to Boombasta, he wants to come with us."

Meya smiled at him, folding her arms. "Really?" she said.

"What?" Lugh said innocently.

"His name! It's not *that* hard to pronounce."

"Maybe for you," Lugh said. "I'm no good at Orcish names."

"I have faith in you. *Bfun*-dasa."

"*Fun*-dasa."

"That's better! You're still off, though. It's like a 'b', a 'p' and an 's' altogether. It's supposed to sound like a drum beat. *Phun*dasa."

Lugh rolled his eyes. "It's like the sound of a *drum* beat, Kyle. Honestly, why do you have such a hard time pronouncing it?"

Meya hit him on the arm.

Something was nagging at Kyle as he and Lugh descended to the training room.

"Is it just me," he said, "or is Meya sort of…touchy?"

Lugh laughed. "I know what you're talking about," he said. "You mean the way she always touches people, right? It's a thing magic users do, healers especially. I think it's because magic is channeled through your hands. Healing works best if you touch the person you're trying to heal, so I guess it becomes a habit. Anyway," he added, "I'm sure you're not complaining, right?"

"Hey!" Kyle said, but Lugh just laughed and galloped his way down the rest of the stairs.

They sparred for a short while before Phundasa arrived. Kyle could tell that he was improving—the more Lugh taught him about combat energy, the less one-sided their training sessions became. Still, he thought, Lugh must be holding back considerably if he were to go by what he'd seen Lugh do in the past.

"Here's another technique that uses force," Lugh said at one point. "You'll be relying on this one a lot. It's called force blocking; you use it when you know you're going to get hit and don't have time to get out of the way." He stood back from Kyle and held his sword out in front of him.

"Put the palm of your off-hand against the flat of your blade, like you were bracing it, see? Then just widen your stance and put your energy into your sword. The idea is to replace damage with distance. If you do it properly, you'll get sent flying backwards, but it won't hurt nearly as much as if you had stood your ground. Make sense?"

Kyle nodded, and tried to imitate Lugh's position as the Selk drew his arm back.

"I'm going to hit you hard—it won't work otherwise."

He leapt forward, sword flashing. Kyle lifted his own to meet the blow. When the two swords met, a wave of force rippled outwards from the point of impact. A circle of blue grew from Kyle's sword, lifting him off his feet and throwing him backwards.

He flew fifteen feet before landing on his rump. It was a surprisingly soft landing; though Lugh's blow had landed on his sword, it felt as though the impact had been spread evenly across his body.

"Well done," Lugh said. "The next step is learning to land on your feet."

At that moment, Kyle realized that Phundasa had come into the room and was leaning against the far wall, arms folded.

"Mind if I join you two?" he said.

Kyle spent the following day and a half in intensive training under each of his four friends. Though most of his time was spent with Lugh and Phundasa, he had another magic lesson with Nihs and a couple with Meya. From Phundasa he learned the basics of what the Orc called *thortnir*, a martial art that mostly involved punches and throws. Secretly, he wasn't sure what the point of learning fist-fighting was—after all, even if he lost his regular sword, he always had his soularm, a weapon that could never be separated from him. But it would certainly help make him stronger, and it couldn't hurt to know how to fight someone without making them explode, an area in which the soul sword was unfortunately weak. Their practice sessions often involved Kyle learning new ways in which he could experience pain, while Lugh laughed at him from the sidelines.

His lessons with Meya were quite a different story. He felt slightly nervous the first time they descended to the training room together; he was still not entirely comfortable around her and was unsure how skilled he would be at healing magic. He still had issues using elemental magic during his lessons with Nihs—perhaps it was because he was from Earth, but he found the whole concept very difficult to get used to.

"All right," Meya told him once they had started, "how much do you know about healing magic?"

"Almost nothing," Kyle said. "I know it gives you power over living creatures. That's pretty much it."

Meya nodded. "You're right about that. We study the three components of living beings—mind, body, and spirit—and how they can be altered. The only real difference between healing and hurting magic is the nature of the alterations you make. We'll start with healing magic. It's easier, and you'll get more use out of it."

"Sounds good," Kyle said.

"Healing doesn't just take energy away from the caster," she told him, rooting through a satchel on her hip, "it also weakens the person that was healed. Magic can only do so much—it doesn't solve everything, it just helps your own body heal faster or fix things it couldn't fix on its own. Healing can do amazing things, but the person who's healed will have to pay for it one way or another."

"That makes sense," Kyle said. Something occurred to him. "Is it…possible to bring people back from the dead with healing?"

Meya gave him a look. "It's possible," she said, "but it's very, very hard, and it gets harder the longer the subject's been dead. I've never heard of someone being resurrected who had been dead for more than a couple of days. I wouldn't be able to do it. It takes a skilled bishop—sometimes more than one—to revive someone."

Kyle just said, "Oh."

Meya produced a small dagger from her satchel.

"Now," she said, "obviously I can't teach you how to heal without one of us getting hurt. It's possible for you to heal yourself, but we should save that for when you get more used to it. I'll show it to you first, then you can try. I'm going to give you a little cut on your palm—nothing serious."

"All right," Kyle said, trying to remain unfazed. He held out his hand.

Meya took his fingers in one hand, then, with a neat little movement, brought the dagger up to his palm and made a small slit.

Kyle winced, but kept himself from pulling his hand away.

"The easiest way to heal is to touch as close to the wound as possible," Meya said, doing so. "You need to give the cut room to mend itself, so don't put your hands right on or in it. After that, it's the same as elemental magic. You have to see the wound closing in your mind's eye. Try to will all of your compassion and desire to see the cut healed through your arms and into the other person. You become aware of their soul underneath the surface when you start to heal…you have to pull at it, willing it to come up and help patch the wound…" her voice trailed off, and she gave a small laugh.

"Sorry," she said, "it's hard to explain to someone who doesn't know how it feels. Let me show you. I'm sure you'll understand once you see for yourself." And with that, she narrowed her eyes until they were almost closed, both hands touching Kyle's wounded one. White light gathered around her, flowing down her forearms and into his palm. He watched as the two sides of the cut sprang together, turning into a red line, a scab, and finally disappearing altogether.

Kyle took his hand back and flexed his fingers. No matter how many times he saw them at work, healing powers amazed him, even more so than the elemental powers of Nihs.

"Think you can do it?" Meya asked, drawing back her own sleeve.

"I'll try," Kyle said. "Be ready to heal yourself if it doesn't work."

Meya smiled. "Don't worry. Just remember what I told you." She drew the blade lightly across her own palm.

Kyle, feeling very nervous and under no small amount of pressure, took her hand in both of his own as she had done. He tried to juggle all of the tips she had given in his mind. It had sounded so simple at the time, but it was much harder to think now that he could actively see her bleeding in front of him.

Ok, focus. Visualize. He tried to recall what it had looked like when Meya had healed him. He imagined the cut pulling itself shut of its own accord and fading into nothingness.

He felt the healing light envelop him, energy rushing down his arms as the magic moved from him to Meya. His hands grew incandescent, and Meya's started to glow as well—but Kyle felt doubt creep into his mind. The cut was swathed in light, but nothing seemed to be happening. Even after several seconds, there was no noticeable difference. A drop of Meya's blood ran down her hand.

"It's not working!" he said.

Meya was unfazed.

"You need to pull at my soul using the magic you've gathered," she told him. "You're still just sitting at the surface. Keep trying. I trust you!"

Kyle tried to figure out what she meant. He knew the cut was not serious, but for some reason it distressed him to see her calmly holding out her bleeding hand. He felt guilty for not being able to help.

He gave her hand a squeeze. *Come on, work,* he found himself thinking.

Suddenly, his senses shifted, and he understood. Meya still stood before him, but now he could sense something else filling the same space as her. It was like a river of energy, a shifting, swirling mass, not always discernible but still obviously there. He looked down at her palm and pressed his fingers near the wound. His fingers dipped into the pool of energy, and when he withdrew them, a part of the mass came with them. His focus shifted to the wound, and the mass followed, rising up over Meya's skin, pushing the blood back inside, knitting it together, sealing it.

The light faded, and Meya pulled her hand back. She brought it up to her face to examine it, smiled and showed it to Kyle.

"Nice work," she said.

It wasn't as clean as the job that she had done; her palm was still rather red, and the cut was still visible as a thin line down her palm. But it was healed.

"That's the feeling you need to go for every time you heal someone," she said. "You need to touch their soul, and give it the power to fix what needs fixing. With elementalism, you're just talking to the physical world, nothing that has a will of its own. With healing, you need to learn to work with the soul of another. Now I think that's enough for today. We probably shouldn't be going around cutting ourselves for too long."

"Right," Kyle said with a small smile.

And so the days passed. When they woke up on the second sun of the third day, the coastline of Eastia was in sight. It was now just a matter of hours until the *Ayger* reached Rhian, and Meya and Phundasa would be leaving them.

Now that they were again flying over land, Kyle spent much of his free time staring out of the ship's picture window. Eastia's topography was an interesting departure from Centralia's; the land was more rugged and wild than the rolling hills near Reno, and the trees were ancient and needled. Mountains appeared in the far distance as they flew—Kyle stared and stared, drinking in the landscape.

They passed over a city by the coast when they arrived. Though it was large and sprawling, it was nowhere near as huge or as magnificent as Reno city. Here and there were signs of modernization, but overall it looked as though the city was very old.

"That's Santrauss," Lugh told him, "big port city. Decent place, I've been there a few times."

More villages passed by as the *Ayger* moved inland, many of them small and simple, built wherever they would fit in the rocky countryside. At one point, Kyle laughed at the sight of a small bundle of houses built on what was practically a cliff face. He couldn't believe that anyone could be so stubborn as to build a village in such a place.

A few hours later, they reached their destination. They had been flying over an extensive mountain range when a crescent-shaped lake came into view. Built upon a high plateau overlooking the lake was the city of Rhian.

Kyle made out a number of small waterfalls on the face of the plateau, feeding into the lake below. As they drew closer to the town, he realized that the falls were actually flowing out of the cliff itself, rather than from the top of the escarpment. In fact, the cliff was not only dotted with holes, but balconies, walkways, and other constructions made of wood and stone.

"That's Kisset," Meya told him. "The Kol of Rhian live there. It's connected to more of their caves in the mountains past the city."

Kyle said nothing, realizing that there was really little he could ask. So this was what a Kol settlement looked like. At first the cliff face seemed solid and natural, until you noticed the telltale signs of habitation and realized that there was probably much more activity under the surface.

"There's an airdock in the back of the city," Lugh said from the wheel. "We can touch down there."

Rhian turned out to be a pleasant mountain town inhabited mostly by Kol, Oblihari, a few Orcs, and the usual smattering of humans and Selks. The sun was bright and the mountain air was clear and refreshing. Most of the buildings were constructed from a kind of white-gray stone, and looked very old. Their facades were stark and smooth, having been worn down over the years by rain and wind. Houses built by the Oblihari stood out from the rest; they were tall and crooked, much like the Oblihari themselves.

None of the urgency displayed by the people of Reno was present here. Townsfolk walked from place to place leisurely, as people do when they know they have little else to accomplish for the day. No runners were present in these streets, and even tigoreh machinery was a rare sight.

Phundasa breathed in and out explosively, stretching his arms.

"Phoo! It is good to be back!"

Though the town was built on a plateau, the ground was far from flat.

Rhian's very existence marked a victory over Eastia's wild topography, and a slight one at that. Streets ran not in straight lines, but along whichever ground was flattest and most convenient. Some houses were twice as large on their second floor as their first, having been built on a steep slope, and others still were skewed dangerously. The roads often transformed into stairs when the slope of the land required it.

Kyle took every possible opportunity to stop and enjoy the view offered. It was breathtaking, if a little dizzying. The lake down in the valley shimmered in the afternoon sun, and the mountains in the distance looked so tremendous as to appear fake, paintings on the sky rather than true masses of rock and snow.

As they walked, Kyle caught signs of the Kol's occupation of the town of Kisset below. There were a number of passages, marked by multicolored lamps, which gave way to steep flights of stairs descending into the earth. Some of the streams flowing through the city mysteriously disappeared into holes in the ground, and Kyle imagined these must be the same streams that ultimately fed the lake below.

They stopped once they reached the town square, and Meya and Phundasa turned and bowed to their three companions.

"Thank you for getting us here," Meya said. "I'm sorry about the eyrioda."

Lugh shrugged. "Wasn't your fault. Besides, that's the kind of thing that keeps us on our toes! But you and Boombasta are going to the hideout, right?"

Meya smiled at the butchering of her companion's name. "Probably, yes," she said. "Us too. So let's stick together for now, and not feel stupid when we say our goodbyes and then head off in the same direction."

And so the five of them turned away from the square, and located the town's only hideout together. It was a large building of wood and stone run by an elderly Oblihari couple, and the inside was clean if not new.

"Is that young Meya?" the husband wheezed, when they approached the counter, peering over a pair of round glasses perched improbably upon his beak. His body was bent and his gray feathers were bedraggled; he stood with the aid of a twisted wooden cane.

"How do you do, Osirde?" Meya said warmly, grasping his hand in both of hers. "It's been a long time, hasn't it?"

"Many years," he agreed, peering at the rest of the group. "And… Phundasa, isn't it?"

Phundasa thumped his fist against his chest in recognition.

"Now, what brings you back to Rhian, my children? Come, sit down, we must chat a while. Would you like a cup of tea?"

"*Tea?*" Lugh said.

Osirde gazed at him over his spectacles. "Too busy for tea, are you? Have somewhere else to go?" He lifted his cane with some difficulty and prodded Lugh in the chest.

"No, I guess not," Lugh said, trying not to laugh. "I've just never heard of a hideout serving tea before."

They allowed themselves to be led to a table and served by Osirde and his wife, Mikasa. Kyle learned as they ate that since so few adventurers came through Rhian, the job of being a hideout master here was not the stressful affair that it was in the big city. In fact, the only other people in the hideout apart from Kyle's party were a pair of Orcs, who left not too long after they arrived.

They ate and chatted, enjoying a last meal together before parting ways. Just as with Rogan, Kyle was saddened by the prospect of Meya and Phundasa's departure; he had already grown used to their company. He wondered what it would be like to travel with only Nihs and Lugh around.

Osirde drew close to their table, bearing a tray, which rattled in his shaky arms. He set it down, unloaded it, and began to gather up their used dishes, joining in their conversation as he did.

"The tea was excellent, Osirde," Meya complimented him.

"Mm, thank you, my dear. Right from Bryan here in town, I've always said that he grows the finest—"

Suddenly, Osirde leapt forwards. Mugs, plates and food were scattered everywhere as he tumbled head over heels across the table and fell off the far side. Meya screamed and Lugh swore, rising to his feet, sword already drawn.

A steel-blue arrow was buried in Osirde's back.

Kyle jumped up after Lugh, drawing his changesword. He did not understand what had just happened, at least not consciously, but some part of him knew that they were all in danger. The window across from them had shattered, and Kyle realized with a sick feeling that Mikasa had been standing in front of it when the arrow flew. She was lying on the ground now, unmoving.

Kyle's companions were all shouting, but he couldn't make out what any of them were saying over the rushing sound he heard in his own mind. He was bewildered and overwhelmed, unable to even feel remorse for what had happened to the old masters.

A twister of magic appeared before them, and two men materialized within it. Apart from the clothing and equipment they wore, they were identical, both with flaxen hair and glassy blue eyes. One of them had a bow drawn and pointed in their direction; the arrow nocked in it was a blue bolt like the one that had struck Osirde. The other, from the clothing he wore, was a spellcaster. For some reason, he was wearing a white bandage on his head that obscured one eye.

"Who the hell are you?" Lugh snarled.

The spellcaster just smiled. "Come with us," he said, "and no one else will be hurt."

Meya stepped forward, her face livid. "You bastards! They were old and innocent! What did they ever do to you?"

"We didn't want anyone to see," he replied, as if this answered everything.

"Give us one good reason why we shouldn't kill you as you stand," Phundasa growled, tightening the riveted gloves he wore on his hands.

The man didn't stop smiling. His—twin?—was doing the same, his bow half-drawn, ready to be fired. Kyle had seen a similar bow before, in the weapon store General Arms. It was constructed not of one arc, but of three separate pieces, and its string was nearly invisible, like a strand of spider's silk. Lugh had warned him about such bows.

Remember the look of these, and be afraid when you see an adventurer using one.

"You can't," the magician said simply. "We will kill you all if you try to fight. We only want Kyle. The rest of you can live, if you surrender."

Kyle's mind was buzzing. The implications of what the man had said were sinking in.

These men are after you. *You're the reason why Osirde and Mikasa are dead.*

Were these more of Radisson's thugs, who had followed them here from Reno city? It was possible. Who was it that wanted Kyle so badly that they were willing to hire these maniacs to get the job done?

In that moment, he knew what he had to do.

"Fine," he said, stepping forwards, "I'll come. But *he* has to throw down his bow."

The men just laughed. "You can't demand anything of us," the spellcaster said. "You have nothing to threaten us with."

We'll see about that, Kyle thought. He stepped in front of the others, spreading his arms wide.

"You need me alive for whatever your boss wants, don't you? How good of a shot *are* you? Good enough to shoot at them without me getting in the way?"

He knew he had been right from the way that the men looked at each other; however, his threat did not have the desired effect.

The sniper looked back at Kyle, and raised his weapon. The arc of the bow spun gracefully about the handle.

"I'm a *very* good shot," he said, bringing the fletching up to his chin.

But his companion, to Kyle's immense relief, laid a hand on his arm, pushing the bow gently downwards. "It's all right," he said. "He said he'd come with us, after all." To Kyle he said, "My brother will not shoot. But he will not throw his bow down either. We will walk outside. Your friends won't follow us. You will go first, and you won't draw your sword. Go on," he added, he and his twin stepping aside to let him pass.

Kyle turned briefly back to the others.

"I won't tell you to trust me," he said in a low voice, "because I don't know what I'm doing. But I don't want any of you to get hurt."

"We'll get you out of this," Lugh hissed back, "I promise."

Kyle nodded and allowed the twins to lead him outside. The spellcaster followed directly behind him, while the sniper lingered to make sure the rest of them didn't try to follow.

Soon the three of them were outside. The bright sun over Rhian seemed unreal as Kyle was marched back toward the town square. The sniper was keeping his bow low, and the other carried no weapon at all, but something about the way they moved must have communicated itself to the people of the town. A murmur arose in the townsfolk, and people began to give them a wide berth; clearly, no one was willing or strong enough to interfere. Kyle's mind was working furiously, trying to figure out a way he might escape. His soul sword was always an option. If what Nihs had said about it were right, nothing on Loria would be able to withstand its attack. But there was little he could do about a skilled magician, and even less against the sniper's lethal ring bow. Whatever the cost, he didn't want to put the others in any danger. He would never forgive himself if one of them got hurt because of him.

They already have.

Kyle shook with rage. He hadn't wanted to cause anyone any trouble, he hadn't wanted to get in anyone's way. And now two people were dead because of him. Some way to repay the denizens of Loria for their kindness. He had brought danger and death into this peaceful mountain town.

The magic user stopped in the square. "Are they watching us?" he asked his twin.

"No, brother."

"Good." He held out his hands.

"You will take one," he told Kyle, "and one of my brother's. Don't squirm."

Hating himself, Kyle took the hand. The other brother approached, holding out his own. A flicker of an idea formed in Kyle's mind. He could have his soul sword out and both of them dead before they even realized it! There was no time to think of it further. He had to act now, while he still had the chance. He tensed to strike.

Suddenly, noise erupted all around him. For a moment, he was utterly confused. The twins cried out, and the magic user withdrew his hand from Kyle's. He wasted no time in drawing his soul sword and pulling it back to strike, but something made him pause. The twin's attention was not on him at all—in fact, they were facing away from him.

"Freeze!" A voice boomed. "This is the Buorish police!"

There were at least twenty of them: armor-clad in their obsidian plate mail, red and gold crests emblazoned on their chests, bows and guns drawn and pointed directly at the twins. They stood in a wide semicircle around Kyle and the thugs, immovable and solid as statues.

The circle opened slightly, and a policeman stepped forward. His uniform was slightly different from the others', and Kyle thought he must be a commander of some kind. His voice rang with authority when he spoke.

"You are under arrest. Step away from the civilian and from each other. Drop all of your weapons. Do not attempt any magic. Any movement contrary to my instructions will be seen as an act of resistance and will invoke both the suspension of your rights and our retaliation."

The twins were standing frozen back-to-back, but they did not move away from each other or drop their weapons. Kyle, unsure of what to do, stepped away from them and withdrew his soul sword.

Suddenly, the magician reached his hands behind his back; the sniper did the same and grasped them. The commander shouted 'stop them!' and a couple of the guards started to move, but magic was already whirling around the twins. A split second later, they were gone.

There was a moment of frozen silence. Kyle stood in a daze as the guards lowered their bows and swarmed around where the twins had been. More of them went off to check the area around the square and more still approached Kyle.

"Are you all right, sir?" one of them asked him.

"Yeah," he said, trying to wrap his head around what had just happened. "Yeah, I'm fine."

He became aware that the others were coming out of the hideout behind him. The guards spun to face them when they sensed their approach, but quickly relaxed.

"Are you this man's companions?" one of them asked.

"Yeah, we're his friends. Hey, what happened?" Lugh said.

"The police got here and they just disappeared," Kyle said.

"Ran for it, huh? Bastards…didn't even give us a chance to pay them back for Osirde and Mikasa."

"Excuse me," the guard asked, "but to what are you referring? Are there wounded inside that building?"

Lugh shook his head. "Dead. That sniper got them both with his ring bow."

Kyle couldn't see the guard's expression, but sensed a tightening of his body language underneath the rigid metal suit.

"I will inform the captain of this," he said. "Pardon me, but if none of you are wounded, then I must go to the aid of my comrades. Please wait here for us." And he strode off, leaving the five of them reunited once more.

"Are you all right?" Meya asked Kyle, drawing close to him.

When he turned to reply, he saw that there were tears in her eyes.

"I'm fine. What about you?"

She looked away, hugging herself tightly across the chest.

"I…I knew Osirde and Mikasa from when I was a girl. I used to visit them when I came to town, and they would give me tea and tell me stories…"

Her voice trailed off, and Phundasa, who had been listening close by, gently laid a huge hand on her shoulder. Kyle could see her jaw clenching as she struggled not to cry. He felt wretched. Angry at the twins, but mostly at himself. He wanted to say something, anything that could redeem him, but the Buorish commander approached them before he got the chance.

"I am captain Callaghnen of the Buorish police," he said, dipping his head to them. "I hope that all of you are well." His manner was stiff and formal, and he kept his hands folded behind his back as he talked.

"Barely," Lugh said. "It's a good thing you got here when you did."

"Alas, had we been present from the start the lives of those brave Oblihari may have been saved. As it is, we arrived far too late." He scanned the group briefly, and his gaze fell on Kyle.

"Excuse me, sir," he said, "but are you Kyle Campbell?"

Unbelievable, Kyle thought. *Does everyone in the world know my face?*

There was no point in trying to deny it. Callaghnen knew; he was just going through the motions. "Yes, I am," he said.

"It is my understanding that a few days ago you applied for a temporary Iden card at the River Street office in Reno city, citing that your memory had been wiped by a magical accident. Is that correct?"

"Yes."

"In that case, I must inform you that a summons to the Buorish court has been issued for you by none other than King Azanhein himself. I will require that you and all of your companions allow us to escort you to the Dark Citadel so that the proceedings may take place."

Lugh was the first to speak. "A summons to court? At the Buorish capital? What for?"

Callaghnen did not answer immediately. When he did, it sounded as though he was reading off a note pinned to the inside of his helmet.

"The court has reviewed the story provided by Kyle, Nihs, yourself, and the one named Rogan Harhoof. The issue was presented to His Majesty King Azanhein, who consented to summon Mister Campbell to the Buorish capital. The court wishes to further analyze the events surrounding his misfortune, and grant him a permanent Iden card if appropriate."

"And destroy his temporary one if appropriate, right?"

"If the court deems it necessary, then yes, the card will be revoked."

Lugh was seething. "How come we have to go all the way to the Citadel for this?"

"I assure you, the court would not have issued the summons if it did not think it completely necessary. You are not under arrest, and we will compensate you for any costs incurred throughout the voyage to the capital."

"And what if we refuse?" Lugh demanded.

Callaghnen tilted his head. "We are authorized to use appropriate force to ensure that the summons are fulfilled."

"So we *are* under arrest, no matter how you present it," Nihs said from Lugh's shoulder. "And now we have to spend a month in Buoria while the court decides what to do with Kyle, all because of one Iden card?"

It was hard to read a Buor's body language, but Kyle thought that the captain looked uncomfortable. He was still standing immobile in front of them, hands folded behind his back, but was starting to broadcast the impression that he'd rather not be.

"I will concede that the court does have additional reasons for requesting that Kyle travel to Buoria," he said, with great reluctance.

"Like what?" Nihs snapped.

"As an example, we believe that he was intimately involved with the events that transpired today? Similarly, we have reason to believe that there exists a connection between Kyle and an abduction that took place in Reno's island district four days ago. The court would like to question him with regard to these events."

Damn, Kyle thought. They were in trouble. The Buors didn't know everything—but it wouldn't take long for it all to unravel if they started to question them. *We're trapped. We couldn't escape if we tried to, and even if we could, we'd have the entire Buorish police force after us.*

Another guard approached the captain and saluted. This one was shorter and slighter than he, insofar as it was possible to tell through the layers of armor.

"We have searched the premises, sir," the guard said, and Kyle realized with a jolt that what he thought was a *he* was a *she*, "there is no sign of any other men nearby, and the two that escaped have left nothing behind."

"Thank you, corporal." Callaghnen tilted his head in her direction, and she returned the motion before joining the other officers a ways off.

The captain addressed them again. "I truly am sorry that the affair must be handled in this manner, but my orders are clear. I am to apprehend Kyle Campbell and his companions, and escort you to Buoria."

"*All* of us?" Lugh asked. He motioned to Meya and Phundasa. "Will you at least let them go? They've only been with us a few days; they hired us to bring them here."

"I am sorry. If they have traveled in your company, then they must come as well. Where is the Minotaur known as Rogan Harhoof?"

"He left us in Reno," Nihs said coldly. "Are you going to hunt him down as well?"

The captain lowered his head. "That will not be necessary. But please, allow me to apologize on behalf of the Buorish court for this inconvenience. It is not often that such a situation arises, and when it does we must all do the best we can to help resolve it. Accompany me to the capital, and I promise that your affair will be handled as quickly and as smoothly as possible."

Lugh opened his mouth to speak, but Kyle beat him to it.

"We'll come with you," he said. "Do we have a choice? You'll just chase us down if we resist, right? And then we *will* be under arrest." He felt bile rising in his throat as the injustice of it all struck him. "All this is happening because of me. I'll come with you, but don't force everyone else to because they were unlucky enough to be with me!"

The captain dipped his head again. He always seemed to default to that motion. "Your concern for your companions is commendable, and I would be all too happy to grant you this boon were it not absolutely necessary that they accompany you to Buoria. I am sorry, but this is the way it must be. We will stay in Rhian for tonight, while the aftermath of what transpired today is dealt with and our ships are serviced. In the morning we will leave for the capital."

They ended up staying at a local inn, since the adventurer's hideout had been sealed off by the police and no one had any desire to enter the building in any case. Guards were posted outside of their rooms, and Kyle was sure there would be more outside. They were told that they would be allowed to move around within Rhian, provided they were escorted, but none of them had any motivation to do so. It was still only afternoon, and the sun was bright and shining, and Kyle felt trapped and forlorn. The knowledge that he was no longer in charge of his own fate was incredibly stifling. There were no guards visible from inside their room, but Kyle sensed their presence as keenly as if they were manacles on his wrists.

They all gathered in Lugh's room for the evening, as they had gotten into the habit of doing. This time, however, the atmosphere was tense, especially when Meya and Phundasa arrived. Phundasa's face was difficult to read, but Meya's anger and distress were palpable from the second she came into the room. Kyle suspected that this wasn't just because of Osirde and Mikasa, and was proven right when her red eyes fell on him and refused to turn away. While Phundasa sat down, she remained standing in the center of the room, her arms folded.

"Well," Phundasa said with a trace of mirth, "looks like we'll be traveling together for a while yet."

Meya ignored him. "Kyle," she said, "who are you?"

Kyle didn't reply. He had no idea what to say.

"When we met in the hideout in Reno, you said people were after you and you had to leave the city as soon as possible," Meya pressed. "Now Callaghnen's recognized you, and *he* said you just applied for a temporary Iden card because you lost your memory? Forgive me, but I think you'll understand why I'm a little suspicious."

"He's not a criminal, if that's what you're getting at," Lugh said.

"Are you sure? How long have you known him?"

"Look, you've got the wrong idea. Kyle's—"

"I'm from another world," Kyle said.

He had no idea what Lugh had been planning on saying, but he did know that it wouldn't be the truth—and at that moment, he couldn't stand the thought of lying to Meya further.

Meya's expression froze. Her arms uncrossed and fell to her sides. Her eyes, and those of everyone else in the room, turned to him. Phundasa sat up in his chair.

"What?" Meya said.

"I'm not from Loria," Kyle said. "I'm from another world, called Terra. I came here less than a month ago. That's why I told the Iden office I'd lost my memory. And we're not sure, but we think that's why those men are after me, too. I know you probably don't believe me, but it's the truth."

This time, it was Meya who couldn't speak. Her mouth opened and closed a few times, and she and Phundasa shared a glance.

"I don't believe you," she said finally, but some of the aggression had gone out of her voice. Kyle hoped that she could sense that he was being honest.

"We didn't either, at first," Nihs said. "It's not something that comes easily."

"You knew about this?" Meya demanded.

"We found him in northern Ar'ac, laying unconscious in a crater,"

Nihs said. "Needless to say we were curious from the outset."

Meya took a moment to reply. She brushed an errant hair away from her face.

"I think," she said finally, "that you'd better tell us the whole story."

It took about an hour. Kyle was surprised, in fact, that it took so little time to tell—it had seemed like years since he had fallen into Loria. Kyle spoke for the majority of the time, though Lugh and Nihs supplied further details. They told Meya and Phundasa about Kyle's fall, his rescue by Lugh, Nihs and Rogan, their journey to Reno and what the scholars Yuma and Oklade had told them, and finally the true version of what happened when they were captured by Radisson's thugs.

By the end of the tale, Meya's mouth was open and Phundasa, who was not easily fazed, had leaned forward in his chair and was listening intently. When Kyle finally stopped talking, there was a long silence.

"And that's the truth?" Meya asked at last. Her voice was half suspicion, half empathy.

"As far as we can tell," Kyle said. "Hard to believe, I know."

Meya looked pensive for a moment, then rose from her seat and approached him.

He recoiled instinctively.

"I want to read your memories," she said. "I don't think that's too much to ask, do you?"

Kyle couldn't argue with this, so he allowed her to touch his temples and force his eyes shut. He'd had his memories read before, but Meya's reading was gentler than the others had been. The images flickered more slowly, and he awoke from it feeling less disoriented than usual. When his eyes opened, he could tell from the look on Meya's face that what she had seen had erased all doubt from her mind.

"They're so *strange,*" she said, putting a hand to her mouth. "Those are memories from your world?"

"Yeah. We don't think that they can be read properly by someone from Loria."

Meya sat back down. "Why didn't you tell us?" she asked, then, "no, that's a stupid question, isn't it. We were only supposed be together for a couple of days, after all."

'Supposed to' was all Kyle heard. "I'm sorry. None of you would be here if it weren't for me."

"Hey, don't you start with that," Lugh said. "It's not your fault all this happened."

"You're not wrong," Phundasa said, "but the question remains: what are we going to do now?"

Lugh shrugged. "Kyle said it all, really. There's nothing we *can* do. Things don't usually end well when people try to outrun the Buorish police."

Kyle just shook his head. He knew he should be worried about the Buors, and what they might find out if they put him on trial, but all he wanted to do was rest and forget about the world. The way he saw it, whether or not the Buors discovered his secret was outside of their power. All they could do was wait and see.

They spent the rest of the day half inside the inn and half out. Since Meya and Phundasa had visited Rhian before, they took Kyle and the others to see some of the town's attractions. There weren't many, mostly because the party wasn't allowed to enter Kisset, but Kyle was grateful for the opportunity to take his mind off of the day's events. The faces of Osirde and Mikasa swam in his mind, and though Meya put on a brave face for most of the day he could sense her deep sadness. At one point she excused herself to visit the town's church alone, and when she rejoined them an hour later her face was downcast and her eyes were red. Though Kyle had only known the elderly couple for a matter of minutes, Meya's grief soon affected him as well, and he found himself unable to enjoy any of their tour. Time and time again he wanted to apologize or at least speak to her—though knowing what she was going through, he knew better than to try and comfort her with hollow words. Instead he walked in silence, Meya's mourning twisting the knife of guilt in his gut.

When the party was relatively alone and Meya found the strength to speak, she and Phundasa asked him questions about his world, and Kyle took an odd pleasure in answering them. At first, it was clear that neither of them completely believed his story, but as the day wore on, their residual skepticism melted away.

And always following them at a respectful distance were Captain Callaghnen's escorting officers. The Buors were polite enough to keep themselves out of earshot as they walked; however, their presence was oppressive nonetheless. In a way, it was infuriating to know that they were being detained by people so polite and well meaning as the Buorish police.

They returned to the inn once it began to get dark, and sorted themselves into their respective rooms. These were small, and unlike the spacious rooms in Reno wouldn't have been able to accommodate someone such as Rogan. Kyle and Nihs shared a room, and Lugh and Phundasa took another while Meya got one to herself. Captain Callaghnen, true to his word, paid for everything.

Nihs entered the overhead once they had settled down. Kyle, who had gotten used to this, simply wondered about whom the tiny Kol was talking to, and what about, before turning over and falling asleep.

Kyle graduated from primary school an honor roll student who had already worked a full-time job; he did not, however, have many friends to celebrate this graduation with, and was frankly happy to be rid of the squat schoolhouse where he had spent the last eight years of his life. It was because of this that the attitudes of his schoolmates on graduation night surprised him.

"Hey! Look at us!" Mark exclaimed when running into him. He spread his arms wide as if to display himself in his finery.

Kyle looked at him in confusion. The two had stopped hanging out together years ago. Why was Mark bothering to approach him now?

"We're off to high school next year," he added, blissfully unaware.

"Yeah, guess so," Kyle said.

"What do you think it'll be like?"

Kyle thought honestly about this. "I think it'll probably be more of the same."

"Haha, maybe. Well, see you around! Nice job on the honor roll, by the way!"

And he moved on.

Kyle, perplexed, did the same.

He worked again that summer, the same all-encompassing hours that he had taken the previous season. As such, he was able to afford new clothes and school supplies when September again rolled around.

The first day of the new term came sooner than Kyle expected. He had not really thought about the transition to high school. He imagined, as he had told Mark, that it would be more of the same; the classes would be a little harder, the rooms would be a bit larger, and the students…well, the students probably wouldn't have changed very much. A couple of the kids from Kyle's school would be going to the same high school as him, but he had no intention of spending time with any of them. His brief stint with Jennifer Vasquez had taught him a thing or two, mostly that people were overall not worth the trouble they brought into one's life. Their time together had been happy, but stressful, and Kyle had wasted a good deal of his hard-earned money besides. But he was not bitter—he told himself that such issues were to be expected, and resolved to learn from his mistakes.

On the first day of term, he got up before his mother and poured himself a bowl of cereal. He ate it staring across the table at his laden backpack, which he had set down in another chair. His mother rose a short while after, and lifted his bag to the ground as she sat down.

"First day of high school," she said, in what she probably thought was an energetic voice.

Kyle said nothing. He had long since run out of things to say to his mother.

"Good luck today," she added, seemingly unaware of this.

He still said nothing. Silently he thought that if his mother still possessed any good luck she should save it for herself. Kyle did not believe in luck. He had resolved to make his way through school and everything beyond through hard work, which had always served him well up until now.

"Do you have everything you need?" his mother asked him.

"Yes."

"Lunch? Binder? Pencils and paper?"

"Yes, Mom."

"Talk to people. Make friends. Pay attention to your teachers, and be careful of bullies!"

Kyle rolled his eyes. "Good grief, Mom, I've dealt with bullies before. I'm not a kid anymore."

"The bullies in high school are bigger," his mother said, and Kyle was surprised to hear how serious she sounded. "And the worst thing about them is that they don't always seem like bullies at first."

For the first time in a while, Kyle looked at her—really looked at her—searching her face, wondering why she had said what she had.

Kyle had never before spent the time to think of his mother, and of the problems she always seemed to have. Now, he found himself slightly curious. But it would have to wait; he had more pressing things on his mind.

"I will, Mom," he assured her, and rose to get ready for school.

Kyle had planned for an uneventful bus ride. He sat in the back and talked to no one, even though the bus was full of chattering people whom he had not met. He looked out the window and tried to shut the noise out, determined to make his first day of school as painless as possible.

A few minutes later, however, the bus slowed to a stop, and the person who came aboard walked all the way to the back and into Kyle's peripherals. He turned to look.

A smallish girl was leaning across his seat and the one in front of it, clearly waiting for him to turn around. She was wearing a look that Kyle had already come to recognize and hate: blonde, but with off-color roots that suggested a darker natural hair color; done up, but inexpertly so, with eye shadow that was far too dark and lipstick that was far too glossy. Her face was rather round, and she was chewing a wad of pink bubblegum.

"Can I sit here?" she asked, pointing to his seat.

"Sure," Kyle said, as if he could really refuse.

She installed herself next to him and immediately started talking.

"What's your name? I'm Kristina. Where are you from? Nice, I'm from around there too. Do you know Emily Porter? She went to…no? Oh. Do you know anyone who's going here? I know like *no*-one, and I'm *soo* nervous. I talk a lot. You probably noticed that, hahaha! Want some gum?"

"No, thank you," Kyle said, with as much dignity as he could muster.

She gave him a look that suggested that no sane man would deny such an offer.

"Are you like, one of those emo kids?" she asked him.

"What?" said Kyle, who had not yet heard this term.

The girl—Kyle had already forgotten her name—had no time to explain this to him, however, for at that moment the bus arrived at its destination, a larger and newer schoolhouse than Kyle's primary one had been.

"See you 'round!" The girl said, swinging her pack onto her back and jumping into the aisle along with everyone else.

Kyle, mystified, eventually followed.

There was a good amount of chaos going on inside the school when Kyle entered. Students were milling around everywhere, shouting to each other in order to be heard, forming into groups and then breaking apart. Some were clearly lost, and were trying to locate someone or something that could help them find their way. Teachers and staff were scattered here and there, trying their best to keep things moving.

Kyle sighed inwardly and skirted a large clump of people on the way to his first class. He had studied a plan of the school beforehand, and was determined not to get lost.

His first class, English, was in a stuffy, nondescript room in the languages department. Signs of classes long gone were spread about the room: a poster here, a project there. *More of the same*, thought Kyle. He sat down at the back of the classroom. There was an obscene picture drawn on his desk; he covered it with his binder.

The students filed in quietly, for the most part. Kyle took in their unfamiliar faces with disinterest. He could always recognize people by how they looked and acted, though he could rarely remember their names.

The door opened, and three boys tramped in. Kyle recognized the type at once. Tough guys, delinquents who people would love to believe suffered deep down from low self-esteem—though the truth was that these boys were confident to the bone, and could chew people up and spit them out. And for the most part it didn't matter that you were smarter than them, because a built-in, animal part of you would always be afraid of them.

Of course, Kyle didn't think of all this. He merely recognized the feeling and hoped that his day wasn't about to become complicated. He realized with a sinking feeling that most of the remaining seats were near him, in the back. And yes, one of the boys tilted his chin in Kyle's direction, saying to his friends, "Hey, let's sit back there."

They sat down in the typical tough guy fashion, throwing their bags to the floor as loudly as possible and plunking themselves down sideways in their chairs. Settling down took another crowded ten seconds.

Kyle avoided their gazes while trying to appear as though he wasn't. He still was not entirely sure how best to deal with these types, although he usually did better than most.

The boy sitting next to him hit him on the arm. It was not a punch, but rather a smack intended to grab his attention.

"Hey," the boy said, "*hey*."

"What?" Kyle said.

"Teach show up yet?"

"No," Kyle said.

The boy nodded and turned to his friend on the other side. He produced a Zippo lighter, flicked it on, and brought it close to his wrist.

"*Hey*!" the other boy yelped, whipping around in his chair while his friend laughed. He punched lighter-man on the arm. Lighter-man just grinned and waved his Zippo at his friend like a sword.

Kyle spotted movement outside the window and made a split-second decision. He could see an opportunity to get these boys on his side, and right now that was far more important than seeing them punished for a small infraction involving a lighter.

He hit the closest one on the arm as the boy had done to him.

"Hey," he hissed, "stash it! Teacher's coming!"

"Oh, shit," the boy said. In an instant, the lighter was gone and the mock fight was over.

The teacher walked in, and class began. Of course, this being the first class, it was nothing more than an introduction to high school—it involved a great deal of handouts and was incredibly boring.

Lighter-man leaned sideways towards him.

"Hey," he whispered, "thanks for bailing me, man." He held out his hand. "I'm Riley." He said it slyly, proudly, as though he were a celebrity that had just revealed his identity.

Kyle regarded him. He was not tall—shorter than Kyle even—though had the wiry frame and dark skin of a boy who spent all of his spare time outside. His face was squat, and his brown hair was curly. He grinned a grin full of mischief bordering on malice.

Kyle took the hand. "Kyle," he said.

The next day dawned bright and surprisingly chilly. The wind had picked up since the day before, and the town of Rhian was soaked with dew. Captain Callaghnen was waiting for them when they came downstairs.

"I have paid the innkeeper for your breakfast," he told them. "Please join us outside when you are finished."

"Not a bad gig, huh?" Lugh said later, as they ate. "We should get arrested more often."

"Very funny," Nihs said curtly.

The squad of policemen was waiting for them outside, assembled in a double column, ten abreast. They were so out of place among the white, worn buildings of Rhian as to look ridiculous, twin lines of military discipline in the middle of a calm mountain town. As they approached, Kyle took in details that he had not managed to notice the previous day.

They all wore the exact same uniform of black, red and gold, with two exceptions: captain Callaghnen's armor was unique, and was not only more impressive but also heavier than the others. One of the guards standing in the back also wore a different uniform—a long black tunic over his armor, and gloves of tough black hide rather than plate.

At first, the remaining eighteen policemen all looked exactly the same to Kyle. But as he looked further, he started to notice the telltale differences between them. They all had different shapes, just like humans did, and Kyle could tell that a good number of them were women. Their suits of armor were shaped to fit their bodies, and Kyle recalled what Lugh had said before about the Buors wearing armor as others wore clothes. They certainly looked comfortable in their uniforms, and moved with a grace that belied their rigid appearance.

Callaghnen strode forward and bowed.

"One of my soldiers will escort you to your ship. Once you have taken off, please remain in a holding pattern over the plateau. We will join you shortly, and send a flight path to Buoria to your ship's map system. Please do not break this path during your flight."

"Gotcha," Lugh said blandly.

They traveled to the airdocks in silence. The guard that accompanied them was slight and lithe. At first, Kyle had thought he was female, but his voice soon gave him away as a younger man. He introduced himself briefly as Didailus, and spoke little afterwards. Kyle noticed that while the Kol he had met so far all had very simple names, Buorish names were always rather complex.

Didailus followed them back to the *Ayger* and supervised them embarking, standing still as a statue with his hands folded behind his back. As Lugh passed him, he pointed to one of the ship's broken windows.

"Your ship has suffered some damage?" he asked.

"Oh, yeah," Lugh said, "we got attacked by some eyrioda on the way here. No big deal."

Didailus was perturbed. "I will inform Captain Callaghnen of this. I believe he will see it fit to schedule a stop to have your windows repaired. A ship should not fly for longer than necessary damaged so."

"Sure, whatever you say," Lugh said, shrugging. "Won't kill anyone, though."

Once they had boarded, Lugh flew straight upwards until they were in full view of the sun, then turned the *Ayger* in a lazy circle to wait for the police's airships. The atmosphere on the bridge was tense. The effect was subtle, but Kyle, who had gotten used to the normal dynamics between his friends, found it unnerving. Lugh wasn't up to his usual banter, and Nihs, sitting in the corner with his books, might as well have been on another planet. Kyle found himself standing beside Lugh at the helm with Meya on his other side, all three staring out of the picture window, waiting for something to happen.

A few minutes later, the police ships rose up through the clouds. They began to circle the *Ayger*, and the communicator crystal on the dashboard lit up and turned red. Lugh put his hand on it, and Callaghnen's voice sounded throughout the bridge.

"Greetings. This is Captain Callaghnen. Private Didailus has informed me that your ship requires repair, and so we will be stopping briefly in the nearby city of Vestwheyr for that purpose. We will transfer the coordinates to your map system now, if you are prepared to receive them."

"Yep, go right ahead," said Lugh. After a moment's pause he added with incredible cheek, "are these repairs gonna be done courtesy of Buoria? Money's a bit tight at the moment, right?"

There was a fraction of a second's pause before Callaghnen replied, and Kyle thought he could detect the faintest trace of mirth in the captain's voice.

"Yes, you may rest assured that I will handle all necessary costs."

"Great!" Lugh said with genuine happiness. He took his hand off the crystal, which faded again to blue. A moment later, it glowed anew, this time with a green light that pulsed on and off. Once it was done, Kyle felt a gentle pull as the *Ayger* turned itself around, following Callaghnen's directions.

Lugh stepped down from the wheel, his role fulfilled. He seemed much happier than before, and Kyle reflected on the fact that the way to Lugh's heart was through his ship.

"Well, well," he said brightly, "free repairs! Breakfast is one thing, but replacing all the windows is going to be *expensive*. I could get used to this!"

"Let's hope your cheery outlook lasts," Nihs said from his corner. "Buoria is not a place noted for its hospitable nature."

"What kind of a place is Buoria?" Kyle asked. "I've only heard bits and pieces."

"It's terrible," Lugh said, laughing. "Or at least, so they say. I've never been there. Not many outsiders have."

"The country is a wasteland," Nihs said, without looking up from his book. "A volcanic island covered in ash and dust. There's precious little there, except for metal, of course, and more stone than anyone knows what to do with. Most of the Buors live near to the coast in their capital city, which is overseen by the king's palace."

"The Dark Citadel," Meya said with a hint of amusement. "We all know about that place, at least. It's supposed to be magnificent."

"The Buors don't really strike me as the kind of people to have a king," Kyle said. "You'd think they'd elect a leader or something."

"The Buorish king is, in fact, elected into office," Nihs said. "The

Buorish definition of 'king' differs from the humans'. They vote for their king based on their ability in combat, their scholarliness and their skill in politics and diplomacy. In other words, they must be the ultimate representative of their race."

"Huh," Kyle said. He was having a difficult time constructing a mental image of a king who was both physically mighty and an avid scholar. In his experience, you could be one or the other but not both.

The city of Vestwheyr was nestled in a flat valley with cliffs on three sides. They flew in from the south, where a gap in the cliffs acted as a giant natural gate. The cliff face directly ahead of them was dominated by a massive waterfall, which fed a large lake that covered much of the valley's floor. Vestwheyr was built in front of, around, and on this lake: Kyle could see from where they flew that the city was built mostly of wood, and a good seventy percent of it was either floating or on stilts. A huge wooden construction framed the wide waterfall, like a massive vine that had grown up from the city below. Kyle couldn't decide if its primary function was as a huge waterwheel, a dam, or both.

Lugh regained control of the *Ayger* and set it down on the city's outskirts as instructed by Captain Callaghnen. The airdocks here were an amazingly crude affair compared to the golden honeycombs of Reno—they were simple raised platforms of wood that looked far too rickety and small to support a ship the size of the *Ayger*. But the landing went smoothly, and before Kyle knew it he and the others were joining the captain and a few of his squad outside the docks.

Some men came to greet them, and Kyle noticed that they were all Orcs. He wondered if Vestwheyr was an Orc city—its construction certainly matched Kyle's perception of what Orcish buildings would look like.

"Welcome to Vestwheyr!" the lead Orc said expansively, spreading his arms. He strode forwards and shook Phundasa's hand, slapping him on the shoulder with the other. "Greetings, kinsman! Who should I speak to?" His voice was a permanent shout.

Behind him, Callaghnen coughed politely. If he was offended by the fact that the Orc had walked right past him, he did not show it.

"Pardon me, good sir," he said, and the Orc turned to look at him, "I am Captain Callaghnen of the Buorish police. My squad and I are escorting these adventurers to Buoria."

"Yes?" the Orc said, clearly confused as to why Callaghnen was telling him this.

The captain seemed not to notice.

"However, their airship has suffered some damage, and we have stopped here in the hopes of having it serviced. Might you be able to repair it?"

Comprehension dawned on the Orc's face. "Of course!" he said. "We are skilled mechanics! What needs doing?"

The lead Orc, whose name turned out to be Bazdul, was somewhat disappointed when he found out that it was not the *Ayger*'s engine that needed work. He supervised his men as they fitted new windows and repaired the damage to the deck caused by the eyrioda alpha. He stood with Lugh and Phundasa as they watched, all the while complimenting the design of the ship and suggesting multiple and slightly insane-sounding improvements to Lugh.

"We have these new cranes, they are almost like mechanical arms! Your ship could lift trees out of the ground by their roots! It would be the work of a moment to fit some in—no? A shame, friend, a shame! This is a great ship, but we could make it greater!"

Lugh shook his head, laughing. "Sorry, friend," he said, "but the captain's paying for these repairs, and something tells me he wouldn't approve."

The refitting of the *Ayger's* windows and the repairs to its deck only took a couple of hours. Bazdul's men swarmed around the ship like ants, working with such efficiency that Kyle was amazed they had never seen a ship like the *Ayger* before.

Once the repairs were done, Callaghnen paid Bazdul for his work, and politely informed Kyle and the others that they would be departing immediately. They took to the sky, and Callaghnen set the *Ayger's* course to Buoria. According to him, the flight to the capital would take them into the day after next, and so they had almost two full days to themselves.

Kyle, who had only become more motivated to practice combat after the events in Rhian, spent every spare moment and every scrap of energy training. When Lugh was busy or asleep he trained with Phundasa, practicing punches and throws until his whole body was sore. This went on for the first three periods of light—however, after Kyle woke up on the fourth morning to find that he could barely stand, it was decided that he should spend the remaining day in recuperation.

Every once in a while, Lugh would call the others to the helm to take a look at Eastia's scenery. To Kyle, it was seeing one wonder after another. He had thought that Loria's alien topography and technology would start to get dated after having seen Reno, Rhian and Vestwheyr, but there was always one more amazing sight on the horizon. The mountains they were flying over climbed higher and higher until they were not flying over but through them. Their ponderous, cragged faces dwarfed even the spectacle that Sky Tower had been. These peaks gave way to golden plateaus and forests that were perpetually wreathed in cloud; stepping outside for a few moments was enough to drench oneself in wet mist. They flew over an Oblihari city, the structures tall and soaring, but at the same time crooked and eclectic. They looked like giant stalagmites that had been hollowed out and painted clashing colors. Nets, rope and huge sheets of hide canvas were bundled and strung everywhere, as if the city had been assembled from whatever was lying around at the time.

They reached the coastline of Eastia in the morning of the second day. From there, it would only be a few hours until they reached the island kingdom of Buoria.

The coast was jagged and rocky; islands dotted the ocean for miles beyond the mainland, all of them different shapes and sizes. It was a wondrous display of natural beauty, but Kyle had no eyes for it. He paced the deck of the *Ayger* anxiously. The memories of Osirde and Mikasa haunted him, and he was desperate for their detour to be over so he could regain control over his life.

The hours of flying over the ocean passed in a blur, and soon a dull black shape began to grow on the horizon. The communicator crystal glowed red, and a familiar voice permeated the atmosphere.

"This is Captain Callaghnen. We will be arriving in the kingdom of Buoria shortly. I will send the necessary landing sequence to your ship's map system. We will spend this day and night in repose within the city before attending court the following day. Please for the duration of your stay keep in mind the unique customs and laws practiced by the citizens of Buoria. If it is your wish, I will have one of my officers provide you with a briefing following our landing."

There was a slight shift in the *Ayger*'s movement as it accepted the coordinates from Callaghnen, and slowly they started to lose altitude as Buoria grew ever closer. Kyle stood on the observation deck with both hands on the railing, staring straight forward, not sure what was awaiting him but determined to face it head-on.

As they approached the island of Buoria, Kyle saw that it was basically triangular in shape, a black spike that rose from a bleak and empty stretch of ocean. They drew closer, and it became apparent that the corner of the island they were flying toward was indented like a crescent moon—it was a port of some kind, ships dotting the sky and sea nearby. Though the edges of the moon rose sharply to become untamed mountains, every flat piece of land between them was built upon. The buildings were all of dark gray stone, and even from this distance Kyle could see the perfectionism in their design. The streets were perfectly straight and buildings were perfectly square or rectangular, the angles so sharp they almost hurt the eye.

Kyle next noticed the city's blatant militarization. Though none of the ships patrolling the sea or sky were armed, there were several long-barreled cannons mounted on the coastline, and numerous guard towers built on the points of the moon and upwards along its ridge.

The island was quite foggy; or rather, Kyle realized, cloaked in dust or ash. More and more of it emerged as the ship descended; street upon street of uniform buildings grew out of the gloom.

A structure materialized in the distance, a sight so grand that without being told Kyle knew what it was: the Dark Citadel, the dwelling place of the Buorish king.

It was a huge castle that sat like a crown atop the city, a mass of walls and turrets that was itself the size of a town. It was built into the face of a cliff that rose up beyond the city, and the dark gray stone construction was sculpted and polished with such expertise that it looked almost alive. Cannons lined its walls and were perched atop its turrets, and a black gate of solid metal cut the castle off from the rest of the world. Light shone from thin windows scattered about its many faces, giving the impression that the castle was covered in eyes watching over the city below. Buoria was a world all to its own, and the Dark Citadel was at its core.

Behind the castle and over the edge of the cliff sprawled more of Buoria's countryside. It was all jagged peaks and gray, dust-covered plateaus. Nothing green was in sight.

Kyle noticed that the bridge was becoming darker. The sky above Buoria was overcast, though whether by normal cloud cover or ash blown up from the volcano-pocked island, he did not know.

They all gathered on the bridge to watch the island draw closer. Phundasa came up from the engine room, and Nihs jumped onto the control panel. Buoria wasn't just a first for Kyle; none of his companions had been to the island before, and they all watched, enraptured, as it grew out of the gloom. Beside him, Lugh leaned on the panel and whistled.

"Damn, that's a lot of guns," he said. "And it's so *square*. Just like the Buors themselves, huh?"

"Sorry I brought you here," Kyle said, noticing that it was getting even darker as they descended.

"Are you kidding?" Lugh said. "This is great! Normally it takes a special permit to land in Buoria! Not many people can say they've been here."

Kyle secretly wished he could share his companions' excitement. He couldn't forget the fact that he was here to participate in a trial—and he didn't feel so comfortable around the Buors now that he had seen their home country. The black ships piloted by Callaghnen and his squad looked much more sinister in the ashy twilight, and Kyle could scarcely believe that the polite, helpful people aboard them belonged to the same race as those who had built this city. He couldn't shake the feeling that their kindness was only a charade.

The *Ayger* swung down low, a hundred feet above the surface of the bay, and glided gently inland. Kyle could see from the observation deck that the water below was gray and ash-stained, with a rough surface carved by wind. They passed over land and came to rest on a large landing plate off to the right of the capital's port.

As the *Ayger* cooled down, Callaghnen hailed them from the communicator. "Greetings. This is Captain Callaghnen. We are pleased to say that the landing went as planned, and that a crew will be present shortly to service your craft. Please meet me and my squad outside."

They did so, the five of them exiting the *Ayger* and together stepping out onto Buorish soil.

Kyle first noticed the heat. It wasn't overwhelming, but it was pronounced, particularly because its source seemed to be the air itself as the sun was nowhere in sight. Black clouds rolled overhead, though Kyle could clearly see the point out at sea where they abruptly stopped and the sky became perfectly blue.

He next noticed the noise, a constant low rumbling that he finally realized was thunder. Red lightning flickered between the clouds, providing an almost constant backdrop of noise.

After the noise were the tremors. They were small, and only lasted for a handful of seconds each time, but came so frequently and consistently that it wasn't long before Kyle could sense when one was due. He soon became convinced that his legs would keep shaking long after they left the island.

Kyle looked around for signs of life. There were some: dockworkers at various tasks, Buors touring the waterfront. But it all seemed muted, as if the activity was taking place at some great distance. Perhaps it was because of the noise—or the thick atmosphere, which dulled both light and sound.

He turned and saw that Meya had been sharing the same view as him; she gave him a wan smile when she noticed his presence.

"Quite a place, isn't it?" she said. Even at this distance, her voice was partially drowned out by the thunder. "Hard to believe it exists in the same world as Reno."

The police ships landed nearby, and presently Captain Callaghnen came out to greet them. He approached their group and bowed deeply as his squad assembled behind him.

"Welcome to the kingdom of Buoria," he said, with something approaching reverence. "Allow me to apologize for the current climate—it is ashfall season, the Heart of Buoria's most active time of year. I assure you it is very rarely dangerous, and that you will soon get used to the sound of the thunder and the shaking of the earth. Some prefer to remain mostly indoors during ashfall. Happily, this is an option that will be open to you should the weather cause you discomfort.

"Please follow me to your place of dwelling. Once there, you will meet officials with whom you may discuss the details of the imminent court proceedings."

"Lead on," Lugh said.

They set off, moving inland toward the city core. The streets were not empty, but they nevertheless carried a distinct feeling of abandonment. Clearly, Callaghnen had been speaking the truth when he said the Buors preferred to remain inside during ashfall.

The people they did pass on the road, however, were all friendly, and without exception nodded their heads and exchanged polite 'hello's as they crossed paths. Kyle was getting better at telling the citizens of Buoria apart; it mostly came down to the colors and shapes of their sashes, for all Buors seemed to wear one, and no two were alike. Some were like large scarves, others were closer to belts. Still more sat on one shoulder and crossed over the chest. The Buors they met going about their daily tasks were not as armed as the policemen were, though everyone carried at least a sword with them at all times.

The buildings were all alike—or rather, they were all different but *looked* alike, as if they had been assembled using the same set of parts. Like the Buors themselves, the differences between them were at first difficult to spot, until small details started to emerge for the eye starved for larger ones. The Buors, as it turned out, were as into personalizing their own space as was everyone else. The front faces of metal doors were fused into interesting shapes or hung with family crests, and yellow light spilled from a number of windows, the contrast provided by the bleak exteriors of the houses adding to its warming effect. Tapestries in many different colors served to frame windows or doors or to add color to the gray stone.

Many of the houses featured small gardens out front, though bereft of anything green to plant, the people of Buoria sculpted theirs from white, gray and black sand, petrified wood, and ornaments made of stone or metal. They were oddly appealing, and reminded Kyle of the Zen gardens that were popular back on Earth.

The streets, as Kyle had seen from the air, were perfectly straight, and those that traveled inland rose at a constant upward grade. Occasionally a wall built across the city would separate two levels of elevation, and perfectly spaced flights of stairs would link the two.

Kyle became aware that Callaghnen was talking; someone must have asked him about the city, for he was speaking of its various districts and providing details on the areas they traversed.

"Interestingly, the land upon which this capital is built was one of the last areas of Buoria claimed by our ancestors…it is not defensible from inland, you see, and in antiquity we had little to fear from overseas…a change in theme of architecture is forthcoming as we pass over this fortification, as it marks the division between the upper and lower, or older and newer cities…as we approach the Citadel, you will notice more impressive buildings, and more frequent works of art displayed on the streets and on the facades of buildings…this area, known as the Upper City, was designed for aesthetic appeal rather than functionality, and serves as the social nexus of the capital. You will notice that the majority of us prefer to congregate in the Upper City during the day…"

Callaghnen, as it turned out, knew his city well, for he had just finished his travelogue when the streets became much more crowded and Kyle noticed a shift in architecture. It was abrupt and slightly shocking, as well as, Kyle realized, entirely Buorish: he could see how the idea of having a city divided into areas specifically for living and socializing would appeal to their sense of style. The social ebb and flow here was much more natural, and comparable to the other cities Kyle had visited previously.

They turned left once upon entering the Upper City. Here they could see the rooftops of the houses below; to their right were grand buildings, statues, fountains, and sculptures. Kyle had never seen so much stone in his life, and most of it was uniformly gray; still, there was a silent grace to what the Buors had made with it.

Occasionally they would pass a guard tower, recognizable by the cannons that sat atop. These were high-tech, mean-looking weapons, sleek and golden, their long, slender barrels pointed at the sky. The juxtaposition between the large artillery and the stone buildings around them gave Kyle an odd feeling. He wondered what the Buors thought they might need them for.

The Buors here were no less polite than those in Lower City, and several stopped to talk to Captain Callaghnen specifically. They passed by groups of policemen on patrol, who all saluted the captain smartly.

They walked along the edge of Upper City for a while. Kyle looked to his left and was surprised to see how far up the face of the mountain they had come. The view was impressive, but intimidating. The city gave the impression of being one giant clock, one was that ticking along perfectly and powerfully, each of its denizens slotted perfectly into place. It was all so well thought-out and efficient, nothing like the disorganization of Reno city. Not for the first time since he had come to Loria, Kyle felt uncouth—the perfection that the Buors had achieved seemed to be mocking his own species' lack thereof. He wondered if this perfection was genuine or only skin-deep.

They reached a square close to the mountain face that was framed on all three sides by a single building. Large metal letters over the door spelled the words *Free Holding Center.*

There were a few rows of tigoreh runners parked outside, and a well-tended garden of metal framed the doorway; apart from this, the building was rather nondescript. Like all the others, it fit in with the those next to it.

Callaghnen led them inside. The interior of the building was significantly warmer than its façade; warm Ephicer light brightened the hallways, and portraits and tapestries adorned the walls. Decorations more colorful and delicate than those outside were on display here: clearly the Buors saved their most precious works for where the volcano's ash could not touch them.

It was a public building of some kind, for they had stepped into a large, symmetrical atrium at the middle of which was a manned desk. The clerk shallowly bowed to the captain when he came forward.

"Good day, captain," he said. "How may I help you?"

Callaghnen inclined his head politely. Kyle noticed that the Buors almost always did this before they began to speak.

"Well met, Elliaran. Is seeker Godraien in the building? He leads the committee meant to welcome these visitors."

"He is," said the clerk, stepping out from behind his desk. "I will fetch him. Please wait here."

"Thank you," Callaghnen said, and the clerk strode off.

The captain bowed to Kyle's party. "I will transfer you into the capable hands of my compatriot, Godraien. He is a personable and knowledgeable individual, and I am sure you will find his companionship helpful during your stay here in Buoria. Though I will be present during your court proceedings, it is unlikely that we will have another opportunity to meet informally—therefore I would like to thank you now for the understanding and cooperation you demonstrated during your escort. It has been a pleasure serving you, and I wish you the best of luck during your ventures."

Kyle was amazed that the captain would go out of his way to thank his prisoners for cooperating; however, he couldn't help but feel pleased. Callaghnen gave the impression of a good person forced to do an ugly job, and Kyle suddenly felt an upsurge of respect for him.

The captain shook all of their hands as the clerk returned with another Buor in tow. The newcomer wore the darkest armor Kyle had seen yet; the gray was more of a coal black, and the sash he wore was black as well. He was shorter and slighter than Callaghnen, and was more animated in his movement.

"Good day, captain," he said, taking Callaghnen's hand. "And to all of you as well! Welcome to Buoria, my friends. I am seeker Godraien, a scholar specializing in foreign studies. Might I know your names?"

"I'm Lugh!"

"Nihs Ken Dal Proks."

"Hi, I'm Meya!"

"Phundasa."

"Kyle."

It might have been Kyle's imagination, but he thought that his handshake with Godraien lasted for a fraction of a second longer than the others'.

"Have no fear, captain," Godraien then said to Callaghnen, "my committee and I will take it from here. I will see you at the courthouse tomorrow morning."

"Thank you, Godraien. I will take my leave of you." He nodded to Kyle's group. "Heed him well, for his advice will be invaluable in the days to come. Farewell, and good luck."

Once the captain and his squad were gone, Godraien clapped his hands together. "Well," he said, "shall we get down to business? First and foremost, allow me to lead you to your rooms. And forgive me if I talk a fair amount in your company—I've been assigned as your guide, and it is my duty to explain and inform whenever possible.

"This is a free holding center: a facility where we house certain temporary visitors to Buoria. As persons called to court by a summons issued here in the capital, you are entitled to stay in this house for the duration of the proceedings free of charge. Please make yourselves comfortable during your stay, provided you respect your surroundings and the rights of the other residents.

"These are the rooms to which you been assigned. Please let me know if you find them unsatisfactory, for I would likely be able to arrange a substitution."

Godraien stopped in front of one of the hallway's many doors, unlocked it, and led them inside. Kyle was struck by how clean, bright and generally well kept it was. It was large, airy, and colorful, with expensive furnishings in wood and tigoreh. Both of the beds were Minotaur-sized, meaning that Nihs would be swimming in his when it came time to rest.

Lugh whistled. "This is all right, isn't it?" he said.

Godraien bobbed. "We do our best to find a common denominator in what the other races enjoy in their personal space; the result is something that we hope will please most visitors. I'm glad to hear that you are happy. May I show you your other two rooms? And then we can meet with my compatriots."

He showed them their other rooms, which were simply the next two down from the first; Kyle found it somewhat amusing that Godraien found it necessary to introduce them to all three. After that he led them to the floor's lobby, talking all the while: he told them about where they could find food and help, what the policies of the free holding center were and what rights they held in their current position.

Waiting for them in the floor's lobby were three more Buors; two wore yellow sashes and the other's was a creamy white. They rose and bowed when Kyle's party stepped into the room.

"Allow me to introduce my colleagues," Godraien said, motioning to them. "Estor Septhiran—" the white-sashed Buor raised a hand to his brow—"a scholar studying Buorish law, he will serve as your legal counsel during the proceedings to come."

"Our counsel?" Nihs said, as Septhiran shook hands with them all.

"Indeed," Septhiran answered. His voice was somewhere between Callaghnen's and Godraien's, smooth and measured, yet frank and confident. "During a trial, all parties have the right to retain at least one personal counsel—I have been assigned to you by the court, and will guide you through any difficulty you may experience. Of course you may hire an additional counsel if you find my services incomplete."

"I'm sure that won't be necessary," Nihs said. "That seems very generous of the Buorish court. Is everyone who's tried here really given such treatment?"

"Oh, yes, but you mustn't confuse my role with that of a lawyer as those in other parts of the world may understand it. My role is not to defend you, but rather to inform, aid in your decision-making, and speak for you if you do not know how to voice your requests."

"And may I also introduce," Godraien said, "seekers Layendis and Errodion, whom I have chosen for their skills in diplomacy and foreign studies. Like myself, they are at your disposal should you require any information or guidance while on Buorish soil."

Layendis and Errodion introduced themselves. They were rather quiet and reserved even for Buors, and Kyle found himself liking their soft-spoken manners. He determined that Layendis was female, and that Errodion was male, despite his high voice and thin frame.

After the introductions were complete, Godraien seated them and bade them farewell, citing that he had other matters to attend to elsewhere. He left them in the care of Septhiran, who produced a leather binder, a pen, and faced Kyle's party like a news reporter.

"Now," he addressed them, "I know that your trip here has been lengthy and that you likely desire to rest; however, as the trial is commencing tomorrow I think we should take some measures to prepare ourselves now. I will start by listing some of the basic rules and procedures followed by the Buorish court. I am sorry if it seems tedious, but the more comfortable you are with the court's rules, the smoother the hearing will go. Of course it is your right to stop the proceedings at any time and consult me for any reason, and you will not be looked down upon for doing so; still, keeping these interruptions to a minimum is desirable. Now, if I may begin…"

Kyle went into this briefing expecting the worst. He thought that Septhiran's explanations would be an impenetrable wall of legal jargon. Instead, he found that the Buorish legal system sounded comparatively straightforward.

Anyone in the courtroom was allowed to speak provided they waited their turn and asked permission. Counselors such as Septhiran were not on anyone's 'side' and were present to inform and clarify rather than to persuade a jury. These did not exist in Buorish court; instead, consensus was reached among all people in the courtroom, and anyone was allowed to protest a ruling provided they had good reason to do so.

Kyle was surprised by many of these rules, particularly the last; he imagined such a system would never be possible on Earth. Then again, he reasoned that it probably wouldn't be possible anywhere on Loria other than Buoria, either.

"Lastly," Septhiran said, "I must list a few rules of communication that are imperative to follow in the courtroom. In fact, most of these apply for outside the courtroom as well, and will certainly earn you the respect of any Buor with whom you are speaking.

"Firstly, never interrupt another speaker. We understand that this is common among all of the world's races; however, here in Buoria we are trained never to interrupt another and find the act extremely jarring. Thus, I ask that you make an effort never to cut off another speaker.

"Also, you should never ignore another speaker. It is practice to repeat oneself in court at another's request, however, asking one to repeat information which was stated clearly before is viewed as somewhat inconsiderate. If someone addresses you directly, make an effort to turn your head towards them—this is a habit that we have developed over the years to make it clear that we are listening, and although no one will think ill of you if you do not, you will garner the respect of your peers if you do.

"Thirdly, stand when you speak, and raise your hand to request the judge's permission before you do so. Do not stand to listen, however, as that suggests you wish to speak immediately after the current speaker is finished."

"So it's akin to interrupting," Nihs said.

"Exactly. Lastly, and I cannot emphasize this enough, do not lie to the Buorish court. We are a logical folk, and while our abilities to divine feelings and implications are scarce, we have trained ourselves over many years to detect faults in reasoning or in argument. I do not prematurely accuse you of speaking falsehoods, but would simply like to warn you that if you do, your deception will not hold. It will be challenged again and again by those attending the court until the truth is revealed. When this happens, you will not be accused of lying or held in contempt, but you will have wasted a large amount of the court's time and of your own. So I implore you—speak the truth from the start. If you are innocent, or guilty, you will be found so in the end, no matter what falsehoods you utter."

Though Kyle couldn't see Septhiran's face, he couldn't help but feel that the lawyer was looking directly at him while he said this, and through the deception he had planned concerning his home world. He looked at a point past Septhiran's shoulder, avoiding the man's eyes. Again he was struck with the impression that the Buors knew far more than they let on.

"With that in mind," Septhiran said, "I will now ask you to please relate to me your version of your story as best you remember it. Beginning with Lugh, Nihs, and Rogan's discovery of Kyle and ending with the event in Rhian after which you were apprehended. At any moment you may depart from me to confer, if you wish."

The next hour was spent in meticulous description of Kyle's stay in Loria. By unspoken consent, they stuck to the story that Kyle, Lugh, Nihs, and Rogan had at first told to the Iden office in Reno. Kyle felt like a criminal going against Septhiran's words just after he'd spoken them, but he wasn't about to share his secret with the Buors, not until he absolutely had to.

Septhiran listened to their tale in silence. He took notes constantly, his head shifting imperceptibly as he listened to each of them in turn. He asked questions on occasion, nodding vaguely at the answers and jotting them down.

Finally it was over and the lawyer closed his notebook. He thanked each of them for their time, then sat, tapping his binder.

"And," he said at length, "do you attest that this account is complete and accurate, to the best of your knowledge?"

"Yes."

"No details have been left out, and none have been altered?" he pressed.

"Yes."

Septhiran bowed. "Then I thank you for your honesty. I am sorry our first meeting had to be one so demanding. If all goes well, it will allow the rest of the proceedings to conclude much more quickly. Please, rest—the remainder of the day is yours. I will leave our information with Elliaran at the front desk should you wish to call upon one of us. We will wake you in the morning when your presence is required. Have an excellent day."

"He knows we're lying," Kyle said later. "It was so obvious. Why didn't he call us on it?"

"Our story was very thin," Nihs agreed, "and people like Septhiran are trained to see faults in reasoning. But he didn't even try to question us."

"This must be how the Buors work people over," Lugh said.

Phundasa laughed deeply. "I think you all worry too much," he said. "Perhaps Septhiran is right, and we will be found out in the end. If so, there is little we can do about it one way or the other."

"So you think we should just tell them the truth?" Nihs said.

"I don't like the idea of lying to them," Meya said, "but if there's a chance that we can get out of here without them knowing about Kyle, we have to at least try."

"What do you think?" Lugh asked him.

"I agree," Kyle said. "If they find out about me later, fine. But there's no point feeding it to them."

With that decided, Meya, Phundasa and Lugh left, leaving Kyle and Nihs to go to sleep. Kyle stretched out in his huge bed with relish. As nerve-wracking as the impending trial was, there was something soothing about being in the Buorish capital. Everything here was so civilized and safe.

Not so soothing was the oppressive heat in the air. What had been only on the edge of discomfort before was now quite stifling under the thick covers. Kyle threw them off and tried not to feel exposed in his undergarments, but failed. He chose the thinnest of his sheets and pulled it back over him.

The ever-present rumbling of the earth far below wasn't any help, either. His attention being drawn to it once by a passive thought, he now found the noise and motion impossible to ignore. He realized that while he might not feel nervous on the surface, deep down he certainly was, and his body was not ready to go to sleep.

He turned to Nihs beside him. The little creature was seated in a meditative pose like the one he usually assumed to enter the overhead. He opened his mouth to speak.

"Yes?" Nihs said.

Kyle smiled despite himself.

"I was just wondering, what does the word 'estor' mean?"

Nihs opened his eyes. "It's a rank in the Buorish legal system," he said, "though I don't know its significance. All trades are ranked in Buorish society, you see, organized by field of study."

"Oh," said Kyle. "So it's like 'seeker' then?"

"Yes. That's a rank for scholars and historians. It's one step up from student. I can't say I'm familiar with many of the ranks, but I know that above seeker are professor and philosopher, and that the highest legal rank is judge—of course, everyone knows that. Buorish judges are world-famous, after all."

"Why?" Kyle asked in surprise.

"Because 'judge' is a class of fighter as well as a rank in law. You see, according to Buorish law, if a judge sentences a convict to death, then they themselves must be the one to carry out that sentence. As such, they must be trained highly in combat to deliver a killing blow to a convict of any level of strength."

"Damn."

"Quite. I've heard that a Buorish execution is something to see. Apparently, the judge does not use an axe to deliver the blow, but a hammer—that way, the victim's mask and helm are crumpled during the execution, and their identity is destroyed completely. The Buors have few criminals, but those they do have they deal with quite expressively."

"Great," Kyle said. He looked down at his bed. "I'm going to sleep *really* well now."

"Oh, you have nothing to worry about. You've committed no crimes that would merit an execution, and besides, you haven't done anything on Buorish soil, which is where their laws are strictest. You'll be fine."

"Right." Kyle, however, wasn't entirely convinced. He glanced out the window. "How late do you think it is?"

"Late enough to be sleeping," Nihs said, eyes already closed.

"But—"

"Trust me. There's not so much of Buoria that you need to start touring it now. You'll need your energy for the trial tomorrow, believe me."

And with that, Nihs curled up and went to sleep; or at least, started ignoring Kyle. Sighing, he turned over and tried to rest.

High school was a life-changing experience for Kyle. This was in no small way due to his friendship with Riley Burnham, the boy he had met on his first day of school.

Riley was a dagger of a boy; small, quick, and cutting, a being full of both energy and not so much malice, but complete disregard for society's restrictions and rules. In fact, Riley loved rules: the more there were, the more there were to break. Kyle often thought that if no one had ever tried to stop Riley from doing what he wanted, he would have ended up a completely normal and well-behaved boy. Instead, teachers, parents, siblings and counselors had all tried to push him down, and he had responded by becoming more destructive and belligerent than ever before. He delighted in incensing the school's authorities, to the point where he was disciplined almost every single day.

Riley skated and smoked, two activities that Kyle had no interest in but accompanied him in anyway. Though Riley was often seen with his group of friends, he spent a surprising amount of time either by himself or with Kyle alone. Kyle felt sometimes like nothing more than Riley's shadow, and though in his own special way he hated the smaller boy, there was something compelling about him that Kyle just couldn't shake.

Over the years, the cause behind this became clear. Riley's friends were all similar in personality to him—they were all tough troublemakers like him, they all skated like him, they all smoked like him. And yet no one *was* him. He was *Riley Burnham.* Everyone knew him. They hated him, of course, for the most part, while being unable to dismiss him from their thoughts. He seemed to be everywhere, and wherever he was you could be sure he'd be noticed. It was a kind of backwards charisma, attraction through dislike—something that Kyle envied and wished to understand. He, Kyle, had never been attractive in any way, to anyone; he felt like a disciple watching a master, trying to figure out what secret technique Riley used to train life's spotlight upon himself.

Riley, for one, had taken an instant liking to Kyle, shunning sometimes even his own friends for Kyle's sake. He found Kyle's sardonic sense of humor hilarious, and envied his intelligence. He seemed never to have any commitments within school or without, and would often urge Kyle to do things with him—explore the sewers under the city, watch and hassle the elementary kids from the school nearby—anything that would satiate his endless desire to rock the boat.

Kyle learned much from his high school years, even counting what he did not learn both consciously and unconsciously from Riley. He saw the social dynamics between the different groups of students, and the effects of gender roles. He watched students around him picking up smoking, drinking, and worse; and he listened to Riley's friend's triumphant and explicit tale of his first time having sex.

It was probably the sex story that made something change in Kyle's brain. His thoughts were churning in his mind all during the rest of the day: on the bus ride home, at home in his room poring over his schoolwork. They flickered around and twisted themselves in knots, as thoughts often do when the brain is forced to crunch a plethora of new information and emotions at once. The main stream of his thoughts teetered between two feelings: one, that Riley's friend was a disgusting, base individual who had, while still too young, done something unspeakable—and supreme, simmering jealousy that Kyle himself had not been the one to tell the story.

Columns of numbers melted under Kyle's wrath as these thoughts tortured his mind. His pencil strokes became thicker and darker, his numbers more clumsy as his hand shook, until finally he was no longer doing math but striking his page over and over again with his pencil, covering it with black lines and denting the desk underneath.

Why? He screamed the question against the inside of his skull. Why was he the quiet one? Why was he the small, pale boy who was good at math and science and nothing else? Why was he forced to crouch over his desk doing sums in this dump of a house with a useless mother and no father, while stupid, dense, idiots like Riley and his friends were reaping everything that life had to offer? Kyle was better than them! He knew it—as surely as he knew the Earth orbited the Sun. So where was it? Where was that invisible particle, where was that key factor that made Kyle such a waste of a life?

He found himself grabbing his textbook from his desk and throwing it as hard as he could, so that it struck the wall heavily and left a dent. Kyle, stunned, stared at the dent, thinking, *that's going to take money to fix.*

He heard footsteps below him. *Damn,* he thought. He hadn't realized how loud he'd been.

"Kyle!" his mother shouted from downstairs. "What are you doing?"

The tone in her voice colored Kyle's vision red.

"*Nothing!*" Kyle shouted back, though this was only a poor shade of what was going on in his head.

More footsteps—she was coming upstairs. His tone must have been a little too hysterical. Though he was incredibly incensed, he still feared the ramifications of his outburst.

She came in. Kyle saw the look on her face shift from irritation to shock.

"Kyle, what's wrong?" she said.

Kyle stood. His mother stepped back from him.

"Kyle—"

"I'm going out." And as though the words had activated Kyle's body, he immediately started walking past her to the door.

"Kyle, it's late already!" she said, but it was to his back. "Kyle!" and her voice was barbed with anger. But what little power his mother had ever held over him was gone now. He turned to face her.

"I'm going out," he repeated. And he did.

She said nothing else.

He wandered the streets of the city for a long time, minutes turning to hours. His excursions with Riley had taught him everything about finding his way around, and so he was in no danger of becoming lost. He wound his way to a park close to his high school and climbed the large, concrete structure that served as an entry point to an abandoned subway station that he and Riley had earlier explored. There he sat, legs apart, arms propping up a torso thrown back to look at the sky.

Kyle felt the cool breeze on his face and made a decision. He was going to change his life. He was going to become a winner, like Riley—no, better. He was going to be the best. He was going to be the one to spearhead every exploration, attempt every experience and vice first. He was going to win more wholly and completely than any student had before. He knew it would be easy because he knew he was better than anyone else at his school. There were nerds who got better grades and punks who were tougher—but Kyle would have some of everything. That was the weakness of the students who entered a clique; no matter how accomplished they were in their particular field, they were always secretly envious of the members of at least one other. This was the case with Riley's respect for Kyle's smarts. Luckily, smarts were one of the hardest of these things to grasp, and this was what Kyle already had.

Sitting atop the subway entrance, Kyle assembled his game plan. He would need a job during school days, because he would need money. He would need to start asserting his dominance over Riley, a feat he was sure he could accomplish—how many times had Riley said something completely inane, an argument Kyle knew he could derail? And the genius part of it was that Riley's power, as absolute as it was, could be siphoned off of him by someone stronger; by ridiculing him, even casually, one made him weaker and themselves stronger.

He would be the new Riley. Riley would follow *him*, as would all the students who had followed the curly-haired boy before. Kyle would be the one drinking and crashing parties; he would be the one getting girls. He would be calling the shots.

Kyle promised this to himself out loud as he sat: "I'm better than all of you. I'm going to beat you, all of you. You can't scare me," and now he spoke to life itself, addressing the sky as though it were a face staring down at him. "I'm going to become the scariest thing there is."

Kyle woke, and immediately curled into a fetal ball under the covers. Afterimages from his dream were assaulting his mind, taunting him with their strangeness and obscenity. For a moment, he was trapped not just back on Earth, but in his teenage form—his frightened, enraged, fanatic counterpart from a decade ago.

His life had not gotten better since his promise to himself. In fact it had gotten much, much worse, to the point of being nightmarish; but Kyle fought back these recollections, wiping them from his mind, hating to look back on them.

There came a polite knock on the door. He heard Nihs stir beside him.

"Kyle," he said mildly, "would you mind getting that?"

"Why me?"

"Well," Nihs said reasonably, "I'm smaller, so I have a farther distance to travel."

The knock came again, slightly louder but still oozing politeness. Kyle shook his head and swung out of bed.

"You're such a dear."

"Don't tempt me, Nihs."

The polite knocker turned out to be Errodion. He bowed deeply when Kyle opened the door.

"Good morning, young master," he said. "Please forgive me if I woke you prematurely. My colleague estor Septhiran wishes to speak with you of a matter of some import and believed that this was an appropriate hour to summon you. He awaits in this floor's lounge. Please join me at your leisure."

Kyle, unfazed, dressed alongside Nihs and then followed Errodion to the room they had spoken in before. Along the way Lugh, Phundasa, Meya, Layendis and Godraien joined them.

Estor Septhiran rose and bowed when they entered. Gesturing for them to take a seat and doing so himself, he said,

"Good morning, sirs and madam. As you know, today was meant to be the day that Kyle's trial would commence. However, I have brought you here today to inform you that the court's resources have been tied up by a problematic issue, and that it will be unable to progress onto Kyle's case today. The officials I have spoken to estimate that the case will likely continue for an additional three or four days, during which your party will, unfortunately, be asked to remain in Buoria."

"Three or four days?" Lugh said. "Damn. What's going on that's taking up all that time?"

"It is the trial of a criminal," Septhiran said shortly. "Without going into an excess of detail, this particular case suffers from being both serious and unique. It is my prediction that some of our laws will need to be rewritten in order to accommodate it. Such cases are universally lengthy."

"Ah."

Septhiran rallied. "I am very sorry that events have transpired as such. Rest assured that we will do our best to accommodate you for the next few days, and that of course all expenses incurred during your stay here will be handled by the Buorish government. I will keep you informed should any developments take place. Until then, you may consider your time spent in the capital leisure time—for the most part. Kyle, I do think that some of our additional time would be well spent acquainting you with the structure of our court."

"Right."

Septhiran dipped his head. "Once again, allow me to apologize on behalf of the court for this situation. Should you have any questions, please feel free to ask Godraien, Layendis, Errodion or myself."

They thanked Septhiran, then rose and prepared to leave. Kyle had taken the news of the delay with indifference. Somewhere in the back of his mind he had already predicted that his trial was not going to start today. Though perhaps this was simply because everything had happened so fast, and that he hadn't had time to think about the trial at all.

They found Godraien waiting for them in the hallway outside.

"Greetings," he said. "Please allow me to say that I am aware of the situation you are in, and am sorry that it could not be prevented. I hope that this occurrence does not cause you ill will towards Septhiran or the Buorish court—we certainly did not anticipate this delay."

"Hey, no worries," Lugh said, "it's not so bad."

"It is kind of you to say so." He bowed, and on rising looked directly at Kyle. "I know it is poor recompense for the inconvenience to which you have been subjected, but allow me to offer you my services as a guide during the days prior to your trial. I am well acquainted with the city and the kingdom surrounding it. There are many marvels, both constructed and natural, present on the island, which I may show to you. There are museums where you might learn of the kingdom of Buoria and view the works of its great artisans. The heart of Buoria is currently active, and so you may climb the escarpment beyond the city and visit our teams of engineers who divert great flows of its magma for use in our machines. Our home may not seem to hold much appeal for the outsider at first glance; however, if you are willing to accompany me, I may bring to light some of the beauty that Buoria hides underneath her harsh exterior."

Kyle had never heard a Buor speak with such a degree of passion, and it almost sounded as if Godraien was begging to do this favor for them.

"We'd be happy to," he said.

And so it was that the next four days were spent touring the island of Buoria. Though Godraien was their primary guide, they were often joined by Layendis and Errodion, and even by Septhiran on a few occasions.

The first place they visited was the Buorish market, a long stretch of road that ran horizontally along the city, a series of indoor shops and outdoor stalls so expansive and populated that it could actually be seen as a band of color when the city was viewed from above. The stalls here were semi-permanent, more like open-faced stores, and the atmosphere was one of cordiality. The skill displayed by some of the Buorish artisans was astonishing; even Kyle, who usually had little interest in art, had cause to stop and stare. Godraien insisted on buying them all a set of Buorish-made clothing, claiming that they would need the thin, durable garments in order to survive the capital's heat and ash. Kyle was surprised that the Buors even made clothing fit for the other races, though he accepted the offer with gratitude. The clothes were for the most part crafted in shades of red and black, mirroring in cloth form the fashion of the Buors' armor. Kyle found it bizarre to see his companions outfitted in clothes other than their usual adventurer garb. Even Lugh and Phundasa looked grave and important in their clothes, while Meya, who wore pants and a shirt instead of her usual flowing white suit, looked very different indeed.

Godraien toured them around the entire island, each day finding something new for them to observe or experience. As promised, he took them to view museums of Buorish history and science in the city proper; they learned much of Buoria's past rulers, exploits, and advances in science and technology. There were museums filled with paintings and works of art, and those that displayed antique weaponry, sets of armor, and scale models of siege weapons used in the kingdom's past.

One day, they rode on massive lifts up the face of the mountain to view the plains of ash that stretched beyond the Citadel. Godraien pointed out flecks of light in the distance—these, he explained, were watchtowers, manned by teams of scientists and engineers monitoring the lava flowing from the Heart of Buoria, the massive volcano at the center of the island. The plains were crisscrossed with perfectly straight lines of bright orange; these were rivers of magma being diverted by the Buors for use in their machines. Some of them even fell in ponderous 'waterfalls' all the way down the cliff face into the city's center.

Later, Godraien showed them the nature of these lava-powered machines. Their guide referred to them as the 'machines of the city', and a more appropriate name could not be had. As the party learned, the city, and particularly the Citadel, were not completely stationary. They were actually capable of shifting and transforming into different configurations, moving on giant robotic arms built into the foundation of the island. These arms, fueled by steam, Ephicers and magma, worked like giant pneumatic pistons, each one over a hundred feet long and capable of moving an entire street. The city could draw in on itself protectively during times of war, streets of houses sliding and shifting, and the canals that ran in between districts could be altered in size in order to accommodate lava flows. As he had been upon first arriving in the city, Kyle was struck by the amazing power and achievement of the Buorish race.

As the days passed, they also learned more about the four Buors with whom they were sharing their time. Godraien was earnest and steadfast, and his enthusiasm and kindness were catching. Septhiran was slightly more conservative, and his comments were often tinged with benign dry wit. Layendis and Errodion were both quiet and respectful, and took their jobs as guides seriously.

When they were not touring the island with these four, Kyle and the party learned more of the Buorish legal system from Septhiran, or Kyle himself learned more of combat from his companions. When they told Godraien that he was training to become an adventurer, the seeker wasted no time in finding them a small, unused training ground for them to spar in.

Layendis and Errodion also taught them a game the Buors played called (as far as Kyle could tell) *mareek-check*. It was played with wooden tiles all colored and shaped differently, and was incredibly addictive. More than once did the party find themselves staying up far past what was a healthy time due to a case of 'just one more game'.

For Kyle, it was a time to rest and relax, and to learn more about the people with which he was sharing his adventure. Each morning when he looked out his window, he saw the outline of one of the defense turrets pointed at the sky, and couldn't help but feel reassured. Nobody could reach him here, in the heart of the safest place in Loria.

During second sun of the fourth day, Septhiran summoned them to tell them that the court was once again free, and that Kyle's trial would be starting the following day. The news was met with genuine sadness; each of them had gained something from their time spent so far in Buoria.

Godraien bowed deeply when they approached him to thank him for his services. Kyle had learned that the Buors did this partially out of courtesy, but also in order to make it clearer who was speaking, since they could not rely on body language or mouth movement for this purpose.

"It has been an honor to keep your company these past few days," the seeker told them. "But do not speak your farewells just yet; I will remain close by for the duration of your trial, and I am sure that we will have the opportunity to speak again in leisure before your departure. Kyle, may I say that having spent time in your company these past few days, I know that you are a man of honor, and I believe that your affair will end well. Have faith in the justice of the Buorish court, and you will find that your trial completes itself all the easier. Good luck, my friends!"

The day of the trial dawned stark and gray. There was little ash present in the air when they awoke, though Septhiran warned them that a heavier ashfall was expected later that day. He gave them time to prepare and eat breakfast in the holding center, before instructing them to follow him to the courthouse. They were accompanied by Layendis, though Errodion and Godraien were not present.

Kyle was caught between nervousness and serenity as they walked. Though he was now quite convinced that no people as reasonable and considerate as the Buors would condemn him for what he had done, he was worried about the agreement he had made with the others about lying to the court. Apart from everything else, he felt it was a terrible insult to the people who had shown them such kindness for the past few days. He found himself wondering if it might just be better to tell the truth from the start, but something held him back from bringing the idea up with the others.

They followed Septhiran down the road and further into Upper City. The lawyer walked casually, carrying his book of notes, and Kyle, who was stepping quickly and nervously, ended up drawing up beside him.

Septhiran must have noticed his apprehension.

"Do not worry yourself unduly about the outcome of this session, Mister Campbell. Simply keep in mind what I have told you and you will find the process painless and pleasantly free of stress. Remember, you are not here as a criminal, and the court has no intention of beleaguering you for your actions."

"Thank you," Kyle said. Septhiran's words had helped somewhat, although whatever the lawyer told him Kyle couldn't help but think of how the court would treat him once they figured out he was lying.

The courthouse was a grand, old stone building far within the Upper City, close enough to the Citadel that Kyle caught glimpses of its gates as they drew close. It was a symmetrical structure with wings extending to its left and right, and a shallow stone staircase leading to a columned entranceway. The doors were great, carved slabs of petrified wood, and there was a legend written above them:

Buorish Court of Law

Innocent or Guilty, The Law Shall Find You So

"Outsiders are often intimidated by the quote displayed above the doors," Septhiran said, reading Kyle's mind. "They misinterpret it as a threat, while in fact it is a reassurance. It promises that your true actions and character shall be exposed, and that you will never be sentenced in a manner disproportionate to your crime or lack thereof."

Kyle didn't trust himself to speak.

There were guards stationed outside the courthouse. Septhiran approached them, pulling a sheet of paper from his notes.

"Good day, sirs," he said, handing them the paper. "I am estor Septhiran, here to assist Kyle Campbell and his companions Lughenor MacAlden, Nihs Ken Dal Proks, Meya Ilduetyr and Phundasa Bar Gnoshen."

"Thank you, estor," the guard said, taking the paper and comparing it to the notes he himself held. He ticked six names off a list, signed Septhiran's paper, and handed it back to him. "The court awaits your participation within; you are familiar with where your party is to be seated?"

"I am, thank you," Septhiran said. He motioned to the rest of them as the guards opened the doors. "Please, this way."

The courtroom began with very little preamble once they entered the courthouse. It was divided from the outside doors by only a small anteroom. As they walked inside, Kyle heard a constant susurration, the soft noise made by many people holding quiet conversations.

The room itself was about what Kyle imagined it to be. Rows of tiered seats lined the walls to the left and right, while the floor was taken up by rows of benches all facing the far wall as in a church. In front of these benches, on the left, was a large table behind which he and his party were meant to sit.

A good number of the seats and benches were already filled. Kyle imagined that there might have been a hundred people in attendance. Seated at the front of the room were the Judge and his retinue.

Kyle's mouth fell open when he saw the Judge for the first time. Like all Buors, he was heavily armored, caped and helmeted, but this particular man was grander and more imposing than any of the other Buors Kyle had met. His suit of armor was a huge mass of dark steel, large enough to host two or even three men inside of it. His armored shoulders were incredibly broad and his hands were large enough to cup Kyle's head. It might have been a trick of perspective, but the Judge looked as though he might have even been larger than Rogan the Minotaur.

That can't be, Kyle thought. All of the Buors he had met so far were human-sized—though perhaps they did come in different sizes and shapes, and he simply had not yet met one of this stature.

The Judge's sash and cloak were black trimmed with silvery white, and he wore a full helm instead of the half helm and triangle of cloth that most Buors sported. He was seated behind a large podium like a judge from back on earth, and propped on the wall behind him Kyle could make out the haft of what must have been a massive hammer.

"Damn," Lugh whispered to Kyle, as they filed into the courtroom.

"You're telling me. Why is he so big?"

"He's not actually that large," Nihs whispered from Lugh's shoulder. "It's an illusion caused by the Judge's magical aura. Individuals of great physical power can distort the space around them, making them appear larger to those of lesser strength."

"Can he turn it off?"

"No more than you can turn off your eyes. Just be thankful that he's seated behind a podium in a courtroom, instead of standing across from us on a battlefield."

The noise in the courtroom changed as they entered, some of the attendees breaking off their conversations in order to watch Kyle's party file in. The room was filled with energy, a kind of noiseless sound made by dozens of people waiting for something to happen.

Septhiran led them down the center aisle, and they sat in a row facing the Judge with Septhiran on their far right. Left of him sat Meya, then Kyle, Lugh, Nihs and Phundasa. Kyle could see from his friends' expressions that they were as nervous as he, as he felt a pang of guilt for dragging them all into this.

There was relative silence for a few minutes after they arrived. The Judge appeared to be waiting for something.

Septhiran rose and stepped into the center of the floor to bow and exchange a few words with him; he then returned to their seat, and said,

"One of the other counselors has been slightly late in reaching the courthouse. The proceedings will commence once he has arrived. I know of him; his name is Erriand, an experienced and well-respected lauster. He is known for his skill in questioning, so I recommend that you slow the pace of your discourse and think clearly before answering his inquiries."

"Got it," Kyle said, his mouth dry.

"I will also tell you that the Judge you see seated before you is known as Judge Somniel. Do not fear him, for he is known for his fairness and openness when speaking and allowing others to speak."

Erriand arrived a short while later, hustling slightly to the front of the room to introduce himself to the Judge as Septhiran had done. He was tall and slight, and his sash was thin and bright yellow. His movements were quick and jerky, giving the impression that he was either full of energy or very agitated.

After he and his two assistants had seated themselves, the Judge raised his hands over his head for attention. The sound in the courtroom died almost instantly as all heads turned in his direction.

"If it is acceptable to all in attendance," he said, "we will now begin the proceedings of case number twenty-seven thousand six hundred and thirteen; the trial of Kyle Campbell and company on the subject of Iden card application, and inquiry into possible association with the criminal activity of others. Is this indeed acceptable?" He waited a few moments for someone to speak. His voice was calm and measured, deep and powerful enough to fill the courtroom with its sound.

He nodded when no one spoke. "I, Judge Somniel, shall oversee the proceedings. Serving as counsel for the defendant is one estor Septhiran; may he rise now?"

Septhiran did, turning to display himself to the audience and bowing slightly.

"Serving as general counsel for the proceedings is one lauster Erriand; may he rise now?"

The other lawyer rose, bowing to the Judge.

Next, Somniel called the names of each member of Kyle's party, requesting that they rise in turn. He introduced his retinue and well as a few other important functionaries in a similar fashion. Once the introductions were complete, he continued.

"For the sake of those in attendance unfamiliar with the current case, I will now summarize it as such. Eight days ago, on the fourth of Nearcross, the defendant, Kyle Campbell, applied to receive an Iden card at the River Street Iden Office in Reno city. When requested to provide his personal information, Mister Campbell cited that he could not, claiming to have lost his memory as the result of an unknown, possibly magical, accident." He shuffled the papers set in front of him, bringing one up to his visor to inspect. "When interrogated further by Iden Office employees Derumnai and Acclairiad, and having his memories examined by the Kol known as Ezki Sol Dal Shend, it was confirmed that Campbell possessed no readable memories and could not recall any details of his past up to approximately ten days previous." He lowered the paper. "Campbell's companions, Lughenor MacAlden, Nihs Ken Dal Proks, and Rogan Harhoof, who is not in attendance, confirmed that they had discovered Campbell in his current state, bereft of any possessions, in northern Ar'ac during an airship flight over the area. As a result of Campbell's interview, he was granted a temporary Iden card, showing here." And to Kyle's surprise, the Judge held up a perfect copy of the card, which he now kept with him at all times.

"The purpose of this hearing is to examine Campbell's case in greater detail, as well as to explore the possibility of a connection between himself and two cases of criminal activity which have transpired within the previous ten days: the first, a suspected kidnapping which took place in Reno city, and the second, an attempted kidnapping and double murder in the city of Rhian. Estor Septhiran, if I may, I would request at this time that you begin the proceedings by recounting Campbell's case in full, beginning with his discovery in the Ar'ac continent."

"Yes, Your Honor," Septhiran said. Before rising to speak, he turned and said to Kyle in a low voice,

"I will request that you listen actively during my discourse, in case I require your clarification or if I falsely recount a detail which you have given me."

Kyle nodded, and Septhiran rose to talk.

He listened with apprehension as Septhiran began telling the court of his story. He still was not entirely settled down in the alien courthouse, and so his attention wavered somewhat as he took in his surroundings. The room was stark and perfectly symmetrical, the walls unfurnished save for a few solid red tapestries. He couldn't tell who exactly formed the audience, though some Buors, such as Erriand's staff, were clearly attending as groups, most had come to the court by themselves, and were watching the proceedings as one might watch a play. Kyle remembered Septhiran telling him that anyone was allowed to attend a Buorish trial, so these must have been normal Buors taking time out of his or her day to observe.

Routinely during Septhiran's account did the Judge request that Kyle or one of his friends confirm a detail; each time Kyle rose to do so, he sat down with his heart beating slightly faster. Septhiran remained largely uninterrupted apart from this, so it was impossible to tell what the audience thought of the story.

Finally Septhiran finished, and seated himself once more.

"Thank you, estor," the Judge said. "The court will now hear the accounts of two witnesses with regards to the criminal events mentioned previously. They are Lieutenant Jendoyle of the Reno police force and Captain Callaghnen of the central Eastia patrol. I will request that the audience hold their questions for estor Septhiran until these two accounts are finished."

Kyle started when he heard the familiar name of Captain Callaghnen, but though he craned his neck to scan the audience, could not make him out in the courtroom.

He did not recognize Lieutenant Jendoyle, who was a well-built police officer sporting a green sash. He was the first to be interviewed, stepping into the center of the room as had Septhiran.

"I bid good morning to the court," he said, bowing. "I am Lieutenant Jendoyle of the Reno police, and was on duty the afternoon that the aforementioned incident took place. At approximately ten o'clock, one of my officers reported having seen an unusual amount of activity within the complex of Sky Tower. As I'm sure many of you are aware, Sky Tower is a great architectural project currently underway in Reno's core. Commissioned by James Livaldi, the head of Maida Weapons, it is not yet meant to be inhabited and is usually empty save for construction crews. Having received this report, I deemed it worthwhile to dispatch a small force to investigate the area. It soon became clear that some sort of criminal activity had indeed been taking place within Sky Tower, as men were fleeing the scene upon our arrival. We managed to apprehend four of the men, who were identified as known members of a criminal gang led by one Michael Radisson. The rest of the men, unfortunately, escaped. Upon the return of James Livaldi, we informed him of the event and requested permission to investigate Sky Tower thoroughly for other signs of criminal activity. We searched the tower in its entirety, yet were unable to find any additional clues."

That's because you didn't search the maintenance floors, Kyle thought. *Or you did, but by then everything had been cleaned up.*

"After interrogating the apprehended men, we discovered that they had received orders to capture a man suiting Campbell's description, though they pleaded ignorance as to the identity of the party ordering the capture. One of them described a man, a blonde human who had at least been in contact with Radisson recently; however, that is all the information that my team has managed to glean."

"Thank you," the Judge said. "May you describe in greater detail the man whom these criminals were told to apprehend?"

"He was described to them as a short human male in his twenties, with black hair and likely a beard, most likely seen in the company of a male, blond sea Selk, a male Kol, and a chestnut-colored male Minotaur, all dressed as adventurers."

"Thank you," the Judge said again. "I will now call Captain Callaghnen to the floor, to tell us of the events which transpired in the city of Rhian four days ago."

Kyle only caught sight of Callaghnen when he reached the floor and began to speak. It was amazing, Kyle thought, how in the past few days he had become so adept at telling one Buor from another, and that Callaghnen's countenance was now incredibly familiar to him.

Before speaking, the captain turned briefly in his direction and gave him a small nod of recognition. Kyle couldn't help but smile and return the nod.

Callaghnen began to recount his version of the story, telling the court of the twins' attack on Rhian and the intervention of his squad. He recounted with gravity the details of Osirde and Mikasa's murder; Kyle glanced once in Meya's direction and saw the sadness on her face as she listened.

The captain quickly went over the remainder of the details—his detaining of Kyle's group, their brief stop in Vestwheyr, and the remainder of their journey to Buoria.

The Judge thanked him as well when he finished, and requested that he and Jendoyle receive seats at the front of the courtroom should they need to be called upon once more.

"I will now open the courtroom for questioning," Somniel said. "Lauster Erriand, do you have any questions you wish to ask?"

"I do," the sinewy lawyer replied, rising to his feet. His voice was high and proper, as if he had received courses in pronunciation and discourse. "If it pleases the court, I desire to reiterate some of the questions put previously to Kyle Campbell, to reconfirm his stance on certain matters."

"Proceed."

Kyle's heart beat in his throat as Erriand rose and approached his seat. He felt both Lugh and Meya tense beside him.

"You do not have to rise during this interview," Septhiran whispered to him from across her. "Simply answer the questions which are put to you completely, yet relevantly."

"Mister Campbell," Erriand said, "I understand that, as a result of an accident unknown, you possess little to no memory of your life beyond approximately a half-month ago. Was the name 'Kyle Campbell' attributed to you after you awoke from your accident?"

"No, it's my real name." Kyle said, "It's one thing I can remember."

"Do you remember the names of your parents, and siblings if you possess them?"

Kyle remembered Septhiran's advice about taking one's time before answering, and he took a moment to let his mind race.

"I can't remember my parents' names," he said. "I don't think I was close to them. I don't remember having any siblings."

"Do you remember your date of birth, including your age?"

"No."

"Do you remember your previous occupation, or your reason for being in northern Ar'ac at the time of your accident?"

"No."

"Upon arriving in Reno, were you aware that you or your companions were in any danger?"

"No!" Kyle said.

"And may you provide a reason why you did not alert the police following the events in Reno?"

"We didn't want to get held up in the city," Kyle said. "I didn't want Lugh and the others to lose time because of me, we thought that if we just left the city we might avoid any more trouble."

"Indeed. Upon arriving in Rhian, did you or your party suspect any additional pursuit or danger?"

"No, we thought they'd given up once we left Reno."

"And either of the two times which you were assaulted, did you recognize your attackers?"

"No."

"Were the two men, the sniper and the sage who were present in Rhian, also present in Reno?"

Kyle shook his head. "I didn't see them."

Erriand nodded. "Thank you," he said, then added to Judge Somniel, "I have finished with my questioning for now."

"Very well," the Judge said. "Are there any others who would like to put questions to the defendant or witnesses?"

There were, and the next half hour was spent answering the questions of Buors all over the courtroom. Most of them were directed at Kyle or Lugh, though some were put to Jendoyle, Callaghnen, Septhiran, Meya, or Phundasa. Kyle's confidence began to grow. The story they had told was holding up surprisingly well, and the court seemed more concerned with the crimes of the twins and Radisson's thugs than with Kyle's honesty.

A Buor in the audience rose and spoke to Judge Somniel.

"Your honor, I believe it would be appropriate to have one of our *irushai* examine Kyle's memories. We will then be able to confirm for ourselves the verity of his recount, as well as possibly glean clues as to his past."

"You speak wisely," the Judge agreed. He addressed Kyle. "Would it be acceptable for this reading to take place?"

"Under our charter of rights you may refuse without penalty," Septhiran told him.

"Thanks," Kyle said, "but it's all right. I don't mind."

The reading was performed by one of Somniel's aides. He wore gloves instead of gauntlets on his hands, and though they were of some kind of leather Kyle could tell that the material was very thin, in order not to interfere with his use of magic. The man approached him and laid his hands on his temples. His eyes closed and his memories began to scroll by.

Just as before, Kyle felt as though the reading went properly, but when his eyes opened again he saw the magic user shaking his head.

"I can confirm the presence of some set of memories," he told Somniel. "They have indeed been corrupted by some outside force. I was able to catch glimpses of places and people, though these are vague impressions and nothing more."

This stirred a murmur in the court, though it died down when Somniel spoke.

"I see. Then I would ask the court: may we at present treat Kyle's claim of memory loss as substantiated, and secondly, does there exist in Buoria or elsewhere one who specializes in recovering lost memory?"

Erriand rose and coughed politely. "To my knowledge, the arts of damaging memory permanently and recovering permanent damage are both forms of complex mysticism. I am unsure that any of our *irushai* would possess the skills necessary to heal him."

"What does *irushai* mean?" Kyle asked Septhiran.

"It is a Buorish word meaning 'those unlocked'. An *irushai* is a Buor capable of using magic. You see, most of us do not possess the ability to use any type of magic save metamagic. However, approximately one in every thousand Buors is born with a soul that is magically 'unlocked', hence the term."

"Oh. I see."

"The corruption of Kyle's memory, however, raises another issue," Erriand said. "If it was damaged by whatever transpired prior to his discovery, then we must suspect the involvement of an extremely skilled mystic. In Reno city, Kyle was captured by men under the direction of Michael Radisson, an infamous criminal lord. In Rhian, he was again apprehended by two individuals of great power, a sniper and a sage."

"To which conclusion are your statements meant to lead?" Somniel inquired.

"Your honor, it seems clear from past events that Kyle has powerful and determined enemies. I would not find it unreasonable to infer that his first 'accident' was brought on by the same party that hired Radisson and the twins to capture him. We must ask ourselves why Kyle is being pursued so aggressively, and what measures should be taken as a result. For instance, if we allow him to leave Buoria, he and his party may be exposed to further danger."

"Indeed," Somniel said, "but there is precious little else we may examine in Kyle's case in order to grant us further insight."

"An unfortunate truth," Erriand agreed. "If I may question Kyle further?"

"Please, proceed."

"Kyle," Erriand said, and Kyle remembered to turn his head toward him, "Captain Callaghnen cited earlier that he had seen you draw a soularm in your defense during the events at Rhian. Is it true that you possess a soularm?"

"Yes, it is," Kyle said.

"Might I request that you draw it now, for the court to examine?"

"I must interject," Septhiran said politely, "and inquire as to why this particular detail is being examined."

"If Kyle possesses a soularm, then it must have been acquired prior to his discovery by Lugh and his party. If we are to examine it, we may gain information as to Kyle's origins. For instance, the make and styling of the sword may reveal Kyle's home continent or country."

"Ah," Septhiran said, "a sound idea. My apologies."

"It is of no moment. Kyle, may you please step to the center of the floor and draw your soularm?"

Kyle rose and stepped into the center of the room, feeling extremely nervous. The court had fallen completely silent in the time it had taken him to stand up. He could clearly hear the whistling of the wind outside as the ashfall that Septhiran had promised took place.

He focused, and the silver and blue sparks danced along his arms towards his palms. He made sure to point his hands into clear air as he pushed them together and watched the silver blade slide out between them.

There was a soft, collective 'ahh' as the audience beheld his glowing soularm. Kyle couldn't blame them. No matter how many times he saw it, the beauty of his soul sword calmed and enchanted him.

"May I examine it?" Erriand asked. He reached out a hand as if to touch it.

"You can," Kyle warned, "but you can't touch it." He had spoken in haste, wanting to avoid Erriand touching by accident, and hadn't thought of how rude he might sound. But the lawyer simply seemed surprised. "Why may I not?" he asked.

"It takes apart anything that touches it," Kyle explained. "We think it's enchanted."

"'Takes apart'? Might you explain further?"

"It explodes," Kyle said.

The court made a gentle gasp of surprise, and Erriand said, "in which case, I will ask that you to sheath your sword for the moment, for safety's sake. Your honor, might I request a demonstration of the abilities of Kyle's sword?"

Somniel nodded. "Provided that it may safely be done within the confines of the court. Is this possible?"

"It should be," said Kyle, sheathing his sword. "It only hurts what it touches."

"Very well. May someone please fetch a disposable item which may be used in the demonstration?"

It wasn't long before a small wooden stool was produced, and placed upon a table in the center of the room, visible to the entire court. Kyle drew his sword and gently touched it to the stool's surface, wincing in anticipation.

The sword touched the stool, and it immediately shattered with a sharp detonation, severed legs clattering on the courtroom floor. The audience gasped once more.

"That is curious indeed," Somniel said, as the remains of the stool were taken away. "And this effect takes place regardless of the object in question?"

"Yes," Kyle said.

The Judge put a finger to his chin. "I believe, then, that at this time it would be appropriate to call to the court an expert in magic, one who may be able to identify the origin of what is clearly a rare and potent enchantment."

One of the Buors seated near the front of the benches rose. "If it pleases Your Honor," she said, "I know of one such expert, a colleague of mine who specializes in magical history. I will bring her here if you desire."

"That would indeed be appropriate," he said, dipping his head to her.

One of the guards posted at the courtroom doors stepped forward from his post.

"I am sorry to interject," he said, "but I must report that the ashfall outside has increased in intensity to a point where it would now be dangerous to leave the building. I would not recommend venturing outside except in a case of emergency."

"Indeed!" the Judge said, and his gaze traveled to one of the windows set high up in the court's walls. Kyle followed his gaze subconsciously, and true to the guard's word, the view outside was obscured by an angry gray-black storm of ash. Now that he was listening for it, the sound the wind made was more pronounced.

"In that case," Somniel said, "I would ask you to delay your errand for the time being. We have debated Kyle's case for several hours now, and if there are no objections I would use this opportunity to consider the court in recess. Is this acceptable for all those in attendance?"

When no one spoke, Somniel said, "Very well. The court is now in recess. We will resume either in an hour or when the ashfall abates, whichever comes first. If the ashfall does not dissipate in an hour's time, we will continue a different line of questioning until it does."

"Your affair seems to be going well," Septhiran said afterward. They had found an empty reception room down one of the courthouse's wings and had settled down there to talk. They had been starved of choice, since most of the courthouse was populated and it was impossible to go outside. This smaller room was lined with windows along one side, and the sound of the wind and ash striking them was almost deafening. If one watched the storm outside long enough, one could see streaks of red lightning flashing within the clouds.

"I suppose so," Kyle said. "It's not really what I expected."

"The method with which we examine our cases indeed differs from what you may be used to," Septhiran agreed. "Our reasoning is that we may only reach an accurate verdict when in possession of all relevant facts, and it is impossible to tell which facts are relevant until the full nature of the case is revealed. As such, we often discuss details that may seem inconsequential. For instance, I am certain that your trial will not end before the mystery of your soul sword is solved."

"We'll be here forever, then," Nihs said. "*We* don't even know what Kyle's soul sword is."

"Have heart, son of Proks," Septhiran said. "I too know of the expert in magical history mentioned by the woman in court. Ecciritae is her name, and her knowledge of ancient and rare magics dating back to the time of *edonus* is second to none. I have great confidence that if anyone may identify the enchantment on your sword, it would be she."

Good luck to her, Kyle thought.

"I guess we'll just have to wait and see what she says," said Meya. "What happens if she can't identify it?"

"I cannot honestly say. We are running out of data with which to analyze the case. Whether or not what we have is enough to grant Kyle a permanent card and dismiss the case is up to the views of those in court."

The storm ended up clearing slightly about forty minutes later. The sky became just calm enough for Ecciritae to be summoned, though the prediction was that it would soon pick up again, and worse than before.

They reentered the courtroom, which had half emptied during the recess, but which was now already full again. In fact, there were more people in the audience than before, and Kyle noticed some of the Buors dusting ash off of their cloaks as they came inside.

They sat down, and watched as Judge Somniel regained his own seat at the head of the room. The noise level was much louder now than it had been when the trial began.

Erriand arrived soon after, followed by a few missing officials. Somniel again raised his hands for silence, and the noise died down.

"We will now resume the trial of Kyle Campbell," he said somewhat informally to the audience. "Prior to our recess, the court was examining Mister Campbell's soularm, which appears to contain an enchantment of unknown origin. The court would now call upon Philosopher Ecciritae, a scholar of magical history and one who may be able to identify the sword. Is she in attendance?"

"She is."

A female Buor made her way to the front of the courtroom, and several heads turned to watch her progress. Though she was petite, she carried herself with bearing; her back was straight as a plank and she moved with confidence. Kyle could not guess at her age, being poor at reading these signs in Buors, though based on her voice he imagined that she was middle aged. Her sash, which draped over her arms like a shawl, was bright green, and she wore a decoration on her helm which looked like a golden headband fused in place.

She bowed when reaching the center of the room. "I am Ecciritae, Your Honor."

He inclined his head to her. "And are you aware of the situation up to the current time?"

"I am."

"Very well. I would ask you to attempt to identify Kyle's soul sword as best you can. Kyle, you may now rise from your position and display your sword to Ecciritae."

Kyle rose as before, standing in the center of the room and letting his sword flow out of his palms into the air. This time, the 'oohh' that traveled through the crowd was much more pronounced.

I wonder if those drop-ins are here just to see the sword, Kyle thought.

"Hmm." Ecciritae brought her face close to the sword, though she did not attempt to touch it. She examined it for several seconds, and then asked him, "and this sword is capable of shattering whatever it touches?"

"I think so."

"What materials, so far, have you destroyed with this sword?"

"Um…wood, stone, other weapons." *And goblins,* he added in his own mind. *And people,* he thought with a sudden shiver of disgust.

"Other weapons? Woven arms, or ones made of traditional materials?"

"Just iron ones, not any woven ones."

"Hmm," she said again, tapping her chin. She returned to her seat and began to rummage through a rucksack she had brought with her.

"I am familiar with the physical construction of Kyle's weapon," she said, as she went through the baggage. "The practice of creating soularms to appear as an imitation of a weapon made of individual pieces is a common one; it is performed in order to decrease the size of the soularm and to render its unsheathing a faster process." She drew several small objects from her rucksack, though Kyle could not see what they were as her back was to him.

"I am also familiar with the family of enchantment that the sword appears to belong to," she continued. "It is known formally as a lysing enchantment, and informally as a shattering or tearing enchantment.

"The philosophy behind such an enchantment is that contact with the enchanted material supercharges whatever touches it, eventually tearing apart the other object's magical structure due to an excess of energy. Lysing may also take place in the form of a traditional spell belonging to the school of mysticism. The strength of a lysing spell or enchantment dictates the amount and density of material that it is able to lyse; in other words, strong materials such as stone, steel, or Buorish obsidian may only be lysed by a powerful enchantment.

"If it pleases Your Honor," she continued, returning to the center of the room and pulling towards her the table on which the stool had sat, "I would now like to perform a simple experiment in order to determine the strength of the enchantment on Kyle's sword. Should it be a powerful lysing enchantment, the sword's possible origins become narrowed down significantly."

"You may proceed," the Judge said with a wave of his hand.

Ecciritae began to place small objects on the table in a row. They were samples of various materials, as some came in geometric bars while others were in chunks.

"I have arranged in front of us a series of materials in order of their structural strength. From right to left as seen by his honor Somniel: iron, steel, Elvish silver—also known as silversteel, Buorish obsidian, vohkorn—commonly known as void iron, and finally vee'nar." She held up to her visor the last of the materials, which looked like a cube made of colored mist. "Also known as Elfglass or magicglass, an extremely rare material that forms in areas of high background magic." She set it down at the end of the table.

"Most lysing enchantments can break through iron, and many can also undo steel and even damage Elvish silver. However, only the most powerful can damage obsidian and vohkorn, and I know of no existing example of the enchantment that can damage vee'nar. Kyle, I would now ask you to touch your sword to each material in order, withdrawing it at my command in order to allow me to examine the sample closely after contact."

"Right," Kyle said. He had a feeling he knew what was going to happen, though he couldn't predict how it would be received.

Carefully, he brought his sword down to touch the materials in turn. Ecciritae did not bother to stop him during the first three, which all shattered with a *snap* when they touched the sword. However, after touching the Buorish obsidian, Ecciritae commanded him to withdraw his sword and carefully picked up the smoking sample. She brought it close to her visor, and Kyle could feel the anticipation present in the audience.

"It appears to be powerful enough to damage obsidian," she said, and the court let out a breath.

"Please, continue."

The vohkorn, which looked like a dull misshapen black marble, was also split along its length when Kyle touched his arm to it. This time, the audience gasped audibly.

"Philosopher," Judge Somniel said to Ecciritae, "at this point I believe I should ask if we would suffer greatly from the destruction of your vee'nar sample. I fear that it may in fact be destroyed and that you will lose this valuable material."

Ecciritae considered this, turning the strange cube around in her hand.

"You speak wisely," she said, "though I desire to continue the experiment for two reasons; the first being that I do in fact possess one more sample of vee'nar, and so I will be able to continue my research should this one be lost. The second being that if this sword can indeed damage vee'nar, I would consider this discovery as important as any I might experience during my research, and well worth the loss of this sample."

The Judge nodded. "Very well."

Ecciritae placed the cube on the table and motioned to Kyle. He eyed the small object warily. It certainly was a beautiful object, shimmering with an inner light much like an Ephicer.

He gripped his sword in both hands and began to lower it towards the iridescent cube. He heard the telltale sound of over a hundred people leaning forward in their seats as he did.

The cube and the sword touched.

There was an immediate loud detonation, so violent that Kyle jumped back and covered his eyes, his sword shooting back into his wrists. It was accompanied by a bright flash of multicolored light, and Kyle saw many Buors' hands raised to their visors.

When the light faded, all that remained on the table was a few tiny chunks of glass and some sand. Quietly, Ecciritae strode towards it and gathered a pinch of sand in her fingers. The room was silent.

"I am amazed," she said quietly. "Not only has the vee'nar been split into fragments, but the magical field that bound it together has been ruptured. What remains is normal glass."

Kyle had thought the room was silent before, but it has been deafeningly loud compared to the hush that now spread throughout the court.

Judge Somniel cleared his throat. "What is the significance of this?" he asked.

Ecciritae didn't reply right away. She was still examining the fragments of vee'nar she held between her fingers.

"As I mentioned previously, I have never before heard of a lysing enchantment capable of damaging vee'nar. In fact, this material is one of the strongest in existence and is by far the one most resistant to magic." She turned to face Kyle, and her mood was vaguely accusatory. "Am I right in inferring that you are not a promoted unit?"

When Kyle hesitated, she explained, "A fighter who has undergone a process of spiritual evolution, and has become what is known to adventurers as a hero."

Finally Kyle understood. "No, I'm not a hero," he said.

Ecciritae pondered this. "Then I am forced to conclude that the weapon Kyle possesses is not a soularm, at least not in the sense that we might understand it. You see, in order for a soularm to be woven into one's soul, one must assure that their own spiritual strength is great enough to contain and control the power of their weapon. Thus the strength of soularm a warrior may possess is bounded by the strength of the warrior. A soularm as powerful as the one Kyle wields would require a soul of immense strength to contain it, one of which Kyle clearly does not possess."

Murmuring broke out in the courtroom at this statement. Somniel ignored it and asked,

"Then what may we conclude of Kyle's possession of the arm?"

"I cannot say for sure," Ecciritae said slowly. "I am loath to use terms such as 'otherworldly' in my description, but the containment of such a powerful weapon in a soul of average power—let alone the existence of the weapon itself—is difficult to reconcile with our laws of magic. Such power does surface in some scholarly conjecture based around the creationist theory. Such theorists believe that particles of otherworldly energy, if brought into a lower-tiered world, could contain an unfathomable amount of power compressed into a miniscule space. That is the only explanation, theoretical or otherwise, that I have come across in my studies which could explain this phenomenon."

"I must protest," Erriand said over the sudden increase of noise in the court. "I believe it is too great a logical leap to jump from Kyle's soularm to the creationist theory. After all, the nature of that theory has been a subject of hot debate among scholars for centuries, and to use it as explanation for these events would be to imply its foundation in truth."

Ecciritae bowed towards him politely. "I do know this," she said, "and I do not wish to make any such implication. I am merely sharing with the court the extent of my knowledge, and the only explanation I have as of yet come across which seems appropriate to the situation."

Septhiran rose and cleared his throat. "If we are to consider an otherworldly origin as a possible explanation for Kyle's sudden appearance and unknown past," he said, "then certain details which before seemed inscrutable may now be seen in new light. For instance, is it possible that the memories present in Kyle's mind are not in fact corrupt, but merely from an alternate reality which cannot be understood by those of us who view them?"

"If that were the case," Erriand said, "then Kyle does not in fact suffer from amnesia, and possesses full memory of the reality he used to inhabit before arriving in ours."

He turned and looked straight at Kyle. So did Septhiran, Ecciritae and Judge Somniel. In fact, Kyle could feel the attention of the entire court on him. He couldn't believe what had happened. How was it possible that they had reached that conclusion so quickly, using only his soul sword as evidence?

Now, the only question was, did he tell them or attempt to continue the charade?

He raked his eyes over his panel again and caught Septhiran's eye. He looked sympathetic, and after a moment he stood up and coughed quietly.

"Kyle," he said simply, "you may call for recess if you so desire, or request time to converse with your companions off the court's record."

Kyle was still stunned. "Yes," he said, "that would be good. The second one." He turned to Judge Somniel. "Is…that all right?"

The Judge nodded slowly, his gaze never leaving Kyle's face. "It is," he said, waving his arm gently, "you may return to your seat."

Kyle walked back to the others on legs made of jelly as the court again filled with noise. It was no problem getting to speak privately with his companions with everyone in the audience holding conversations of their own.

"Hey, Septhiran," Lugh said, "would you mind giving us a moment?"

Septhiran nodded and made to rise, but Kyle interjected.

"No, Lugh, it's all right."

Puzzled, the lawyer settled back down.

Kyle leaned closer to him.

"Look, I'm pretty sure you've known for a long time that I was from another world. Ever since we told you our story when we first got here. Right?"

Septhiran spread his hands gravely. "It would be too strong a claim to say that I *knew*," he said, "for indeed the implications of such a truth are vast and the conclusion is not to be reached lightly. But yes, it is true that my colleagues and I have suspected this even before your arrival in Buoria."

"*What?*" Lugh said.

"You knew," Phundasa said, "and yet you did not expose us."

"It is not the Buorish way. There was no need to confront you when we believed that the truth would be ousted in time through normal course of logic. As events have transpired, the truth shall be revealed in public, after a rigorous, recorded and civilized debate. My colleagues and I have discussed this at length, and agreed that it was the optimal way of handling Kyle's case."

"So what do we do now?" Nihs asked him in a tone only Nihs could manage. "Does the rest of the court know about Kyle already? How do we make the confession?"

"I will handle the confession, if you so desire," Septhiran said. "However, once the statement is made, the onus will again be put on you to recount your true story in full."

"That's fine," Kyle said, nodding, "that's what we get for lying in the first place." A wry smirk appeared on his face. "I guess you were right, Septhiran, lies don't last long here."

"It was only natural to do as you did," Septhiran reassured him, "and I thank you for having the courage to tell the truth in the end. You are shielded by it now; the court shall not find you guilty, I am sure of it."

He began to rise, but paused, and turned back to face Kyle.

"So it *is* true, then," he said. "You are, in fact, from another world?"

"Yeah," he said, staring into the expressionless face, "it's true."

Septhiran bowed gently, though he said nothing. He rose and raised a hand to Somniel, signaling that his group was finished conferring. Somniel raised his arms in turn, and silence abounded.

Septhiran stepped onto the floor.

"Ladies and gentlemen of the court," he said, "my client desires to make a confession pertaining to his origin, pleading that his previous recount was tainted by falsehood yet assuring that he now speaks the truth to the best of his ability. The overarching reason behind all of the bizarre events and facts surrounding Kyle is, in fact, that he is not from our world of Loria."

The court erupted into noise, and for the first time, Judge Somniel was forced to raise his voice to restore order.

When the noise had again died down, Septhiran continued. "As I myself am not in full possession of the facts, I would recommend that we allow Kyle and his companions to recount their story once more in its complete and true form before we take any other action."

"A wise statement," Somniel said. When he spoke again, Kyle detected a hint of displeasure. "However, before even this I would ask Kyle for what purpose he intended to deceive the court, and whether he now truly attests that he is, to his knowledge, an otherworldly being."

"I'm sorry," Kyle said, rising to his feet. "We were lying. We were afraid of what would happen if people found out what I was—that they'd think I was crazy, or that they'd want to capture me or kill me. But it's true that I'm not from Loria. I can remember my life from before I came here."

The Judge leaned forward in his seat to peer at Kyle more closely. Strangely enough, Kyle no longer felt nervous. Perhaps Septhiran had been right; now that he was speaking the truth his confidence was returning, and the weight of his secret was removed from his shoulders.

"Very well," Somniel said, not unkindly. "Please begin your story again, beginning this time with a brief summary of the world you previously inhabited and the circumstances which lead up to your arrival in ours."

It took hours and hours. Every detail Kyle mentioned about his world only gave rise to more questions, and Buors all over the courthouse were standing up in their seats to request permission to ask him another. Some were skeptical, and more than once the point that he may just be insane was raised, but these comments were eventually quelled in the face of overwhelming evidence that Kyle was telling the truth.

He told them of the geographical layout of his earth, of the differences in technology and the absence of magic; he told them of his own life leading up to the accident on the *Caribia* and of course all the events which had transpired since his arrival in Loria.

His soul sword was again examined with the new evidence in mind, and Nihs told them of his theory that the sword was in fact Kyle's nuclear soul, compressed into his being by Loria's magical atmosphere.

His memories were read again and again, by various members of the court. Each one attested to viewing the strange and garbled memories left over from his time on earth. Kyle's companions were questioned about his personality, his behavior, and what he had told each of them.

Paper was brought from somewhere, and Kyle sketched out as best he could the shape of Earth's continents, labeling whatever countries he knew and showing them where in North America he used to live. He went into far more detail about his world than he ever had to his companions or anyone else.

Finally Somniel again called for silence and everyone returned to their seats. The energy in the room was now palpable. Kyle never could have believed that the Buors were capable of becoming so animated or excited.

"Ladies and gentlemen, please, please," Somniel said, as noise still persisted. When the room finally fell silent, he said,

"We have interrogated Kyle extensively for many hours now, and it has grown very late. I too share in the excitement exhibited by the members of the court; however, it would be unfeeling of us to continue our interrogations any further tonight. Kyle has been very understanding and cooperative toward us, and it is now time for us to return the favor. I declare this session closed for the night. We will resume in the morning when everyone is well rested and has had time to thoroughly weigh the questions they wish to ask." He lifted his gaze heavenward. "I see that the ashfall has abated, and that it would now be safe for all to return to their homes. Court will resume three hours after sunrise tomorrow."

Several Buors in the audience nodded, and soon the court began to empty. As quickly as that, the session was over.

Kyle had been talking so much over the past few hours that he had become hoarse, and now that the court was emptying he became aware of a persistent rumbling in his stomach.

Septhiran breathed out explosively. He had been talking nearly as much as Kyle, helping him out at every turn and deflecting as many questions as he could. Over the course of the session Kyle had come to infinitely appreciate his assistance.

"Well!" he said, "I believe that will do for the night. Gentlemen, my lady, we should return to the free holding center for tonight."

"Yes, please," they chorused.

No one felt like trying to sleep once they reached the holding center. Instead, they had a meal in the common room and played mareek-check well into the night. They thanked Septhiran profusely for his help, and he bowed modestly and thanked them in turn.

The overall feeling within the group was a triumphant one. Though they had still not technically won their case, they each felt deep down that the court had begun to sympathize with them.

Since Kyle's description of his world to the court had gone into more detail than ever before, his companions all had a plethora of new questions to ask him about Earth. He didn't mind; it wasn't nearly as exhausting to talk to them as it had been to an audience of hundreds.

Finally Septhiran poked his head into the common room to tell them that they really should sleep, as it was only a few hours to sunrise. What he found was Lugh—who was slightly the worse for a bottle of wine—already asleep on the carpet, with Nihs curled up nearby and Meya dosing off on Kyle's shoulder. Kyle and Phundasa were still attempting to continue their game of mareek-check, though since the others had all been playing it had fallen apart somewhat.

Septhiran paused in the doorway, and Kyle could *see* a smile forming behind his visor.

"Good sirs and madam," he said, "tomorrow will be another long day, and the floor is hardly an appropriate place to spend your night. I do recommend that you take to your beds."

"Right," Kyle said, while Phundasa laughed.

Kyle gently took hold of Meya's shoulders and lifted her off. Nihs woke quickly, though it took a slap from Phundasa to get Lugh off of the floor. They shuffled into their rooms and finally fell asleep.

James Livaldi, head of Maida Weapons Inc., was very, very busy.

It was a natural state of being for him. Maida, after all, was a massive company, and Livaldi was not a strong believer in delegating work. Even though his employees were handpicked from the best and brightest Reno city had to offer, there were few people within the company that Livaldi would trust with his work anyway. Better to do it himself, quickly and properly, than give someone else the chance to do it wrong.

The door to his office opened, and in stepped his personal magician, Saul. He made his way to Livaldi's desk on silent feet, trying to gauge the young master's mood based on his expression.

"The twins have returned, sir," he said finally.

Livaldi looked up from his paperwork. "I suppose it would be a waste of breath to ask if they brought Kyle with them?"

"I'm afraid so, sir."

Livaldi sighed. "Somehow I thought that might be the case. Oh well…call them in."

Saul dipped his head and left back the way he came. He knew better than to say anything else.

A moment later he returned, herding the twins ahead of him. Lian and Lacaster looked much worse for wear; they were sullen and pouty, and Lian wore a bandage over his still-bleeding eye.

Livaldi steepled his fingers. "And where exactly have you two been?" he said.

The twin's expressions grew darker, but neither of them answered.

"While I'll admit that I wasn't necessarily expecting you to return with Kyle, I at least hoped you would have the decency to show yourselves if you failed. You've been gone for days. What happened? Did you get lost?"

"We had to escape," Lian whined, spurred into talking by Livaldi's insult. "The Buorish police caught up with us."

"Really? That must have been terrifying. What happened to your original plan? I suppose Kyle's sword was enough to fend off a swarm of eyrioda?"

"Their party had changed," Lacaster said, while his brother whimpered and clutched at his eye. "They had a bishop with them."

One of Livaldi's eyebrows shot up. "Really?" He was smiling, but there was no warmth in his expression. "So they escaped. Where are they now?"

"We don't know," Lian said. "We think the guards took them."

Livaldi didn't reply right away. He got up and drew a cup of coffee from his favorite machine. The twins watched him as he took a sip, sighed contentedly, and walked over to an expensive wooden filing cabinet on the other side of his desk.

"If Kyle ran into the Buorish police," he said, setting his mug atop it and opening one of the drawers, "then they have taken him to Buoria. They would never let a man with such a suspicious past go free for long. He's probably being tried in their court as we speak."

Livaldi drew a long, thin box from within one of the shelves, shutting it again gently and taking up his mug. He strode back behind his desk and set the box down.

"I must say," he continued mildly, "that it would be very difficult for me to be more disappointed in the two of you than I currently am. Not only did you fail to capture Kyle on two different occasions, but you *also* managed to cause an immense amount of collateral damage at the same time. You've murdered no less than twenty people and caused a commercial trading vessel to go missing—a trail of crime a mile wide for the police to follow. Every person who disappears, every sighting of you that takes place, is one more clue that ultimately leads them back to me. Can't you *think?* Now I have to deal with the fact that Kyle is in Buoria, the safest nation in the world. Do you have any idea how terrible it would be if the Buors found out about what he is and decided to offer him their support?"

Livaldi had the amazing ability to lose his temper without losing his temper. By the end of his lecture, both twins were cringing back from him as if they'd been shouted at. But Livaldi never shouted. When he became angry, his diction only improved; his words became sharp and clipped, each one a small barb that cut into the skin of whoever was on the receiving end of his displeasure.

"Thankfully," he continued, "in this particular case, your incompetence may end up serving us for the better in the long run. In your failure, you've given my engineers the time to complete a weapon that I am certain will make our lives easier."

At the mention of a weapon, the twins' faces lit up. They looked with renewed interest at the box Livaldi had brought from the drawer. Not deigning to notice their hungry expressions, Livaldi revealed the box's contents.

It was a single arrow, similar to the metal bolts which Lacaster used in his ring bow. It was pure black in color, glossed with some kind of material that gave its edges a white sheen, like a thick coating of glass.

Livaldi lifted it from its silken bed and handed it to Lacaster, who took it greedily. It felt cold to the touch.

"What does it do?" he asked, his eyes full of its sheen.

"It's not your job to know what it does. Your job is to shoot Kyle with that arrow in a place where he'll recover. Once he has left Buoria, I will ensure that you are put in a position where such a shot will be possible. You will notice I am giving you only one arrow. Needless to say that if you miss, you may consider yourselves fired."

"I never miss," Lacaster said.

"I hope for your sake that you are right. Run along, now. I have business to attend to."

They were woken early again the next day, much to their chagrin. Kyle heard a knock on their door as the sun was coming up.

"Good sirs?" came a voice from the other side.

"Kyle," said Nihs, "could you—"

"Yeah, yeah." Kyle was puzzled, though. The voice hadn't sounded like Septhiran's.

He opened the door to find Godraien waiting for them in the hallway, hands folded politely behind his back.

"Godraien!" he said in surprise, shaking the seeker's hand. "What are you doing here?"

"I heard of the progress which was made during yesterday's court session," he replied, inclining his head, "and decided to take the day off in favor of attending today's proceedings. If I have judged correctly, then it will have been well worth my time to do so."

"That's great," Kyle said, as Nihs got out of his bed and walked up to them. "So…you heard about where I'm from?"

"Indeed I did," Godraien said.

His tone made Kyle add, "you knew already. Right?"

Godraien nodded. "We had suspected for a while that you were not all that you seemed, and following your interview with the estor our suspicions were all but confirmed. But there is more to this tale, and not all of it should be revealed by me—and particularly at this moment, as you will soon be needed in court! Please, the others are downstairs."

Kyle was perplexed by Godraien's words, but he had no time to push the issue and thought that he shouldn't anyway. The Buors had a tendency to go at their own pace and he usually found it best to let events play out.

Nihs scrambled up onto his shoulder as they made their way downstairs.

"I was meaning to ask you," Kyle said. "Ecciritae was talking about promotion yesterday and I don't really understand how it works. It sounded like it was some kind of big event. I thought it was just when an adventurer got a new title."

"It is both," Nihs said. "A promotion is a magical event that takes place when an individual reaches a certain level of power and spiritual advancement. A new part of their soul becomes unlocked, allowing them to achieve their true potential and grow more powerful than they currently are."

"Wait—becoming more powerful makes you more powerful?"

"If I may," Godraien said politely, "in Buoria, promotion is often described using the following metaphor. Imagine for a moment that you were born with one of your lungs sealed shut. If you trained your body, you would become able to hold your breath for longer and longer with your single lung—however, you would never be able to achieve your maximum potential due to that significant crutch. Therefore, promotion is akin to the unsealing of that lung, the breaking down of a physical, mental and magical barrier preventing you from becoming more powerful."

"That's a very good way of putting it," Nihs said, sounding surprised as he always did when another contributed to his lectures. "When you undergo promotion, your overall level of strength increases dramatically, and a powerful aura of magic surrounds you and re-sculpts your body. Promotion can even warp the clothes you're wearing or other impressionable items nearby. Think of it as a magical overload that transforms you permanently."

"Wow," Kyle said, "and this just happens at some point while you're training?"

"Promotion is a different process for each individual," Godraien said, "and in each case it is a different event which triggers it. In some cases, it is traditional for a powerful weapon to be presented to one who is believed to be ready for promotion—such is the case with knights. In this instance, the presentation of the weapon is the event that triggers the process. Others are brought on by dire or near-death circumstances, or magical rites of passage designed to test one's strength."

"Right," Kyle said. He had many more questions he wanted to ask, but they would have to wait for later.

Breakfast was already underway by the time they reached the common room; Septhiran, Errodion and Layendis had joined the others at their table. Kyle and Nihs sat down and began to eat ravenously.

"Good morning," Meya said. "Sleep well?"

Nihs nodded with his mouth full and Kyle said, "Well enough." He smirked and looked at Lugh, whose eyes were closed and whose face was drawn. "How about you?"

Phundasa grunted as he reached across the table. "I'm glad he and I aren't married," he said. "His snores were like a beast growling all through the night."

Lugh made a rude gesture in his direction as the others laughed.

As soon as they were done eating, Septhiran leaned forward in his seat to speak. "We should be on our way shortly. The court will be expecting you soon."

When they arrived at the courthouse, it was to find a certain level of commotion outside. Kyle was stunned to see a closely packed crowd of Buors blocking the doors, waiting to be let inside. One of the court's guards was standing on a platform near his station, making an announcement to the mass of people. As they drew closer, they were able to hear what the he was saying.

"…all remaining space is to be used by the party of Kyle Campbell, and other functionaries of the court whose presence is essential. I am sorry, but I must deny entry to those of you beyond this line."

A murmur passed through the crowd and a couple dozen Buors at the back nodded and turned to leave. As they passed by the party, Kyle noticed a couple of stares.

They finally reached the doors and were called over by the same guard who had let them in the previous day.

"Ah, estor…and Kyle and his company, excellent. As you can see, word of your trial has spread throughout the capital and there are many who wish to witness its conclusion. You may proceed directly to your seats, as I believe Judge Somniel is prepared to resume the case."

They thanked him and entered the courtroom. Kyle was amazed by the sight that greeted them. Every single seat in the room was occupied, and in the case of the benches lining the sides of the room, Buors were wedged in next to each other to allow the maximum possible number of people to occupy them. But most shocking was the number of men and women who were standing—standing on every available tile of flooring, leaving only the aisles leading to the Judge's podium perfectly free.

Kyle felt hundreds of eyes on him as he followed Septhiran down the aisle. He couldn't believe what was going on. Were these people here to support him or watch him get prosecuted?

They were all seated, and soon Somniel raised his hands for silence; clearly he had been waiting on Kyle's arrival to begin. The hush was almost immediate.

"Yesterday," Somniel began, "we reviewed the case of one Kyle Campbell, a man who recently applied for a temporary Iden card citing that his memory had been modified by a magical incident of unknown origin. After reviewing Kyle's case, it was discovered that…"

Kyle let his mind wander as Somniel encapsulated the events of yesterday's court session. His gaze wandered across the Buors amassed in the hall, trying to get an impression of how they felt.

Somniel completed his summary and then addressed the court. "In order to assure that our debate proceeds in the proper direction, I propose that we settle the case of Kyle being an otherworldly being before we touch any other issue. I am sure you will all agree that this decision will have a direct and significant bearing on any others we arrive at throughout the proceedings.

"As such, in light of the extensive evidence that Kyle has provided concerning his origins, I now ask for any individual who wishes to examine why Kyle may *not* be from Terra to voice their questions and concerns. Is there any who has spotted a possible flaw or falsehood in our reasoning?"

There were several, and the next couple of hours were spent examining in excruciating detail every aspect of Kyle's story, picking it apart to ensure that it was absolutely airtight. The questioning was intense, but Kyle faced it with optimism. Now he was telling the truth, and talking about a world with which he was intimately familiar. He answered every question quickly and completely, without having to watch his words or bend the meaning of his statements. His confidence must have shone through, for eventually Erriand rose from his seat to speak in his defense.

"Ladies and gentlemen of the court, I believe it is quite clear that we are not dealing with a fabricated story or the result of a magical prank. The authenticity of Mister Campbell's story has been tested time and again through logical and magical means, and we have yet to detect any sign of weakness. Even if one were to accept that an illusionist could create such a powerful and convincing alternate past, this does not explain the origins of Kyle's soul sword."

"You speak well," Somniel said. "Then I will ask the court again: are there any who do not believe that Kyle is, to the best of all parties' knowledge, an authentic otherworldly being? I will leave ten seconds for objection, at the end of which my ruling shall be to declare him so. Are we agreed?"

Kyle's heart pounded in his chest as the seconds ticked by. Some conversation broke out in the courthouse, but to his immense relief no one raised their voice in objection. Finally, after what felt like an eternity, Somniel said:

"Very well. By the authority vested in me as a Judge of the Buorish court, I declare Kyle to be a legitimate denizen of the world known as Terra, and *not* a native inhabitant of our world of Loria."

Kyle felt a wave of joy and relief wash over him as a smattering of applause broke out in the courtroom. Meya squeezed his shoulder and Lugh whooped out loud.

Somniel called again for silence.

"Clearly," he said, "this is a historic moment, and I am sure that many of our texts, both legal and scientific, shall have to be amended in light of it. However, as far-reaching as the implications of this declaration are, we must withhold for now our desire to discuss them. For there is still the specific case of Kyle Campbell to be addressed, and though we may wish for him to remain in Buoria for further discussion and questioning, it would not be within our legal rights nor within the bounds of courtesy to do so. As a member of the human race, he holds the same basic rights as any other man.

"Therefore, we must now turn our discussion to the three specific incidents related to Mister Campbell's case which may have legal implications. First, Kyle's application for a temporary Iden card. Second, the attempted kidnapping in Reno city. Finally, the attempted kidnapping and double murder in the town of Rhian."

Septhiran rose. "If it pleases Your Honor, I propose we consider the situation as such: in cases two and three, Kyle and his companions were clearly victims. In these cases, the only charge which may be laid against the party would be their failure to report an incidence of crime. In the case of the Iden card, the party may be charged with deceit, or more specifically failure to provide true and complete information during official government business."

"Indeed," Somniel said gravely. "Let us first handle the party's failure to report an incidence of crime. It is widely known that this is a common practice in many parts of the world, and consideration may be taken for the fact that Kyle's party intended to leave Reno city immediately after the incident took place. However, in this case a follow-up crime took place, one which resulted in the death of the Oblihari Osirde and Mikasa."

Kyle's elation drained out through his shoes. Somniel's tone had changed quickly, and the names of the elderly couple threw up terrible memories in his mind. He didn't dare to look at Meya beside him, though he could tell that she had tensed with the mention of their names.

"We must then ask ourselves if Kyle and his party should be held collaterally responsible for their deaths; for if the original crime has been reported, this additional crime may have been avoided."

A Buor at the center of the audience rose, and Kyle realized that it was Captain Callaghnen.

"If I may, Your Honor," he said politely. "I wish to bring to the attention of the court the following facts. Firstly, while I do not believe that Kyle acted appropriately in failing to report the crime, I can attest that his actions throughout the second incident were noble and responsible, seeking as he did to protect his comrades and prevent further bloodshed at the cost of his own freedom. Secondly, judging by the persistence and professionalism with which Kyle has been followed, I am loath to believe that the party's report of the incident could have prevented future incidents entirely."

"Indeed," agreed Somniel, "but it is also true that these incidents may have been delayed, or the criminals responsible captured, as a result of cooperation with the police."

"I cannot deny this. But I beg the court to display lenience nonetheless. Remember that we are speaking of an individual who has only just recently arrived in our world, and who sought only to move through it silently and unmolested."

"Thank you, captain, your words will be considered. Are there others who wish to voice their opinion on this matter?"

There were a few, some of them in favor of pardoning Kyle, others who thought that Lugh, Nihs and Rogan should be held responsible if not him. One Buor dressed in deep blue rose in the center; Kyle recognized a man who had spoken a few times before.

"Ladies and gentlemen of the court," he said, "I beseech you to consider my argument. I believe that the charge of negligence placed upon Kyle's party should be dropped, for a number of reasons. As stated previously, it is very common for crimes to remain unreported by witnesses. In most cases, the consequences of these unreported crimes are impossible to divine, and are thus impossible to punish accordingly. I ask you, does it appeal to your logic that a man and his entourage, pursued by criminals and wishing only to protect their own, should be persecuted for failing to involve themselves with the police? Kyle's party wished to protect his identity in the interest of his own safety, and they correctly predicted that involvement with our police would cause this identity to be revealed. They failed to report the crime not out of malice or guilt, but out of simple desire to remain anonymous and unmolested. No one could have foreseen the later ramifications of this act, and I am sure that if these results had been considered by Kyle's party, the decision would have been made to report the crime after all."

"Very well spoken," Somniel acknowledged, as the blue-sashed man sat back down.

"Yeah, thanks," Kyle said under his breath.

More opinions were heard, though now many of them agreed with what the blue-sashed Buor had said. Kyle couldn't believe his good luck, and was considering asking Septhiran who the man was so that he could thank him later. In the end, the court ruled that the charges should be dismissed.

Lugh let out an explosive breath, and leaned over to Kyle. "You know," he said, "sometimes I can't tell if you're the luckiest or unluckiest person in the world."

Kyle smiled thinly, more relieved than he was willing to admit.

"And finally," Somniel said, "we have yet to decide what is to be done on the subject of Kyle's Iden card. Judging from the attitude of those at court, am I wrong in suggesting that neither Kyle nor his party should be held responsible for withholding information during the application?"

Somniel's impression was correct, for this debate was a short one. It was soon agreed that Kyle was not guilty in this case either. The court even decided to grant him a full Iden card. Kyle was overjoyed, though he was waiting until they were safely out of the courtroom to celebrate.

"If we are then decided on that subject," Somniel said from his bench, "then I believe that this case is closed. A final opportunity to voice any objections will now be given. Does any person in attendance wish to object to any of the following rulings: that Kyle Campbell and his company will be found innocent of all charges; that Kyle will officially be declared as an otherworldly creature; that Kyle will receive a fully useable Iden card in accordance with the basic rights of man?"

Another tension-filled ten seconds passed, throughout which several conversations broke out in the courtroom yet no one raised their voices or stood to speak. The seconds ticked by. Across the aisle from them, Erriand sat silently, his arms folded across his chest. Beside them, Septhiran was also silent.

"Very well," Somniel said. "This case is closed."

The courtroom broke into applause. Kyle, who had been wound tight for the past several hours, sank into his chair and rested his forehead on the table, drained of energy. Meya grabbed his shoulder and Lugh reached across her to pound him on the back.

The applause lasted for several seconds, and the packed room quickly filled with noise. Eventually it died down, and the courtroom began to empty, the members of the audience in the back exiting to make room for everyone else.

They rose and stepped into the aisle once they had the space. Kyle and the others swarmed Septhiran in order to thank him, while he in turn congratulated them on their success.

"Kyle," he said, shaking his hand, "I must commend you for the way you handled yourself during the trial. Clearly you have made an impression on those in attendance here, and they have judged you as a man of honor and character."

Septhiran followed up by saying that they should exchange some words with Judge Somniel before leaving. They approached the bench, which was still manned by the Judge's entourage. Erriand was already standing on the floor before him, speaking with him over the din. When he noticed their approach, he turned and extended his hand to Septhiran.

"You spoke and reasoned well, estor," he complimented in his sinewy voice. "I must admit I was surprised by the outcome of this trial. Upon entering this room, I never suspected that I would leave it having voted for a man to be declared an otherworldly creature."

"Nor I, lauster," Septhiran agreed with a trace of humor. "It was a privilege to attend this case in your company. I see why you are so well-respected by the members of our profession."

Erriand inclined his head in acknowledgment, then shook each of their hands briefly, saying, "I must be going soon, and as much as I would like to speak with Kyle further I am sure that he desires nothing but rest. Good-luck to you, Mister Campbell. I hope that our world treats you well."

"Thanks," Kyle replied. The yellow-sashed lawyer departed, leaving them free to speak with Somniel.

Septhiran bowed deeply to him. "We thank you for lending this case wisdom and guidance, Your Honor," he said respectfully.

Somniel inclined his head, though he waved his hand as is to brush away the compliment. "You do me too much honor, estor. I merely perform my duties as would any other Judge—and I must congratulate you on your own success, estor. I see in you a great future in the world of law, should you choose to pursue it."

"Thank you," Septhiran said gratefully.

"Now—" the Judge rose from his bench, and made his way around it to join them on the courtroom floor—"if you may grant me this, I wish to shake the hand of the man who fell into our world. Never before have I had the opportunity to seek such a unique honor." And reaching their group, he proffered his hand to Kyle.

Kyle almost whimpered. Up close, Somniel was an even more fantastic apparition. Though Kyle knew that his immense size was an illusion, the man still appeared at least as large as Rogan, and was made taller and wider by his massive iron suit. The palm of his gauntleted hand was as large as Kyle's own hand in its entirety.

Gingerly, Kyle took the hand and shook it. The grip was surprisingly soft and warm, feeling more like a real hand than it should. Kyle wondered if this had anything to do with how masterfully the Buors crafted their armor.

"I wish you good luck with your affairs, Mister Campbell. The good estor will be able to provide you with the details of acquiring your new Iden card once you have exited the court."

"Thanks!" Kyle said, still too overwhelmed to think.

The Judge then acknowledged Lugh, "Captain MacAlden."

"Oh yeah," Lugh said, smirking, "I *am* a captain, aren't I? Why don't *you* call me Captain MacAlden, Nihs?"

"Because you'd hate that as much as I would, as you know very well."

Finally the introductions were over and the courtroom had emptied to the point where it was possible to leave. They stepped outside with the intention of heading back to the holding center; however, as soon as they left the courthouse they ran into a crowd of Buors standing around the entrance.

Several heads turned, and after a moment a number of people came over to greet Kyle and shake him by the hand. Kyle, who had never been in such a position before, was amazed by the number of people who wanted nothing more than to say hello to him.

Not everyone who came to greet them was a stranger; Captain Callaghnen came by shortly to speak with them, as did Godraien. Though his congratulations were effusive, he politely declined their offer to come back to the holding center with them, claiming that he had business to attend to. He took his leave of them waving heartily and promising that they would meet again.

They made their way back to the holding center, chatting animatedly the entire time. Kyle felt as though an enormous weight had been lifted from his shoulders, and he could tell that his companions felt the same way. Even Septhiran was catching their good humor.

They were all dying to eat by the time they got back, so they sat down to eat while Septhiran spoke to them.

"If it suits you, later on today we may proceed to the Iden office and have your new card printed," he told Kyle. "Other than that, you are now officially free of any obligation in Buoria. The holding center will remain free for you to use for two more days, if you so desire to stay here. If I may ask, now that your trial is over, where do you mean to go?"

Kyle swallowed a mouthful before he spoke. "Proks," he said, nodding to Lugh and Nihs. "We think the Kol elders might be able to help me."

Septhiran nodded. "A wise choice indeed, for there are few who can match the elder council's knowledge of magic and mysterious phenomena. Well, if you require any supplies or assistance before you depart, simply speak with me and—" he cut himself off as another Buor, a smaller man with a bright red sash, stepped into the room and waited politely in the door-frame for him to finish talking.

"Yes, good sir?" Septhiran asked him. "Do you have business with us?"

The man bowed, and approached their table. His hands were folded smartly behind his back.

"Excuse me, good sirs and madam," he said, his voice clipped and professional, "are you estor Septhiran and the party of Kyle Campbell?"

"We are," Septhiran said.

"My name is Herraine. I am a page serving His Majesty King Azanhein of Buoria. I would like to extend His Majesty's greetings to Kyle Campbell and his companions…and to invite them to a private audience and dinner with His Majesty taking place this evening at two o'clock." And with that, he unfolded his hands from behind his back and gave to Kyle what he had been holding: a thick black envelope trimmed with red and sealed with the crest of the Buorish king.

Kyle took the envelope and stared at it while the page's words sunk into his mind.

Lugh beat him to it.

"What!?" he said, leaning across the table at Herraine. "An audience with *King Azanhein?*"

"Indeed," the page replied, stepping backwards slightly. "His Majesty wishes to extend his congratulations to Kyle, as well as discuss certain matters whose natures are unknown to me."

Kyle had never seen Lugh at a complete loss for words before. He himself had no idea what to say. He opened the thick envelope and unfolded the paper inside, getting only an impression of the letter written upon it.

"Um…" he said.

"We will certainly attend," Nihs said, "it would be an honor."

"Excellent. Then may I find you here approximately thirty minutes prior to the appointed time, in order to escort you to His Majesty?"

"Of course," Nihs said.

Herraine turned to Septhiran, who seemed no less shocked than Lugh.

"The invitation has been extended to you as well, estor. It is my understanding that your colleague, Godraien, will also be in attendance."

"I…I will absolutely attend, if His Majesty seeks my company," Septhiran replied.

"Perfect. I will inform His Majesty. Farewell, good sirs and madam. I will return here at one-thirty tonight."

They waited until the door shut behind him before they fell to talking.

"By the Saints," Septhiran said, "never would I have thought that my involvement in this case would result in an audience with His Majesty. Kyle, I must thank you for granting me the opportunity to receive this sublime honor."

"This is amazing!" was Lugh's comment. "I can't believe we're going to meet King Azanhein!"

"Is it that rare for people to speak with the king?" Kyle asked.

"Rare enough for the Buors, I should think," Nihs said, "and practically unheard of for adventurers like us."

"Huh," Kyle said, poring over the letter Herraine had given him. It was fairly straightforward, mostly repeating what the page had told them. At the bottom was a large signature in black pen—Azanhein's.

"When's the dinner again?" Lugh asked him, nodding at the letter in Kyle's hand.

"Two o'clock," Kyle said, looking down at it. "Look…I know I should have asked this before, but how do you measure time here? Three can't be right, can it? That's the middle of the night."

"Two in the evening means two hours from sunset," Nihs said. "Each time the sun rises or sets, the clock begins counting from zero. It's not the most convenient system, but it's the best one we have, ever since the meteor threw off the world's rotation."

"The art of timekeeping is not an easy one," Septhiran agreed. "In order to be accurate, a clock must incrementally change the length of its days and nights on a constant basis. Such machines are difficult and expensive to produce. As such, it is common practice in many parts of the world to be lenient with timekeeping, and use the position of the sun and moon in the sky as tools for estimation."

"'Many parts of the world'," Kyle repeated. "Not here, though, I bet."

Septhiran laughed. "You are correct in your assertion, Mister Campbell."

Meya was tapping her chin. "Should we be getting clothes to meet with King Azanhein? We're not exactly dressed for royalty."

"It is not necessary for you to wear finery when dining with the king. Provided that you are well groomed and that the garments you wear are of reasonable quality and cleanliness, no one in the king's court will object. We do not stand so on ceremony, and I am sure that His Majesty will take into consideration your situation."

"Still," Lugh said thoughtfully, "it's not every day you get to have dinner with a king. Might as well do it properly, right? We've got half the day left. We were going out to Kyle's Iden card anyway. If we've got the time, why don't we pick up some fancy clothes?"

"Oh, yes," Nihs said sourly. "While we're at it, we can put the *Ayger* up for sale to pay for them."

"Hey, if you can't spend your money on looking posh for the king of Buoria, what can you spend it on?"

So it was that after lunch, they headed once more into the Upper City, following Septhiran's lead. First, he brought Kyle to the Iden office, where a slightly awestruck clerk walked him through the process of creating his new card. This was exactly the same as what Kyle had gone through before in Reno, with the one difference that he had to surrender his old card first. When the clerk snapped it in two, there was a brief flash of light and it was immediately stripped of all its information, turning into two blank plates, which the clerk disposed of in a neat metal basket next to his desk.

Once Kyle had his complete Iden card, they set out for the Buorish marketplace to find some formal wear. Kyle, Lugh, and Phundasa were easy, since none of them were particularly knowledgeable about fashion and were more or less happy with the first suits they found. Nihs, for his part, refused to buy anything, favoring instead traditional Kollic robes he kept on the *Ayger*. Meya was slightly more difficult, and Kyle couldn't blame her. As a human shopping in Buoria, her array of choices was far from limited—in fact, it was quite dazzling. Finally, she came out of a store carrying a large box and wearing a pleased expression.

"What did you *get?*" Lugh asked her, as they fell into pace.

"You can see it once I'm in it."

They had time to kill once they were finished shopping, but decided to spend it at the holding center rather than wander around the capital. Once there, they were surprised to find that Godraien had arrived in their absence, and was chatting with the clerk at the front desk. He turned when he saw them come in, and immediately went to welcome them.

"It is good to see you again," he said, bowing. "I apologize that our meeting following the court session was rushed so. I did not have the time to properly congratulate you on the outcome of the trial!"

"No problem," said Kyle. "I heard you're coming with us tonight to meet Azanhein."

"That is correct," Godraien said, in a voice filled with awe. "I am honored to be able to say so. I have in fact met His Majesty once before; I had only hoped that one day circumstances would allow me to do so once more."

"Wait, really?" Lugh said. "You've met Azanhein? You have to tell us about it! Come on, we need to know what to expect!"

Godraien laughed, and Kyle could tell from his body language that he was immensely pleased to be able to talk of his experience.

"To begin with, I must say that his reputation as both a mighty warrior and a great scholar is well deserved—when I first encountered him, his aura nearly overwhelmed me and it was difficult for me to organize my thoughts.

"He is always seated with his armor donned and his arms by his side. To his left, the massive shield known as the Crest of Buoria. To his right, his weapon, the transarm known as the Will of the King."

"I hate to sound stupid," Kyle said, "but what's a transarm?"

"It's like a changearm, but more intense," Lugh said. "A transarm moves through different classes of weapons when it transforms. Like a sword that becomes a spear."

"Indeed," Godraien said. "Though it is usually kept next to the throne in the form of a sword—as it was during my audience—the Will of the King can be any of a sword, a spear or an axe as the situation requires. It is a weapon of massive size and weight; only Azanhein possesses the strength necessary to wield it."

Kyle was impressed and intrigued by the stories about Azanhein, though these feelings were still tinted by disbelief. He had not been a very credulous person back on Earth, and thought that claims like the one Godraien had just made were more likely to be hyperbole than actual truth.

"Despite all of this," Godraien added, "I found him to be very soft-spoken; calm and reserved, yet in possession of a quiet confidence that is found often in diplomats—which is only fitting, as His Majesty has received such training. If I may be so bold as to provide you with some advice, we Buors do not place much emphasis on ceremony and appearances, but we do believe strongly in authenticity, honesty, and respect. King Azanhein, of course, is no exception. I do not know what he means to discuss with you, Kyle—though I may guess that it relates to your unique situation—but whatever the subject of discussion, I recommend that you hold these values close to your heart."

Kyle nodded. "Septhiran said something like that to us when we were going into court."

"It is no coincidence, I am sure. In any case, rest assured that your goal is not to impress the king or please him in any way. Remember that he was the one who sought you out, and that you are his guest! I am sure that everything will go smoothly."

Soon after, they left the common room to dress and prepare. Kyle had acquired a stylish black coat that fastened diagonally across the chest. The collar was a thick scarf that wrapped around the neck, emulating the sashes that the Buors wore. He donned it without too much trouble, and headed back to the common room. Lugh, Phundasa and Nihs were already there, waiting for him and Meya. Phundasa was looking gentlemanly in a type of maroon doublet, his normally unkempt hair brushed back neatly. Nihs' outfit wasn't much different from what he usually wore, but he looked dignified regardless. Lugh, meanwhile, managed to look laid-back even when dressed up. His coat was similar to Kyle's, but blue, with a dark red sash that flowed down his back. He was lounging on a sofa, legs outstretched and arms folded behind his head.

Meya emerged some time later. She was clothed in a flowing, floor-length dress in red, trimmed with loops and curls of black lace. The dress cut off at her shoulders, but the loops of black lace continued down her arms. Tight around the torso, it flowed down in soft ripples towards the hem. The dark elegance of it suited her surprisingly well.

"Looking good," Lugh said, from his spot on the sofa.

"Thanks! It's not too much?"

"You look great," Kyle said. He wouldn't have said it out loud, but Meya looked even better than that. The otherworldly beauty of her red hair and eyes, coupled with her dress, was something Kyle had never seen back on Earth.

It was another half an hour until Herraine arrived. It was a half hour spent nervously making conversation and doing a lot of nothing. This meant that Kyle had plenty of time alone with his thoughts. He had a lot to think about, from the battle with the eyrioda and the twins' attack, to everything he had seen and done in Buoria. He also had plenty of time to worry about his upcoming audience with King Azanhein.

Finally, Herraine returned to the holding center. "Excuse me, sirs and madam," he said, bowing, "if your preparations are complete, then I will ask you to now accompany me to the Citadel."

"I believe that they are," Godraien said, rising from his seat.

"Very well. Please follow me. His Majesty awaits."

Herraine walked them laterally across the city towards its center, and then turned left onto the wide, sloping main road that led into the Citadel. The massive edifice loomed larger and larger as they approached. The sense of scale experienced from looking up at the castle's towers was dizzying, and the multitude of lights and windows mounted on its dark surface made it appear like a sky dotted with stars.

Kyle couldn't help but feel a passing fear on seeing the castle, and not for the first time was grateful for the knowledge that the Buors were on his side. He wouldn't want to be one of their enemies.

When they first approached the Citadel, it was completely sealed off; the wall ahead of them was blank and Kyle could see no sign of a gate. The street leading up to the wall was flanked on both sides by guardhouses, and a half-dozen soldiers stood before it, looking for all the world like inanimate statues. Herraine approached the guards and drew a seal from his belt, holding it up to show them. A few words were exchanged, and Herraine rejoined them a moment later.

"You will have to surrender your weapons before entering the Citadel," he told them. "Please follow me into the guardhouse."

They did so, and once they had been relieved of their weapons exited the guardhouse to be greeted by a deep groan coming from somewhere within the castle. To Kyle's amazement, the barrier ahead of them began to pull itself apart—what had seemed like an unbroken wall was in fact the castle's gate, two halves which interlocked seamlessly at the center of the road.

The gates opened to a width of ten feet, and Herraine hustled them forwards, claiming that they would only remain so for a matter of minutes. The walls were at least thirty feet thick, and closed up behind them the second they were through. Beyond these were two more pairs of gates, the third pair finally opening up to the inner courtyard.

The courtyard was almost completely paved, though it was dotted with a few monochromatic patches of garden. It was a huge space that easily could have fit several thousand people; a parade ground of the likes that Kyle had never seen. It was walled in on all sides by black stone, and

Kyle had to crane his neck to see sky above them. Paths crisscrossed the grounds at perfect right angles to one another, leading to the far edges of the courtyard where gates and doors led into the castle walls. Turrets that each looked the size of the Empire State Building stood at the corners of the courtyard like unfathomable stone sentinels.

A hush fell upon the group as they stepped forward into the world of the Citadel. It was a beautiful, soaring, yet incredibly intimidating structure. Kyle felt like an ant trespassing in a world of giants, an uncouth figure tiptoeing around this symbol of strength and architectural perfection.

"This is unbelievable," Meya said. Her voice was full of fascination, but tinged with disapproval. "How long did it take you to build this place?"

"The Citadel is the product of hundreds of years of planning and labor," Septhiran said quietly. "It represents the greatest single effort in the history of our race, and to this day it is constantly maintained, improved, and refurbished."

"But *why?*"

"At its core, the Citadel has three primary purposes: to defend the Buorish king and the treasures of our race, and to serve as an invincible fortress in the event of a dire emergency."

"Who could possibly attack that you're so afraid of?" Meya asked.

"It is not a matter of who might attack," Septhiran said patiently, "but of what may be lost if the attack were successful."

"What's that?" Kyle asked. He realized that he shouldn't have, but Septhiran had clearly been expecting the question.

"The secret of our race. Our identity," he said simply. "The Citadel serves the same purpose as the masks we wear upon our faces, and the armor with which we cover our bodies. It protects our appearance, our racial identity. What we are, and how we fit in with this world. It is not a secret in the traditional sense—one which could be written down, or that I could tell you, or even that could be truly revealed if I were to remove my mask at this moment. But if the right people were to gain access to the deepest parts of our Citadel, there lies evidence of the Buorish identity to be gleaned, and that must be avoided at all cost."

Kyle was burning with curiosity at this point, and he could tell that the others were, as well. But it was just as obvious that questioning Septhiran more would lead to nothing. So instead he asked,

"Why is it so important that no one finds out what you are?"

"That, alas, is a reason that must be kept as secret as the thing itself. Mister Campbell, I know that my explanation has likely done more to spark your curiosity than to quench it, but I must ask you not to inquire further, to myself or any other Buor, about our racial secret. It has never been revealed by any Buor in history and we remain confident that it never will. Thus, any questions you may ask will only have to be deflected, to the inconvenience of both yourself and the affected party."

"Oh. Sorry."

"You needn't apologize. It is to be expected of one learning of our secret for the first time. And indeed, anyone looking at our fortress would be moved to ask as to why it is necessary! But we insist that it is so."

By this time they had reached the far end of the courtyard. An iron gate barred the entrance to a great lift that went up the side of the fortress. On either side of the lift was a turret several hundred feet high built into the castle wall. Perched at the top of each turret was a massive artillery gun. These were much larger than any of the others Kyle had seen, and were pointed at the parade ground directly in front of the lift. Each one was the size of a house, with a barrel that Kyle could have lived in. They were gold in color, and mounted on huge swivels to allow for three hundred and sixty-degree shooting. They shone even in the dusty twilight of Buoria, like a pair of glittering dragons keeping watch over the castle.

Septhiran said nothing as they approached the lift, and Kyle didn't dare speak. He tried to block out a sudden mental image of the cannons' barrels swiveling to face him.

The lift was a large, heavily gated metal platform that could accommodate a hundred people. It was built into the side of the Citadel's wall and was barred shut when they approached. Herraine put his hand on a communicator crystal set into the wall nearby, and spoke quietly to whoever was on the other end. A warning alarm went off above the lift, bathing the party in red light. The heavy iron gates swung open and they stepped inside.

"Please mind the rapid ascent of the lift," Herraine told them. "Do not be alarmed if you sense a change in pressure."

There was a loud *clank* of iron and the lift started to move. It ascended smoothly up the face of the Citadel, slowly at first, but accelerating quickly. Kyle's vision became blurred, his ears popped, and his legs were ready to buckle. Meya clung to Phundasa for balance; only the three Buors in their party remained solid as rock, their hands folded politely behind their backs.

The lift flew upwards so quickly that they were soon above the courtyard walls, and the Citadel increasingly came into view. It seemed to go on forever; there was always another wall, a higher turret, another layer of security that Kyle had yet to see.

Phundasa strode forward with difficulty to place his hands on the iron bars and get a better view.

"Very impressive," he said to Herraine. "How do you power this lift so that it moves so quickly?"

"There is another lift connected to this one which serves as a counterweight, descending as this one ascends. That, coupled with the power of our steam and Ephicer engines, allows us to reach this measure of speed."

After a minute of ascent, Kyle felt a shift in the lift's movement. To his surprise, the shaft it was traveling through began to bend inwards, so that the lift moved in towards the Citadel's core. Its speed remained unchanged as it slowly leveled out. Herraine warned them all to find a handhold for support, and soon the lift was traveling horizontally, zooming through the stone corridor like a solitary subway car.

Finally the elevator quickly decelerated and came to rest against an iron grille leading into the Citadel. It slid open, and they passed through a Spartan anteroom before entering a large hall. It was a muted, warm space, hung with tapestries and impressively furnished. Hallways and staircases led off in all directions.

"Welcome to the Citadel," Herraine said.

"Nice place," Lugh said, with the dry humor that he always adopted in serious situations.

Herraine, apparently, was not amused. "Indeed, sir. Please follow me."

He led them to the far end of the hall, where a pair of guards stood in front of a huge double door. He spoke briefly with them, flashing the same seal that he had shown the guards outside. They nodded, and swung one of the doors open slightly.

"I must now leave you to inform His Majesty of your arrival," Herraine told them. "Please wait here. I will return shortly."

With that, he stepped through the door and left them to themselves. Kyle, who had nearly forgotten about his meeting with Azanhein after seeing the Citadel, began to feel nervous again. He looked at the large doors Herraine had passed through. Was the Buorish king seated just beyond them?

His companions were obviously feeling the same way. Meya kept adjusting her dress, and even Lugh was pacing back and forth, his thumbs in his belt.

Herraine returned a moment later, bowing to them smartly.

"His Majesty is prepared to see you. Please follow me."

Kyle's heart was pounding as Herraine led them through the doors, but it was not the throne room, only another anteroom with another pair of double doors at the far end. A formidable-looking guard stood at attention in front of each door. Their uniforms were trimmed with gold and white, and they were armed with thin, magnificently crafted lances. They were each at least seven feet tall—or rather, Kyle realized, they *looked* seven feet tall due to their level of power.

The guards did not acknowledge their presence or even flinch when they entered. Herraine, likewise, did not engage with them at first, but rather addressed the party.

"You are about to enter the presence of Azanhein, king of Buoria," he said. "Please remain civil and courteous at all times, and do not approach His Majesty without his express permission. Please note that there is a magical seal in effect within the throne room that prevents spells from being cast; you may sense some discomfort upon entering, but rest assured that the seal is not harmful. Needless to say, any violent words or actions within the throne room will not be tolerated. Mister Campbell, as your soul sword is inseparable from you, you will be permitted to bring it inside; however, you may not draw it save at His Majesty's request."

"Right," Kyle said. He had decided that he didn't like Herraine. He was as formal and polite as all the other Buors Kyle had met, but was lacking in the warm undercurrents he had sensed in Godraien and the others.

"If you are all prepared, we will now enter the throne room," Herraine said. When they all nodded, he drew the seal from his belt and held it up to the guards at the door. "Page Herraine, escort to the party of Kyle Campbell, requesting permission to audience with His Majesty."

The guards nodded in perfect unison, and, extending their arms, swung the huge doors open.

"Your majesty!" they called into the cavernous throne room. "The party of Kyle Campbell!"

Azanhein.

The second the doors opened, Kyle felt the king's presence billowing towards him, washing over and enveloping him, flooding his senses. Though the figure at the far end of the throne room was a couple hundred feet away, Kyle felt as though his eyes were being pulled towards that spot, so that there was no other possible place to look than at the king.

So this was what Nihs and Godraien had talked about—the strength of a powerful magical aura. It was like a dream, a dream where he wasn't in control of his body, forced to move and look a certain way. He was dimly aware of walking forwards along the marble floor, passing by rows of the royal guard on his way to Azanhein. His companions were still around him, but they might as well have been separated from him by panes of foggy, soundproof glass.

After what felt like both a very short and very long stretch of time, they reached the throne. Kyle couldn't help but take in every detail about the man seated upon it.

Azanhein was huge, or at least seemed to be. Though he knew his senses were lying to him, Kyle would have said that the Buorish king was easily two feet taller than Rogan the Minotaur. The armor he wore was a mass of black plate, exquisitely crafted and trimmed with gold and white, the pauldrons wider across than Kyle was tall. Azanhein wore a cloak of black, white and gold that spilled over the sides of the throne and onto the floor, fastened under his neck by a brooch the size of a grapefruit. Like all Buors, he wore a full helm that completely concealed his masked face.

Fused to the helm was a great crown of black iron, a mass of spikes a foot tall.

Leaning up against the throne to Azanhein's left was a tower shield seven feet tall and four feet wide. It must have been the Crest of Buoria, Azanhein's famous shield. To his right was the largest and most magnificent sword Kyle had ever seen. It was gold and black, polished to blinding perfection, and easily eight feet long. The Will of the King, Azanhein's transarm.

As Kyle took in every minute detail of the king's armor, his initial hopeless stupor somewhat ebbed. Some of the shock of being exposed to Azanhein's presence wore off, and his senses returned to him. He still found himself unable to look anywhere but at the king, however. If he made an effort, he could quickly glance at one of his companions, but his vision almost immediately snapped back to the king's visor. Looking away was like trying to keep one's eyes open when extremely tired.

The king's head tilted somewhat as they approached; a gauntleted hand rose to his helm, and he appeared silently pensive.

Herraine strode to the foot of the throne and sank to one knee.

"You majesty," he said, "the party of Kyle Campbell."

Kyle didn't wait for someone to tell him to bow, though he hadn't thought at first that he would bow deeply if it wasn't required of him, it now seemed foolishness to do anything but show as much respect as he could for the formidable being in front of him. He bowed low as he had seen the Buors do, holding it for a few seconds before he rose. His companions did the same, and Godraien and Septhiran fell to one knee, their hands over their hearts.

The king made a lifting motion with his hand. "Please, rise," he told them gently.

Kyle had been expecting a voice that was deep and booming, as powerful and fearsome as Azanhein appeared to be. The reality was almost the exact opposite: the king's voice was high, slightly higher even than Kyle's own, and amazingly soft. Though he spoke quietly, his enunciation was impeccable, and Kyle could hear him as clearly as if his voice had arrived through a pair of headphones.

Godraien and Septhiran rose to their feet at once, rejoining the party.

Azanhein dipped his head to all of them in recognition.

"Thank you, all, for deigning to meet with me on such short notice. I am sorry that the invitation I sent you could not have given you more time to prepare."

"It is of no moment, your majesty," Godraien said. "I am sure that I speak for all of us when I say that we could never be inconvenienced by such an invitation."

"Your words are generous, seeker Godraien, and I thank you for them. But it is a poor king who assumes that his subjects are prepared at all times to submit to his will. But enough of that. Herraine, thank you for escorting these individuals to me. You are now dismissed."

As Herraine bowed and left, Kyle took a moment to glance around the throne room. The path leading up to the king was lined with members of the royal guard, and there were also two uniquely-dressed guards standing on either side of the throne. One carried a lance, while the other had a large shield strapped to each arm.

"Thank you again for your attendance," Azanhein said, once Herraine had gone. "I am glad that I have had the opportunity to meet you before your departure from Buoria. I do not believe that we have been formally introduced. I am Azanhein, king of Buoria. Pleased to make your acquaintance," and he inclined his head politely.

Godraien, who was on the far left of their party, strode forward and bowed. "I am seeker Godraien, your majesty. We have met before. I am honored to make your acquaintance again."

"I remember you," Azanhein said. "You provided me with a briefing on the current state of Reno city some months ago. It is good to see you again, seeker. Do your affairs treat you well?"

"They do, thank you, your majesty."

Septhiran was next to introduce himself. "I am estor Septhiran, your majesty. I served as Kyle's legal counsel during the trial proceedings."

"I am pleased to meet you, estor. From what I have heard, you were a great asset to Kyle and his companions during the trial. I am glad to hear that the fine traditions of our practitioners of law are being upheld in those such as yourself."

"Thank you, your majesty."

One by one they went down the line, introducing themselves to the Buorish king. Soon it was Kyle's turn. As his gaze met Azanhein's, he felt the king's aura wash over him once more. His eyes were glued to the black slits in the king's visor, and the silence stretched on forever.

"I'm Kyle Campbell," he said, bowing.

"Yes." The king's voice was subdued. "Kyle Campbell, the man who only earlier today made history in our court. I never thought the day would come that I would address one who came from another universe; and yet, this is the reality we find ourselves in." The king sighed wistfully. "What a strange world it is, that in such a short time all of our knowledge can be challenged so. Your arrival here will undoubtedly change the lives of so many. But these are heavy thoughts so soon in our meeting. It is my desire that you will join me for a meal within the Citadel—once our appetites have been sated and we have had the opportunity to acquaint ourselves in a more informal manner, perhaps we can then turn our minds to more serious matters. Would you accompany me?"

Azanhein rose from his throne, and they followed him into a cavernous dining hall adjacent to the audience chamber. It was strange to see the Buorish king mobile; Kyle had started to think of Azanhein as a permanent fixture of the castle. Though he moved gracefully, each of his steps was accompanied by a clang of metal.

The dining hall was large, but welcoming and ornately decorated, dominated by a long table of solid wood. Three separate tigoreh chandeliers lit the room brightly, and merrily crackling fireplaces lining the walls made it pleasantly warm.

Azanhein strode to the far end of the table, motioning for the others to take up chairs as they wished.

"Good seeker and estor," he said, "would you care to sit one at each of my sides? It would be my pleasure to share with you a *rouk* pipe."

Their guides looked ready to panic at this offer.

"Your majesty, we couldn't possibly!" Godraien said.

But Azanhein waved aside their protests. "You are my guests, and the sharing of *rouk* is a tradition whose practice should never depend on the stations of the individuals involved. I must insist!"

The two were torn between their desire to be humble and their desire to please their king. In the end, they bent to his will and seated themselves at his sides. Kyle sat next to Godraien, with Meya and Phundasa beyond him; across from him sat Nihs and Lugh.

"My head chef, Ishmaal, should be along shortly," Azanhein told them. "You will be pleased to hear that he is trained in the traditional culinary arts, as practiced by the other races—in fact, I believe that he relishes the opportunity to prepare such meals, and will surely outdo himself given such an opportunity."

They made small talk as they waited for Ishmaal to arrive. Azanhein addressed each of them in turn, making sure they all had an opportunity to speak. He was genuinely interested in everything they had to say, and the points he contributed to their discussion proved that he was taking in every detail. Kyle noticed all of this, as well as the fact that Azanhein was deliberately not bringing up his origins. It was nerve-wracking—Kyle knew that this subject must have been of interest to the Buorish king, and had come prepared to speak about it.

A door behind Azanhein opened, and a small Buor stepped out, accompanied by a two-man escort. He was more energetic than any Buor they had met so far; each of his steps was more of a skip, and when he stood beside Azanhein to address them, he wrung his hands together constantly.

"Your majesty, honored guests! I am Artisan Ishmaal, and it will be my pleasure to serve you tonight. I am happy to inform you that I am learned in the art of creating traditional meals for members of all races to enjoy. It is one of my passions, and I hope that my creations for the night will please you. If you will indulge me, I have prepared a brief introduction for the course that tonight's meal will take. We will begin with…"

Judging from Ishmaal's introduction, they would be eating well into the night. The cook was unable to resist telling them about each course in great detail, going so far as to tell anecdotes about how he had developed the recipe in question. Kyle couldn't believe that anyone could care so much about food.

After he had finished speaking, he asked them if they wanted any drinks in waiting; Lugh, with his typical cheek, asked for ale.

Ishmaal addressed Azanhein, "Your majesty, how may I serve you tonight?"

"Good Artisan, it is not for my sake that you select a *rouk* for tonight, but my guests'—if you would, acquaint the good estor and seeker with the usual menu, and prepare whatever pleases them."

He threw up his hands for silence before Septhiran and Godraien had the chance to protest. "I must insist. My tastes are sometimes uncommon, and it would be churlish of me to invite you to share in my meal and then set the menu myself."

Ishmaal departed to the kitchens, and servants came out with their drinks. Their conversation resumed, much the same as before. Whether because of nerves or growing comfort, they were all very talkative. Azanhein questioned the others about their pasts, and Kyle himself was often surprised by the answers. In a way, it was unsettling to learn so many new things about the people he'd been traveling with, and he was reminded of the fact that he had only known them for a handful of days.

"If I understand correctly, miss Ilduetyr," Azanhein said to Meya, "you were in Eastia at the time of the Orcish conflict four years ago."

"That's right," Meya said. Her demeanor changed, and Phundasa looked up from his meal to listen to her. "I was right in the middle of it—I was studying at the church of Saint Miren when the fighting broke out."

Azanhein's hands were steepled under his chin as he listened. "I am sorry," he said. "It must have been a traumatic experience."

"It was," Meya said without any hint of hesitation. "But I learned a lot about myself and the world because of it. And of course that's how I met Das."

At the mention of his name, Phundasa reached over and put his hand on her shoulder.

"I still can't shake some of it from my mind," Meya went on, "but in a strange way I'm glad it happened to me. It made me realize just how much of the world I was shutting away by living in one place and studying magic. That's why we became adventurers once we managed to escape to Centralia."

Azanhein nodded. "It is incredible in the most horrific of ways, the acts that men and women can be moved to commit when society's foundation has broken down, and the animal inside the spirit is roused. But you are right; it is an inevitable part of life as long as life persists, and in pushing it from our minds we commit only the sin of apathy, and ultimately solve nothing."

Meya nodded quietly, staring at the table in front of her. Kyle had heard her mention the war before, but only in an offhand way. He'd never seen her like this before. He was struck with both the desire never to discuss it again, and a terrible curiosity to find out more about what had happened.

Azanhein, sensing the dark mood emanating from their side of the table, turned to Lugh across from them.

"Captain MacAlden," he said, "I have inquired about the subject before, but I must admit my curiosity has gotten the better of me. Might you enlighten us further as to the wager you made which won you the *Ayger?*"

Kyle smiled as the attention around the table focused on Lugh. Lugh lowered his mug slowly, scratching his chin.

"I'll be honest, your majesty," he said, "I don't like talking about it in mixed company. I'll put it this way: it was something my friend thought I would never do."

"It must have been, for if I were in possession of such a fine ship I do not believe I would ever risk losing it."

The doors to the kitchen opened, and Ishmaal entered, followed by a long procession of golden serving carts piloted by his kitchen hands. He reintroduced the meal that he had prepared as the carts fanned out around the table and the dishes upon them were uncovered.

Kyle wasn't listening. The second the lids came off of the dishes, steam poured out, and a delicious smell filled the dining hall. It made Kyle realize just how hungry he'd become in the last few hours, and he couldn't wait to be served.

At the head of the table, Godraien, Septhiran and Azanhein had been presented with a large and ornate *rouk* pipe. A servant next to Azanhein brought out what looked like a cheese wheel wrapped in paper. He removed the wrapping to reveal the *rouk* cake, a dark disc that looked hard as rock. He opened a vent near the base of the pipe and slid it in, then flipped a switch that turned the heating element on.

Once they were all served, Ishmaal bade them an excellent supper and retreated into the kitchens along with his helpers.

Azanhein spread his arms.

"Please, you may begin."

Dinner was delicious. Ishmaal was clearly an artist; Kyle didn't know the first thing about cooking, but he did know that this was possibly the best meal he had ever eaten. For a short while, there was little conversation. In the beginning it was awkward eating in the presence of Azanhein, but as Kyle watched him pass the rouk pipe to Godraien and Septhiran, his nervousness abated. He wondered if this was because Azanhein himself was comfortable, and the rest of them were still caught up in his aura.

It was entertaining to steal glances at their Buorish companions as they ate. They clearly deeply respected, even revered Azanhein, and were intimidated by his presence. When each accepted the rouk pipe, they would insert it near the chin of their helmet with a faint *clunk*, hold it there for a few seconds, and then pass it on.

Once their eating momentum had died down, and Lugh had already finished and was asking for more, King Azanhein began to make conversation again. This time, several of his questions touched on the subject of Kyle's home world, and Kyle found himself going over numerous details while Azanhein listened with interest.

"It amazes me to hear of your world, Mister Campbell," Azanhein said. "To think that something so fantastic could exist, and be described in such perfect detail by one of its denizens, and yet never be reached by anyone in Loria."

"No kidding," Kyle said. "I still have a hard time believing it all."

His gaze fell as he said this. As he had done many times since his arrival in Loria, he wondered how his life had ever reached this point. He'd gone from being a jobless programmer in Ohio to a sword-fighting adventurer who dined with the kings of strange lands. How had it all happened so quickly? Suddenly, he found the confidence to broach a topic with Azanhein that he felt the conversation had been ultimately steering towards.

"Your majesty," he said, lowering his glass and looking straight at Azanhein as he had been taught, "during my court case, I was told that by the time I got here, the Buors already half knew that I was from another world. How did you find out about me?"

Azanhein matched Kyle's gaze, and kept his hands crossed underneath his chin as Kyle spoke. Once he was done, he said,

"Mister Campbell, I wish to be honest with you, and I would like to preface my answer to your question with an apology. Unfortunately, it has been necessary for us in this matter to conceal the truth from you in many ways; we have done this partially in order to make you more willing to complete your journey to the capital, and mostly to protect you and your friends from danger and detection. Yes, it is true that we knew of your origins well before you reached the capital."

"How?"

"I plead that you bear with me in the recounting of the tale. It is not overly long, but I wish to provide you with the truth in its entirety—after all, this is what you have given us, and it would be disrespectful, to say the least, not to reciprocate."

"Of course," said Kyle.

"Then I will begin in Buoria itself, in the plains of ash that extend beyond the city. I believe you are familiar with these plains, and how they are uniquely cultivated by the sons and daughters of Buoria. We control the rivers of lava that flow across them for our own uses, and have built a network of observation towers for this purpose. The plains are also the home of some rare flora and fauna, and among these are some truly dangerous monsters."

Kyle couldn't see how any of this had anything to do with him, but he listened respectfully as the king continued.

"In current times, these monsters pose little threat to our fortifications, as each outpost is outfitted with members of our military and various artillery. However, approximately one halfmonth ago, a new type of monster was discovered by one of these towers. Shortly after, it was destroyed by that very same monster. Needless to say, we immediately deployed soldiers and artillery to dispatch it, a task at which we succeeded. The monster, however, left behind a remnant of itself when it died—a glowing, blue core that reacted violently with everything and anything that it touched."

Kyle understood. "You mean, in the same way that my soul sword reacts to things."

"Precisely. Once the core was discovered, we attempted to recover it and study its strange properties. But, as you might imagine, it was impossible to move the core from its resting place. Only after a series of violent detonations did it finally stabilize and come to rest in a crater in the plains themselves. Our scientists traveled to this area, to study it as best they could. However, another misfortune awaited us. Less than a day after we slew the creature, another one spontaneously formed around the core. This beast was just as potent as the first, and we were ill prepared to deal with it. We managed to corral it inside a valley in the plane of ashes, and erect sentry turrets around its perimeter to discourage it from attempting to leave. But no matter how many times we defeat it, we are unable to destroy it completely.

"You may be wondering what this has to do with you. As you may have noticed, the date that the beast appeared matches somewhat the date upon which you were discovered. I must say as an aside that your descent from the sky did not go unnoticed, as your friends originally believed. You were seen by several individuals in the surrounding area, and word eventually made its way to the Buorish police, and thus to the capital. Though we only discovered your contact site after you had been recovered by Captain MacAlden and his companions, we did find the crater you left upon landing. It was remarkably similar to the one created by the monster's core, and our *irushai* there detected trace amounts of an unknown form of magic. It was at this time that we drew a connection between the two events.

"By the time you applied for your Iden card, all of Buorkind had been alerted to the situation, and had been instructed to remain vigilant for any strange happenstance. The crater you had left upon falling was roughly human-shaped, so we had gotten so far as to suspect that we were searching for a living being. When Acclairiad, the Iden office clerk you spoke with, reported the existence of a human with an unreadable set of memories and no past, we decided to contact you and see if we could persuade you to come to the Buorish capital. Unfortunately, you were attacked in Reno city before we were able to locate you. By considerable chance, one of lieutenant Jendoyle's men spotted your assailants in transit to Sky Tower, and we converged upon the building. You, of course, will be familiar with the story from here on out. You escaped both Radisson's men and the Buorish police, and it was not until the events in Rhian that we were able to detain you.

"As you can see, our reasons for apprehending you and bringing you to the capital were threefold: one, we wished to protect you from the assailants who sought you; two, we were interested in testing your legitimacy and learning more about you; and three, we had a favor we wished to ask of you."

Kyle had been following up until this point. Now he said, "A favor?"

The king sighed delicately. "Mister Campbell, I cannot apologize enough for the way that we have treated you. We have detained you, kept the truth from you, and inconvenienced you; and now we have the audacity to ask something of you. So before I progress further, I wish to give you and your party the opportunity to refuse me outright. If you feel that we have not earned the right to ask anything of you, then you may tell me so, and I will pursue the subject no longer."

Kyle wasn't sure what to say. On one hand, the Buors had certainly inconvenienced him, and he now had to face the ugly truth that some of the hospitality they had shown him may have been strategic rather than sincere. But whatever their intentions, they had treated them with kindness, and captain Callaghnen had saved him from the twins. Besides, even if he weren't in the Buors' debt, what harm could it do to hear Azanhein out?

"Your majesty," he said, "what is it that you need us to do?"

Azanhein inclined his head. "I thank you for your consideration," he said. "Remember that this is only a request, and if you find the task too dangerous or otherwise undesirable, you need only say so.

"As I mentioned before, we have been unable to slay the beast in the ash plains no matter what techniques we employ. But you, Mister Campbell, have access to a destructive force unlike anything our world has ever seen. It is possible that you and this beast are somehow linked, and if what the scholars who have studied the core believe is true, then you may be the only person alive who is capable of permanently destroying it. That is what we wish to ask of you: that you and your party travel to the plains of ash and attempt to defeat the beast with your soul sword."

Kyle had been expecting something like this. But he knew so little of combat and of what his companions were capable of.

"I'm willing to help," he said, "but I can't speak for the others. And I don't know how strong this monster is, or if we'd be able to kill it."

"Of course we'll come with you!" Lugh said, leaning back in his seat. "Killing monsters is what adventuring is all about!"

Phundasa nodded his head in agreement. "The opportunity to engage and slay a rare foe is one that no true adventurer would shrink away from."

"If we can help, we should," Meya said. "Even if there wasn't anything in it for us."

"Nihs?"

The little Kol sniffed. "It would be selfish for us to refuse. And foolish for us to back away from a possible opportunity to learn more about Kyle."

"All right," Kyle said. "Let's do it."

Later on at the holding center, Godraien and Septhiran bade them goodnight and left. Azanhein had been pleased that they had chosen to help, but had refused to provide more details that night, insisting that they rest and tackle the creature the next day. He promised that he would send Herraine down to the holding center in the morning.

They held a meeting in Kyle and Nihs' room as they had many times before, talking about Azanhein and of the Citadel, and a little of what awaited them tomorrow.

"What could that monster possibly be?" Nihs mused. "No one else fell off the boat with you, did they, Kyle?"

"Not that I know of," Kyle said. "There was a sailor on deck with me, but I don't know what happened to him. But if he came to Loria too, he'd be human like me, wouldn't he?"

"Hmm. You're right, of course. No monsters on the boat with you, I suppose."

Kyle laughed, but the question of what the monster was still plagued him. They decided to call it a night soon after, and Kyle sank into bed, the constant rumbling of Buoria's soil below rocking him to sleep.

On the bus to school the next day, Kyle reviewed his plan to become the dominant player in his high school world. It was a simple one at heart, formulated around what Kyle had found to be his main weakness in the past: his overall passiveness and failure to seize social opportunity. Before, he had never seen the sense in going to social gatherings or even in maintaining a large group of friends. Now, he could clearly see that even if he didn't *like* his friends, they needed to exist as a kind of medal, a way of keeping Kyle's place on the social scoreboard. And the only way to accumulate them was to become a more desirable friend himself. He could accomplish this by being more active; going to parties, participating in groups, and putting himself in front of people in any way possible. It was like advertising, he thought to himself. As long as people recognized his face, it didn't matter how they had come to do so.

The bus pulled up next to the school and Kyle stepped out. *Well Kyle, this is the first day of the rest of your life.*

And so Kyle changed. There were teething troubles, but overall the plan went smoothly. In fact, it was almost depressing how easy it was to reinvent himself. He kept up with his schoolwork but spent less time on it than before, so that his grades dropped slightly but stayed nevertheless high. He worked part-time, bringing in a steady stream of money so that he never had to worry about going out with friends. And he started being sociable. Kyle was an introvert by nature, but if he focused he could force himself to be around people, force himself to care about them and interact with them at a more than basic level. He found that he had a talent for pretending to be concerned with other people's issues, and to say whatever it took to wring the proper reactions from them. He had always been an observant person and his mind was sharp, so it wasn't long before he could detect exactly what to say or do in any given situation that would raise his stock with the largest possible number of people. He knew which boys to joke with and which to casually abuse, which girls to flirt with and which to coolly ignore.

Drinking came onto the scene once Kyle was entering tenth grade. The stories were always floating around to some degree, of the crazy party at X person's house where Y person had done Z. Kyle ignored them for the first little while, partially because he ignored most of what people said and partially because most of these stories were fabricated. But by grade ten, the stories had become more numerous, and it was clear that many people in Kyle's grade *were* drinking consistently.

And so it was that Kyle's choice to start drinking was not a choice at all—it was a necessity. It would not do for other people to be participating in what was becoming an increasingly large part of the social scene while Kyle was left in the lurch. He had attended a good number of parties by this point, but alcohol had not been present at any of them. Kyle decided he should fix this himself.

Taylor was an older boy—a twelfth grader—whom Kyle had befriended for this reason uniquely. He himself couldn't buy alcohol, but he had an older brother who could, and often did. Kyle had met Brian, a large man with a blonde beard who loved causing chaos among his younger brother's impressionable friends. Kyle had won him over by giving him what he wanted, which was a measure of respect tempered with awe. So when Kyle gathered up over a hundred dollars from his friends and persuaded Brian, through the mouthpiece of Taylor, to show up at their next party with over a hundred dollars' worth of alcohol, he complied.

Needless to say, Brian got his wish of witnessing a mob of out-of-hand, drunk teenagers get up to no good. There weren't many people at the party who knew how to drink; Kyle, unfortunately, was among them, but he reasoned that since he was so much more intelligent than his classmates while sober, the difference would probably still exist when drunk, and that was all that mattered.

The pivotal moment came when Brian gathered Kyle and six of his friends for some drinking game or another. They sat in a circle and watched as he poured shots of vodka from a clear bottle.

"Everyone gets a shot before we start! S' your first time drinking, right, buddy?" he asked Kyle with a grin.

Kyle nodded, his expression cool. "Yeah."

"Well then," Brian pulled another glass towards him, "you get a double to celebrate."

Kyle heard the others snicker as Brian filled the glass. *Double?* he thought. *Not enough.*

Instead, he leaned forward, reached past the offered glass, and grabbed the bottle. He lifted it up to eye level and guessed there were four shots' worth left inside. Before anyone could react, he tipped it back and drained it.

He had known, to a degree, what to expect, but the fire he felt in his throat as the vodka went down was worse than he had imagined it could be. He forced himself to finish the bottle, though it took all of his self-control to keep himself from coughing. He knew that as long as his performance was perfect, he'd impress everyone—but if it was anything less, he'd just embarrass himself.

He got it all down and managed to keep eye contact with Brian without so much as a wince. The older boy stared at him for a moment, and then roared with laughter.

"You've got balls, kid! Who's next?"

Kyle couldn't remember much else of that night. He had vague impressions of talking more than he had in a very long time, dancing with random people all throughout the house, and laughing at even the most inane jokes the others told. Brian managed to get more drinks into him, clearly seeing great promise in him. Through some miracle, he avoided being one of the three people who had thrown up by the end of the night.

At one point, he stood up and delivered a speech to his schoolmates about some subject he couldn't remember. He could recall, however, the raucous laughter that accompanied it, and Brian pointing at Kyle screaming, "this guy is friggin' *hilarious!*" over and over. Kyle had never felt so good about himself.

It had felt like a dream that was both amazing and horrible at the same time. Kyle's emotions swung wildly between social bliss, brooding depression, fierce anger and hysterical joy. Loud music pounded at his ears and his throat hurt from shouting; he wandered about the house on random errands to find some person or seek another drink. A girl grabbed him—or rather, fell on him—and they ended up dancing passionately, their bodies pressed together, her hair inundating his senses with her presence. Once they had exhausted themselves after what felt like days of dancing, Kyle sat down, thinking that the girl had gone for good. But she reappeared, sitting on his lap and wrapping her arms around his neck with shameless intimacy.

"What's your name?" Kyle shouted at her.

"Natalie!" she shouted back. She reached down, and Kyle jumped when he felt her hand on his leg.

She laughed, leaning in. "Give me your phone!" she shouted.

Oh. Kyle reached into his pocket awkwardly and handed it to her. She punched her number into it, her forehead leaning against Kyle's for support. She handed him the phone back and kissed him on the cheek, her breath sending shivers down Kyle's neck. She got up, and before Kyle knew it, she was gone.

The next day, Kyle woke up feeling absolutely horrible, and it was all he could do to drag himself out of bed, have a huge drink of water, and make himself breakfast. He had the strange feeling that nothing that had happened last night was real, but when he checked his phone, he saw Natalie's number saved into it. When he went to school the day after, everyone was talking about the party, and Kyle was the main focus. One of his friends approached him.

"Heard you hooked up with Natalie over the weekend," he said with a huge grin.

Kyle squinted, still trying to convince himself that it had happened. "Sorta," he said. "I got her number. Where's she from?"

"She's in the year below us. She's hot though! One of Kelsey's friends. Apparently she's liked you for a while. Nice job getting her number!"

Kyle accepted the high-five distractedly. He was staring at the number in his phone while some thoughts arranged themselves in his brain. *Natalie, huh?* He hadn't even known about her before the party, but she *had* been attractive, and she had come to him without him even trying.

Really, he'd be a fool to refuse her advances. He didn't have a girlfriend and hadn't had one yet in high school. Besides, this wasn't primary school, where being in a relationship basically meant nothing, and was destined to go nowhere.

Sure, he thought to himself. *Why not?*

There were a multitude of lifts that climbed the escarpment beyond the Buorish capital. The smaller lifts, designed for single passengers, ran almost constantly from top to bottom. The two largest ones, which sat on either side of the Citadel, could easily carry hundreds of men or tons of equipment, and made their ponderous ascent only a few times per day. It was on one of these lifts that Kyle and the others rode on their mission for King Azanhein.

Beyond the escarpment lie the ash plains, the rocky, sand-blasted desert which comprised the majority of Buoria. As impressive as the Buorish capital was, it covered only a tiny fraction of the country—the rest was a harsh wilderness, almost completely untamed and uninhabited.

Kyle and the others had ridden the lifts before, as part of the tour Godraien had given them. They had been allowed the ride to the top of the cliff face, so that they could visit the large outpost there and look down on the capital. Looking in the opposite direction had provided a less inspiring view—Kyle had seen nothing but gray for miles and miles. Gray ash, gray sand, gray rock…and gray smoke, billowing out from the Heart of Buoria somewhere in the extreme distance. Red lightning had struck over and over, and Godraien's reassurances that it only ever struck the intended lightning rods had not been very comforting.

As happy as Kyle would be if this were the extent of his experience with the ash plains, these were the home of the mysterious creature that Azanhein had tasked him with killing, and that meant that he was going to become familiar with them whether he liked it or not.

Though they hadn't seen Azanhein since their dinner the previous night, the king had sent several of his men to the holding center in the morning to help them plan out their attack. Chief among them was an older Buor who introduced himself as Drunamoh, commander of one of the many defense platoons that patrolled the capital. He was a dignified individual who clearly had years of experience behind him, and the party had listened intently as he unrolled a map of the area they were to be assaulting.

"The creature has been corralled inside this large valley," he had said, pointing with a mailed finger to an irregular blotch on the map. "As large as the beast is, it cannot climb, and we have erected guard towers around the valley's perimeter which fire upon it whenever it attempts to. In order to engage the creature, you will have to enter the valley. We will be observing you throughout the battle and will strike from the guard towers if necessary."

They had refused Azanhein's original offer to have a squadron of Drunamoh's soldiers accompany them on their mission, but the king was determined not to allow any of them to come to harm. He had insisted that they take a guard with them, and so five of what the Buors called defenders—heavily armored soldiers who carried huge shields—had been dispatched to lend them aid. Each one was tasked with protecting one of Kyle's party, and Drunamoh had assured them with a touch of pride that they would not suffer so much as a scratch as long as his soldiers were there.

At first, their defenders had acted like steel-clad shadows, following close behind but rarely speaking unless addressed. After some time, however, they began to open up, and Kyle took a liking to them. His own defender was Darcelin, a large man who wore an ocher sash and was gifted with an odd sense of humor. He displayed a slightly frightening level of enthusiasm at the prospect of facing an unknown creature with an inexperienced adventurer as his charge.

Kyle, watching the city shrink as the lift ascended, said to him, "So tell me again what we know about this monster." His nervousness was showing—he'd long ago gleaned everything of use from Drunamoh and the other advisers.

Darcelin, armor clanking, folded his arms across his chest. "At first, the creature seems not unlike the elementals which form in the plains. It is humanoid, but often favors four-legged movement. Its flesh is as hard as stone, and it is deceptively fast and intelligent. We believe, however, that it is somehow malformed. It is susceptible to fits of rage, and is not always in control of its body. This I think will make our task easier, if not, in fact, easy."

"What's an elemental?"

"A creature that forms in areas of high background magic. If a location holds a concentrated amount of some kind of magic, there is a chance that particles of that magic can run together and form an elemental.

The ash plains are a place of power, and elementals are quite common there. Most often they form of stone, metal, or magma, but sometimes as well of ash, dust, sand, or smoke. We are quite used to dealing with them, and normally the threat is minimal, but this creature is larger and more powerful than the average elemental. And, of course, we are not sure if it can be killed."

"Don't remind me."

"Ah, but we have nothing to fear!" Darcelin said happily. "The creature may not be easily toppled, but neither are we! I have yet to face a foe that could not be quelled by an iron defense and a surplus of mettle."

"That's great and all, but I hope to have more than mettle between me and that monster when the fight starts."

"You may rest assured that you will, my friend!" Darcelin clanged his massive shield against the ground.

As the Buors were not known for their elaborate place names, the outpost at the top of the escarpment was simply called Overlook. It was a compound of buildings clustered around the lifts, and was more functional than anything else. Most of the structures were temporary storage for the resources that the lifts brought up. Though no one lived permanently in Overlook, many Buors worked there, moving shipments of materials on and off of the lifts.

Beyond Overlook, the only signs of civilization were the outposts that dotted the ash plains. Buorish scientists, engineers and soldiers populated these outposts, channeling the Heart of Buoria's lava flows, performing research and preventing dangerous creatures from making their way to the city.

The lift ride, for all Kyle's nervousness, was uneventful. He and his companions waited in silence as the city slid smoothly away from them. Lugh and Phundasa stood at the railing, admiring the view. Meya was chatting with Ashiren, her defender; somehow, they had all come to the agreement that the only female member of the defense squad should be paired with the only female member of Kyle's party.

The wind picked up as soon as the lift rose over the lip of the escarpment. Kyle reached for the black scarf he'd been given and fastened it over his mouth and nose as he'd been shown, then pulled out his pair of protective goggles and pulled them on as well. Though the ash-filled winds that blew from the plains might provide the Buors with food, they could quickly reduce non-Buors to fits of coughing.

Overlook was quiet even by the standards of Buorish civilization. Few people were out working, and those that were returned to their jobs after the shortest of greetings.

The group split into two and boarded a pair of tigoreh vehicles called drifters, which were like all-terrain hover cars made for skimming over the treacherous ground of the plains. It was Kyle's first time riding in a tigoreh vehicle other than the *Ayger*, and though the drifters were essentially boxes with engines attached, the ride was fast and exhilarating. Kyle spent the time staring out at the ash plains, watching the black clouds roll overhead and the lighting strike again and again. He felt like he was on the surface of the moon, the farthest possible place from the civilized capital city he'd left behind. Jagged peaks of stone rose into the sky like daggers of obsidian, and the ground underneath alternated between huge drifts of ash and cracked and pitted stone blasted clean by the wind.

The ride in the drifters took an hour. At one point, the winds were too fierce to stare out the window, so Kyle retreated to safety under the drifter's canopy. He caught Lugh's eye, who was sitting across from him.

"Nice place, huh?"

"Yeah, lovely."

Eventually, they drew up to one of the guard towers overlooking the valley the monster had been corralled in. This was more of a crater than a valley, and was positively huge; the ridge they drew up to disappeared into the darkness in both directions, and Kyle could barely see the valley floor from their vantage point. His heart was thrumming, and he realized that he was expecting the monster to emerge out of the darkness at any moment. But the world was silent and muffled, and strain though he might, Kyle could neither see nor hear anything.

The guard tower was small—at least compared to some of the buildings Kyle had seen in the city—and had been hastily built, but nonetheless was large enough to host a half-dozen soldiers and a swiveling artillery gun. They stepped briefly inside to greet the tower's crew and share information.

"None of the towers have reported seeing the creature for several hours now," one of the operators told them. "It was last sighted by tower nine, across the valley. We believe it is learning to keep away from the valley's edges, and so is likely somewhere close to the center."

"Great," Lugh said. "So we'll have to wander around until we can find it? You can't see *anything* out there."

"Our advice would be to head first towards tower nine. Failing that, if you turn northwards and travel lengthwise up the valley, your chances of encountering the creature will be rather high. We will remain in crystal contact with your squad and will alert you if the creature is spotted."

They left the guard tower and assembled on the valley's lip, adjusting their scarves in the face of the wind blowing from below. Visibility was terrible, and Kyle squinted instinctively as particles of dust struck his goggles. He looked around at his companions. Lugh appeared fearsome in his scarf, until he noticed Kyle's attention and winked. Phundasa, on his other side, was looking positively thuggish. For once he was wearing a heavy shirt that covered his arms, and with his scarf pulled up high and his goggles on, it was almost impossible to see where he was looking or what he was thinking.

"Well," he said, cracking his enormous knuckles, "shall we get started?"

Kyle had thought it was hard to see standing on the ridge, but it had been nothing compared to what awaited down in the valley. The ground was stone, with a thin layer of ash covering it that muted all sound. Dust hung in the air, and the second the ridge behind them was swallowed by the darkness Kyle lost all sense of direction. The party shuffled quietly across the valley, their footsteps stirring up the ground and leaving a trail of short-lived prints behind them. The defenders' armor clanked softly as they followed.

None of them felt like speaking into the quiet, so they made their way slowly and silently across the valley floor. Kyle listened intently and strained to see into the distance, but neither he nor any of the others caught wind of the monster.

Half an hour passed, then another. Finally, the ground in front of them began to slope upwards, and Kyle saw the dim outline of a guard tower above them. Darcelin stopped and craned his neck upwards, then touched his finger to the crystal set into the collar of his armor.

"Tower nine? This is defender Darcelin. We've reached the edge of the valley and you are in sight. Do you have any information for us? Has the monster been spotted by any of the other towers?"

He took his hand off the crystal, and a moment later it lit up again. "This is tower nine. A possible sighting took place at tower fourteen approximately forty minutes ago. We recommend that you travel northwest and attempt to intercept it."

"Thank you. We will proceed at once."

"There is something else you should know. A dust storm is anticipated to blow in from the north in anywhere from two to four hours. If you are unable to find the creature soon, you will have to be extracted and attempt this mission some other time."

Lugh groaned. "Let's stop wasting time and find it, then!"

"Thank you for the information," Darcelin said. "We will remain in contact whenever possible." He took his hand off the crystal. "I must agree with Captain MacAlden. The valley is small enough that we should be able to locate the creature well within time. Let us make haste!"

Kyle didn't know how good of an idea it was to race against Buoria's brutal weather, but he still trusted Darcelin not to put them into serious danger. They set off to the northwest, at a slightly quicker pace than before.

This time, only fifteen minutes had passed before Nihs hissed for everyone to stop moving. He jumped from Phundasa's shoulder up to Darcelin's, where he unfurled his ears and sat stock still, listening intently.

"Heard something?" Lugh asked.

"Perhaps I would, if you would be quiet!" Nihs snapped.

Lugh chuckled. "The Kol have great hearing," he whispered to Kyle. "Even if you speak really quietly…"

"*Lugh!*"

He grinned.

Nihs shook his head and hunkered down, his ears twisting back to their usual position. "I thought I heard something, but I couldn't say which direction it came from, and *some* people were being too loud for me to make out anything else."

"How rude," Lugh said from his position at the back.

"Good sir," Darcelin said, "perhaps you should remain at the front of the group, with me, so that we may put those excellent ears to better use."

"A sound idea. It's comforting to know that at least one of us has a little sense."

They carried on, Kyle growing more and more tense with each passing minute. He didn't know if he should be worried or relieved that they had yet to find the monster. If they failed, they'd likely just take up the hunt another day. They'd still have to face it eventually, and delaying their meeting wouldn't get him any closer to finding out what connection he had with the creature, if any. Even still, it was hard to wish for an encounter with a monster that even the mighty Buors couldn't topple.

Suddenly Nihs' ears pricked up again. He reared himself up to his full height on Darcelin's shoulder, and pointed ever so slightly to the left of the direction they'd been headed.

"That way!" he said, in a tone that brooked no argument. "I can hear it!"

Darcelin hoisted up his shield and turned to the others. "Comrades, may I suggest that we make some haste? We have, after all, little time, and quite a lot of monster to slay."

As they sprinted in the direction that Nihs had made out, the monster's presence became detectable by those who weren't gifted with the Kol's hearing. Dull thuds that might have been footfalls came out of the gloom, and Kyle felt tremors that weren't part of Buoria's usual makeup.

The creature's silhouette emerged so abruptly that Kyle skidded to a halt, shocked by its appearance. Darcelin stepped forward immediately, putting himself between Kyle and the monster. His companions formed up around him, subconsciously creating the fan shape that fighters adopted when facing Loria's larger beasts.

And it was large, very large, at least fifty feet tall by Kyle's estimation.

It was moving, its steps slow and laborious, though in which direction it was impossible to tell in the dim light. They approached it slowly, fanning out further, trying to make out the creature's movements and anticipate where it was headed.

All in a moment, Kyle realized that it had turned and was moving towards them. It paused; a deep groan came from its mouth. Then its footsteps came one after the other, faster and faster, until it burst out of the gloom and instantly swung a huge fist down at Lugh, who leapt out of the way at the last second. Just like that, the battle erupted.

Kyle's instincts took over, and instantly he was no longer afraid, but drawing his soul sword and circling the creature, sizing it up as Lugh had taught him. It did, vaguely, have the shape of a human, but its form was so distorted that this wasn't apparent from the start. Its body was dark, almost black, and looked to be made of a kind of stone or metal. It stood on two feet, but often fell to all-fours. When it did so, it looked much less human and much more feral. Black tendons held its body together like roots binding a clump of earth; its head was small, nestled between two gigantic shoulders, and the only features of it Kyle could make out were two glowing eyes.

And wedged in the creature's chest, nestled at the center of a crater that nearly bifurcated it, was a light that shone blue so intensely that it almost hurt the eye. Kyle squinted at the glowing core, then held up his soul sword to compare the two. Yes. Even the shade of blue was identical.

Looks like that's where I stick my sword.

Cautiously, he closed the distance to the monster. Lugh and Phundasa were baiting the creature, slipping under its ponderous blows and landing hits whenever they found themselves in a blind spot. It was working; the monster was big, but slow, and had none of the deadly bloodlust that Kyle had seen in the eyrioda alpha. It struck at Lugh and Phundasa whenever they fell under its gaze, but it was an undisciplined and thoughtless attack, a giant swatting at bugs rather than an animal fighting for survival. Whatever it couldn't see, it ignored.

Lugh ducked under the monster's arm and started chopping at its right leg. Not only did he fail to wound it, but it didn't even notice his attacks. He swore, striking at the same spot over and over as if trying to fell a tree. Sparks flew, but the sword bounced off without making a scratch, and a moment later Lugh had to jump backwards as the creature swatted at him. His defender leapt forward and parried the blow while Lugh danced out of range, falling in beside Kyle.

"Damn!" he said, testing the edge of his sword with his thumb. "This thing's not going to last much longer at this rate. Hey, Darcelin! I thought you said the monster could be killed!"

"The beast is resilient," Darcelin conceded, "but can be harmed by traditional weaponry if struck solidly enough. That, however, is not the goal of this operation. All we must do is ensure that Kyle is able to deliver a finishing blow."

"Well, let's get on that, then. Nihs! Aim for the head and see if you can distract it. I get the feeling that the more confused we can make this thing, the better. Then the four of us can close in and Kyle can do his stuff."

They ran forward, flanked on both sides by their defenders. Up ahead, Phundasa was toying with the monster, ducking under its attacks while making sure that its attention was always on him. He had clearly long since given up trying to attack it, but still managed to keep it engaged. His defender stood poised nearby.

Lugh stopped and hovered at the edge of the creature's range, then dashed forward as a gap in its defenses opened up. Kyle followed him, bringing his sword back for a strike. He ran straight for the left leg and struck a solid blow with his soul sword. A chunk of the monster burst off, and a split second later its fist came crashing down on Darcelin's raised shield.

"Press the attack!" Darcelin shouted as the monster raised its arm again. "I will not let you come to harm!"

Kyle didn't question this, and circled around the leg and struck two more times. Rock and metal fell from the creature's frame, but it didn't even slow its pace. The leg lifted up, and Kyle dove out of the way as it came down again. He scrambled to his feet but was fielded by Darcelin, who had to push him back away from a flailing fist.

They backed off together as the monster, enraged, fell to all fours and made for them, but a moment later its attention was taken up by Lugh and

Phundasa on its right. Kyle ran between its limbs and struck the wounded leg again and again. His sword clashed against something and he winced from the recoil. It was the first time he'd met resistance striking with his soul sword, and the surprise shocked him as much as the impact. Confused, he stared at the leg. A revelation hit him just as the creature reared up again, and he was forced to run back.

From a distance, what he had suspected became obvious: the black tendons that crisscrossed the creature's body all sprang from the crater in its chest, and it was one of these that the soul sword had failed to cut. The leg Kyle had been hacking at was completely shattered, but the tendons remained, and supported the creature as if no damage had been done.

"This isn't going to work!" he shouted to Darcelin over the monster's bellows. "My sword can't cut the leg! We need to see if I can take the core out!"

Darcelin, panting, surveyed the creature. It was clear that even when on all fours, its core would be well out of reach. They couldn't cripple it, and trying to climb it would be suicidal even if Kyle weren't so inexperienced.

Kyle came to this conclusion at the same time as Darcelin, who said, "I believe we will have to enlist some outside aid if we are to accomplish that. The creature will not be felled only by the likes of us."

"That's fine," Kyle said, "but who's going to come help us?"

Darcelin didn't answer, but raised his hand to the crystal in his lapel. "Tower fourteen? Please respond. This is Darcelin of Kyle Campbell's defensive squadron…"

As he spoke, Meya approached them with Nihs on her shoulder. The little Kol was looking slightly wan, as he often did after using too much magic, though both he and Meya were unscathed.

"What's going on?" Meya asked him. "Are you hurt?"

"Darcelin's calling for help," Kyle said. "I'm fine. How are you two?"

"Feeling a little useless," Meya said with a slight smile. "Those defenders do their job, all right."

"Better useless than with too much work to do," Nihs said. "But I'm more concerned about what this creature is made of. Why can't your soul sword harm it?"

Kyle had his suspicions, but wasn't in the mood to discuss them now. Darcelin came to them a moment later.

"We have a plan," he said happily. "The guard towers have determined our position; we are close to the western ridge of the valley. Tower five will be within range shortly if we travel westwards. If we can coax the creature in that direction, the tower will be able to fire upon it. Such firepower will be able to cripple the beast."

"So all we have to do is get it to follow us to the edge of the valley," Meya said.

"Precisely."

Meya turned back to the battle. The creature was flailing madly at Lugh and Phundasa, bellowing constantly.

"Great."

Getting the plan across to Lugh and Phundasa was hard enough with both of them engaged, but once this was accomplished they were faced with the much larger task of keeping the monster's attention. As angry as it seemed while attacking, it quickly forgot about them and wandered off if they fell out of its line of sight. At one point it headed off in the complete wrong direction, and Lugh was forced to sprint in front of it and pester it until it turned back around. In this manner they made painful progress westwards for nearly twenty minutes. Kyle was becoming exhausted from the sheer effort of controlling distance to the monster, and what was worse, the weather had started to deteriorate. The wind was picking up, and dust was stirring from the valley floor. It wouldn't take much more to make it impossible to see.

But none of them could think of an idea better than Darcelin's, and so they carried on doggedly, hoping against hope that the valley wall would rise up in front of them before the storm did behind them.

Finally, a dim silhouette appeared in the distance. A few of them actually cried out with joy, and they had to keep themselves from running right at it. It was still a painfully long time before Darcelin's crystal lit up again, and they heard one of the guard tower's operators speak through it.

"Darcelin, this is tower five. We have a visual on the monster, but it is as of yet out of range. Please lure it closer if possible. The ballistae have been moved to the valley ridge and are being primed. We will alert you when we are ready to fire."

It was just in time—Lugh and Phundasa were drained from baiting the creature, and the rest of them weren't faring much better. The wind was coming faster, dust and ash almost obscuring their view of the valley wall.

They brought the monster ever closer, until their backs were nearly up against the escarpment. The monster had finally started to pursue them of its own volition, and was now advancing almost too quickly. Kyle watched its every move, all the while waiting for the guard tower's confirmation.

Darcelin's crystal lit up. "The creature is within range. Firing ballistae," the operator said.

A deep, thrumming sound came from above, as if a giant drum had been struck in the sky. A twisting metal snake came flying out of the gloom, shooting by over their heads. It struck the giant in the shoulder, and Kyle realized that it was a huge bolt attached to a massive length of chain. Pieces of the monster's shoulder came exploding out behind it, and it rocked backwards, nearly toppling over. A moment later, another bolt flew from the right and struck the monster's leg. The chains grew taut, and it struggled to regain its balance with the bolts jutting out from its body.

"The creature offers resistance," the operator said through the crystal, "but I believe we will be able to pull it off-balance. Please standby while we attempt this."

None of them needed telling twice. Even their defenders were drained after watching out for the safety of the others. They stood for a moment and waited, while the chains above them twisted and groaned.

The monster was now bellowing, not from the pain the ballistae had caused, for it seemed to feel none, but from the restriction to its movement. It struggled against the chains, bewildered and frustrated. It fell to all-fours and then reared up again, waving its arms. Still the chains tightened, pulling its leg and shoulder in opposite directions. Then, with a long, deep groan, its leg was pulled out from underneath it, and it toppled backwards, falling onto the valley floor in a cloud of ash.

"*Now!*" Lugh shouted, and they ran forward, skirting the monster's massive body and navigating its flailing limbs. An arm flew at Kyle and Darcelin deflected it, sending it skidding along the ground. Kyle wasn't paying attention. He came up to the creature's armpit and looked around frantically for a way up onto its chest. Seeing none, he panicked for a moment, until Darcelin came forward and crouched down, making a platform with his shield. Kyle vaulted upwards and scrabbled for a handhold, but couldn't find one and started to slide off. He drew his changesword and stabbed downwards, wedging it between two of the metal tendons in the creature's chest. Using it as a handle, he pulled himself up.

The creature was pitching and swaying as it swung its limbs around, struggling to rise. It was like a turtle on its back, and Kyle had a moment to reflect that it had probably never had to deal with losing its balance before. He danced his way to the glowing core, drawing his soul sword. He reached the lip of the cavity in the monster's chest, and was nearly blinded by the blue light pouring out from it. He planted his feet and raised his sword over his head, but before he could strike, the creature lurched and he lost his balance. Staggering, he grabbed on to the ballistae bolt jutting out from the monster's shoulder to avoid falling off.

There came a deafening *crack* as the bolt holding the monster's leg in place broke off by the chain. The creature pitched this way and that, trying to get its legs underneath it. It rolled over, and Kyle had to run along its waist to keep from getting crushed. He was no longer thinking. His blood was pounding in his ears, and though he was dimly aware of his companions shouting below him, he could focus on nothing but the swaying, thrashing body beneath him.

The monster had come to rest on all-fours again. Kyle ran to the bolt embedded in its shoulder and clung to it for dear life. What was he supposed to do now? The core wasn't visible from this side of the monster.

Unless...

He waited for a lull in the monster's movement, then, dancing along its back, came to the center of its chest. He held his sword aloft and plunged it down, shattering the creature's back. He struck again and again, until blue light started to come through the back of the creature. Around the core, the black tendons crisscrossed like spider webs, and Kyle grit his teeth and cursed as he tried to find a gap in the latticework. Finally he revealed an opening where blue light poured out. He thrust down with his sword.

The monster exploded. Kyle flew through the air, wind rushing past his face. The sky and the ground spun and merged into one being; then he hit the ground and his vision went black.

He came to with Meya hovering over him, a hand on his forehead. Her mouth was concealed by her scarf, but her red eyes glowed when she saw he was awake.

"Saints be. How do you feel?"

"Terrible. What's going on?"

Meya laughed. "The monster's dead. It fell apart after the core was destroyed. Everyone's safe, so don't worry."

Kyle groaned and lay backwards, stars exploding in front of his eyes. He felt Meya touch his chest, and winced in pain.

"That was incredibly stupid of you," she said professionally. "I think you're spending too much time with Lugh. His bravado is catching."

"You're in a good mood."

"I'm glad to find you all in one piece. I was afraid we were going to have to scrape you off the valley floor." Having finished, she brushed his cheek affectionately before helping him to his feet.

Kyle's head was spinning as Meya walked him back toward the others, who were gathered around the remains of the monster. They all came to greet him when they saw him approaching. Lugh slapped his shoulder and Darcelin laughed, clanging his shield against the ground.

"Splendid!" he said joyfully. "A maneuver worthy of the greatest of heroes."

"Kyle keeps on pulling this stuff, doesn't he?" Lugh said. "We're going to have to have a talk with you one of these days if you don't cut it out."

"If we're all done celebrating," Nihs said, "I believe we have something rather important to address. Kyle, if you'll follow me…"

Nihs led him through the remains of the monster. Chunks of rock and metal, and twists of the strange black tendons, were strewn everywhere. They drew up to the lip of a large crater, at the center of which was a small, shiny object.

"I believe that the core is inactive," Nihs said. "But we still thought it best that you be the one to recover it. Just in case."

Kyle wasn't really listening. Bemused, he stepped forward into the crater. He stared at the elemental's core, then, dropping to his haunches, picked it up. He heard Meya gasp as he did so, but he was not remotely afraid of such a familiar sight.

He stood up, his back to the others. He could practically feel their curiosity burning through his armor. Slowly, with his eyes still glued to the item in his hand, he made his way back to them.

They gathered around him. He held the object up for inspection.

"What *is* it?" Nihs asked, perplexed. Kyle still couldn't believe the answer, even when he gave it to him.

"It's my cellphone."

The storm was picking up, and the wind was howling, but none of them paid it any mind. They were standing in a huddle around the twisted piece of metal in Kyle's hand. The reality of it still hadn't quite struck him, and all he could do was stare at it in silence. It was barely recognizable. There was a hole right through the middle where Kyle's sword had penetrated, the screen was shattered, and the case was partially melted as if it had been struck by lightning.

"Let me try to understand this," Nihs said. "That's a telephone—one of the devices the people of Terra use to speak with one another?"

"Yeah."

"How did it end up *here?*"

The memory came rushing back to Kyle. "I lost it right before I fell off the *Caribia*," he said. "One of the crew was trying to get me back inside and he knocked it over the edge."

"And it fell into our world on its own?" Meya said.

Nihs was tapping his chin. "That does fit with everything else that we know. The monster appeared right around the time we found Kyle. As for the distance, perhaps there's no accounting for where in the world an object will fall when it comes through a portal."

"But why did it turn into a monster?" Kyle asked.

"There's precedent for that, as well." Nihs was starting to sound excited. "Your own soul turned into a soul sword when you came to this world; its energy was adapted into a form that made sense within the context of our world. Your phone held energy of its own, and when it came to Buoria, our world fitted it to a different role, the core of an elemental."

"That is all well and good," Phundasa said, "but I concern myself with something else. The Buors said that the monster reforms every time they kill it. Is it truly dead now? Can we go and tell Azanhein that he need not worry himself any more, or will another monster spring from Kyle's hand as we sit here talking?"

All eyes fell on the broken phone. It certainly looked innocuous. It was so mundane, an object Kyle had seen nearly every waking hour during his life back on Earth.

"I believe that we are safe," Nihs said. "But of course one should always be willing to back up his claims. Kyle, hand me the phone."

"Are you sure that's a good idea?" Lugh said. Nihs ignored him, holding his palm out to Kyle. Kyle dropped the phone into it.

There were a few sharp intakes of breath, and Nihs himself flinched a little for all his confidence, but nothing happened when the phone touched his skin. He turned the object around in his hands, looking pleased with himself.

"It's as I thought," he said. "It's broken—which is to say, its magical potential has been released. What's more, it has been reunited with Kyle, so I think that it would be safe even if he hadn't shattered it."

"How so?" Kyle asked, taking the phone back.

"A magical phenomenon known as 'subsumption'. Think of it this way: why did your other possessions, such as your clothes, not turn into monsters when you came to our world? Because you still had ownership of them; their magical potential had been subsumed into your own soul. Objects, by themselves, have very weak magical potential, and no singular purpose. So, it is easy for their aura to be absorbed by a more powerful soul when in close proximity to it."

"Oh."

"In any case," Nihs continued, squinting out across the valley, "I believe we've overstayed our welcome. What do you say we get out of here?"

He was right; the storm, which had picked up towards the end of the fight, was getting progressively worse. Kyle could barely see anything in any direction.

"A sound idea," said Darcelin. "We have completed the task we set out do, and not with a moment to spare. Let us first ascend the valley wall and take refuge in tower five. We will see if transportation can be arranged from there."

The inside of tower five was identical to that of the tower they had visited before. Kyle wasn't particularly surprised to find this out. The operator who had been speaking with Darcelin greeted them warmly, if quietly, when they entered. He went upstairs to contact Overlook, and returned soon after.

"I'm afraid I have some bad news," he told them. "The storm has increased in intensity and Overlook believes it would be too dangerous to extract you now. Their recommendation is to spend the night in this tower, as lightning strikes are common during ash storms and these towers are insulated against them."

Kyle found himself relieved by the news. He was more tired than anything else and would thankfully have slept anywhere provided he got to rest. The tower was a little cramped with all of them inside, but at least it was inside. Blankets and sleeping rolls were provided, and though the tower held little in the way of food they all got some rations to eat. The wind grew louder and louder as they settled down, until Kyle became worried that the tower was going to be uprooted.

Lugh rolled a supply barrel to the head of his bedroll and leaned against it, elbows holding it in place.

"Not the greatest victory celebration," he said, looking around the small room, "but something tells me it's going to be a little different once we get back to the capital."

"I wouldn't be surprised," Nihs said from his nest. "Azanhein doesn't strike me as the kind of person to ask such a favor of someone and then fail to show his thankfulness."

"Azanhein doesn't strike me as the kind of person who has to ask favors very often."

"You're right about that."

They talked for a little while longer, but it was clear that they were all exhausted and it wasn't long before Nihs announced that he was going to bed. The rest of them followed suit, and soon the only sounds that could be heard were those of the storm outside.

Kyle leaned against the wall, picking out details in the room as his eyes adjusted to the dark. He was completely worn out, but somehow still didn't feel like sleeping. Absent-mindedly, he pulled his phone out and stared at the shattered screen. How many times had he made that exact motion before? Suddenly he wished that it was still working, just so he could scroll through the menus or play some inane game—something, anything to remind him of Earth. But there was little chance of that now. He sighed, and slid the phone back into his pocket.

The storm outside was deafening, but that, in a way, was comforting. Kyle turned over and tried to sleep.

Transport arrived the following morning in the form of a pair of drifters similar to those they had ridden in before. They were carrying food for Kyle's party and supplies for the guard tower. They also, to Kyle's surprise, contained Herraine, the page who had invited them to dinner with King Azanhein, and Ecciritae, the expert in magic who had run the tests on Kyle's soul sword.

The two greeted them as they met outside the guard tower, Herraine with stiff cordiality and Ecciritae with slightly more warmth but no less stiffness. When Lugh asked them what they were doing out in the plains, Herraine said, "King Azanhein has heard of your professed victory over the monster blighting the ash plains, and has instructed us to take stock of the situation before further action is taken. As you know, the creature's core is extremely unstable, and must be deemed safe before it is taken closer to the city. Might we be led to the site of the creature's demise so that Ecciritae may examine it?"

Lugh laughed. "No need for that," he said, "Kyle's got it right now."

Herraine gasped. "But—instructions were that the core was not to be moved! It could be incredibly dangerous."

"I will take responsibility for this," Darcelin said. "When I saw the condition that the core was in following the fight, I judged that it was safe to be moved. The young Nihs, putting his own safety as risk, verified that it could safely be touched by denizens of Loria."

Ecciritae spoke before Herraine had a chance to reply. "Regardless of whether or not instructions were followed," she said, "if the core *is* safe, then no harm has been done. If it is not, a new monster is in danger of spawning, in which case it is imperative that I examine the core as quickly as possible. May I see it, Mister Campbell?"

Kyle held his phone out for Ecciritae to look at. She did not touch it at first, but hovered close to it, peering at it intently.

"What a strange object," she said, fascinated. "I cannot for the life of me divine what it is."

"We kind of figured that out," Kyle said sheepishly. "It's my phone—something of mine I lost right before I fell into Loria."

Ecciritae glanced at him sharply. "I believe some explanation is in order?"

Once they had finished, and Nihs had provided his unsolicited theories, Ecciritae gingerly took the phone from Kyle and brought it close to her visor. "Fascinating," she said. "If this is truly how objects from Terra react when entering our atmosphere…in any case, it is clear that the core—your phone—no longer holds any energy. I cannot imagine that it would not be safe to bring back to the capital."

Herraine cleared his throat primly. "In that case," he said, "I will inform you that King Azanhein has pronounced that you may continue to use the Free Holding Center for as long as you remain in Buoria. He also requests to know on what date you intend to leave, so that he may see you off before you depart."

"At least one more day," Meya said firmly. "Kyle isn't completely healed, and we all need time to rest."

"I second that motion," Lugh said. "Besides, we're in no hurry. How about we leave second sun tomorrow?"

They all agreed, and Herraine said, "I will inform His Majesty of your decision."

The trip back to Overlook went smoothly. The skies were clear and the sun was bright, even over the ash plains. The capital positively gleamed when it came into view, and Kyle realized that it must not have been hit by the storm.

Overlook was busier than it had been the previous day, and several of its citizens came over to them to congratulate them on their victory. Kyle had noticed that word traveled very quickly among the people of Buoria.

They took one of the smaller lifts down the city and returned to the Free Holding Center, where another surprise was waiting for them in the form of Godraien, Septhiran, Errodion and Layendis. They congratulated the party warmly, and Godraien stepped forward to offer Kyle a gift, which turned out to be a dark red bottle of Buorish spirits.

"I have heard that it is a tradition among certain adventurers to enjoy a drink once a difficult mission is completed," he said. "I thought I might sponsor your celebration."

Lugh's eyes nearly popped out of his head when he saw the bottle. He took it from Kyle and examined the label. "This stuff is *crazy* expensive! You didn't have to get us this!"

"I beg to differ," Godraien said, clearly pleased. "It is the least I can do for having had the pleasure of working with all of you."

"Well then, since you insist…" Lugh unstoppered the bottle.

"*Lugh*."

"Don't give me that. That's what it's *for*. Now come on, everyone gets some."

The spirit was unlike anything Kyle had ever tasted. It was fiery and sharp, but modulated with a strange flavor that he just couldn't place. Lugh offered some to their Buorish entourage, but Godraien waved it away, laughing.

"I am afraid that we Buors are incapable of drinking. It is one of the reasons why our spirits are so difficult to come by. There is not much of a local market for a good we cannot use."

After Godraien and the others bid them farewell, they all took some time to make themselves presentable, and then met in the common room to eat and rest. Kyle was feeling surprisingly good considering what he'd been through, but his body was still stiff and sore and his head was tender where it had struck the ground.

They chatted, played mareek-check, and generally took advantage of the calm atmosphere inside the holding center. The night passed almost entirely in this tranquil way, though they were paid a surprise visit by Drunamoh, the commander of Darcelin's squadron.

"I heard of your victory and wanted to personally congratulate you on your success," he said, shaking all of their hands. "I also wished to put forth a proposition that was first suggested to me by King Azanhein. The reason I am doing this now is because I wanted to provide you with ample time to consider it."

"Go for it," Kyle said.

"We know from the unfortunate events of Reno city and the town of Rhian that you have powerful enemies in Loria. As you have done King Azanhein a considerable service in eliminating the monster, he is willing to provide you with soldiers to serve as an escort during your travels. If you wish, these can be the same squadron of defenders who accompanied you in the ash plains."

At first, Kyle wasn't sure how to take this. Expand their party of five to one of ten? He would certainly feel safer if Darcelin and the others stayed with them, but somehow it didn't feel right. He liked them, of course, but having five Buorish soldiers with them at all times might attract unwanted attention. He searched his companions' expressions and made up his mind.

"Thank you for the offer," he said, choosing his words carefully, "but I don't think we'll need that many people. I know I have enemies, but I don't want to take soldiers away from Azanhein, and it might be easier to move around if we keep to a small group."

The others were nodding their heads in approval, and Lugh added, "It's not like adventurers to run around with a ton of firepower like that. Besides, Kyle needs to grow strong on his own, and he'll never do that if he has a defender following him everywhere he goes."

Drunamoh nodded slowly, as if he'd been expecting that answer. "Very well," he said, and his tone was not disapproving. "I will inform Azanhein of your decision." There was a moment where it seemed like he was done speaking, but then he said, "Out of curiosity, sirs and madam…I do not suppose you would consider adding a single member to your party, instead?"

His tone had changed, and Kyle wasn't sure what to say at first.

"Who did you have in mind?" Nihs asked shrewdly.

"I would like you to consider my son, Deriahm. He is young, and does not have the experience of a veteran soldier, but is trained in a number of combat styles. He is also an *irushai*, and possesses at least elementary skill in all of the magical schools."

"We couldn't possibly accept," Nihs said at once. "*Irushai* are far too valuable to be sent away with random groups of adventurers."

"On the contrary," Drunamoh said, "I believe that such an endeavor will be beneficial for all those involved. Deriahm is a diligent student, but his experience of the world outside of Buoria is limited, and I believe that travel abroad will serve to unlock more of his potential. When he does return to Buoria, he will be a more valuable asset to his country than ever before."

Kyle caught the earnestness in Drunamoh's voice, and realized that the commander desperately wanted them to accept his offer.

Lugh scratched his chin. "So you send him off with us so he can learn a little about the world, huh? Heh, I've heard that one before. What do you guys say?"

"Why not?" Phundasa said. "One Buor can move with a little more stealth than five."

"An *irushai* would be a powerful ally," Nihs said. "If you're truly willing to provide one, we'd be foolish not to take you up on it."

"Kyle?" Meya said.

Kyle nodded. "Sure. He can come with us."

"Excellent. I will ensure that he is ready to depart with you tomorrow."

"That reminds me," Lugh said, "what about you two? I guess you'll be going your own way now that the Buors aren't after us."

He said this to Meya, and for a moment Kyle had no idea what he was talking about—then he remembered that she and Phundasa had been meaning to leave them back in Rhian.

"Oh, yes," Meya said, brushing a strand of hair away from her face. "Actually…Das and I talked it over, and we'd like to come with you, if that's all right."

Lugh grinned. "You're caught up in it now, are you?"

Phundasa laughed. "Not all adventurers have the chance to take part in events such as these," he said. "We are lucky to have this chance, and none of our business is so pressing that it can't wait."

"Can't argue with that," Lugh said. "Besides, I get the feeling that we're going to need more of your help before this adventure is over."

Meya gave him a wan smile. "Let's hope not."

The day of their departure dawned bright, with a swift wind blowing down from the escarpment. There was clearly another storm brewing over the ash plains, and the rumble of lightning was ever-present in the background. As he dressed, Kyle reflected on how quickly he'd gotten used to Buoria's schizophrenic weather. He barely noticed the earthquakes any more.

Drunamoh was waiting for them below, with another Buor in tow. He was male, and slightly on the short side, only an inch or two taller than Kyle. His sash consisted of two strips of cloth attached to his collar, one blue and the other green. He was wearing black gloves instead of the usual metal gauntlets, and had a sword and shield slung to his back.

Drunamoh bowed deeply as they approached, and after greeting them stood aside for the other Buor to step forward. He too bowed, and said,

"I am *irushai* Deriahm. Pleased to meet you." His voice was youthful and sincere.

"You're the son, huh?" Lugh said, taking his hand. "Welcome to the crew!"

"Thank you. It is a great honor to take part in such a company. I hope to be of service to all of you."

"I'm sure you'll do fine," Nihs said from Phundasa's shoulder.

"Yeah, you can't go wrong with a Buor on your team! I'm Lugh, by the way. The annoying one's Nihs, the big one's Phundasa, this is Meya and this is Kyle."

Kyle sized Deriahm up as the two shook hands. The newcomer seemed polite and reserved and little else. He couldn't tell how old Deriahm was, partially because he didn't know how Buors aged compared to humans. If he had to guess, he'd say that Deriahm was younger than himself. Even more so than most Buors, kept to himself when not the focus of attention, and didn't move with the same self-assurance that Kyle saw in his father. For a moment, Kyle wondered if they hadn't made a mistake by agreeing to bring Deriahm with them; then he remembered how inexperienced he himself was.

They ate breakfast in the holding center, as there was still some time before they were meant to meet King Azanhein at the airdocks. Deriahm sat with them, hands folded politely in his lap.

Lugh raised a bite of food up to his face and sighed. "I'm going to miss this place," he said. "It'll be tough cooking for myself again."

"If you could call what you normally do 'cooking'," Nihs said under his breath.

"So, Deriahm," Meya said, "what do you do for a living?"

"I am still finalizing my studies," he said.

"You're a student?"

"In a manner of speaking. All Buors are submitted to mandatory education until a certain age; at that point, they can choose to either continue their studies or begin working in their chosen fields. I have completed my required work, but…I am not yet decided as to what craft I should pursue. As an *irushai*, I have an obligation to continue searching until I find one that will maximize my potential."

"Oh, I get it," Lugh said. "That's why Drunamoh wanted you to come with us."

"Yes. The experience will be invaluable, and it will be an opportunity for me to acquaint myself with the world outside of Buoria."

"So you've never left the island?" Meya asked.

"In a small number of controlled instances, yes. But never for an extended period of time."

The discussion was cut short by the appearance of Herraine, who strode into the common room and made a beeline for their table.

"Sirs and madam," he said, "King Azanhein will be arriving at the docks shortly. May I escort you to your ship?"

They followed Herraine down to the city's waterfront. Deriahm walked slightly behind the rest of the group, his armor clanking softly. While Kyle and the others had brought little with them from the *Ayger*, Deriahm was carrying a large pack slung over one shoulder. Kyle wondered what he possibly could have brought. Did Buors change suits of armor like humans changed clothes? They must not, and besides, the pack was too small for that.

A number of people had already gathered at the docks near the *Ayger*; word of Azanhein's appearance must have spread. Even when they were forming a crowd, the Buors were astonishingly polite. Kyle and his party passed through with not a single problem, and entered an open space created by members of the royal guard.

Soon after, a fanfare rang out over the docks, and an excited hush fell over the crowd. At first, Kyle couldn't see what was happening, until the entire crowd collectively fell to its knees and the royal procession became apparent. The royal guard, its members marching in perfect unison, was resplendent, but the figure of King Azanhein was a more magnificent sight still. He stood head and shoulders above the rest, and had slung to his back his massive sword and shield. Following him came a half-dozen Buors carrying lavish cases and even more members of the royal guard.

As Azanhein approached, Kyle felt his vision swim as it had a couple nights ago. He and the rest of the party took to one knee. The king stood over them and regarded them kindly, and said, "Please, rise. There is no need for such formality."

Kyle wasn't buying that for a second, but he stood anyway. Deriahm was the last to regain his feet. He was obviously terrified by the presence of his king.

Once they had risen, Azanhein addressed them again, in a voice that carried over the crowd. He named each of them in turn, inclining his head as he spoke. "Kyle Campbell. Lughenor MacAlden. Meya Ilduetyr. Phundasa Bar Gnoshen. Nihs Ken Dal Proks. You have done Buoria a great service on this day. You have rid us of a dangerous beast that even our bravest knights and most powerful weapons could not quell. Furthermore, you performed this task for us out of goodwill, as a favor, even after your affairs were interrupted by your summons to court. For this, may I offer my sincerest apologies and my greatest thanks."

The cheer that erupted as a result of this short speech was tremendous. Azanhein raised his hand, and silence fell instantly. "Yes, thank you, on behalf of every brother and sister of Buoria," he said solemnly. "My friends, I am sorry that your travels were delayed by your involvement in this matter. As thanks, I will keep my farewells short—I do not want to impede your business much longer than I already have, and I know that we Buors have a tendency towards verbosity when left unchecked.

"However, I'm afraid that I must delay your departure for a short time still. For it would be churlish of me to accept your aid and offer only my thanks as recompense."

The six Buors carrying the large lavish cases stepped forward. They sorted themselves into a horizontal line, each of them facing a member of Kyle's party, their cases presented in front of them.

"I have prepared a small reward for each of you," Azanhein said. "I hope you will accept them."

By this point, Lugh was practically dancing with excitement. Meya elbowed him from his other side, but it didn't accomplish much.

Azanhein strode to the first case and flipped it open. He took out two silver, ring-shaped objects glowing blue with Ephicer light and gave them to Phundasa.

"To you, Bar Gnoshen, I give bracelets made with accelerated armor technology. Worn on the wrists or on the ankles, they will enhance your natural abilities and grant you additional striking power. They also project a magical field that will protect your limbs from harm."

"A priceless gift." Phundasa touched a knuckle to his forelock and bowed deeply.

The second case was for Nihs, who was riding on Phundasa's shoulder. It was small and square, and its contents turned out to be a beautiful dark red cloak inlaid with golden designs.

"A sagecloak," Nihs breathed, before Azanhein even had a chance to speak. He took it, and sat passing the material through his fingers, staring at the swirling patterns.

Azanhein laughed softly. "Indeed it is, Nihs of the Ken folk. Though the skills and materials necessary to weave such cloaks are scarcely found in Buoria, we do possess a limited number of them. This cloak was made approximately four years ago, and is infused with some of the Heart of Buoria's volcanic power."

It took Nihs a few seconds to reply; he was still staring at the cloak. When he finally managed to tear his eyes away from it, he said, "thank you, your majesty," in a hushed voice.

Azanhein stepped to the next case. This one was so tall that the Buor holding it had stood it up on its side. Azanhein opened it and drew out a long staff made of a dark, heavily burnished metal. Simple and unadorned, it tapered slightly towards the top, where it split into two curved prongs of metal, one longer than the other.

Azanhein gave the staff to Meya. "To you, Miss Ilduetyr, a staff made of Buorish obsidian that will serve as a focus for your magical abilities, and as a rather formidable melee weapon. It is expertly woven, and very strong for its weight."

Meya hugged the staff close to her body. "Thank you very much, Your Majesty!"

Lugh was next. He was wearing a massive grin and bouncing on the balls of his feet. Azanhein paused before him and Kyle would have sworn he was returning the smile from behind his visor.

"You seem rather excited, Captain MacAlden," the king said.

"Who, me?"

Azanhein opened the next case. For the first time, Kyle recognized the contents, and he knew instantly that Azanhein had picked the perfect gift. It was a composite weapon, similar to one Lugh had shown Kyle back in Reno but of even greater quality. It glowed silver and golden, lighting up Lugh's face as he took it with shaking hands. Kyle had never seen someone so happy.

"A composite weapon," Azanhein said, "manufactured by Adenwheyr. It is made out of silversteel, a material known for its ability to hold a keener edge than almost any other metal. I'm afraid that this weapon is not bespoke, but I hope that it pleases you anyway."

"To be honest, Your Majesty," Lugh said, "I think I'd like to marry it."

Meya, who had been covering her mouth with one hand, finally burst into laughter, and it caught, spreading through Kyle's party to Azanhein and then to the crowd. Lugh was unrepentant, and hugged his weapon close to his chest as Meya had.

When the laughter finally died down, Azanhein came to the last case and laid his hand upon it.

"For you, Mister Campbell," he said, "a rather special weapon that I hope will be of use to you."

He opened the case and drew out a sword. At first, Kyle thought it was his own changearm: it had the same wide blade, single edge, and silvery sheen. But then he realized that it was larger and more ornate than his own weapon. There was a dark blue Ephicer set into the hilt that was several times larger than those he'd seen in other weapons.

He took the sword reverentially. It gleamed in his hands, and he turned it this way and that, feasting his eyes on the intricate mechanisms that the blade revealed. He looked up at Azanhein, who said:

"During your sparring sessions at the holding center, your entourage noticed that you were very partial to your current weapon, and considering your level of skill I did not want to present you with one vastly different. However, this sword is made of stronger materials than your current weapon, and has been designed to make use of your unique abilities."

There was a touch of pride in Azanhein's voice as he went on, "After witnessing your remarkable soul sword, certain bright minds within the city began to consider how your power might be better controlled. The result was this sword, the creation of which was completed just this morning. Unlike your current changearm, it has not two, but three forms: two standard forms, and one which is activated when you draw your soul sword with it in hand. It is only a prototype, but we are certain that the technology is sound. Please, try it."

Kyle, despite himself, was dubious. He'd never tried drawing his soul sword with something else in his hands and wasn't convinced it was a good idea—but he wasn't about to refuse the king of Buoria his request.

He gripped the handle with both hands so that the blade was pointing upward; the sword was heavier than his old weapon. He focused, forcing the blue and silver sparks to climb his forearms and into the hilt of the sword.

There was some resistance at first, but then the barrier broke, and the Ephicer on the sword's hilt glowed. The blade collapsed in on itself, the machinery inside the sword splitting it apart like a metal flower. A thick blade of intense blue light burst from the hilts, extending to a length of four feet. Though Kyle still felt the weight of the hilts, the blade was as light as air. Kyle heard a sigh of wonder pass through the crowd.

"Excellent," Azanhein said with satisfaction. "The weapon is functional. You see, no force in our world can contain your soularm; however, with your cooperation, it can be channeled and morphed into a different shape. This blade will not strike with as much raw power as your soularm, but it can be lengthened or shortened at will, and will only lyse when you desire it—rather than pose a threat to enemy and ally alike whenever it is drawn."

Lugh whooped with excitement. "That's great!" he said. "Now you won't have to worry about accidentally killing us every time a fight's on!"

Bemused, Kyle withdrew the sword. The blue blade sunk smoothly back into the hilts and the flower closed up. He knew that the gift Azanhein had just given him was priceless; there was likely not another sword like this in the entire world. He bowed deeply to the king of Buoria.

"Thank you, your majesty," he said, "I promise to make good use of it."

"That is good," Azanhein said, "I am glad that it pleases you." Then, the king did something strange. He leaned forward and placed a hand on Kyle's shoulder. In a much lower voice than before, he said,

"Mister Campbell. You are an individual gifted with a unique fate and fantastic powers. There is nothing you cannot accomplish here in Loria. With a soul of your strength, one could raise empires…or topple mountains into the sea. It is a great blessing, and also a grave responsibility.

King though I may be, I have not the authority to command anything of you. I can only implore you, as a friend, to follow a righteous path, and not to turn your immense strength against this frail earth."

Kyle looked into the king's dark visor, at the mountain of a man standing before him who was nevertheless practically pleading with him. All he had ever wanted to do was leave Loria in peace. He hadn't asked for a sword that could kill anything with a touch. He hadn't asked for people to die because of him, or for a monster to terrorize Buoria. He hadn't wanted any of it.

"Don't worry, your majesty," he said, "that will never happen."

To everyone's surprise, especially Deriahm's, Azanhein also had a gift for the young *irushai.* He proffered a small box, which Deriahm opened gingerly. Inside was a strange object that looked like a flat rock with a delicate metal antenna fixed to one surface.

"A lodestone," the king explained. "When a communication crystal is placed atop it, it will increase the range of said crystal, allowing you to speak with whomever you desire wherever they happen to be. Though you are leaving your home country of Buoria, you need never be alone as long as you carry this stone."

Once Deriahm had thanked the king timidly, Azanhein addressed the group once more.

"I have one last gift to present to all of you," he said. "I'm afraid that its significance may be slightly obscure to those not from Buoria, but I believe the young *irushai* will be able to explain its purpose."

Deriahm jumped slightly at the mention of his name. Azanhein drew out a round package wrapped carefully in dark blue cloth. On the front of the cloth was a large seal that Kyle recognized as Azanhein's.

Deriahm gasped. "That is a cake of king's *rouk*. It is the most valuable kind of *rouk* in existence. It can only be prepared by the king's entourage and given by him as a gift. While you yourself cannot eat it, possessing it marks you as one who has won the king's favor. If you made a gift of it to another Buor, you could instantly win them to your side. All the sons and daughters of Buoria know the value of that *rouk* cake."

"Aw, shucks, your majesty," Lugh said, "if you keep giving us stuff the *Ayger*'ll be too loaded down to take off."

Azanhein laughed out loud. "You needn't fear, Captain MacAlden, for now I am done. My friends, may I thank you one last time on behalf of all Buoria for your actions. I wish you the best of luck in your affairs, whatever they may be. And, young *irushai*, I know that you will make us proud."

And so it was that they left Buoria in the highest of spirits, with the king's kind words and the cheering of the crowd ringing in their ears. As the *Ayger* took off, Kyle looked back at the bleak island country, with its tremors and storms and dust and ash, and thought he'd never been anywhere so inviting.

No sooner had they boarded the *Ayger* and loaded up a flight path to Proks than Lugh dragged Kyle down to the training room to test out their new weapons. Ecstatic wasn't a strong enough word for what Lugh was. He was as excited as a child at Christmas, and wouldn't let Kyle's hesitation nor Nihs' reprimands change his mind. So Kyle resigned himself to his fate, and the two of them sparred for well over an hour, breaking in their new arms.

Kyle didn't take to the weapon Azanhein had given him as quickly as he had his old one. This one was heavier, and often required two hands to swing, but Kyle knew that it would be amazingly potent once he could master it.

Because they were both using unfamiliar weapons, their levels of skill were closer together than normal, and at one point, completely by accident, Kyle managed to strike a blow against Lugh. He'd come to think of his friend as being untouchable in combat, and never bothered to check his blows. He was therefore shocked when a swing made it through Lugh's guard and struck him in the chest. Kyle gasped and dropped his sword, afraid that he'd wounded him, but Lugh just jumped back, wheezing slightly, and put a hand to his stomach.

"Phew! You got me with that one. You don't give a guy a break, do you?"

"How aren't you hurt?" Kyle asked, dumbfounded.

"We haven't told you about soul shields yet, have we?"

"No, you haven't," Kyle said, picking up his sword. "Am I ever going to run out of things I don't know?"

Lugh laughed. "A soul shield is like…natural armor powered by your soul that keeps you alive. Once you get strong enough, your aura starts to extend outside your body, right?"

"Right."

"So when something comes along that would normally hurt you, it gets deflected if it hits your aura first. Like a shield that covers your whole body. But it takes energy, same as using magic does, and if you use it too much, things will start to get through it." He felt his chest again. "If you'd kept hitting me I'd be looking at more than a bruise."

"Do you think I have a soul shield?" Kyle asked.

"Maybe, maybe not. You're right around the level of power that one starts to form. I could hit you and find out."

"I'd rather not. At least not with *that*." Kyle jabbed his sword at Lugh's own deadly weapon.

They sparred for a little while longer, this time without incident. Kyle was still bemused that he'd managed to get through Lugh's defense. He didn't think Lugh had been going easy on him, or at least too easy. He could tell that Lugh was still more skilled than he, and much more experienced besides, but the thought that he could even be approaching his friend in terms of power was alien to him.

They returned to the bridge to find Meya chatting with Deriahm; Nihs was off in his own world as usual. Because Kyle had just been testing out his new weapon with Lugh, he noticed that the little Kol wasn't wearing the exquisite red cloak that Azanhein had given him.

Meya shot the two of them an amused look when they came in. "Had a good session?" she asked.

"Not bad," Lugh said. "I'm getting old, though, Kyle got one past me. Hey, have you had your combat level tested, Deriahm?"

"I have; I was tested just recently before departing."

"And?"

"I am level twenty-eight, sir," he said.

"All right. That makes you closer to Kyle than I am. How about the two of you train together for a while? That'll give me time to catch up on my sleep."

Meya laughed. "You didn't get enough while we were in Buoria?"

"What can I say, the more I sleep the more I'm reminded why I love it so much."

As the three of them talked, Kyle took the opportunity to observe the new addition to their party. Though Deriahm was taller than both Meya and Kyle, he didn't give the impression of being so. He seemed to shrink in front of Meya and Lugh, even though their posture was relaxed and his was straight-backed. His hands were folded behind him. Kyle wondered why so many Buors were fond of this pose.

"Anyway," Lugh was saying, "I need to save up on my sleep before we get to Proks. I've heard horrible things about the Kol sleeping on rocks. Isn't that right, Nihs?"

He directed this question across the room, but Nihs was still absorbed in his book and didn't make any indication he had heard. Lugh waited for a moment to see if there would be any activity, then shook his head. "Unbelievable. *NIHS!*"

The tiny Kol looked up angrily. "I'm going to assume there's a reason for all the shouting?"

"I was trying to ask you a question."

"Well, what is it then?"

"Is it true that the Kol sleep on rocks?"

Nihs shot him a venomous glare, and Kyle had to look away to keep himself from laughing.

When Nihs went back to his book without answering, Lugh said, "No, seriously, what are we in for when we get to Proks? We should have a plan for how we're going to handle this."

That was enough to get Nihs to close his book. "Fine," he said. He waddled over to the center of the room and clambered up onto the pilot's stool.

"We want to see what the elders know about people like Kyle, right?" Lugh said. "That means we'll have to tell them about him. Is that dangerous?"

Nihs took a moment to think. "It shouldn't be. Provided the elders, or older Kol in general, are the only ones we tell. It's no secret that the Kol mistrust the other races, and the older they are the worse they are in that regard. The elders would have no reason to spread information about Kyle outside of the city. The younger Kol are a different story, however. Many of them have friends or relatives in Centralia, and love to gossip on the overhead."

"So we keep quiet until we're in front of the elders. How easy will it be to talk to them?"

"It…may be difficult," Nihs said. "It certainly isn't a given. My family has no small amount of status within the city, but I'm not the most respected member of my family, either. In any case it's likely we'll have to wait for an audience."

"What if we tell them it's important?"

"That's not how it works." Nihs pressed a palm to his forehead. "All we can do is get ourselves into the council chamber and show them irrefutable proof that Kyle is from another world."

"What, get him to chop up more vee'nar with his soul sword?"

"It wouldn't hurt."

Lugh shook his head. "Damn. Your elders should have just listened in the *first* time we had to prove where Kyle was from. Now we'll have to do it all over again."

"It's not going to be easy to convince them we're telling the truth, let alone enlist their aid," Nihs admitted. "But we have to try nonetheless. The elders' assistance will be invaluable if we can secure it."

"Great. I guess we'll just have to see."

Lugh lumbered off to bed not much later. Nihs also left for the privacy of his own room, claiming that he had some catching up to do on the overhead; Kyle suspected this had something to do with their imminent arrival in Proks. Phundasa joined them on the bridge, and so Kyle found himself talking with him, Meya, and Deriahm—though Deriahm, for his part, wasn't saying much. He was even quieter than Kyle had been when he first came to Loria, and always registered surprise when one of them tried to include him in the conversation. He clearly wasn't used to holding long conversations, or comfortable being the center of attention. As an outsider of sorts himself, Kyle felt empathy for him, but he also hoped that Deriahm's lack of confidence wouldn't make him a burden. He resolved to put Lugh's idea in motion and start training with him as soon as possible. He felt that they would both benefit from it.

The rest of the day passed uneventfully. In the evening, Kyle went out on deck to watch the scenery pass by. The *Ayger* had left Buoria far behind, and was now hugging the coast of Eastia on its way south. After a day's flight, it would cut inland, over the mountain range that lined the east coast of the continent. Nestled somewhere in those mountains was Proks, the Kol capital of the world, and the home of the Kol elders.

He wouldn't have said it out loud, but Kyle wasn't feeling very confident about how much help the elders were going to be. Nihs himself, who was normally so sure of the Kol's superiority, wasn't convinced that the elders knew anything of use—and even the Buors, with all of their scientific and technological might, hadn't been able to help him. In fact, they had asked it *of* him.

He thought back to the plea that Azanhein had made as they left Buoria. *I can only implore you not to turn your immense strength against this frail earth.* Did Azanhein know something that Kyle didn't? Sure, his soul sword could break almost anything, but it wasn't a weapon of mass destruction, and its owner wasn't exactly an expert in combat. He wouldn't last long if he tried to turn his power against the people of Loria.

Kyle found himself staring up at the sky, his thoughts turning to Earth. Was time passing there? Though he hadn't been gone for very long, it was more than enough time for him to become a news story. If he ever did make it back to Earth, that might cause a few problems.

But there was no point in worrying about that now. Do the job that's in front of you, Nihs had told him once. Before he thought about what would happen once he got back to Earth, he had to figure out just how he was going to get there.

It wasn't long after the party that Kyle decided to pursue a relationship with Natalie, the girl he had danced with at the end of the night. At worst, he thought, it could end up being a non-affair lasting one or two bad dates before falling apart. At best, he could have a girlfriend to call his own for the rest of his high school career. It was definitely worth the risk, especially if he was careful not to spend too much money on her, a mistake he'd seen many of his classmates make. Of course, many of his classmates could also rely on their parents for financial support.

Kyle hadn't even met Natalie before the party, and so had no idea of what to expect from dating her. What he got was a surprisingly fun, if exhausting, relationship with a girl who possessed unlimited energy and no small amount of mischievous tendencies. She was a year younger than him, and looked even younger than that, but if the prospect of dating someone outside her year daunted her, she never let it show. In fact, she enjoyed showing their relationship off whenever possible, and Kyle was often subjected to public displays of affection. At first, he found this worrying, but after watching the other students he realized that this was nothing out of the norm. Boyfriends and girlfriends were, after all, a symbol of status; what was the point of having one if you couldn't show them off? So Kyle played along, and was rewarded with even more affection both in public and in private.

At first, Kyle was concerned that Natalie would forget about him once summer came along and they stopped seeing each other every day, but he needn't have worried. Natalie wanted to spend every moment that she didn't spend working with Kyle. On the rare occasions that he had access to his mother's car, Kyle was able to drive them wherever they wanted to go; otherwise, they made do, usually ending up at Natalie's house, which was often deserted.

One day towards the end of summer, Natalie texted him saying that her parents would be gone all weekend, and would he like to come over? The promise that one sentence held made it hard for Kyle to focus on work for the rest of the week. He prayed that his mother would let him borrow the car.

The weekend came, and Kyle made his way to Natalie's house. She greeted him in the usual way, smothering him with kisses or rather one kiss that lasted several minutes. She then disappeared downstairs, a place Kyle had come to think of as where all of her parents' alcohol was stored. Though Natalie often raided their fridge, she had to do it in small doses to avoid being found out. Today, however, was different. She reappeared with an entire sealed bottle of raspberry liqueur.

"It's mine," she explained gleefully at the sight of Kyle's expression. "I got a friend to buy it for me." She immediately twisted it open, and Kyle knew the bottle wouldn't last through the weekend.

The time passed too quickly. They watched movies, swam in the pool, and worked their way through most of the liqueur bottle. Later in the evening, when the drink was starting to wear off, Natalie jumped into his lap and touched him on the nose.

"I've got a surprise for you," she said.

"Really?"

She grinned and kissed him rather clumsily. "Wait right here," she said.

Kyle wasn't sure what was coming, but he had some suspicions, and wasn't sure whether to be excited, scared, or both. He waited on the couch, listening to Natalie walking around upstairs.

She came back down carrying a number of objects in her hands, and spread them out on the table in front of him. Kyle looked down, and then silently reached out and picked up a small plastic bag full of green herbs. He'd never seen any before, but didn't need to be told what it was. He was amazed. He looked at Natalie, who was clearly waiting to see his reaction.

"Where did you *get* this?" he asked.

Natalie just laughed. "Don't worry about it." She took the bag from him and started filling a glass pipe with its contents. She'd obviously done it many times before. Kyle was troubled; throughout his relationship with Natalie, he had always assumed that he was the older, more experienced one. Now, he wasn't so sure any more, and the feeling disquieted him.

Natalie, meanwhile, had produced a lighter, and had brought the pipe to her lips. Smoke escaped from her mouth as she held it out to Kyle, smiling.

"Wanna try some?" she asked.

There wasn't any question of Kyle refusing, so he took the pipe and awkwardly turned the mouthpiece towards him.

"Make sure to hold it in for as long as possible," Natalie said, "or else it won't work."

The rest of the night passed in a haze. Time stretched out, and Kyle's memories dissolved the second they were made, leaving him lethargic and bemused. Natalie became even more shameless in her affection, clinging to him and kissing him over and over again. She ran her lips up the side of his neck, ending at his ear.

"Want to move somewhere else?" she said.

Kyle turned to her, struggling with the question. She was wearing a look on her face that he'd never seen before. A suspicion started to build within him.

"Where were you thinking of?" he asked.

She grinned wickedly. "How about my parents' room?"

Kyle found that shocking even in his current state. He wanted to protest, but the words wouldn't leave his mouth, and Natalie was smothering him with kisses and dragging him to his feet. He allowed himself to be led upstairs and through the large double doors he'd only ever seen closed. He didn't have the time to take in the details of the room before Natalie grabbed hold of him and pushed him down onto the massive bed.

The *Ayger* was silent and deserted when Kyle woke up the next morning, which suited him just fine. He stood on the observation deck and looked through the picture window, trying to sort out the thoughts that were running through his mind.

When someone finally did join him on the bridge, it was Lugh. He clomped into the room, rubbing his eyes and trying to push his mane of hair out of his face. He yawned, waved at Kyle, and leaned on the control panel, also staring out the picture window.

"Nice day, huh?" he said.

"Yeah." Kyle joined him at the control panel, arms folded.

"You sleep well?" Lugh asked him.

"Sort of. I keep having dreams."

"Oh yeah? What about?"

Kyle thought back on the dream he'd had last night, and decided to generalize. "Things that have happened to me back on Earth."

"No kidding. How often do you get them?"

"Almost every night, I guess."

Lugh laughed in amazement. "You should have told us. Nihs' gonna freak out when he finds out."

"Why?" Kyle said. He had no idea why Lugh cared so much.

"I don't know what it's like in your world, but here, dreams are what happens when magic gets into your head while you're asleep. Your mind's defenses are down when you're sleeping, right? So if there's anything around that can influence it, you end up having weird dreams. I bet it's no coincidence that you're dreaming about your world. We should let Nihs know about it."

Try though he might, Kyle couldn't force himself to care. He would rather forget his dreams than dwell on them, and it was very early in the morning besides. He didn't say anything more, and neither did Lugh.

Phundasa and Deriahm were the next to wake up. Kyle still had to get used to Deriahm's presence on the ship, and could tell that the *irushai* felt the same way. Kyle remembered the resolution he'd made about training, and put it forth to Deriahm once he came onto the bridge.

"It would be a pleasure, sir," Deriahm said. "We can begin at once, if you wish."

"Breakfast first," Lugh said. "Remember, we're not Buors, we can't get away with eating once every few days."

"Ah—my apologies," Deriahm said, flustered.

"Hey, I was just kidding around, don't worry about it."

Deriahm bowed in Kyle's direction. "I will head down to the training room and begin my morning exercises while you eat. Please join me at your leisure."

"Scout him out for me, Kyle," Lugh said once he had left. "I want to know what we're getting into with this fellow. Now, I heard something about you making us breakfast."

Kyle hadn't been sure what to expect from sparring with Deriahm; if anything, an easier version of his sessions with Lugh. However, the difference in style between his two partners was remarkable. Deriahm was a much more defensive fighter than Lugh, and more conservative and strategic in style. At first, Kyle mistook this for lack of skill, but as they continued sparring, he realized with growing respect—and frustration—that this was not the case. Rather, Deriahm reacted to every move that Kyle made, countering and striking back methodically. As Kyle continued to test his defenses using the different tricks Lugh had taught him, he realized that Deriahm would always react to the same kind of technique the same way, without fail. Kyle quickened his attack and tried to slip through Deriahm's defenses, all the while barely protecting himself against the inevitable counterattacks. Deriahm either could not or would not strike back with enough force or speed to be seriously threatening, but more than once he caught Kyle by surprise.

Kyle finally sank to the ground, leaning on the hilt of his sword.

"How do you *do* that?" he asked, noticing Deriahm was barely out of breath.

"Repetition is the key," the Buor replied. "During military training, we are drilled in the same list of techniques every day. Eventually, the movements that comprise them become etched into the mind, so that it knows no other way to react when presented with a certain situation. Beyond that, you must simply keep the mind in a calm state and allow it to react to your opponents' movements."

"You've got to teach me how to do that," Kyle said.

"I'm afraid that any lessons I could give you would be incomplete, and we do not have the time for the discipline to be instilled in you as strongly as it is in me. But I would be happy to share with you as much as I am able."

"That'd be great."

The others were all up by the time Kyle and Deriahm returned to the bridge. Phundasa, for once, was not down in the engine room, but leaning against the counter of the mini-kitchen with a mug of something in his hand. He, Lugh, and Meya were having a rapid-fire discussion about some political issue, while Nihs kept his face buried in his books, as he had done ever since the party had left Buoria.

Since Deriahm and Kyle had nothing to contribute to the discussion, they decided to break it off and find some other way to pass the time.

"How about a game of cards?" Lugh said. "Do you play Siege, Deriahm?"

"I am familiar with the basic rules, but I have never played it myself."

"Great, we'll teach you." He stepped over to the control panel to check the *Ayger's* systems. He was about to turn around and say something to Nihs, when his eyes were dragged back to the picture window.

"Huh."

"What is it?" Phundasa asked, walking over with his mug in his hand.

"Oh, nothing. Another ship just came out through those mountains. They must not be using a flight path."

"Hmm." Phundasa peered closer. "I don't recognize the make. Looks like it was built in Reno, though."

A slight chill went down Kyle's spine at the mention of Reno city. He knew he was being paranoid, but he joined Lugh and Phundasa at the control panel nonetheless. He followed Lugh's pointing finger and saw the ship up ahead. It was slightly smaller than the *Ayger*, and was about to pass by them on their left. It was sleek and golden. Phundasa was certainly right about it being from Reno; Kyle knew he'd seen a similar design somewhere in the city.

Lugh put his hand on the communication crystal as the ship drew closer. "This is captain Lughenor MacAlden of the *Ayger*," he said. "Your course is taking you across a flight path. You might want to reroute."

By this time, they had all gathered to watch the ship, even Nihs. Lugh took his hand off the crystal, but the other ship didn't reply.

Phundasa frowned. "What's that mounted on their deck? It looks like a cannon."

"Can't be," Lugh said dismissively. "You can't put a gun that size on a ship."

Kyle's nerves, which had already been jangling, hit a fever pitch as he saw the weapon mounted on the other ship's hull. He didn't care what Lugh said: it was a cannon, he knew it, and he also knew without a doubt that this ship was here for him.

He opened his mouth, struggling to put his fear into words. He saw the barrel of the cannon swivel around slowly, just as it slipped out of view of the picture window. He heard a low whine start to build up, and suddenly found his voice again.

"*GET DOWN!*" he shouted.

An explosion rocked the ship, lifting them all off their feet. Kyle tumbled sideways and slammed into the far wall. As he struggled to rise, there came another explosion, and he heard the sound of shattering glass and tortured metal coming from the *Ayger's* hull.

He managed to get his feet under him and stood up. His companions were splayed everywhere, and alarms were going off on the control panel.

"Lugh!" Nihs shouted. He was trying to disentangle himself from the broken furniture and piles of books that had spilled everywhere. "Lugh, get us away from them!"

Lugh had fallen off to the left of the control panel. He was sitting upright, but was stunned. His eyes were wide and he made no indication he'd heard.

Phundasa bounded past him and took hold of the *Ayger's* wheel. He twisted it to the right, all the while pulling upward. There was a jolt as the ship broke off from the flight path and started to rise sharply. The engines were flaring, but it still felt agonizingly slow, and a moment later they were hit with another shell.

"No good!" Nihs shouted. "Take it into a dive!" He scrambled over to the control panel and climbed on it.

Phundasa growled and pushed the wheel in. The ship swooped sickeningly downwards, and Kyle nearly lost his footing on the sloped floor.

"We need to fall faster!" Nihs snapped.

"We'll crash it into the ground at this rate!" Phundasa shouted back through gritted teeth.

"The alternative is being blown to pieces!" Nihs shouted back.

Phundasa grunted and pulled back on the throttle. Kyle felt himself getting lighter as the ship fell rapidly. Meya had run over to help Lugh, and Deriahm was standing in the middle of the bridge, shocked into inaction. Nihs, meanwhile, had climbed over to the alarms going off on the control panel.

"Hull breaches," he said, "but the engines are still intact."

"Little good that will do us if we can't fight back," Phundasa growled. "What are we supposed to do against a ship with a cannon mounted on it?"

Nihs didn't answer.

The ground below was coming up rapidly. Phundasa pulled the *Ayger* out of its dive at the last possible moment, and the ship went skimming through the air just above ground level. Wherever the other ship had gone, Kyle couldn't catch sight of it.

There was a moment of relative silence as they sped away. Kyle's heart was beating, and with every second he expected another attack.

"I don't see them behind us," Phundasa said, his eyes on the control panel. "They're in one of our blind spots."

"Could it be we're out-flying them?" Nihs said.

"I doubt it. They're—"

Kyle heard a booming noise coming from above. To his horror, he saw the strange ship descend into view directly ahead of them. It wheeled about sharply, the cannon mounted on the hull coming to point directly at them.

Phundasa swore sulfurously and heaved on the wheel, pulling them into a sharp ascent. But it wasn't enough; the *Ayger* was too large and too slow to out-maneuver the mystery ship. It fired again, and the blast lifted them all off their feet and flung Phundasa away from the wheel. The picture window shattered, and Kyle raised his arms to protect himself from the shards of flying glass. The bridge was suddenly full of wind and noise, and the *Ayger* started to pitch and sway with no one at the wheel to stabilize its course. Alarms blared, and if any of his companions were trying to speak, Kyle wouldn't have known.

The ship lurched and rocked again and again. Their opponents were peppering them with smaller shots. As soon as Kyle managed to struggle to his feet, another explosion knocked him off-balance. He fell on all fours, and a shard of glass sliced open the palm of his hand.

"This is madness!" Phundasa roared over the din. "We can't keep this up! We have to get off the ship before they shoot us out of the sky!"

Lugh, who had been in a daze since the first impact, finally woke up on hearing these words. He rose to his feet, bracing himself against the wall as the ship pitched once more.

"No!" he shouted. "We can get out of this!"

He dashed over to the control panel and seized the *Ayger*'s wheel, straining against it as it tried to jump out of his hands. The ship's course stabilized somewhat, and it began to climb again, though wind was still whipping through the bridge and alarms were still sounding.

"Come on!" Lugh shouted, though whether this was to the others or to the *Ayger*, Kyle did not know.

The mystery ship came into view, pulling up on their left. Kyle flattened himself against the wall and managed to keep to his feet as they fired again. There was a sickening shriek of metal, and the ceiling of the bridge crumpled inwards, spilling its innards of tigoreh wiring. Lugh ducked reflexively, but remained fixed to the wheel.

"Lugh!" Nihs shouted, as the enemy ship circled around in front of them, "we need to get off the ship *now!* Kyle can't leap, he's going to need help!"

"*No!*" Lugh shouted back, his long hair whipping around behind him.

"*Lughenor!*" Phundasa bellowed. "*We are going to die if we stay here!*"

Lugh didn't answer. Phundasa cursed and ran over to Meya, who was crouched in a corner near the far wall. He helped her to her feet and took her over to Kyle and Deriahm.

"All of you, get downstairs!" he shouted at them. "We have to jump off the ship. It's the only way we're getting out this alive. I'll lower the ramp."

"But Kyle can't leap!" Meya said.

"He's going to have to learn. We don't have any other choice."

"What about you?" Meya demanded, grasping his arm as he turned away.

He put a hand on her shoulder. "I'm going to get Lugh out of there if I have to drag him. Don't worry about me. I'll be down in a second."

Once the others had run downstairs, Phundasa turned to the task at hand. Lugh was still at the wheel, gripping it stubbornly with white-knuckled fingers. Nihs was standing on the control panel, shouting at him, trying to convince him to let go. Phundasa would have been furious if there had been any room in his mind to be so. At the moment, all he cared about was getting them all off the ship in one piece.

He dashed across the empty room, praying that their enemy would not strike again. He collided with Lugh at the wheel, and latched onto his arm, both to keep his own balance and to drag Lugh away.

"Nihs," he said, "lower the boarding ramp and get downstairs with the others. I'll get Lugh out of here."

"But—"

"Don't worry, I won't let your friend die on me. But the others are going to need help."

Nihs looked terrified, but nodded his understanding. He climbed across Lugh's arms and pressed the button that lowered the ship's ramp, then leapt down and fled the bridge. Phundasa, relieved by Nihs' level head, turned his attention to Lugh.

"Lugh," he said, as clearly and calmly as he could manage, "you can't save the *Ayger*. We're out of time. Don't throw your life away for the sake of a ship!"

"Don't do this to me, Phundasa!" Lugh shouted back, his voice modulated with hysteria. "I've still got a chance! I have to try!"

The enemy ship fired again. Phundasa clung to the control panel for support, then whipped his head around to assess the damage. His heart sank—a fire had blossomed down one of the hallways.

"Lugh—" he said again, then stopped himself. He had realized that Lugh was no longer there, at least not in a way that could be reasoned with.

If he wanted to get Lugh off the ship, he was going to have to drag him.

There was no time for second-guessing. Phundasa grabbed him with both arms, hauling him away from the wheel while Lugh thrashed in resistance. Phundasa strained, pulling as hard as he could to no avail; Lugh was nearly as strong as he was, and had a more reliable grip.

Just as Phundasa was wondering if his efforts were hopeless, the enemy ship drew up in front of the *Ayger* and fired directly through the picture window. The shell struck the observation deck, and both Lugh and Phundasa were blown away from the control panel. The ceiling buckled further and Phundasa felt heat wash over him as the magical shell exploded, releasing its potential inside the bridge.

Phundasa leapt to his feet, and reached down to pick Lugh off the floor. Lugh no longer struggled. He was screaming in agony, clutching both his hands to the left side of his face. Phundasa took this opportunity to lift him from the ground and dash down the stairs, leaving the bridge to collapse in on itself.

Kyle and the others fled down the stairs, bracing themselves against the walls as the ship rocked. They made their way to the off-ramp, and stood panting, waiting for it to open as Phundasa had promised it would. Kyle and Meya clung to each other for support, and Deriahm sank to the ground, his elbows resting on his legs and his hands clasped in front of his face.

"What did Phundasa mean by jump?" Kyle asked, speaking directly into Meya's ear to make himself heard over the noise.

"If you leap from a height," Meya said, "you can survive falls you wouldn't normally be able to. If we all leap before the ship hits the ground, we should be all right."

"But I can't leap!"

Meya put her hands on his shoulders and looked directly into his eyes. "You have to," she said. "Don't worry, you're strong enough now to make it work. If you can will yourself to do it, you're most of the way there. Just do what we do and you'll be fine."

The ramp hummed into life, and slowly lowered. The view the portal offered was dizzying, and wind howled into the room, tugging at them as if wanting to pull them through the opening.

Meya squeezed his hand as the opening yawned wider and wider.

Then, suddenly, there was an awful tearing noise and the ramp was torn free of its bearings, spinning off into the empty air. Kyle watched in shock, his breathing ragged and his chest pounding.

"How long do we wait?" he asked Meya.

"As long as we can. The closer we are to the ground, the better."

They clung to the room's support beams, gripping all the tighter every time the ship lurched. Deriahm sat farther back, meditating.

Nihs came down the stairs, pale and afraid. His clawed toes clacked against the metal floor as he drew up the gaping hole left by the ramp.

"Where are Lugh and Das?" Meya shouted at him.

Nihs' face was agonized. "Still on the bridge," he said. "Lugh went into shock. I couldn't get him to let go of the wheel. Phundasa said he would try to bring him."

Meya didn't answer. Kyle couldn't bear to look at her face.

They waited in silence for a few unbearable minutes. Nihs stood dangerously close to the portal, his arms folded in front of him. He had never looked so small and vulnerable. Kyle panted, his lungs struggling to bring in the air that was whipping around the room. He strained his ears, listening for the sound of Phundasa and Lugh coming down the stairs. But all he could hear was the roar of the *Ayger's* engine, the sound of the wind, and the agonized screech of metal as the enemy ship continued its bombardment.

The ground was drawing closer, though how close it truly was or how much time they had Kyle couldn't tell. Still there was no sign of Phundasa or Lugh.

Nihs said, "We don't have much time left. We may have to—"

Phundasa crashed into the room, with Lugh in his arms. Meya let out a wordless cry of joy and Kyle felt a wave of relief wash over him. The left side of Lugh's face was a bloody mess, and he had his palm pressed against it, but both he and Phundasa were alive.

"Are we ready?" Nihs shouted over the wind.

"I don't know about Lugh," Phundasa said. "He's hurt. Meya might have to—"

But Lugh put his free hand against Phundasa's chest, and attempted to swing out of his arms. Phundasa, surprised, set him down on his feet.

"I can make it," Lugh said grimly, blood oozing between the fingers of his left hand. "I'm not getting any of you killed because of me." He was shaky on his feet, but there was determination in his voice, and he kept his balance even after Phundasa let go of him.

"Whatever we're doing, we need to do it now!" Nihs shouted, his eyes on the ground.

"All right!" Lugh said. "You all jump, Kyle and I will go last! Kyle, watch the others to see how they do it!"

Nihs ran towards the ramp and leapt into the empty space. Within a fraction of a second, he was gone. Meya, Deriahm, and Phundasa followed. From what Kyle could tell, all you had to do was run and jump.

"Think you've got a handle on it?" Lugh asked him.

"Doesn't look like there's much to it!" Kyle said.

"That's right. It's just like all the other metamagic you've learned! Just will it to work and it will. You'll be fine! Go on!"

Kyle had no other option but to obey. Terrified, he ran towards the opening, hoping with every fiber of his being that the others' confidence in him was well-placed. Heart pounding, he kicked himself away from the ship once he reached the lip of the ramp, and flew out into the empty air.

Kyle had no idea what a leap was supposed to feel like. What it *did* feel like was nothing short of a free fall. His arms windmilled as he soared through the air, leaving the *Ayger* far behind. He plummeted to the ground, accelerating rapidly. He was at least a hundred feet from the ground, and Kyle's heart leapt into his throat when he looked down. He was absolutely certain that he was going to die. There was nothing to break his fall, no slow descent, nothing to indicate that he was in control of the leap. Kyle closed his eyes and grit his teeth as the ground came up to meet him.

The landing was hard, but nowhere near as hard as he thought it would be. He was thrown from his feet and tumbled painfully along the ground, rolling several times before his momentum was spent. A lance of pain shot up his arm as his cut palm struck the ground, and he picked up several other cuts and bruises as well. But none of his bones were broken, and he staggered to his feet a moment later.

He looked around, dazed and bemused. He was part terrified, part elated to be alive. He caught sight of the *Ayger*, drifting low over the ground, fishtailing in a strangely graceful way. Several fires were burning where the enemy's shells had hit, and even from this distance Kyle could see where the ship's hull had crumpled. Part of him couldn't believe what had happened, and another part didn't want to. The *Ayger* had been his home ever since he fell into Loria. Lugh's prized ship, with which they had the freedom to travel wherever they wanted. What were they going to do without it?

He watched it as it fell into the distance; his heart was in his throat as it crashed into the countryside. He could hear and feel its impact from where he was standing. He was shocked, but had more pressing matters to worry about. He had to find the others.

Kyle picked his way silently across the countryside, heading away from the wreckage of the *Ayger*. He scanned the ground for signs of his companions and the sky for signs of the ship that had shot them down, but saw neither.

After a minute or two, he heard someone calling to him, and found Meya walking through the brush, Nihs riding on her shoulder. She sighed in relief when she saw him.

"I'm so glad you're safe," she said. "I was worried that you wouldn't be able to leap. Are you hurt?"

"Not really," Kyle said, showing her his cut palm. Meya touched it gently, and shook her head.

"I'm sorry, but it'll have to wait. I don't know how much healing the others are going to need."

"That's all right."

"You haven't seen anyone else?" Nihs asked him.

Kyle shook his head.

Nihs scanned the countryside, his face pale. "All right," he said. "Let's keep looking."

Thankfully, it was only a short time before they found Phundasa and Deriahm, both unhurt. Meya ran forward and threw her arms around Phundasa's broad waist while Kyle and Nihs greeted Deriahm.

"You seem to have come through unscathed," Nihs remarked drily.

"Indeed. I am glad that we could locate you so quickly."

"Did you see where Lugh landed?" Nihs asked. He couldn't quite keep the panic out of his voice.

"I am afraid not, sir."

"Sorry we didn't call out," Phundasa said over Meya's embrace, "but I'm afraid that our friends may be out to get us. We need to find Lugh as soon as possible."

"I couldn't agree more," Nihs said, his tone turning businesslike. He leapt off of Meya's shoulder and on to Phundasa's. "What's our approach? Do we fan out and try to find him?"

"We stick together," Phundasa said firmly. "We can't risk being picked off by whoever attacked us."

"I may be able to help in this endeavor," Deriahm said hesitantly. "I have some skill in mysticism and am able to douse for signs of life. I am not powerful enough to locate Lughenor at any great distance, but I may be able to prevent us from missing his location through oversight."

"That's a start," Nihs said. "Let's go find him."

It was a tense, wary group that set out to search for its missing member a few minutes later. The countryside they had landed in was sculpted and dramatic, rugged hills rich with vegetation that gave way to the mountains of Eastia in the near distance. It was late afternoon, and the sun hung low in the sky, drenching the plains in golden light. But none of them had an eye for this beauty; they were straining their senses, scanning the ground and listening intently, hoping to pick up on Lugh's location. Between them walked Deriahm, his head bowed and his hand to his forehead. A soft purple light escaped from between his fingers, and when Kyle came close to him, he heard the whisper of magical energy being spent.

Wind was blowing over the hills, and the air was chilly. The ground was deceptively treacherous, and going was slow. They curved around the area where they had found Phundasa and Deriahm, then closed in obliquely on the *Ayger's* crash site. It was a massive fire, a pall of greasy smoke rising from the distant valley where it had fallen.

As the *Ayger* drew closer and closer, Kyle started to seriously worry about Lugh. He'd been in a poor state when Kyle had jumped. What if something had gone wrong? He grit his teeth in frustration, wishing there was more he could do to help find him.

Finally, they reached the wreckage of the *Ayger*. The whole ship was in flames, and they didn't dare approach it. They stood on a nearby hill, watching the oddly compelling sight. Kyle wanted to be upset that the *Ayger* was no more, but his mind didn't seem to be working properly. All he could think of was how pleasant the warmth generated by the fire was.

"I can't believe it," Meya said softly. "It was such a beautiful ship. What's Lugh going to say when he sees this?"

"I don't know," Nihs said, just as quietly. He then cleared his throat and said, "speaking of Lugh, this isn't getting us any closer to finding him. We need to keep searching." He cast his eyes over the hills. "Let's head back, along the next ridge over. He must be somewhere close."

It was painful to head out again, and Kyle felt more helpless than before. The sun was starting to set, and the long shadows it cast made searching all the more difficult.

They had not gone a hundred feet, however, when Deriahm said, "I believe I can sense life nearby. Please, allow me to divine the direction."

They all stopped at once, tension buzzing throughout the group. Deriahm stood stock-still, his head bowed. He spun about gently, extending his arm in front of him. Finally he pointed.

"I cannot be sure, but I believe the signal originates from over there."

They set off again, their desperation modulated by hope. Kyle's pace quickened even though he was telling himself not to get too hopeful. They crossed over a few ridges with no result, and Kyle's spirits started to fall again. They stopped once more to let Deriahm focus, and stood completely still as he tested his surroundings. Then Nihs' ears suddenly pricked up.

"Do you hear that?" he said. His ears unfolded and started to undulate in the air. A second later, he bounded off of Phundasa's shoulder without saying a word and dashed through the undergrowth.

They ran after him, calling for him to slow down. Nihs didn't listen, and they nearly lost sight of him as his small green body darted this way and that. They ran around the hill, bushes snagging at their legs and rocks sliding underfoot.

All of a sudden, they turned a final corner and found Lugh. He was reclining on the side of a hill, occupying a gap in the undergrowth. His clothes were slashed and burnt, and he still had his palm pressed to his forehead, but he was grinning from ear to ear. He waved at them lazily with his free hand as they swarmed around him.

"Thought I heard you all crashing through the bush," he said, his voice strained. "You ought to try and make less noise. Though I guess it worked out all right."

"You idiot!" Nihs shouted. "Why didn't you come looking for us, or at least get up and make yourself visible? We would have missed you if Deriahm hadn't sensed you!"

"Lay off it, Nihs," Lugh said, pushing him away. "I was going to come looking for you. Just catching my breath first." He looked up at Meya. "I think my eye might be a little cut up. Mind taking a look at it?"

"Of course." She fell to her knees by his side and lifted a hand to his forehead.

"You'll have to move your hand," she said gently.

"I know." He took a deep breath, then peeled his hand away from his face. "All right, be honest. How ugly am I?"

Kyle sucked in his own breath when he saw. The entire left side of Lugh's face was a mess of blood, and his eye was nowhere to be seen. Bits of white skull showed through, and part of Lugh's brow had crumpled inwards.

Meya started to cry softly. "I'm so sorry, Lugh," she said, "but your eye's gone. It's beyond healing."

Lugh made a face, closing his good eye, and leaned backwards in the grass. "So the old girl took a part of me with her, did she? I was always afraid she'd break my heart. What a day, huh?" He laughed bitterly.

None of the others said anything. Kyle didn't trust himself to. Meya, still crying, had put a hand on Lugh's arm, and was using her other to repair what she could of the wound on his head. Nihs, all trace of his haughty demeanor lost, sat near Lugh's shoulder.

Slowly, Lugh opened his eye again, and blinked back a few tears. "Still, though, we all got out of it alive, right? We can't complain. Least we're all still alive." He craned his neck to bring Phundasa into view. "I didn't thank you for saving my skin back there. Sorry I acted like such a jackass."

"You would have done the same for me," Phundasa said.

"You *are* a jackass," Nihs said.

"Thanks, Nihs."

"It's like you said," Meya said gently. "At least we all made it out safely."

"Yeah. Oh, by the way…" he pointed to the ground beyond her.

Kyle looked to where he was pointing and saw, to his surprise, that their weapons—his own sword, Lugh's composite weapon and Meya's staff—were piled in the grass a few feet away.

"Thought I'd grab the important stuff before I jumped," Lugh said, coughing. "After all, we're gonna need them if we want to beat the hell out of the people who did this to us."

Nihs looked from Lugh to the weapon pile and back.

"You idiot!" he shouted again, color rising in his cheeks. "You had little enough time as it was and you went back for *weapons?*"

"The training room was right next door," Lugh said, waving his hand. "Besides, King Azanhein gave them to us."

"We could have salvaged them from the wreckage afterwards!"

Lugh leaned back. "Nihs," he said, "shut up, will you? I just lost an eye, all right? Could you give me a rest, just this once?"

Nihs sighed, the anger leaving his face. He sat down next to Lugh and pouted.

"I'm not happy about it," he said.

Slowly, Lugh laughed. "Good. You know I'm only happy when you're not happy."

Kyle heard a shout coming from his left. Before he could react, he was knocked off his feet by a massive body that bore him to the ground. He heard an unworldly shriek, and a massive, soul-wrenching pain exploded in his gut. His whole body was encased in fiery agony, and a fraction of a second later, he was swallowed by darkness.

Lugh, sitting across from Kyle, saw the bolt a moment before it struck, but could do nothing to prevent it. He had heard the high-pitched whine of its flight growing closer for a few seconds before that, but hadn't realized what he'd been hearing until it was too late.

Ring bow, he thought. *The twins.*

Time slowed as he watched the same realization dawn on Phundasa's face. The Orc dove sideways, bowling into Kyle and wrapping his thick arms around him, shielding him with his body.

The bolt plummeted out of the sky, a deadly streak of black. It struck Kyle and Phundasa, its momentum slamming them against the ground and causing them to roll a few feet in the undergrowth. Blood sprayed everywhere, and Lugh felt a few drops touch his cheek.

Meya screamed, and flew to where the two of them had landed. Nihs swore loudly and Lugh rose to his feet, ignoring his protesting body. He swayed, and almost lost his balance due to his missing eye, but willed himself not to fall over.

"Nihs, Deriahm!" he shouted. "Get Kyle!"

He himself ran over to Meya, who had crouched over Phundasa's inert body. As he drew closer, he saw at once that it was hopeless. The bolt had pierced Phundasa's chest, directly through the heart. His ribcage had shattered outwards, and blood was already pooling around him. Lugh knelt down and pulled back an eyelid. Phundasa's eyes, normally black, gold and glittering, were gray and dead.

Lugh's mind was on fire, and his head was swimming. He forced himself to think rationally. Phundasa was gone, but Kyle had been struck as well. He turned to Nihs, trying to drown out the sound of Meya's sobs.

"Nihs! Is Kyle alive?"

Nihs' face was white. "He's alive," he called back, "but dying."

Lugh nodded grimly. He looked back at Meya, and what he saw filled him with despair. She was sobbing hysterically, and her hands were on Phundasa's chest. Magic was cascading down her arms and into Phundasa's corpse—she was trying to heal him.

Lugh grabbed her by the shoulders and forced her away from Phundasa. She screamed, trying to fight him off.

"*Meya!*" Lugh shouted, "you need to help Kyle!"

She shook her head violently, trying to speak through her sobs. She reached out towards Phundasa. She didn't need to speak for Lugh to understand—she thought she could still save him.

"Meya," he repeated, "you can't. I'm sorry, but you can't. You're wasting your magic. You have enough left to save Kyle right now, but you won't if you keep doing this! Listen to me!"

Finally he got through to her, and she sat back, sobbing but no longer pouring magic into Phundasa. Lugh helped her to her feet and walked her over to Kyle, who was laying on his back, staring blankly into the sky. Deriahm was crouched over his body, infusing him with magic as Meya had been doing to Phundasa. Nihs stood at Deriahm's side, his hand clamped to his wrist, sharing his magic with him.

This time Lugh recognized the whine as soon as it reached his ears. He flew into a dash, knocking Meya over as a second bolt, this one blue, drilled into the ground where they'd been standing a moment before.

Lugh swore bitterly as his skull throbbed with pain. He leapt to his feet before helping Meya to hers.

"We have to get away from here!" he shouted to the others.

"How?" Nihs said. "They have a ring bow, there's no way we can outrun them!"

Lugh racked his brains desperately, trying to think through the stabbing pain in his forehead. He looked across at Meya, who was shaking with grief. It was time to see if what he'd expected of her was true.

"Meya," he said, "do you have enough magic left to escape all of us?"

"Are you *mad?*" Nihs shouted. "Of course she doesn't! And even if she did, she'd have none left to save Kyle by the end of it!"

Lugh ignored him. He put a hand on Meya's shoulder, who turned away, hugging herself tightly.

"Meya, please," he said. "We don't have any other options."

Meya started to cry again. "I don't…Phundasa…" she stammered.

Lugh followed her gaze back to Phundasa's corpse, and he understood. Part of him wanted to scream that it didn't matter, but another part of him knew that it did.

"We'll take him with us," he assured her.

"*Lugh!*" Nihs snarled.

"There's no time to argue, all right?" Lugh snapped back. "Deriahm, help me!"

The two of them ran over to Phundasa's body, and between them hoisted him off the ground. They carried him over to Meya, who now had Nihs riding on her shoulder and her hand clamped to Kyle's wrist. Lugh came close to her and she grabbed his arm with her other hand.

Meya started to radiate magic, and the air around her glowed white. Wind whipped around the group, and Lugh felt the ground beneath him start to fall away. The world was dissolved by blinding light, and then the magic picked them up and whisked them away in a soundless vortex.

Lacaster, standing on a hilltop several miles away, lowered his bow. His face registered both satisfaction and frustration.

"You got him, brother," Lian said, as a statement of fact rather than a question. Lacaster's aim was very good, and besides, what one of the brothers knew, so did the other. Lian sometimes wondered why this was the case. Perhaps the special link that all twins enjoyed was stronger between him and his brother than it was for normal folk. He could only guess as to why. Just one of the many fascinating and delicious questions that magic posed, he thought.

Lacaster rarely thought much about anything. He was a man who knew what he liked: first and foremost, the company of his brother. Beyond that, all he cared about was hitting his target, whether from a distance with his bow or up close with his twin swords. As long as it had a life that could be snuffed out, he cared not whether it was a monster or an animal or another person. He dimly understood that the killing of certain things was not correct or allowed, and only very grudgingly did he allow himself to be bound by these restrictions. It was for this reason that he was so overjoyed when a person like James Livaldi not only told him who to shoot, but offered to pay him for the pleasure.

Right now, he was upset. Yes, he had struck Kyle as Livaldi had asked, and had even managed to kill the Orc at the same time, but the party had escaped before he could pick off any of the others. He hadn't, strictly speaking, been told to do so, but he figured that the companions of the one they were told to capture were free game. His brother hadn't objected.

Shooting down the *Ayger* had been great fun. The ship that Livaldi had supplied them was swift, agile and deadly. Lacaster had come to think of it as much like his bow, only in a larger form. It was a shame the day had to end on such a disappointing note.

"I got him," he said to his brother, "but they escaped. And that stupid Orc ruined my shot."

Lian nodded. The botched shot was worrying. Lacaster's aim was perfect if his target wasn't moving, which was just as well—shooting someone with a ring bow without killing them was almost more impressive than the alternative. But the Orc's interference may as well have ruined everything. Kyle couldn't be allowed to die. "We have to find them as soon as possible," he said. "We must ask Livaldi where they've gone."

Lacaster couldn't agree more. He hated the thought of his quarry getting away.

They re-boarded their nameless ship, which they had touched down on a ridge several miles from the *Ayger's* crash site. Inside, Lacaster brooded while Lian contacted their employer.

Or, at least, tried to. Livaldi's schedule was busy, and he often refused to speak with the twins directly regardless. This was one of those cases; the voice that came to them through their communication crystal was that of Livaldi's manservant, Saul.

"I assume you have an update on our project?" he said, his voice, as always, stern and disapproving.

"We struck Kyle with the black arrow," Lian said, "and the Orc is dead. But the bishop escaped them before we could capture Kyle. We need Livaldi to tell us where they are now."

"You killed one of Kyle's companions?" Saul snapped. "Was this necessary?"

"Oh, yes," Lian said.

"The young master is very busy," Saul said, his voice cold. "He will contact you with Kyle's new location once his schedule permits. In the meantime, you are *not* to take any more innocent lives. May I remind you that other mercenaries can be hired to complete your work if you prove yourselves inadequate. Do I make myself clear?"

Lian pouted. "Yes," he said sullenly.

"Good," Saul said, in a voice that indicated it was not good at all. The crystal's glow faded before the twins could answer.

Lacaster keened in annoyance. "We have to wait? Why?"

Lian put a comforting hand on his brother's shoulder. "Don't worry, it won't be long now." He let his eyes drift back to the smoking wreckage of the *Ayger*. "They can't run away from us forever."

Lugh and the others spun through the ether, their world filled with light and speed. The experience was intense, but short-lived; it wasn't long before blotches of green ground appeared below them, and blue sky above them. A few seconds later, the magic vanished, and they all fell to the ground.

Lugh's head was pounding and he was feeling faint, but there was no time to waste. He jumped to his feet and spun around, scanning their landing site with his good eye. That was the problem with escaping—it was a kind of teleportation that sacrificed accuracy for distance. It could fling a party of people across a continent or even across the world, but with no control as to where they would land. A last resort used to escape death, but one that often resulted in death nonetheless.

Thankfully, wherever they had landed looked safe enough. The countryside was not dissimilar to where they had been flying before; Lugh could see mountains in the distance, but couldn't tell if these were the mountains of Eastia or some other range. He listened intently with his water ears and thought he heard the ocean both to the west and to the south of them, but this wasn't much help either. It was just as likely that they had ended up near the southern coast of Westia. Lugh fervently hoped this wasn't the case.

He joined the others, and was relieved to see that Meya was already bent over Kyle, pouring magic into him. Deriahm was with her, lending her whatever power he could. Nihs stood nearby, and caught Lugh's eye as he strode over.

"Looks like our luck hasn't completely run out," Nihs said. "That was a risky move."

"I know. Look, let's not talk about it. We're all here, aren't we? And can you get on the overhead and find out where 'here' is?"

Nihs didn't argue. He only nodded and walked to the top of a nearby hill before sitting down and unfolding his ears. Lugh had always been thankful for Nihs' ability to put his bickering aside when the situation called for it.

With that done, Lugh looked around for Phundasa's corpse. He saw it laying in the grass nearby, but couldn't bring himself to approach it. Instead, he made his way carefully over to Kyle, trying to keep his balance between his missing eye and throbbing brain.

Meya, her face grim and tear-streaked, sealed the wound around the arrow as best she could. Deriahm squatted next to her, his hand on her shoulder. Lugh lowered himself down on her other side.

"Need magic?" he asked quietly. Meya nodded. Lugh put his hand on her shoulder, and felt the slight draw of magic being pulled out of him through his arm. He looked back down at Kyle. The man had always been pale, but now he was positively ghostly. He was shivering slightly, and the sight of the black bolt sticking out of his stomach made Lugh sick to his.

"Can't get the arrow out?" he asked.

Meya shook her head. "It's resting on his heart. I wouldn't be able to keep him alive if we pulled it out now. We need to get him to a hospital or a church."

Lugh nodded. He resolved not to think about how that was going to happen before Nihs told them where they were.

A minute later, Nihs joined them, sitting across from them and folding his hands in his lap.

"Good news," he said, "we're still in Eastia. About a thousand miles southwest of where we were."

Lugh sighed with relief. It was better than he had dared hope. "Churches?" he asked.

"I spoke with a Kol from a village south of here. They have a church there."

"Can they come fetch us? We need something that can carry Kyle without hurting him. And we have Phundasa's body, too."

Nihs looked dubious, but sat down and entered the overhead once more. When he resurfaced, he said, "there's a man with a carriage who's willing to come get us. That's all, unfortunately."

Lugh put his hands on his hips, staring up at the sky. "It'll have to do," he said. "There a road nearby where we can meet him?"

"South of here," Nihs replied. "Meya, is it safe to move Kyle?"

Meya's expression was haunted. "It won't help," she said. "But neither will staying here."

"Good point. Deriahm, you help Meya. I'm going to get Phundasa's body."

He rose and made his way over to Phundasa's corpse. It was a sorry sight. There was a gaping wound in his chest, and his limbs were splayed everywhere. Lugh shook his head sadly. He'd barely had the chance to meet Phundasa, but had already come to consider him a friend. Not to mention that it was because of him that Lugh had only lost his eye to the *Ayger*, rather than his life.

Lugh removed his undershirt and bound it around Phundasa's chest. Now, at least, he looked somewhat more whole. Lugh arranged his limbs, and then grit his teeth and lifted the corpse off the ground. As he had expected, it was tremendously heavy. He rose to his feet with difficulty and rejoined the others.

The road was only a short way away from where they had landed, but by the time they reached it, Lugh's back was breaking and the sweat running down his face was making his wound sting. He gently set Phundasa down, as Deriahm had done with Kyle, while they waited for help to arrive.

It felt like an age before rescue came. A horse-drawn carriage came into view down the road, moving at a steady trot. The driver was a human man, likely in his thirties, with a tanned face and simple garb. He could have been from a completely different world as Lugh and his companions, and in a very real way, he was. Riding with him was a Kol who looked much like Nihs, though to be fair, many of the Kol looked alike from Lugh's point of view.

The man dismounted and shook Lugh's hand, introducing himself as Harlan and his companion as Rihn. His face was stern as he looked over their party, but all he said was, "We'll have to go at a walk with wounded on board. Going to take a few hours to get back. Your man going to hold on for that long?"

"I'll sit in the back with him," Meya said. "I'll keep him alive until we reach the church."

"I'll accompany you," Rihn said. "I have magic I can share."

"Thanks, both of you," Lugh said. "You've saved at least one life today."

Harlan grunted and helped them load Kyle into the back of the carriage. They wrapped Phundasa up in a canvas blanket and put him in the back. Lugh didn't envy being in Meya's position for the ride. The thought of keeping one friend alive with the body of a dead friend next to him was horrifying.

They set off, Meya and Rihn riding in the carriage, while Deriahm and Lugh, with Nihs on his shoulder, walked alongside it. The trip went well for the first hour, but not long after Lugh started lagging farther and farther behind. The pain in his head was piercing, and the healing Meya had performed on him had sapped him of his strength. He sat down at the side of the road, panting.

"You guys go on," he said, waving the others away. "I'll catch up with you later."

Nihs exchanged a look with the others. "I'll stay with you," he said. "This is no time for one of us to go off on their own."

Lugh nodded and sat back in the grass, letting his fatigue wash over him as the carriage rolled away. He hadn't had the time to process any of what had happened to them, and it looked like it would be a while before he had the chance. Nihs sat down next to him. There was silence for a few minutes while Lugh got his strength back.

"Lugh," Nihs said quietly, "we're in trouble. A lot of trouble."

"I know that, Nihs."

"What are we going to do now? We don't have a ship to get to Proks even if Kyle does survive."

Lugh rose to his feet and started walking. "I know that, Nihs," he said.

Nihs fell into stride beside him. "If those assassins come back, we're finished. Meya won't be able to escape us again so soon and we wouldn't be able to match them even *if* Phundasa and Kyle were there to fight."

Lugh stopped short. "I *know* that, Nihs!" he snapped, his voice shaking. "So what are we supposed to do? Abandon Kyle and run away? Wait for those assassins to find us and finish us off?"

"I never—"

"All we can do is stick together and help each other out. We've got a friend who's dying, and we need to get him safe. What's the point in worrying about what comes next?" He started walking again.

Nihs exploded. "You can't always drift through life telling yourself that everything's going to work out!" he shouted at Lugh's back. "One of us is already dead! Haven't you even *realized* that? What about Meya? Have you thought about what this will do to her?"

Lugh turned around. He fixed Nihs with a piercing glare from his good eye, though his vision was blurring.

"You think I haven't thought about that?" he said. "Think I don't know what she's going through?"

Nihs' anger burned away once he realized what Lugh had said. "I didn't mean—"

Lugh shook his head. "Just forget about it, all right?" He looked up at the sky, and the wind soothed the burning pain he was feeling on his face. "All I'm saying is, we have to keep going. We've never had it this bad, I know, but we can't give up. We owe it to the others. Especially Phundasa. Right?"

Nihs nodded, tight-lipped, and they resumed their trudge across the countryside.

The uninhabited brush that lined the road soon turned to farmland, which then gave way to Harlan's village. It was nestled alongside a hill, and was barely larger than the village in Donno at which they had stayed in before the raid on the goblin mine. At the top of the hill, overlooking the village, was the church.

They reached the stone pathway that led up the hillside and started to climb. Someone inside the church must have seen them approach, because they were less than halfway up the stairs when the doors opened and half-dozen clerics came out to meet them. Lugh almost cried with relief at the sight of their white robes.

The priests led him up the stairs, one of them already examining his cut face. There was a mixture of men and women, but they all wore identical white robes and all spoke with the same soft reassurance. They welcomed him into the church and asked after his well-being.

"What about the others?" was all Lugh wanted to know.

"Kyle will survive," one of the clerics said, "thanks to the efforts of Meya and bishop Abel. They've removed the arrow and sealed the wound, but he still hasn't awoken. Bishop Abel says that his soul is thin, and that it will take a while for him to recover. We were afraid that the arrow was cursed, but that doesn't seem to be the case."

Lugh breathed a sigh of relief. He had been worried about the arrow, as well. He wasn't too familiar with ring bows, and had hoped that the black arrow was just another ammo type he hadn't known about.

The inside of the church was decorated in muted tones. Candles burned in sconces all along the main chamber, and the air was thick and warm. At the end of the chamber, presiding over the space, was a statue of a slight, youthful man with curly hair, who was clothed in a robe similar to those worn by the clerics. His arms were spread in welcome, but he wore a somber, almost sad expression.

A female cleric approached them once they came inside. She shared a few hushed words with one of the other priests, and said,

"Your friends are in one of the back chambers with bishop Abel. I'll take you to them. Follow me."

Kyle's recovery room was a small chamber down in the left wing of the church; it was one of a number of rooms used to house the sick or the homeless. Lugh, with Nihs on his shoulder, stepped inside to find Meya, Deriahm, and an older man, who must have been bishop Abel, gathered around Kyle's bed. Kyle was still pale and shaking, but looked much better with his wounds dressed, his clothes swapped out for clean linens, and most importantly, without the ugly black bolt in his chest. They must have just finished treating him, as Meya and Abel both had blood on their hands and sleeves.

The three of them turned around when they heard Lugh and Nihs enter, their guide stepping in after them.

"How's he doing?" Lugh asked.

"He'll live," Meya said, wiping her forehead carefully on her arm. She was pale from magic overuse, and her whole body was trembling. "The worst is over. I only hope he wakes up soon. It'll be a long time before he's at full strength again."

"Right. How about Phundasa?"

The cleric who had brought them in cleared her throat. "Now that Kyle is stable, we can prepare his body for burial. I can take you to him," she said to Meya.

Meya opened her mouth to answer, but then turned back to look at Kyle.

"I shouldn't," she said. "They might need me here—"

"Kyle is safe for now," Abel said gently, laying a hand on her arm. "You have done more than enough, Meya. Go. Let us take care of him now."

Meya wiped her eyes again. She returned Abel's touch, and strode out of the room without another word, the other cleric following her.

Abel shut the door gently behind them. "Poor soul," he said, shaking his head. "Even when her heart is bursting with grief, she does not neglect her duties as a cleric. She refused to take rest, and lent us her magic all throughout the healing process." He turned his wrinkled gaze to Lugh and Nihs. "You must be the friends she spoke of. Lugh and Nihs, I believe?"

"That's right," Lugh said, shaking his hand. "You must be bishop Abel."

Abel, reaching up to shake Nihs' tiny hand, nodded. "I am the deacon of this church of Saint Marc," he said. "Rarely are we ever confronted with a situation this dire. I am glad you were able to reach us in time."

"Us, too." Lugh walked over to Kyle's bed. "Is he going to be alright?"

Abel nodded. "He was barely clinging to life when he came to us. If it hadn't been for Meya's magic he certainly would have died. But the danger passed once we combined our power to bring him strength, and removed the bolt. He is weak, and will remain so for some time yet, but he is safe." Abel examined Lugh's face. "But what of your own wounds, young one? They need looking after."

This comment brought Lugh's attention back to the pain coming from the left side of his face. He'd been rather successfully ignoring it up until now. He grinned as his head throbbed.

"Oh, I'll be alright," he said, since he knew it was the sort of thing he had to say. "I'll stick a patch over it and let it sort itself out."

Bishop Abel laughed. "Now that won't do. Come, I will have some of my clerics see to you."

An hour later, Lugh's head was freshly healed and bandaged, and he was enjoying a welcome relief from the pain that had been consuming the left side of his face. The clerics had mended everything they could, though they had confirmed Meya's diagnosis that his left eye was beyond saving. Lugh took the news with a strange ambivalence. He realized that he might be in shock, but decided to enjoy his good mood while it lasted rather than squander it.

He wandered around the church, taking his time to examine every last detail. The building wasn't very large, so even going slowly didn't take long. He walked to and fro, trying to get used to his reduced field of vision. His depth perception was off, and whenever his focus wavered he started bumping into things. He fought back his feelings of loss and panic by telling himself that it would just take time for him to adjust.

He paused at the statue of Saint Marc, looking up into its grave expression. The statue matched his gaze, and gave the impression of knowing exactly what was on his mind.

Lugh had enjoyed the services the church provided from time to time, but had never been one for the religious aspect of it. Now, though, he wouldn't mind having someone to talk to.

"Hey," he said. The statue didn't answer.

"Nihs was right, huh? We've never had it this bad. Lost my eye, lost my ship. And we all lost Phundasa."

Still no answer. Lugh looked away.

"You know, this is going to sound terrible, but part of me's glad it all went at once. I think that's what's keeping me from caring about the small stuff. Phundasa's what really matters here. I've got another eye, and, well, we can get another ship, but there was only one of him. Now I wish I'd had more time to get to know him. Really was a hero…saved my life and Kyle's."

Lugh frowned. "Kyle's going to blame himself for all this," he said, in sudden realization. "That's the kind of guy he is." He'd have to remember that for when Kyle woke up. There was a chance he'd do something stupid if Lugh left him to his own devices.

He sighed. The next little while was going to be tough, there was no doubt about it. But Lugh knew that they would pull through. He looked up at Saint Marc, and allowed himself to smile.

"I'm off to find Meya," he said. "She's the one who lost her best friend. She'll need all the help we can give her."

The statue didn't answer, but Lugh didn't mind. He patted Saint Marc's foot.

"Good talk," he said.

His meeting with Meya was a short one. He found her in one of the back rooms of the church, watching over Phundasa's body. It had been cleaned, clothed, and laid on a stone dais surrounded by votive candles. Meya was sitting by his side, looking not unlike a statue herself. She was sunk so deeply in grief that her head barely moved in recognition when Lugh came in. She responded to his words with kindness, but he could tell that what she really wanted was to be left alone. He excused himself a few minutes later and quietly shut the door behind him.

He ran into Deriahm in the corridor outside. The young *irushai* was waiting in the hallway, apparently for him, with his hands folded behind his back. He looked even more awkward and out-of-place than usual. Lugh felt a pang of sympathy for him. Deriahm hadn't been traveling with them for three days when all this happened.

"Hey there," he said. "How are you holding up?"

"I am well," Deriahm said shortly, clearly not wanting to talk about himself. There was a slight pause before he added, "I was wondering if I should meet with Miss Ilduetyr and offer my condolences."

Lugh looked back at the closed door. "I'll be honest," he said, "I think it's better that we leave her alone for now. I don't think she wants company at the moment. And you can call her Meya, by the way."

Deriahm nodded, not fully managing to hide his relief. He fell into stride beside Lugh as he made his way back to the central chamber. Lugh watched Deriahm out of the corner of his eye as they walked. He clearly had something on his mind, but was unable to voice it.

"I am sorry that I was of so little help in the attack," Deriahm said finally. "If I had been able to take action more quickly, I may have—"

"Don't you blame yourself," Lugh said, cutting him off. "The only people whose fault this is are the ones who attacked us, all right? Besides, it's not up to you to keep us all safe. That's why your dad left *you* with *us*."

Deriahm looked down at the floor, not answering. He did this rather often. Lugh thought he'd have to help break that habit, but now wasn't the time.

"Is there anything I can do?" Deriahm asked. "There must be some way in which I can contribute to the well-being of the group. Please, tell me if this is the case."

Lugh understood where Deriahm was coming from, but still didn't know what to say. "Honestly, if I knew what we should be doing right now I'd be doing it. I think that all we can do is wait for Kyle to get better…and Meya, too."

"Do you believe we are safe here?" Deriahm asked then. "I am concerned that our assailants will find a way to locate us."

Lugh had thought about this, too. It was impossible to trace where someone had teleported with escape magic, but the twins had been uncannily good at tracking down their party before. Lugh suspected there was some greater force at work here.

Their chances of survival if the twins found them again weren't good, especially with the party in its current state. Four adventurers against a sniper and a sage who were twins, a single deadly fighting unit. To make matters worse, Lugh was missing an eye and Meya was grief-stricken. Grief, and the fury that often came with it, could be powerful tools in combat—but not for someone whose magic was fueled by empathy and compassion.

He surfaced from his musings to answer Deriahm's question. "The twins have no way to track us here. But if they do, we'll just have to give them the best fight we can."

Deriahm looked at the floor again. "Yes," he said, "I suppose you are right."

They buried Phundasa the following day. The ceremony was a simple and private affair; the only attendants were Lugh, Meya, Nihs, Deriahm, and a few members of the church. None of them but Meya had known Phundasa for long enough to say more than a few words, and Meya was in no condition to speak, so the event passed largely in silence.

Once the burial was complete, Phundasa's grave was fitted with a dark blue headstone donated by the church. These headstones, imbued with an ancient magic, carried an enchantment that made the stone glow with a soft blue light as long as the one buried beneath them was remembered. The light preserved the stones, and turned graveyards around the world into places of beauty.

From that day onward, Meya spent her time grieving before his grave rather than inside the church. The nature or intensity of her grief, however, hadn't changed. Lugh was starting to worry about her. He didn't want to think of what would happen if she fell into depression.

Some good but completely unexpected news came the next day in the form of Deriahm. One of the clerics approached Lugh in the hallway and told him that the *irushai* wanted to see him in his room. Lugh, puzzled, made his way there to find Nihs already sitting on the bed, with Deriahm standing nearby looking nervous but excited. He closed the door after Lugh came in and locked it.

"What's up?" Lugh asked. "Why all the secrecy?"

Deriahm lifted his pack up onto the bed and rooted through it. "I beg your pardon, sir," he said, "but I have acquired something that may be of use should we be discovered by our assailants, and I thought it best to keep its existence as secret as possible."

Lugh was even more confused now. "What did you get? And how?"

"Following our conversation two days ago, I made the decision to contact my father Drunamoh with the lodestone and explain our situation to him. I reasoned that Kyle was in very real danger of being captured, and that it was necessary to enlist whatever aid we could. The result of my contact was this." He pulled from deep inside his pack a thick red scroll, sealed shut with black wax.

"An indictment!" Nihs exclaimed, astonished.

"Indeed," Deriahm said, giving him the scroll. "It was written by the supreme Judge of the Buorish court, and should thus be very potent."

Lugh had heard about the special kind of metamagic practiced by Buorish Judges, which centered on exposing and punishing the guilty, but he had never seen an indictment before. He could only guess how Nihs knew what one was supposed to look like.

"How does it work?" he asked, taking the scroll from Nihs. It was heavy, as if made of something more than paper and ink.

"It is a magically charged text which condemns the party guilty for the murder of Phundasa Bar Gnoshen," Deriahm explained. "The spell will only work against that party, but will provide us with significant assistance should they approach us again."

"This is great," said Lugh. "We might actually stand a chance against the twins if we use this! I don't know what favors your dad had to call in to get this, but he might have just saved our lives."

He handed the scroll back to Deriahm. "Why don't you hold on to it? It's your cavalry, so you should be the one to call it in."

"Thank you, sir," Deriahm said, tucking the scroll into a pouch by his hip. "It is my sincere hope that it will go unused." His tone of voice made it clear that this hope was as slight as it was sincere.

The following day brought no signs of danger with it, and neither did the one after that. The church, and the village around it, were peaceful and quiet.

Meya was doing better, although her mood was still highly variable. At times she was well enough to join them for meals and talk with them; at others she would lock herself in her room, or spend hours sitting beside Kyle in his sickroom or Phundasa in the cemetery. Her face, robbed of its usual calm smile, was tired and drawn.

One day, when Meya was in one of her better moods, Lugh decided to broach a certain topic with her. He found her standing in front of Saint Marc's statue, looking up into the marble face.

"Hey," he said, drawing up beside her.

"Oh. Hello, Lugh," she said. Her smile was strained, but it was there.

"You doing all right?" he asked.

She nodded silently.

Lugh himself looked up at Saint Marc. There was still something about the statue's expression that attracted the eye.

"I don't know a whole lot about the different Saints. What was it that Marc did?"

"He was a pilgrim," Meya answered. "He spent his life traveling around the world, healing people who had no church to go to. He was known for never slowing down or taking rest; he believed that it was every person's duty to use each scrap of energy they were given to accomplish as much as they could with their lives."

"Huh." The statue's sad expression had a little more context now.

Lugh gave Meya a sidelong look, gauging her mood. "I've been meaning to ask you," he said, "why have you been hiding the fact that you're a bishop?"

Meya glanced at him sharply. She searched his face, looking for a sign of malice. When she found none, her eyes drifted back to the statue.

"You found out?" she said.

"I always thought you were powerful for a healer. But I was only sure once the *Ayger* got attacked. Why hide that you're promoted?"

Meya sighed. "It's easier this way. People expect so much from healers. When they go to a church, or when a pilgrim shows up in town, they think all of their problems are going to melt away. And with bishops it's even worse. They expect you to be a miracle worker."

She shot Lugh a piercing gaze. "I'm powerful, but I'm not a miracle worker, Lugh. I was promoted while Das and I were traveling around the Orcish territories. I guess I'd been using my powers so much that they spilled over. But I didn't feel like I'd earned it. As a bishop, people wanted even more from me than before, and it broke my heart every time I had to tell them I couldn't help them. In the end it was easier to tell people I was just a regular cleric. It's become a habit since then."

Lugh nodded. "I thought it would be something like that. Well, I won't tell the others if you want to keep it secret. But I think Nihs is getting a little suspicious."

"It's all right," Meya said, turning her eyes to Saint Marc again. "I'll have to start being honest at some point."

Lugh laughed. "We wouldn't be adventurers if we each didn't have a secret or two to keep."

"No," Meya agreed, "I guess we wouldn't."

Kyle finally started stirring later that day. Though this was a small improvement over the way he'd been before, the change came as a relief to the rest of the party. Meya now spent more time in his room than before, as did bishop Abel, the two trying to coax him out of whatever state the arrow had put him in. Lugh paid them a visit the following morning to see if any progress had been made.

He found them sitting on either side of Kyle's bed, not currently infusing him with magic, but watching the play of expressions on his face. His unconsciousness now looked more like fitful sleep; his eyes were squeezed shut and he was tossing and turning.

Lugh walked over to the bed, shaking his head.

"I still don't understand," he said. "If that arrow wasn't cursed, then how come he's taking so long to wake up?"

"He was as close to dead as he could be when we brought him in," Meya said softly. "We poured a lot of magic into him to keep him alive. But I think you're right. There was something wrong with that arrow. We just can't figure out what it was."

The three of them watched Kyle in silence. Lugh felt sorry for him.

Poor guy hasn't been able to catch a break since he got here, he thought.

A moment later, Deriahm came bursting into the room. He was panting, and his usual reserved manner was gone. He had something clutched in his hand; it was a red scroll sealed with black wax, glowing with an angry red light that bathed the entire room. The scroll thrummed with energy, shaking in Deriahm's hand as if there were a creature inside struggling to be released.

"They have found us," Deriahm said.

Meya gasped, rising to her feet. "Is that what I think it is?" she said.

Lugh nodded. "An indictment. It's written against the assassins who killed Phundasa."

Meya's expression hardened once the realization struck her. Her red eyes glowed, and the corners of the room grew dark.

"Listen," Lugh said, afraid that her anger was going to make her foolhardy, "remember what happened in Rhian. We need to make sure everyone in the church keeps away from the windows so they won't get shot at. Deriahm, how long do we have?"

"A matter of minutes, or less. It is possible they are already within range."

"All right. Does anyone know where Nihs is?"

No one did. Lugh ground his teeth in frustration. "He'll turn up," he said, half to himself. "Let's focus on going through the building and telling everyone what's going on." He looked at Kyle's bed, then at the large, open window that was allowing sunlight to stream into the room.

"We can't wait for those guys here," he said, "but we can't leave Kyle here either. Can we move him? And is there anywhere safe we can put him?"

Bishop Abel had been watching the conversation in shock and concern. He rose, shaking, from his seat by the bed.

"There is a vault in the back of the church," he said. "But what is going on? Who has found you?"

"The guys who put a bolt through Kyle. They've been following us for a while. Meya escaped us the last time they attacked us, but it looks like they've found us again. I'm sorry. We didn't mean to bring our problems here."

Abel's expression was sympathetic, but his eyes also contained a righteous anger. "They wouldn't dare attack you here?"

"I'm afraid they might," Lugh said. "I don't think they're the kind of people who care about the rules."

"Good sirs and madam, we must make haste," Deriahm interjected.

"Right. Come on and help me with Kyle. Could you show us the way to the vault, bishop? And then please, warn everyone and get them somewhere safe. I don't want any of your deaths on my conscience."

Together, he and Deriahm moved Kyle to the vault Abel had mentioned. It wasn't the most secure of rooms, but at least it was windowless and only had one method of entry. It was a risky move, but their choices were limited. Lugh hoped that whatever it was that allowed the twins to pursue them wasn't accurate enough to pinpoint this room.

Word of the impending attack spread quickly throughout the church, and it wasn't long before Nihs emerged from one of the back rooms, scampering across the stone floor. He scurried up onto Lugh's shoulder and wasted no time in contributing his own thoughts about the situation.

"This is going to go very badly. You *do* realize that we're four regular adventurers planning to fight against two promoted assassins, don't you?"

"Do you have a better idea?"

"Almost anything would be. But I don't suppose we have any other options. Meya, you can't escape us again, can you?"

Meya shook her head while Lugh said, "even if she could, we tried that, and all they did was track us down again. And next time we might not be so lucky with where we land."

Nihs' expression was sour. "Hm. Then I suppose we'd better figure out our combat strategy."

"Right. First thing that happens, Deriahm uses his indictment. Then he and I go for the sniper while you two go for the sage."

Nihs nodded. Pitching physical and magical fighters against each other was a common tactic. It led to longer and less risky fights, since skirmishes between spellcasters and fighters didn't often last very long regardless of who won.

"The most important thing is to keep the twins from fighting as a unit," Nihs said. "We'll get overwhelmed if we each have to focus on two of them at once."

They assembled at the doors of the church, waiting for a sign of the twins. The indictment Deriahm wore at his side was still glowing, but all around them was peaceful and quiet. Lugh was uneasy. They were going into this blind, not knowing where their enemies were or what they were capable of. He hoped that the twins weren't sophisticated enough to have set a trap for them.

Thinking back, he realized that a part of him had known all along that they weren't safe inside the little church. Maybe it was the fact that the twins had found them after leaving Buoria, but he got the distinct impression that they would never be safe until those two were dead. He grit his teeth, and rubbed the linen dressing that concealed his shattered eye. *Well*, he thought, *it's us or them.*

A moment later, a bolt came screaming out of the sky, plummeting towards Meya. Lugh shouted a warning and she spun out of the way at the last moment. It drilled into the earth not a foot away from her.

Lugh swore and spun around. The twins were nowhere to be seen, not even from their viewpoint at the top of the hill. He looked at the bolt, and the angle at which it was sticking out of the ground.

"They're behind the church!" he shouted in realization. They sprinted to the back of the building, but just before they rounded the last corner Lugh had a sudden vision. He threw his arm out and bore the rest of the party backwards.

"No, no, wait, stop!"

Another bolt flew across their path, striking the corner they'd been rounding and gouging part of the wall. Bits of shrapnel struck Lugh's face, but he ignored them and bulled around the corner.

At the back of the building was the graveyard. It was small, but neat and well-kept, tended by bishop Abel's flock. Lugh hadn't been in the mood to notice much else on the day they had buried Phundasa, and he didn't have the time now. He skidded to a halt, and drew the composite weapon he'd gotten from Azanhein.

The twins were there, among the graves, and both of them had smiles on their faces. The sage was leaning against one of the larger tombstones, his loose clothing stirring in the slight breeze. As for the sniper…Lugh felt bile rising in his throat. He was standing *on* one of the tombstones, his legs spread for balance and his bow in his hands. The tombstone belonged to Phundasa.

Lugh heard Meya scream with rage when she saw this, and was quick enough to grab her wrist and stop her before she ran past him.

"It's what they want," he hissed at her, hoping the twins couldn't hear. "Keep a cool head, all right? The only way to get back at them is to win this fight."

The two assassins were smirking, though whether this was because of Meya or some private joke Lugh couldn't tell. The sage eased himself up from his reclining position.

"I'm glad you came out to see us," he said. "It's such a nice day, isn't it?"

The sniper sheathed his bow and jumped down from Phundasa's grave, drawing his twin swords smoothly. Lugh forced himself to keep calm, and struggled to keep both twins inside his limited field of vision.

"Who are you?" he said. "And why are you following us?"

The smiles broadened.

"I'm Lian," the sage said.

"I'm Lacaster," his brother said.

"Pleased to meet you," they said in unison.

"Real funny. You still haven't answered my other question."

"We told you before, didn't we?" Lian said. "All we want is Kyle. He's inside the church, isn't he? Won't you take us to him? Otherwise we'll have to go looking ourselves."

"Not so fast, friend. We haven't talked about what you did to Phundasa."

"The Orc?" Lacaster said. "It was his fault he died. I was aiming for Kyle, and he got in my way. And now *you're* in my way."

Lacaster was circling around to the left side of the group. He was getting dangerously close to Lugh's blind spot, so Lugh felt this was as good a time as any to dispense with the formalities.

"I think we've just about run out of things to say to each other," he said. He slid into a lower stance and leveled his sword at Lian, who seemed to be the leader of the two. "If you want Kyle, you'll have to get through us. Simple as that."

The air between the two parties crackled with hostility as Lian smiled. "With pleasure," he said.

Lacaster leapt, blades flashing in the air. But before he could reach them, Deriahm dashed forward to meet him, the indictment in his hands. He threw the scroll forwards and it unraveled in the air, its seal broken. As it came open, it exploded into a roiling, red and black mass of smoke and lightning, blowing Lacaster backwards and consuming a large part of the graveyard in the process.

Stunned, they all watched as the smoke twisted around on itself, coalescing into a solid form. Threads of black ink wrapped around the smoke like chains, binding it together. An oblong form emerged, which grew legs, arms, and finally a head. Lugh heard Meya gasp beside him.

Phundasa the Orc stood before them, larger and more threatening than he had ever been in life. A shade made of smoke and ink, his form shifted and wavered, yet it was undoubtedly Phundasa, and there was something terrifying and real about his presence. Red light spilled from where his eyes should have been, and when he opened his mouth to emit an unearthly roar, more light escaped from between his teeth.

The shade of Phundasa charged without wasting a single moment more. It bore down on Lacaster, who barely managed to vault to his feet before two huge fists smashed into where he'd been lying. The shade chased after him, punching over and over again with no regard for its own safety. Lacaster's twin blades came up to meet the fists, and though they cut away pieces of the phantom with each block, they did nothing to deter its assault.

There was a massive thunderclap; a lightning bolt sizzled through the air and struck the shade in the back, carving a hole in the smoke. For a second it looked as though the shade might fall apart, but then the smoke billowed back into place and it turned, its wrathful gaze now fixated on Lian. He was floating a few inches off the ground, swathed in magic, already preparing another spell. The shade charged after him, and Lian was forced to vent his magic and teleport further away.

Lugh dashed forward, tapping Deriahm on the arm as he passed.

"Come on!" he said. "Lacaster's ours, remember?"

He didn't wait to see if Deriahm had heard; he couldn't give Lacaster the time to rally and start harassing the shade. Lugh had no idea how much damage the indictment could suffer before dissipating, but knew that it wouldn't be infinite.

He ran across the uneven ground, vaulted over a tombstone and brought his sword down hard. Lacaster lifted his own blade to parry, and immediately followed with a cut aimed at Lugh's stomach. Lugh barely had enough time to block it, and the impact sent him reeling.

Deriahm advanced beside him, shield raised. Lacaster circled him, weighing his new target. He lashed out and made a few cuts, which Deriahm blocked—but Lugh could tell he wouldn't be able to hold Lacaster off for very long.

Lugh dashed forward and cut again, making sure to keep Deriahm on his blind left side. He and Lacaster shared a few blows; Lugh grit his teeth in concentration and Lacaster grinned. Deriahm lowered his guard and struck out with his longsword, and soon Lacaster's arms were a blur about his body, parrying and striking back against two assailants.

Even two-on-one, their fight was evenly matched. Lacaster struck incredibly quickly and with surprising power. It was something that everyone forgot about archers: nothing built upper body strength like learning to draw a ring bow.

They danced through the graveyard, Lacaster leaping to and fro. Lugh and Deriahm's swords flashed as they struck again and again, trying to get through his defenses. Lugh was terribly grateful to have Deriahm beside him. It was his first battle with only one eye, and if Lacaster had been able to exploit this weakness Lugh wouldn't have lasted a second.

Outside of the graveyard's boundaries, a very different fight was taking place. Nihs, Meya, and the shade of Phundasa were harrying Lian, forcing him away from his brother. It was tough going. Even though they had the shade on their side, they had to be careful. Lian was obviously extremely powerful, and their advantage of numbers would mean nothing if they got caught in one of his magic blasts. He was a sky sage, a promoted mage who specialized in the elements of wind, ice and lightning. Fighting him was like fighting a storm; he was swift and unpredictable, melting into immateriality and reappearing farther away when threatened. The bolts of lightning he fired were incredibly strong and extremely hard to dodge or deflect.

The shade pursued him with mindless persistence, sprinting after him and trying to crush him with its powerful fists. Lian could avoid it easily, but it threw off his rhythm, forcing him to act defensively where otherwise he'd be planting his feet and gathering huge amounts of magic.

Meya and Nihs watched him carefully, controlling the distance between them. Meya was using the staff that Azanhein had given her, though Nihs hadn't donned his sagecloak. They lashed out with magic whenever they got the chance, and had grazed Lian's soul shield a handful of times, but more often than not he was able to avoid their attacks and their energy was wasted.

Lian teleported to the top of a hill and crouched down. The sky grew dark as he channeled magic out of the air. The spirit of Phundasa sprinted up the hill, roaring, but Lian blew it backwards with a blast of wind and ice.

Meya, shouting, ran after Lian, firing a blast of hurting magic at him. Lian deflected it, and it flew off into the empty sky. He brought his palm forward and shot a bolt of lightning. Meya blocked it with a shield of energy, though she could feel her magic being burned away by the hit.

Lian made a claw with his hand and raked it upwards. Both Meya and Nihs were forced to leap sideways as a spiky mass of ice erupted from where they'd been standing. Lian took the opportunity to weave more magic. Clouds twisted in the sky above him and the temperature dropped. He was stirring up the air, creating a storm that would grant him more power. Meya and Nihs saw this and assaulted him with magic, trying to force him to stop. He ignored their attacks for a moment, allowing them to fizzle against his soul shield, then finally teleported away, laughing. His laughter chilled the heart. It was childish and carefree, letting everyone know that its owner saw all of this as a game.

Meanwhile, Lugh, Deriahm, and Lacaster were fighting full bore. Sparks flew through the air, and ill-calculated blows tore up clods of earth and took chips off of tombstones. They wove all throughout the graveyard, giving and taking ground equally but not managing to scratch each other.

Individually, Lugh and Deriahm would not have been a match for Lacaster, but together they were just enough to keep him fighting defensively. Lacaster couldn't bear down on his target as ruthlessly as he normally would, and since he carried no shield, it took effort to keep his defense up.

But Lugh was worried. The battle was quickly becoming a question of who would run out of energy and start making mistakes first, and he was afraid that that person would be him. Deriahm was heavily armored and could afford to make a few blunders, but Lugh had always relied on his agility and precision to keep out of trouble, and these had both suffered as a result of his injury.

We've got to find a way to mix this up.

He risked a few glances in Meya's direction. She and Nihs were having a hard time with Lian, even with the indictment on their side. The hills were dark and flashing with magic. Lugh couldn't see exactly what was happening, and hoped that it wasn't the same thing that was happening with them and Lacaster.

He blocked Lacaster's next blow and ended up shoulder-to-shoulder with Deriahm. He leaned in close and hissed, "circle left!"

Deriahm probably didn't understand, but he obeyed nonetheless. Carefully they circled Lacaster until he was the one with his back to the other fight. Now Lugh could watch what was going on with the others. He saw Lian blow Phundasa's shade back with a wall of ice, and it occurred to him how little the spirit was contributing to the fight with the sage. It was only enough to engage Lian, not seriously threaten him. Lugh thought about how much trouble Lacaster had had with the spirit, and realized that that was the key. Meya and Nihs would have a hard time holding off Lian on their own, but if they could get the phantom to attack Lacaster, they might stand a chance of defeating him.

There was a problem. As far as Lugh understood it, there was no way of controlling what the phantom did. It attacked whatever it saw first, or whatever drew its attention.

Lugh fought alongside Deriahm, warding off Lacaster's blows while trying to find an opportunity to talk to him.

"Force him back," he managed to say, hoping his voice wouldn't carry to their opponent. "Get Phundasa after him."

Deriahm gave an imperceptible nod, and Lugh was flooded with relief. The two redoubled their efforts, trying to force Lacaster outside of the graveyard and toward his twin. Whenever he leapt to the side, Lugh and Deriahm followed him, corralling him. It was tough going. Even though Lacaster didn't realize what they were doing, he was an agile fighter who was as likely to slip under attacks as he was to back away from them. It went well until they got to the boundary of the graveyard, when Lacaster suddenly sprang to the side, twisted away from Lugh's sword, and ended up behind him and Deriahm. Lugh took the opportunity to vault over the fence, and Deriahm followed. Lacaster grinned in boyish confusion when he saw what they were doing. He paced for a moment, then sheathed his swords and started to skip backwards.

Lugh swore. "He's drawing his bow!" he shouted at Deriahm. *This is bad.* If Lacaster got out of range, he could rain arrows down on the two of them with impunity. Their only option at that point would be to chase after him.

Deriahm pointed his sword at Lian. A fireball grew in his fist and skimmed down the length of the blade. Lacaster saw it coming and danced out of the way, but also stopped backing up, leaving his bow half-drawn. Lugh could practically see Lacaster's brain working. He hadn't known that Deriahm could use magic, and was now wondering how powerful he was. His bow had a greater range than any spell, but if he had to dodge magic all while getting to that range it wouldn't be worth the effort.

Deriahm started to draw magic again. Lacaster eyed him, still smiling, and for a second Lugh was afraid he'd follow through. But then he sheathed his bow and sprinted forwards, drawing his swords. He launched himself into the air and Deriahm's fireball flew underneath him. Lugh braced himself for the impact, but was still thrown backwards when Lacaster cleared the fence and slammed into him. A flurry of blows knocked him off his feet, and he parried desperately as Lacaster bore down on him, blades raking across his soul shield. Deriahm came up from behind and Lacaster was forced to jump away. Lugh sprang to his feet and wheeled around just in time to parry Lacaster's next blow.

They were closer to the others now. Lugh could feel the chill wind stirred by Lian's magic and hear his companions' shouts. He could see the phantom chasing after Lian, but had no idea how they were going to draw its attention.

Lacaster paced, spinning his twin swords in his hands. He was panting, gathering up his energy before the three of them clashed again. Lugh saw that his main focus was on Deriahm, who was drawing magic again. Lugh groaned inwardly. What was Deriahm thinking? His magic had served its purpose before, but it wasn't strong enough to seriously threaten Lacaster. He would just end up wasting energy, or worse, making Lacaster realize how little he had to worry about the *irushai*'s powers.

Deriahm launched the spell before Lugh could stop him. Lacaster had been ready to dodge it, but it wasn't necessary. The spell skimmed by him on his right, making him eye Deriahm in amused confusion.

"What was that?" he said. "Some kind of joke?"

Lugh shrugged. He was forcing himself to look at Lacaster and not over his shoulder. "Maybe," he said. "I don't know. The Buors have a strange sense of humor."

That made Lacaster pause. His eyes narrowed, and he locked gazes with Lugh. "What are you talking about?" he snapped. His tone was petulant, as if he were a child who knew that adults were making a joke at his expense.

It was Lugh's turn to grin. "Come on," he said, "let's forget about it. Deriahm missed, all right? Now are we fighting or what?"

Lacaster gripped his swords, clearly upset. He sank into a combat stance and started to advance, then a moment later realized what was going on and spun around.

He was too late. The phantom, which had been struck by Deriahm's spell, had wheeled around and caught sight of Lacaster's back. It charged down the hill, bellowing, winding up a massive punch. Lacaster turned just as the blow landed, and there was a sickening crunch as the fist collided with his shoulder. A barely perceptible blue light that had been surrounding Lacaster broke apart, with the faint sound of glass shattering far in the distance. Lugh's heart soared: the blow from Phundasa had broken through Lacaster's soul shield.

Lacaster was blown towards Lugh, who gripped his sword in both hands and dealt a blow to his chest. Lacaster, now unprotected, squealed in pain as the blade sheared through his armor and into his skin. He fell off the side and then sprang to his feet, his face red with rage and pain. He lunged at Lugh, but was intercepted by the spirit, who had found a target and was now attacking relentlessly. Lacaster shrieked in anger and cut at the spirit, snapping apart the tendons of ink that held it together.

Lugh and Deriahm circled around and struck at him, trying to keep him from damaging the spirit, but rage had given Lacaster strength. He dodged away from their blows, not bothering to strike back at them but instead targeting the spirit. Parts of it were now in tatters, and smoke was leaking out of its frame—it was clear that the enchantment was almost spent. Worse, it was still bulling forward, forcing Lacaster backwards and crowding Lugh and Deriahm out of the fight.

"*Come on!*" Lugh shouted, partially to Deriahm and partially to himself. He tried pushing the offensive, but Lacaster was flailing around angrily, making any approach dangerous. He couldn't see where Deriahm was or what he was doing.

Suddenly Deriahm came into view, charging headlong at Lacaster. His armored body smashed into the sniper, knocking him off balance. Lacaster lashed out and landed a flurry of blows, but he was not strong enough to break through Deriahm's heavy armor. Deriahm clung to him, trying to pin him down.

The spirit, growling, approached the struggling couple and threw a hook punch at Lacaster. The blow struck home; he was knocked out of Deriahm's arms and spun away, losing his grip on one of his swords.

Lacaster desperately tried to right himself as the phantom charged after him. He raised his remaining sword just in time to plunge it into the spirit's chest, but this did nothing to stop the mighty blow it had been winding up. Lugh heard Lacaster's ribs crack as he was flattened against the ground. The spirit landed on top of him, and brought back both arms for an overhead strike.

Lacaster shrieked, seeing what was coming but having no way to defend himself from it. He threw his hands out in front of him, and for a brief moment Lugh felt pity for him.

"No! No!" he screamed. "Brother, help me!"

The fists descended. There was an appalling cracking noise, and

Lacaster's voice cut off. His arms dropped to his sides and his body went limp.

Lugh heard an agonized wail coming from the hilltop. It was a mindless scream of pain and loss, modulated first with fear and sadness, and then with a burning rage and the promise of revenge.

The battle with Lian had been tense ever since the shade's departure. No longer having to flee from its relentless offense, Lian had been able to plant his feet and channel magic freely, feeding energy into the storm he was brewing. A wide area around him was now darkened by a canopy of cloud, and beset by icy wind. The weather grew worse, and Meya and Nihs' power was sapped just as Lian grew stronger. Nihs couldn't match his level of strength, and offensive magic wasn't Meya's forte. Once the shade stopped hounding him, it was all they could do to keep Lian distracted and stay out of the way of his deadly magic.

Lian turned on the spot, and a vortex of icy particles descended from the clouds above. They whipped around him faster and faster, until his form was completely concealed inside the blizzard. Nihs and Meya backed far away, staying outside of the storm's range. Meya leaned on her staff, gripping it with both hands. Even at this distance from Lian, her breath was visible in the summer air and her body was shaking. Lian's ice magic wore on the soul, and Meya felt close to the limit of her power. She grit her teeth in anger. She couldn't lose, not against *him.*

Nihs was nearby, though if anything he was faring worse than Meya. The green color was leaching out of his skin, as happened to the Kol when they used too much magic. He was panting heavily, and his ears were unraveled and hanging by his sides.

Breaks in the blizzard started to appear. Meya crouched, ready to sprint, watching it intently. Finally the spell dissipated, and Lian's shape emerged. Both she and Nihs dashed forwards, spells in their hands. But Lian turned, and they saw too late that he was holding an orb of energy close to his chest—the power of the blizzard, appropriated into a new spell.

Lian threw his hands outwards, and shards of ice exploded in every direction. Meya braced herself and put all of her energy into her staff. The ice shards broke and shattered against her magical shield, and though the impact jarred her she kept to her feet. Nihs wasn't so lucky; Meya heard the dreadful sound of his soul shield breaking beside her.

Lian, smiling broadly at the sight of their distress, followed up his attack with a bolt of lightning aimed at Nihs. The little Kol was now so weak he couldn't even react, but Meya leapt in front of him and absorbed the blow. Lian laughed out loud and sustained the spell, bearing down on her, turning the air between them into a mass of electricity. Meya strained against him, though she could feel her soul shield burning away under the assault. She couldn't move or Nihs would get killed, but neither would she be able to hold out for more than a few seconds.

Suddenly, Lian's attack started to falter, and his attention was taken up by something behind her. She couldn't risk turning around, so she didn't see the shade of Phundasa bearing Lacaster to the ground. But she heard his desperate cry for help, and then the crack as his skull was smashed in by the phantom.

Lian screamed. It sounded like no noise that a human should have been able to make. It would have been heart-wrenching if Meya hadn't been feeling a sick satisfaction: Lian was the leader of the twins, but Lacaster had been the one to fire the arrow that killed Phundasa. The joy she felt at his death made her feel guilty, but it also filled her with a new resolve. One of the twins was dead, and in a moment Lian would have to fight all of them at once. Victory was within their grasp.

Lian was still screaming, his whole body shaking. Magic was roiling around him; his emotions were making it go wild. In this state he was dangerous and unpredictable, but he was also vulnerable, and Meya now felt stronger than she ever had before.

Shrieking, Lian flew towards his fallen brother, his blue cloak streaming out behind him. Meya ran into his path and shot a blast of hurting magic. He staggered, confused, then saw her standing in front of him, staff raised, blocking his path to his brother. He gathered up an enormous amount of magic and launched twin bolts of lightning from both hands. Meya slipped past them, closed the distance to Lian, and swung her staff, striking him in the chest. Lian lost his footing, then broke his fall and flipped backwards. He fired a beam of ice at Meya, who blocked it and answered with another blast of hurting magic. Lian teleported out of the way, reappearing in the distance. At first, Meya couldn't tell why he did it; then she heard the footfalls behind her and Phundasa's ghost barreled past her.

Her heart caught in her throat, as it did every time she saw the shade. In a way the indictment felt like a cruel joke, but she knew that they wouldn't have stood a chance against the twins without it.

Lugh and Deriahm drew up beside her. Overcome with relief, she allowed herself to lean against Lugh for support.

"How's it going?" he asked mildly.

Meya laughed despite herself. "Finally decided to come help, have you?"

Lugh grinned thinly and raised his sword.

"Come on," he said, "let's finish this. For Phundasa?"

"For Phundasa," Meya agreed.

The shade had caught up with Lian, who was now blasting it with magic in a blind fury. The phantom was in tatters, and often was no longer recognizable as Phundasa, but it still held together. Meya, Lugh, and Deriahm dashed across the field to join it, leaving Nihs recuperating on the hilltop.

Lugh got there first. He leapt at Lian and struck down; the sage spun out of the way and answered with lightning. Deriahm came between them and took the blow on his shield. Meya ran around Phundasa's other side and fired hurting magic. Lian screamed in frustration and teleported away. Before they could see where he had gone, the ground underneath them froze over, and tendrils of ice grasped at their feet, binding them in place. Meya cried in frustration and hacked at the ice around her with her staff—she had no magic that could affect the physical world. Lugh and Deriahm broke free, and she waved them away when they came to help her.

"Don't worry about me!" she shouted. "Get Lian!"

After they ran off, Meya took a moment to draw on her last reserves of strength. She braced her staff against the ground and pulled herself upwards. Finally, the ice cracked and gave way. She turned, scanning the hills, and found Lian being attacked by Lugh and Deriahm.

She ran after them, and to her surprise was joined by Nihs along the way. He was still pale, but his face was set in determination. Meya closed the distance between them, and Nihs, getting the hint, jumped up onto her back before climbing to her shoulder.

Together, they reached Lian. He was no longer thinking straight, and was blasting magic at anything that got close to him. Lugh and Deriahm were dancing around him, trying to find a safe opening. The phantom, which was now missing most of one leg, was limping after him, its attacks finally slowing down. Meya and Nihs stopped at a distance to Lian and started firing magic at him, no longer worrying about technique. He didn't even try to avoid their attacks, and let his soul shield absorb every blow.

Meya knew it was over. Casting spells drained one's soul shield, but Lian was forced to use magic to keep Lugh, Deriahm, and the phantom at bay. With Meya and Nihs attacking his defenses from a distance, he wouldn't be able to last long. He was clearly aware of this, and his expression grew more enraged the worse his situation became.

Finally he teleported again, this time only a dozen yards backwards. Meya felt him building up a great mass of magic. The air turned pitch black and the ground shook. The wind picked up, and a spiral of fog and debris started to build up around Lian. Meya gasped. She'd only ever heard of spells like this, but had never seen one performed.

The funnel kept growing, swelling in size and pulling more of the earth and air into it. Soon it was a full-fledged twister, and they all fell back as it began to advance slowly but inexorably. Meya was frightened. All of Lian's fear and anger had been given shape, and the result was terrifying. The tornado roared as it moved toward them, trying to pull them in to be destroyed.

They retreated further and further back, struggling to keep out of the tornado's suction. Meya had no idea how they were going to fight against it. She couldn't see Lian inside the twister, and didn't want to risk slowing down to cast a spell.

A figure ran directly at the twister. At first Meya was dismayed, until she saw that it was the remains of the indictment, charging full bore into the storm, trailing tatters of ink and smoke behind it. It spread its arms and then clamped them together, grabbing hold of something at the center of the tornado. For a moment, it was lost inside the swirling cloud of debris. Meya thought she saw it coming apart, its form finally dissolving into nothingness. But as the last threads of ink snapped, the red core of the phantom glowed. As the magic binding it together faded, the spirit exploded violently, venting all of its energy in one final blast.

Inside the tornado, Lian screamed. The storm faltered and then dissipated as he was thrown dozens of feet away, his soul shield falling in shards around him. His limbs flailed, but he couldn't right himself before he fell. He slammed down on his back, bounced, and then rolled to a stop in the dirt.

Meya and the others converged on him, warily at first. But it soon became clear that Lian had nothing left to fight them with. His clothing was in tatters, and his whole body was bruised and cut. He was crawling, pulling himself slowly along the ground, spitting blood from his mouth.

They gathered around him. He rolled onto his back, and shot all of them a gaze of pure hatred. For a moment he said nothing, grinding his teeth together in pain and trying to take control of his shaking body.

"I hate you," he spat then. "I hate you! I hate you, I hate you—"

"Meya?" Lugh said. "I think this one's you."

Meya nodded, her mind numb. She leveled her staff at Lian's chest, and red light started to build up between the two prongs. Lian was still shouting, working himself up into a childish tantrum.

"*IhateyouIhateyou—*"

"Saints forgive me," Meya said.

There was a flash of red, and Lian's voice cut off. His body stopped convulsing, and then collapsed gently to the ground.

All at once, the world was silent. No one in the party moved or spoke a word. The moment stretched on and on. Meya still had her staff pointed at Lian's limp form; Nihs had climbed onto Lugh's shoulder and was watching silently. Deriahm stood on Lugh's other side, sword point stuck in the ground.

Finally Lugh folded his arms.

"Well," he said quietly, "I guess that's that. We did it."

Meya barely heard him. Her vision was becoming cloudy, and waves of fatigue were washing over her. She saw Phundasa's tattered spirit charging into the tornado, exploding into a million pieces in her mind's eye. She heard Lugh ask her a question, but couldn't hear what it was. He put a hand on her shoulder, and suddenly she sank to her knees and cried until there were no tears left in her body.

Bishop Abel's face blanched when he saw the weary and bruised party re-enter the church.

"By the Saints," he said. "Are you all right?"

"We're alive," Lugh said, "which is more than I can say for the other guys. Sorry, Bishop, we might have torn up your graveyard a little bit. The townsfolk won't be happy about that."

Abel shook his head. "Never mind that. Is it safe for everyone to come out?"

Lugh nodded. "We got the guys who were after us. We should be safe now."

"Their bodies will need taking care of," Nihs said from Lugh's shoulder. "We can hardly leave them where they are."

"I will inform the clergy that the danger has passed," Abel said. "We will arrange to have the bodies dealt with. But first, let us look to your wounds."

As intense as the battle had been, they had gotten off without any serious harm. Soon, normal activity within the church had resumed, and the bodies of Lian and Lacaster were brought inside. The shade's work had rendered Lacaster unrecognizable, but Lian's body was mostly intact. The clerics laid them down side by side and started preparing them for burial. The party, along with Bishop Abel, came in to watch the process.

"There was something wrong with those two," Lugh said, eyes on Lian's blank face. "I've never met anyone who acted the way they did."

"No two souls are entirely alike," Bishop Abel said, "and sometimes, through defects of birth, the soul can be twisted as can the body and mind.

These twins were clearly the product of a strange birth. Perhaps their death was a kindness."

"You might be right," Lugh said. "They shouldn't have been running around loose, that's for sure. Whoever hired them has got a sick sense of humor."

Dr. James Livaldi, president and CEO of Maida Weapons, Inc., had gotten an early start to his day. At least, anyone who saw him sitting in his office an hour before sunrise would have assumed as much. He was steadily working his way through the mountains of paperwork that reached his desk every single day. A steaming mug of coffee sat on the desk beside him. Even though it was so incredibly early, it wasn't his first or even his second for the day.

The door to his office opened, and his manservant, Saul, slid quietly into the room. He was carrying an ornate wooden tray laden with a sumptuous breakfast. Carefully, he glided across the office floor, found a vacant spot on Livaldi's desk, and set the tray down.

"Good morning, sir," he said, folding his gloved hands in front of him. "I anticipated that you had not eaten, so I took the liberty of having breakfast prepared."

Livaldi's eyes hadn't moved from the paperwork in front of him. "It's hardly morning, yet, Saul," he said, though he reached out absently and took a hot buttered roll.

"Has the young master been up all night?" Saul asked.

"The young master has a great number of responsibilities, and cannot always share in the luxuries enjoyed by those who do not," Livaldi said. He yawned, something he normally only ever did when alone, and took another sip of coffee.

Saul knew that no ground would be given on this subject, so he mentally moved to the next item on his list. He drew a slim black notebook from the side of the tray and flipped it open.

"I have some issues that require your attention. May I begin?"

Livaldi leaned back in his chair. "All right, then," he said, "let's hear them."

"Very well." Saul cleared his throat. "Don Gomes released a statement recently which..."

James listened with disinterest as the litany went on, though anyone who knew him personally would know that not a single word of it escaped him. He picked away at his breakfast while Saul meticulously addressed each item on his list. By the time Saul had finished, James was drumming his fingers on his desk, his eyes fixated on some point in the distance. He reached for his coffee again, and found the cup empty. He rose from his desk and went to draw another one from his favorite machine.

"You know, Saul," he said, his eyes on the steaming liquid pouring from the machine, "sometimes I wonder what the world would be like if people like me didn't have to concern ourselves with problems like these. If I had just one employee whom I trusted enough to deal with these issues, I might actually have the chance to get something productive done."

He sipped at his coffee. "Don Gomes can wait. He's merely filling the world with unnecessary noise. The factory can follow normal cleanup procedure. Tell the shareholders that I refuse to comment on the falling stock. They'll see their precious returns soon enough." He took another sip. "As for the progress on the Albatross...how long has it been since my last workplace inspection?"

James heard the flip of notebook pages. "A month and a half ago, sir," Saul said.

"I'd say we're about due for one, then, aren't we? Perhaps I'll pay them a visit later today and strike some fear into them. But before we get to that," he added, sitting back down behind his desk and folding his fingers on top of it, "tell me about our other project. Have the twins reported back?"

Saul's face was always severe, but at the mention of the twins his lips tightened all the more. He flipped to a different page of his notebook.

"I...do not know where they are, sir," he said. "After you provided them with Kyle's new location, I received one more transmission from them claiming that they were in pursuit. Since then, their ship has not moved, and I have not heard from them again."

Livaldi sat at his desk, unmoving. For a moment he said nothing.

"It is possible that they have gone rogue—" Saul began.

"No. Lian and Lacaster wouldn't let a quarry escape them once they had given chase. Either they've run into complications with Kyle's capture…or, somehow, he's managed to overpower them."

"The twins reported previously that Kyle's party had grown once more," Saul reminded him. "A Buorish soldier was traveling with them."

Livaldi tilted his head pensively. "Could it be that those two fools attacked them and were defeated?" He gave a small laugh. "What a captivating end to their existence that would be. No matter. At the very least they've struck Kyle with the black arrow. I was becoming concerned that they wouldn't be able to manage even that."

"Yes, sir."

"We'll wait for a few days longer. If they don't respond, arrange to have their ship recovered."

"Yes, sir."

Livaldi drained the rest of his coffee and checked his watch.

"Excellent. In two hours' time we're paying a visit to the weapons development laboratory. They're not to know this. After all, our engineers always appreciate surprises, don't they?"

"Of course, sir."

James smiled thinly. "You're dismissed, Saul."

Saul bowed shortly and turned to leave. On the elevator ride down from Livaldi's office, he reflected on the young master's mood. James hadn't been very upset to hear about the twins' absence; on the contrary, the news had seemed to amuse him. Saul shifted his feet uncomfortably. James had always been prone to harshness, but it wasn't like him to act so unfeeling, even when talking about people such as the twins. Then again, it wasn't like him to deal with people such as the twins in the first place. Saul had felt all along that their employment had been a mistake, but had refrained from commenting. James was nearly impossible to sway once his mind was made up. It was a trait that he shared with his late father, and his father before him.

Saul was worried nonetheless. He was starting to believe that this whole Kyle Campbell business had gotten out of hand. James was pursuing it with a directness and callousness that Saul had never seen before. It was as if the young master had been caught up in a fever and was no longer thinking straight—and straight thinking had always been Livaldi's strength. He was sleeping less and less, and the strain was showing itself in the lines on James' face. Not for the first time, Saul wished he could take away that damned coffee machine and smash it to pieces.

But he would do no such thing. Saul had served the Livaldi family his entire life, and he knew that his place was at James' side, wherever that happened to lead him. He could only hope that it was somewhere good.

Kyle slept, but he didn't rest.

His mind was a mire of jumbled senses. He floated through a confusion of colors, sounds, and impressions, half-formed thoughts and memories that merged together and split apart before he could make sense of them. People that Kyle had known on Earth invaded scenes from Loria, and monsters and magical happenstance interrupted memories of Earth.

Above all else, the common thread that bound all of the dreams together was the pain. It was a deep, familiar ache that sat at the very center of Kyle's being. It was such an integral part of him that he found he could ignore it, as he could ignore the beating of his own heart. But every once in a while, it would float to the surface and eclipse everything else in Kyle's mind. These times were the worst of all.

The memories faded and shifted. Kyle found himself back on Earth.

After the summer with Natalie, Kyle left his hometown to study at college. He was unbearably excited for term to start. He couldn't wait to be free of his high school, his hometown, his house, and all of the people that came with them. He was looking forward to a fresh start, and, like everyone else, had heard stories about what college life was supposedly like. His current existence felt fake and immature; he couldn't wait to see what was waiting for him on the other side.

At first, Kyle had been afraid that he would have to sink himself into debt in order to pay for college. His mother wouldn't be able to help him, and the money he'd made working wouldn't stretch nearly far enough. To his amazement, however, salvation did come: his mother's father, his grandfather, offered to subsidize him provided he took his studies seriously and kept his grades up. Kyle was shocked, since he'd never been very close to his grandfather, and couldn't understand why the old man would do such a favor for him. He accepted, promising not to disappoint and knowing that he wouldn't. He'd been given this chance to make his life better, and had no intention of wasting it.

Of course, that didn't mean that Kyle never had the chance to relax along the way. Especially in first year, most of his classes were laughably easy, and Kyle was never in danger of having his grades fall below the threshold he and his grandfather had agreed upon. He employed the same strategies here as he had in high school, and found they worked just as well if not better. He quickly climbed to the top of the social ladder; he attended every party and was the host of many himself, but at the same time was dependable, smart and mature. At some point, every student needed advice, friendship, or help with classes, and Kyle's door was always open.

The effort it took for Kyle to keep this all up was tremendous, but he was determined. He wouldn't be outdone, not in anything. He filled his schedule with club meetings and parties and dates, and convinced himself that this was success. He had heard what college what supposed to be like, and tried as hard as he could to bring the fantasy to life.

The pain returned, and his memories wavered. The past dissolved, falling away from him. Sights and sounds, muffled and distorted, assailed him from all sides. Then, suddenly, his mind became clear once more.

He was still at college, entering the cafeteria at the beginning of the day. He threw his backpack down at the entrance, then retrieved some breakfast and sat down. After a moment, someone else came up and sat down beside him.

Kyle was used to this, and shifted in his seat to give the newcomer room. He looked up briefly, prepared to greet one of his friends, but found that he didn't recognize the other student's face.

He was male, slight and of above average height, but what immediately stood out about him was his paleness. His skin was nearly white, and his hair was so blonde that it looked bleached. His eyes were a glassy blue, and his features were delicate.

Kyle stared at him in confusion. He was certain he didn't know the man, but at the same time, there was something familiar about him.

The man had brought his own breakfast with him, and had started to tuck into it when he felt Kyle's eyes on him. He looked over and gave a casual wave.

"Morning," he said, "how's it going?" He spoke as if he and Kyle knew each other well.

"Fine," Kyle said, confused. "Hey, do I know you?"

"I'm Todd, remember? Todd Wilder. We met at the party last night."

Kyle didn't remember. Had there been a party last night? His memory didn't seem to be working. He thought there was something wrong about this situation, but it kept eluding him. He stared at Todd, trying to figure it out.

"Oh, by the way," Todd said, in between bites of breakfast, "you need to make it to Proks, all right? Make it there and I can help you."

Kyle was still bemused, but something in that sentence had grated against his subconscious. Warning signals went off in his mind, and he felt the cafeteria around him dissolve.

"What?" he said.

"Proks. Make it there. Meet me in Proks and I'll help get you home."

"Who are you?" Kyle asked, nearing panic. The cafeteria was shaking and falling apart; a sense of wrongness and fear permeated the atmosphere. The air was growing dark and Kyle's senses were jumbled.

"I'm a friend," the man continued in the same casual tone. "My name's Todd. Try to remember when you wake up, all right?"

Kyle reached out, but Todd disintegrated into immateriality. The cafeteria shattered like a dropped mirror and Kyle found himself falling through a black void. The pain in his core worsened until it was nearly unbearable. As it peaked, a crack appeared in the darkness, and light flooded in. It was harsh and invasive, and brought more pain with it, but it also felt real. The crack opened wider, and the world beyond the light came slowly into focus. Kyle's eyes were open. He was awake.

The first person to know was a church cleric who had been attending him. After making sure Kyle was all right, she ran off to tell everyone he was awake. Kyle, however, was still bleary and disoriented, and must have slipped back into unconsciousness. He couldn't remember anyone entering his room, but the next time he opened his eyes Lugh was sitting on a chair by his bed, occupied with something in his hands.

Painfully, Kyle propped himself up and tried to focus his eyes.

"Finally awake, huh?" Lugh said. "This is becoming a bad habit of yours. How's it going?"

"Fine," Kyle said, though in truth he felt far from fine. His grip on reality was still rather tenuous, and his whole body ached deeply. He felt as if he could drop off to sleep again at any moment.

"That's good. You had us worried for a while. But I knew you'd come out all right."

Kyle didn't say anything. He was sorting through his memories, figuring out which ones were real and which were not. He stared at Lugh, and then at the object in his hands. In this moment, it was easier to focus on this small detail than try to take on the rest of the world.

"What are you doing?" he asked.

Lugh looked up at him and grinned. "You like it? I think this is going to be my new eye patch. What do you think?"

He reached up and tied a small disc to his face with a strip of cloth, covering his left eye. It had a stone surface carved with a number of intricate symbols, and four oblong holes around the perimeter, two of which Lugh had threaded the cloth through.

"What is it?" Kyle asked.

"Selkic stone coin. We used to use them as money, but stopped making them once the Nell took over. They're supposed to be good luck. I figure that if I'm going to be a one-eyed adventurer, I might as well do it right."

Kyle only picked up on one part of this. "One-eyed?"

Lugh gave him a sidelong glance. "How much do you remember, friend?"

Kyle rubbed his head, figuring it all out. His memory of the last few days was blotchy at first, but the picture started to come together as he thought about it more.

"We left Buoria…and we got attacked?" he said. "The *Ayger* was shot down? Did that actually happen?"

Lugh nodded slowly. "Hate to say it, but it did."

Kyle knew how much Lugh cared about his ship, and wanted to talk more about the *Ayger,* but also had to follow his train of thought to the end. "We all jumped, didn't we? You were hurt and we couldn't find you." He looked at Lugh's eye patch, assuring himself he was right. "And then…"

"You got shot," Lugh said. "Remember the twins who attacked us in Rhian? The sniper and the sage? It was them who shot the *Ayger* down. And then the sniper got you with this guy." He rose from his chair, lifted a black bolt from a nearby table, and held it out for Kyle to inspect. It was a twisted, nasty looking weapon, and Kyle felt his insides squirm at the thought of it lodged inside him.

"I got shot with that?" he asked. "I can't believe I'm alive." He felt gingerly at his bound chest.

Lugh had his hands on his hips. "I think they kept you alive on purpose," he said. "They were just trying to put you out of commission so they could take you away. But no worries, we're safe now."

Something in Lugh's voice made Kyle pause. He looked around.

"Where *are* we?"

"Meya…well, I'll explain how it works later, but she teleported us away. This is a church in southern Eastia."

Mention of Meya's name made Kyle think of something else. "Is everyone else safe?" he said, feeling guilty it had taken him this long to ask. "What about Nihs and—"

"Nihs is fine," Lugh said quickly. "Meya and Deriahm too."

There was a name missing. It was the only one Lugh had left out and the only one Kyle heard.

"What about Phundasa?" he said.

Lugh didn't answer. Kyle sat up straight, his heart beating.

"Lugh," he said, "what about Phundasa?"

A moment later, Kyle had vaulted out of bed and was trying to locate his belongings in the small room. His body was still aching and his head was pounding, but these were nothing compared to the searing pain he felt in his heart.

"Kyle," Lugh was saying, "listen to me. It's not your fault—"

"It doesn't matter whose fault it is!" Kyle shouted, turning on him. "If it weren't for me, he'd still be alive. It's not the first time this has happened and it won't be the last, not if I stay with you. I'm not going to be responsible for getting all of you killed."

"You're not responsible," Lugh said. "It was our choice to help you."

"I don't care! Every time they come after me, someone dies. I'm leaving before it happens again." He found his sword and armor in a corner of the room and piled them on the bed.

"It won't happen again. The twins are dead."

This made Kyle pause. He turned around to watch Lugh's face. It didn't look as though his friend was lying, but Lugh might have been a better liar than he thought.

"Really?" he said.

"Really. They did come after us again, a few days after we got here. But we won the fight. They won't be bothering us any more."

Kyle looked away. For a moment, he hesitated. He shook his head.

"It doesn't matter. Whoever's after me is just going to send someone else. All of you are in danger as long as you stay with me."

For the first time Lugh was angry. "Were you not listening? No one forced us to come with you, Kyle! We all knew what we were getting into. Danger's part of being an adventurer, and even if it weren't, you're our friend. We're not going to abandon you and let you get captured."

"You should. Then you might be safe."

Lugh sighed. "Kyle," he said, "I know you're upset. But there's only one person responsible for Phundasa's death, all right? The person who shot that arrow, and he's dead now. Don't blame yourself for it. Meya wouldn't want you to do that and I know Phundasa wouldn't, either."

Kyle felt tears welling up in his eyes. He was ashamed of himself. No matter what he did, he inevitably brought ruin down on anyone who tried to help him. And what was worse, his friends wouldn't recognize it.

"I'm leaving," he said softly. "It doesn't matter what happens to me. I'd rather be captured than have someone else killed."

"You know," Lugh said, "sometimes you're as stubborn as all hell. We're not leaving you, and I won't let you leave us."

Suddenly Kyle was enraged. He drew his sword from the bed and leveled it at Lugh. His body screamed in protest but he ignored it.

"Get out of my way," he said.

Lugh folded his arms. "Come on," he said, "you really think you're going to get past me?"

Kyle lunged. Lugh drew his own sword and deflected the blow. Kyle staggered off-balance and his weapon clanged to the floor.

"Stop it, Kyle," Lugh snapped. "You need to save your energy, and you'd be no match for me even if you had all your strength."

Kyle was inflamed. He knew that Lugh was right, but his friend was forgetting something. He put his hands together and started to call forth the blue and silver sparks from inside him.

Lugh's eye widened when he saw what Kyle was doing. It was half realization, and half disbelief—he clearly hadn't imagined that Kyle would draw his soul sword on a friend. But Kyle was determined, and it was the one threat he knew would have an effect on Lugh.

He focused, willing the sparks to appear. But something was wrong. The elated feeling that normally accompanied his soul sword was missing. It was replaced with a sense of deep discomfort that suddenly transmuted into pain. There was light gathered around his hands, but instead of the blue he was used to, it was a writhing mass of black and white. His hands and chest felt like they were on fire, and he started to scream in pain. Lugh was looking on in fear, but didn't dare approach.

Kyle collapsed to his hands and knees, the light and the pain fading as his focus did. He heard Lugh run out of the room, shouting for help.

A few minutes later, they were all gathered in Kyle's room: Lugh, Nihs, Meya, and Deriahm, plus a few clerics and an elderly man who was introduced as bishop Abel. Kyle was seated on the edge of his bed, trying to calm his racing heart and overcome the aching pain he felt in his chest.

"It's that black arrow," Nihs hissed. "I *knew* it was cursed! That's what's binding his soul, I would stake my life on it."

"How is that possible?" Meya asked. She was seated on the bed beside him, a hand on his shoulder. "Kyle's soul sword was supposed to be unstoppable."

Nihs plucked the arrow from Kyle's bedside table and ran a claw along its shaft. "Yes, it was," he said darkly. "Binding a soul is easier than destroying it, but this is frightfully powerful magic nonetheless. Whoever gave the twins this arrow is very, very dangerous."

"You don't think it was theirs?" Lugh asked.

Nihs shook his head.

"Neither of the twins had the power or skill to create something like this. It must have been given to them by their employer. It's no coincidence that Kyle was the one they shot with it. It was meant to weaken him, and make him vulnerable for capture."

"The curse is advanced," Deriahm said, "but may it not be broken via the concerted effort of all inside the church? There is a significant amount of power held within these walls."

"We will certainly try," bishop Abel said. "Though this curse seems rooted in mysticism, all of our power combined may be enough to shatter it. But we should wait for Kyle to regain some of his strength first."

Kyle had his arms wrapped around his chest. The existence of the curse made him feel unclean, as if there were a parasite inside of him. Though it never manifested itself outside of when he tried to draw his soul sword, he could sense its presence constantly.

"So what do we do now?" he heard Meya ask. "Even if we can break the curse, we're far from Proks."

Lugh scratched his chin. "We'll have to find our way there somehow. We can hitch a ride or make it there on foot, if we have to."

Kyle wasn't listening. The name 'Proks' had brought something else to the forefront of his mind.

"Uh," he said to bishop Abel, and all heads turned to him. "I don't want to be rude, but could we be left alone for a moment? I have something to tell everyone."

"Of course," said Abel, and he and the other clerics filed out of the room and closed the door behind them.

Lugh raised an eyebrow. "What's this about?"

Kyle wasn't so sure himself. "I…don't know if this means anything," he said, "but I had a dream while I was unconscious."

Part of him expected his companions to laugh at him, but none of them did. Nihs climbed up on to the bed and sat down.

"Go on," he said.

"I wouldn't have brought it up, but Lugh told me before that dreams can mean things in Loria, and I think this one might have meant something."

"Lugh is right," Nihs said. "The mind is open to magical influence while asleep. Considering what's been happening to you, I don't think it's unreasonable to examine your dreams closely. What was it about?"

"I've been dreaming about Earth almost every night since I got here. I did again just before I woke up. But this time, there was a man in my dream that I'm sure wasn't someone I knew from Earth."

Nihs was hanging on every word. "It's a good thing you're telling us," he said. "It could be a mystic from our world inserting himself into your dreams. What did he look like, and what did he say?"

"He was human, about my age. He was really pale and he had white hair. He said his name was Todd Wilder and that I should meet him in Proks. He said he was a friend and wanted to help me go back home."

Silence greeted his words. Nihs' brow furrowed in thought, and Lugh put his hands on his hips. "Todd Wilder? What kind of a name is that?"

"It sounds made up," Meya said. "The kind of name an adventurer would have."

"It sounds familiar," Nihs said, his tone pensive. "But I can't imagine why. If only I still had my books!" He shook his head. "Let me ask the overhead. I know I've heard that name somewhere before."

Without waiting for anyone to reply, he sat down, shut his eyes and unfolded his ears.

Lugh smirked. "Once Nihs' on the case he's hard to shake off. We'll leave him to it." He folded his arms. "It is strange, though. This guy goes to all the trouble of coming to you in a dream, and all he tells you is to go to Proks?"

"It is possible, albeit difficult, to intercept magical signals sent over long distances," Deriahm said. "If this man is truly at Proks, perhaps he feared having his message detected by an enemy."

"I'm more worried about who he is," Meya said. "It's easy to *say* that you're a friend, but how do we know he's telling the truth? He could be someone else out to capture you."

"Let's wait and see what Nihs finds out," Lugh said. "Something tells me that name's going to mean something."

Nihs, however, was slow in coming back from the overhead, so they ended up talking about their plan for after they left the village.

"Whether we're going to Proks or not," Lugh said, "we're going to need some kind of transportation, and for that we'll need money."

"How much do we have now that the *Ayger's* gone?" Meya asked.

"Not a lot. But I think we'll be able to make some of it back. We have the twins' weapons now."

"That's right! Those will be worth more than enough to get us to the city."

"Yeah, but only to the right person. Something tells me no one in this village is going to want a ring bow. We'll have to get to a bigger town and find a weapon shop."

At this point, Nihs came back from the overhead. "I knew it!" he said at once.

"What is it?" Lugh asked.

"Todd Wilder is the human name of Rosshku the Archmage. It's not often used, so I'd forgotten who it referred to."

At first Kyle assumed that this name would mean something to the residents of Loria, but Lugh's expression made him realize this wasn't the case. "Rosshku? Who's that?"

"A figure that appears in Kollic folklore," Nihs said. "According to our legends, he is an immortal vagabond whose life is dedicated to studying magic. Some of our magical discoveries are attributed to him, though no one these days knows if he's a real person or not."

"Great. So what do we do about the fact that he showed up in Kyle's dream?"

"We don't know that he did. Whoever it was used Rosshku's name and likeness, but that doesn't mean it was actually him."

"Is Rosshku supposed to look like the person in my dream?" Kyle asked.

"To a degree. He likely altered his image just enough so that it would fit in with the rest of your memories; otherwise, he'd run the risk of having your subconscious reject it. But Rosshku is supposed to be a human, and an albino. So the man you described fits."

"The question remains," Deriahm said, "do we trust the message? Rosshku, if he indeed lives, has not had contact with the outside world for hundreds of years. Is it possible that the vision was authentic? For we know also that Kyle has enemies of significant power. It would not be unreasonable to suspect that this is a ruse, and that they are the ones responsible for it."

"We were going to travel to Proks anyway to meet with the elders," Nihs pointed out. "If this is a trap, and Kyle has enemies waiting for him there, then we'll have to abandon that idea and look for help elsewhere."

"What do you think, Kyle?" Lugh asked.

Kyle wasn't sure what he thought. His emotions were still in turmoil. The fever he had felt upon hearing of Phundasa's death was gone, but the anger and the guilt remained. He'd sworn that he wouldn't let anyone get hurt because of him, but it had happened anyway, and he suffered no delusions that he'd be able to keep it from happening again in the future. But, he could at least try to keep his friends as far away from danger as possible.

"I don't think it's a trap," he said. "It doesn't feel like one, anyway. It's too strange. There are probably much better ways of getting me to go somewhere than pretending to be some ancient mage that I don't even know about."

"I agree," Nihs said. "If it is a trick, it's a very bizarre one. Not to mention the fact that whoever is after you clearly has some way of tracking where you are. They'd be more likely to pursue you than to wait for you to come after them."

"Speaking of which," said Meya, "do we have some way of keeping them from finding Kyle? We can't go on like this, worrying that there will be assassins waiting for us everywhere we go."

Nihs' face was dour. "Unfortunately, we don't know how they're able to follow him. The escape magic you used should have been enough to keep almost anyone off his tail. I have no idea how they're doing it."

"It is possible to sense—and to conceal—souls using mysticism," Deriahm said. "Though the amount of power it would take to track an unfamiliar soul at any great distance would be unprecedented. As for a counter charm, a sufficiently skilled mystic should be able to provide one. I am afraid that my own strength would not be adequate."

"Hey, don't worry about it," Lugh said. "It was enough to find me after the *Ayger* crashed, so I won't complain."

"We're going to Proks, then?" Meya said.

"Yes," Nihs replied. "We'll speak to the elders as planned, and see what's going on with this man claiming to be Rosshku."

"But first we have to sell those weapons so we have money to travel with," Lugh added. "And if we run into a mystic who can make us a charm for Kyle, all the better."

"Before any of that, we have to deal with the curse the twins put on him," Meya said. "We need Kyle's soul sword, and even if we didn't, I'm worried that it might have other effects we don't know about."

"Sounds like we're going to be busy for a while," Lugh said. "Let's get to it, then."

They decided to wait until at least the following morning to try and break Kyle's curse. He was still weak from his unconsciousness, and Bishop Abel warned that the process would be difficult and painful. They instead spent the rest of the day planning their next move. They received directions to a town ten miles southeast of where they were, which Abel assured them would be large enough to have all that they needed.

"I don't know if anyone in town will be willing to lend you horses," he admitted. "I'm afraid you may have to walk the distance yourselves."

"Eh, we've done that before," Lugh said. "We're going to need supplies, though."

"These we are able to provide," Abel promised.

Kyle had planned on going to bed as soon as they were done sorting everything out. It was getting dark, and he was, besides, exhausted. But as he bade goodnight to his friends he realized one of their party was missing.

"Hey, Lugh," he said, "where's Meya?"

Lugh looked around. "She's probably at Phundasa's grave," he said. "It's out back."

"Oh."

He didn't want to face Meya alone, not after everything that had happened. But he knew he couldn't avoid her, either. It was the least he could do to go and see her, and offer his condolences, even if she didn't want them.

She was in the graveyard, as Lugh had guessed she would be. The battle with Lacaster had torn up some of the ground and damaged some of the tombstones, but it wasn't noticeable in the dim light. What was noticeable was the soft blue glow coming from some of the tombstones. It was a beautiful, haunting sight, and Kyle had no idea what caused it.

Phundasa's grave was one of those that glowed blue. In fact, it was one of the brightest in the graveyard. Meya was kneeling in front of it, praying. She turned when she heard Kyle approaching, and rose to her feet when she saw who it was. Kyle immediately felt guilty.

"Kyle," she said, smoothing the front of her dress.

"I'm sorry, I didn't mean to interrupt."

"No, it's all right," she replied, half turning back to the grave. "I just wanted to spend a little more time here. We'll probably be moving out tomorrow and I might not get another chance."

"Right." He drew up beside her and they both looked down at the grave. Kyle felt compelled to say something more, but the words stuck in his throat. Instead he said, "Sorry if I'm quiet. It's just…I know there's nothing I can say that can make it better, and I didn't know him very well, so…I'd rather say nothing at all than say something stupid."

Meya gave him a smile. "I understand. Thank you for coming anyway."

For a while neither of them said anything. Meya hugged herself, bracing herself against the cool air, while Kyle stared into the soft blue light and let his thoughts wander.

"It's funny," Meya said eventually. "I've always felt that Das had the soul of a protector. I used to tell him that when we were traveling together. Everyone else saw him the same way they see all Orcs—as a big brute. But he had the kindest soul of anyone I've ever met. He protected me during the war, and then…he died, protecting you."

She turned sharply, realizing what she'd said. "I'm sorry, I didn't mean to—"

"No, it's all right. Meya, I should be the one who's sorry. You lost your friend because of me."

Meya's voice became stern. "Kyle, I lost my friend because of two assassins who were sent by some maniac to capture you. It's not your fault."

Kyle couldn't bear to look at her. He stared down at the tombstone, struggling to keep his emotions in check. "That's what Lugh said, too," he said. "It doesn't make it much easier."

He felt Meya's hand on his shoulder, then her other hand on his far shoulder. She steered him around until he was forced to look into her red eyes.

"Kyle, I just lost my best friend in the entire world. The last thing I need right now is to lose you as well. Do you understand? Das gave up his life for you. He knew you were worth saving, and I know that too. Now *you* need to realize it. Don't spend the life Das gave you consumed by guilt, all right? He wouldn't want that."

Meya's eyes were locked on to his, and for a moment she held him there. It was painful to match her gaze. It felt as if she were forcefully keeping her words at the forefront of his mind. For the first time in years, Kyle started to question his view of himself. Could it be that there was truth to what Lugh and Meya had said? Had Phundasa really thought that Kyle was worth saving? He thought about the Orc, his glittering eyes and his booming laugh, and suddenly felt resolve. He'd been training to become a stronger person since he came to Loria. Now, perhaps, he could try to become a better one as well.

"You're right," he said to Meya. "I won't blame myself any more. I promise."

There was still gravity in Meya's eyes, but slowly, a smile formed around it. She didn't speak, but drew him into a brief embrace, and when they broke apart she kept her hand clasped to his. They watched the grave for a while more, though the air now felt cool and refreshing rather than stifling, and the blue glow that permeated the graveyard was soothing and serene.

The next day, bishop Abel gathered all of his clerics together to try and break the arrow's curse. With Meya and Deriahm participating, there were more than fifteen people present to lend their aid. The way Kyle understood it, only Meya and Abel would actually be working to break the curse, while the rest were there to provide the extra magic that would no doubt be needed.

They gathered in the center of the church, before the statue of Saint Marc. Bishop Abel performed a brief prayer, invoking the power of the Saints, and placed a hand on Kyle's chest while Meya took hold of his shoulder.

"This is going to hurt, a lot," Meya had warned him. "Your soul is twisted in on itself. We have to try and unbind it, and for that we'll have to almost kill you. But I promise you won't be in any real danger, all right?"

Now, as Abel neared the end of his prayer, and Kyle felt magic start to build up around him, he grit his teeth and prepared himself for the worst.

Meya and Abel unleashed their power in tandem, and Kyle immediately dropped to his knees. A pair of clerics held on to his arms, keeping him from collapsing entirely. He felt as though an auger were drilling into his chest, tearing him apart from the inside out. He would have screamed, but he couldn't muster the strength. His body went completely limp as his vision swam. He was aware that the others were saying something, but couldn't make sense of any of it. Black flames flickered in front of his eyes, and his chest was on fire.

Whether the ritual went on for ten seconds or ten minutes Kyle would never know, but finally the pain faded and Kyle was allowed to sink slowly to all fours. His whole body was shaking, and his chest was still raw with pain, as if the curse were a spiteful monster inside of him that had been roused by the ritual.

After a moment, he was helped gently to his feet. The clerics holding his arms looped them around their shoulders while he steadied himself.

Bishop Abel's face was grim. "I'm sorry," he said, "but the curse remains. We can't break it, not without more power, and not without endangering you in the process."

"Can't say I'm surprised," Lugh said, hands on his hips. "Something told me it wouldn't be that easy."

Kyle wasn't surprised, either, but the failure still stung. The curse didn't feel unpleasant, but he hated knowing that it was there, and didn't care for the idea of traveling without his soul sword. It had always been his final fail-safe, and Loria felt much more dangerous without it.

With nothing left for them to do at the church, they decided to leave later that morning. The walk to the next village would take a few hours and they wanted to get an early start. They thanked Bishop Abel and his clerics profusely for all of their help, and Lugh donated nearly all of their remaining money to the church. Abel thanked them in turn, clasping each of them by the hand and wishing them a safe journey. Before they left, he blessed their party, calling upon Saint Marc to protect them.

They were in high spirits when they finally set out on the winding road leading southward. After all of the hardship they'd been through, it was pleasant to do something as simple and as physical as walking. The air was crisp and refreshing, and the countryside was quiet and peaceful. The road wound mostly through farmland, with green and golden fields stretching out over rolling hills. Occasionally, they passed through a more heavily wooded area, and Kyle noticed that many of the leaves on the trees were turning golden. Some had already fallen, and were crunching underfoot as they walked by. It was a pretty sight, but it also got Kyle thinking.

"Wasn't it summer back in Reno?" he asked the group at large. "How do seasons work in Loria?"

"Nihs," Lugh said.

Nihs, who was riding on Lugh's shoulder, heaved a dramatic sigh and turned around in his seat. "You remember how the sun crosses over the earth twice each day, correct?"

"Right."

"So, on any given day, there is a point somewhere on the planet known as the cross—the location over which the sun passes directly twice in one day. The cross sits at the center of the Earth vertically and shifts slowly to the west as the year goes on. In terms of the seasons, the hottest time of the year—midsummer—is the time when the cross is exactly overhead. The point on the world opposite the cross is in midwinter. East of the cross is autumn, and west of it is spring. In essence, the seasons divide the world vertically into four quadrants, which rotate westwards as time passes."

"So it was summer in Reno and it's fall here."

"Yes. And it's currently winter in Westia and spring over the western part of Centralia."

"Speaking of which, it's almost midsummer in Reno," Lugh pointed out. "That's when the new year starts, since Reno is the center of the universe. They have a huge festival there on On-Cross and then party halfway through the month."

"A shame we left just in time to miss the festivities," Nihs said. He didn't sound particularly upset.

Though Kyle still felt weak from his arrow wound, he was grateful for the opportunity to get outside and stretch his limbs. He could feel himself being rejuvenated by the bright sun and cool air. Whenever they reached a high point in the path, they could see fields and forest for miles around and the mountains of Eastia in the distance.

After a couple hours of walking, the farmland gave way to low foot-hills. They followed the now-winding path upwards into the hills and eventually came to the town Abel had described. It sat on the edge of a small drop-off, nestled between a pair of lakes. Kyle was no expert, but it looked very old. The houses were wood and stone, weathered with age. Here the air was chillier, and a thin mist hung over the town.

"All right," Lugh said, once they passed through the town's gates, "we're looking for a weapon shop and a place to stay for the night. And we need to think of how we're going to get to Proks. Do we buy some horses or some runners or do we see if there's an airship we can hitch a ride on?"

"An airship," Nihs said. "It's going to be a long trip if we go over land—three full days at the very least. And we can't exactly afford the best of the best in terms of vehicles."

"We may not have a choice," Meya pointed out. "It doesn't look like this town has an airdock."

Nihs scowled as he realized this was true. "Hmph. I suppose we'll have to manage with what we can find."

"This area is known to have a large Kol population," Deriahm said. "It's likely that some method of transport exists for those who wish to travel between the Kol capital city and here."

"We can only hope, I suppose."

"Let's stop talking and start looking," Lugh said.

The town was quiet, and there was little activity in the streets—though whether this was normal or as a result of the chill fog they couldn't tell. Those people they did see were a mix of human, Kol, Oblihari, and a few Orcs. The streets were narrow, and the town's contours were dictated by the lakes it sat between.

At first Kyle wasn't confident that they would find what they were looking for, but soon they hit a main street of sorts lined by shops, inns, and stables. Nihs wrinkled his nose at the very suggestion of horses and Kyle had to admit he was with him. He'd never ridden a horse back on Earth and was hoping he wouldn't have to start here. But before they thought about transport, they had to make some money.

They found a weapon shop that faced the main street, and went in to see if they could sell the twins' weapons. Kyle found the idea of pawning the weapons slightly disturbing, but none of his companions treated it as strange, so he took it in stride.

There was a younger man working at the counter when they came in. His eyes bulged when he saw what they wanted to sell, and he went into the back of the store to fetch the owner. The owner turned out to be a large, middle-aged Orc. He was well spoken, good-natured, and clearly very knowledgeable. He examined each of the weapons in turn, telling them more about the bow and swords than they ever wanted to know.

"These two are good quality," he said, tapping the twin swords, "but the real beauty is this one here." He lifted up the ring bow for inspection for the umpteenth time. "This is one of the deadliest models ever made, and it's been customized by someone who knew what they were doing." He leaned back, his arms folded. He stared at the weapons, thinking hard. Finally he said, "I can give you fifteen hundred each for the swords and…six thousand for the bow."

"Sounds good to me!" Lugh said.

Once the trade was made, Lugh leaned on the counter. "To be honest," he said, grinning, "I was worried that no one here would have the money to buy that stuff."

The owner laughed. "I'm not so sure I have the money myself, but I couldn't let that bow pass me by."

"How's business here? You're kind of out in the middle of nowhere."

"If there's one thing I've learned over the years," the owner said, "it's that you can find adventurers anywhere in the world. I'm the only weapon shop around here, so I get more business than you might think."

"Out of curiosity," Lugh said, "we'd like to head to Proks next. Are there any airships that land around here? We didn't see an airdock on our way in."

"We've been trying to have one built for a few years now," the Orc replied. "There's a cruiser that comes in every few days, but right now it has to land outside of town. There's an old Adenwheyr mine down the road with an airdock, so it drops down there."

"Great," Lugh said, "when's it coming in next?"

"You just missed it yesterday, I'm afraid. Next will be in two days."

Lugh shrugged. "That's all right. Better luck than I thought we'd have. You've got a hideout here, right?"

"Of course. It's on the next street over. Got a guild symbol hanging out front."

"Perfect, thanks."

The town's hideout was small and nondescript, run by a quiet, sallow-faced man. There clearly wasn't much activity here. Lugh rented them a few rooms and they dropped off their provisions before heading back outside. The town didn't have much to offer, however, and they were all still edgy from the twins' attack, so it wasn't long before they retreated back to the hideout to spend the night.

The following two days passed in more or less the same fashion. They had time to kill, but none of them particularly felt like taking advantage of it; they were all restless, waiting for the cruiser to arrive so they could continue their journey. Whenever they stopped back at the hideout, Nihs went up to the counter to peruse job postings, but there was never anything available that interested them.

They were all relieved when it came time to head out to the cruiser's landing site. The road to the airdock was obviously well-trod, and they made the trip with a few of the town's residents.

Kyle had seen other airships docked and flying over the sky of Reno city, but had never boarded one other than the *Ayger* before. He wondered how this ship was going to compare to Lugh's. Surely it couldn't be as magnificent as the luxury ship Lugh had been so proud of.

The road wound through the foothills, skirted the base of a small mountain to their right, and then broke off in the opposite direction, heading downwards into a large valley. The landing pad was on the valley's ridge, and had a view of the old Adenwheyr mine below. The earth in the valley had been churned and scraped clean of greenery, but other than that there was no sign of the mine's existence—none of the discarded equipment or abandoned camping sites that they'd seen during their raid on the mine in Donno.

As if he'd been reading Kyle's thoughts, Lugh said, "Another mine, huh? Probably a goblin or two hiding out in this one, too. They love places like this."

"The mine feels like years ago," Kyle said.

"No kidding. Hard to believe it's only been—getting on a month, now, I guess." Lugh gave a small laugh. "I wonder how Rogan's doing."

Kyle had completely forgotten about Rogan in the events of the previous days. Suddenly he missed the Minotaur's comforting presence. He wondered if he'd see Rogan again before he left Loria. If he ever *did* find his way home.

"Hey," Lugh said, "looks like that might be our ship."

Kyle turned his gaze skyward, and saw the ship drifting lazily toward them. It was at least as large as the *Ayger,* but nowhere near as elegantly designed. Its hull was larger relative to its wings, and though the original golden color of the ship was shining through in places, the rest of its body was marred in various ways.

They waited at a safe distance for it to touch down on the landing pad, and lower its boarding ramp and allow passengers to disembark. A few workers jumped down from the airship to direct traffic, but apart from that there was little ceremony. It was more like boarding a bus back on Earth than an airplane. Clearly the denizens of Loria didn't have much need for high security.

This reminded him of something else, and as they were queuing up to board he asked Lugh in a low voice,

"When we were attacked by the twins' ship, you said it was impossible to put a gun on a ship like that. Why?"

"No one's been able to figure out the science yet," Lugh said. "See, you can use small machines on an airship, but anything the size of an artillery gun steals power from the engine and causes the ship to crash. I have no idea how those two did it."

"James Livaldi runs a weapon company," Kyle pointed out.

"That he does. Well, if he really is the one responsible for this, all we can do for now is keep away from him."

Kyle nodded. "Think we'll be safe in Proks?"

"Not as safe as we were in Buoria, that's for sure. But outsiders don't come to Proks often. Any funny business would draw a lot of attention. Then again, the last people we fought didn't try too hard to be subtle."

"Yeah, right."

They reached the front of the queue, and the man selling tickets eyed them as they approached. He was dressed in a rather snappy green-and-blue uniform.

"Adventurers?" he said.

"Yep."

"All together?"

"Yep."

The man nodded, and counted out five tickets. "No drawn weapons on board and no magic except with the crew's permission," he warned.

"Sure thing," Lugh said wryly.

There were no private rooms on the cruiser—at least, none that Kyle could see. Instead, there was a large open room that was divided via furniture and half-walls into dozens of smaller areas. They claimed one of these for themselves and set down their equipment.

"I'm gonna watch us take off," Lugh said, as the ship's engine revved into life.

"Suit yourself," Nihs replied. He'd made himself a makeshift nest out of some of their equipment packs and was sulking inside of it.

"I'll go with you," Kyle said.

Meya and Deriahm opted to stay with Nihs, so Kyle and Lugh made their way to the far side of the room by themselves. There was a huge window here that ran almost the entire length of the wall. There was a gap between the floor and the wall, blocked off by a railing, over which one could lean to see another floor below.

Kyle stood in silence for a moment, and then voiced something that was on his mind. "That conductor didn't seem too happy to see us."

Lugh laughed. "In this job, people either love you or hate you. It's all part of being an adventurer. The man who helped us into town when you were out wasn't too fond of us either."

"Why's that?"

"Some people think that adventurers are more trouble than they're worth. They're not totally wrong—you get ones like that from time to time, though if too many complaints about you come in you get kicked out of the guild. But a lot of us fall a tad on the strange side anyway. You can't always know what you're in for."

"What do you mean?" Kyle asked, confused.

Lugh smiled in return. "Normal people don't become adventurers," he said. "That's something my brother told me when I was young. Took me a few years on the job to realize how right he was."

"Really?" Kyle tried to reconcile what Lugh was saying with the person who was saying it. His friend looked the same as he always had, save for the stone eye patch he now wore.

"Absolutely. Makes sense, when you think about it. No one leaves home to go travel the world and kill monsters because their life's going exactly to plan. Adventurers are all misfits in some way or another. They've each got something to hide, or that they want to leave behind. Take us, for example. See if you can tell me what's wrong with each of us."

"I'm not doing that!" Kyle said, laughing despite himself.

"I'm serious. We'll start with you. You're not normal."

Kyle was about to protest, until he realized that he was probably the least normal person in existence right now.

"All right, all right." He paused for a moment, thinking seriously about the others. "With Nihs it's his family," he said. "He doesn't get along with them, especially his father."

"You got it," Lugh said. "It's going be hard for him to go back to Proks. That's why he's been in a bad mood lately."

"Meya and Phundasa…they were in that war together."

"Right. I don't know exactly what they went through, but I'm sure it wasn't too pleasant."

"Deriahm doesn't fit in because he's an *irushai.* And I don't think he has a lot of experience with the outside world. His father sent him with us to keep him from being a shut-in."

"Yep. See what I mean?"

"What about you?" Kyle said.

Lugh stared out the window. "It's a long story," he said. "Let's just say that the brother I just mentioned isn't around any more."

"Oh. I'm sorry."

"It's all right. Maybe I'll tell you the whole story later. For now, let's focus on what's in front of us."

"Right."

By this time, the ship had risen over the trees and hills and was swinging around to face its destination to the northeast. *Proks*, Kyle thought. The Kol capital had been their ultimate destination for a while now. He wondered what it would be like, and if there really were answers waiting for them there. There was only one way to find out.

Since they were banned from using weapons on the airship, they couldn't exactly spend the time training as they usually did. Instead, they spent the time talking, sleeping, and wandering around the cruiser. That was, until Deriahm revealed that he'd brought with him a miniature set of mareek-check blocks; then they spent the time losing to him in mareek-check. He was frightfully good, in a way that suggested he'd spent a huge amount of time playing the game. He could anticipate plays that were coming far in the future and counter them long before they had taken place. Kyle reflected that Deriahm played mareek-check in much the same way that he fought.

Deriahm was settling into the group fairly well, though a level of separation still existed between him and the others. His shyness never manifested itself outright; he spoke up often and could carry a conversation as well as any of the others. But there was a guarded stiffness about him that never completely went away. He still acted like a guest in their party—a welcome guest, but a guest nonetheless.

Kyle couldn't stop thinking of what Lugh had told him. *Normal people don't become adventurers.* He wondered if what he'd guessed about Deriahm was the full story. Kyle's experience with Buors was limited, but Deriahm reminded him of the way captain Callaghnen had acted when he'd first apprehended the party. Polite, friendly, but holding something back.

Kyle also couldn't help but dwell on what else Lugh had revealed during their talk—the existence of his brother, who had died in some way that Lugh wasn't ready to reveal. He had promised Kyle the rest of the story, though, and to Kyle's own surprise he found himself looking forward to hearing it. On Earth, he'd never cared about his friends' so-called problems. Perhaps it was because people on Earth had a different view of what constituted a problem. Or perhaps it was because the people Kyle knew on Earth hadn't really been his friends.

Despite everything, Lugh seemed in good spirits, as always. Kyle had no idea how he did it. He'd lost an eye and his beautiful airship all in the same day—but he never even mentioned the *Ayger* any more, and only had one thing to say about his missing eye.

"At least I've got another one. I'm going need you to help me brush up on my fighting skills once we've got the chance, though. As nifty as this patch is, I think it's set me back a few threat levels."

Though Lugh's spirit was indomitable as ever, Kyle wished he could say the same for the rest of his companions. The closer they got to Proks, the more irritable Nihs became. He spent more time than usual on the overhead, and often refused to join the rest of the group in whatever they were doing.

"Next chance we have," Lugh said in a low voice, "we're getting him some books."

"Is he angry about the ones he lost with the ship?" Kyle asked.

"Probably not. I don't think he had anything too rare on him. But reading's how he calms down. He just needs something to stick his face into. He thinks that if he reads enough he'll eventually learn everything there is to learn."

Meya also tended to keep to herself during the voyage, though this was out of sadness rather than irritability. She went through ups and downs, but overall she spoke and smiled less than she used to. If she ever went through more serious grief, she kept it to herself, but her depression still weighed heavily on the others. Kyle felt a throb of guilt whenever he saw her in one of her more somber moods, but he kept it to himself, knowing that it would do more harm than good to express it.

The foothills below them became larger and more rugged as they flew east. Soon, there was not a patch of level ground to be seen. Kyle had seen plenty of the mountains of Eastia during their flight to Buoria, but the sight of them still amazed him. The ship climbed higher and higher, matching the mountains' height and escaping the thick mist that blanketed them.

Finally, the city of Proks came into view. Lugh was the first to see it, being the only one of their party who was up at the time. He came galloping down the stairs from the second floor.

"Guys!" he said, "you need to see this!"

"Let me guess," Nihs said without looking up, "the doors of Rhann."

"Yeah! You never told me how cool they were!"

Nihs rolled his eyes. "You're far too easily impressed. All right, then, I suppose we have to get ready to leave in any case."

They followed Lugh back to his position near the window on the second floor. The airship was flying down the length of a valley shrouded in mist. It was lush with trees and there was a river flowing down its center. At the other end of the valley was a massive structure that must have been the doors of Rhann.

And it was, essentially, a giant pair of doors. They were carved out of a dark, bluish rock, and were each several hundred feet tall. They were fitted snugly into the face of the mountains at the far end of the valley, and looked as eternal and immovable.

"Wow," Meya said. "You'd think we were back in Buoria."

Nihs sniffed. "The doors allow the people of the city to control the amount of water flowing out of the caves. And, I imagine, to show the people of Reno that they're not the only ones who can waste money on large, unnecessary structures."

"I like it," Lugh said, placing his hands on his hips. "If no one ever took the time to build stuff like this, the world would be a dull place, right?"

"The city of Proks is not a city in the traditional sense," Deriahm said. "It sprawls across a vast network of caves and has no defined borders. Perhaps these doors are a way of establishing a formal entry point into the city. A front door, as it were."

"If I didn't know any better, I'd say they don't like guests," Lugh said, grinning. He jostled Nihs, who was sitting on his shoulder. "Eh? Eh?"

Nihs was not amused. "The Kol of Proks do *not* like guests. This isn't Reno city. There aren't many non-Kol who live here and you're bound to draw attention unless you keep a low profile. Our situation's very delicate, and if we make a nuisance of ourselves our chances of being allowed to consult the elders are second to none. So *please*, Lugh, try to restrain yourself once we're inside."

Lugh dropped his smile and folded his arms. "All right, all right. We'll all be on our best behavior. Promise."

Nihs said nothing else, but his speech had been sobering. Suddenly Kyle wasn't too excited to visit Proks after all.

He watched the doors of Rhann grow larger in the near distance as their airship approached. They were firmly shut from what Kyle could see, though presumably there was some way inside. The doors sat on the lip of a steep incline that had clearly been carved out by the valley's river; the ground directly underneath was rocky and swept clean of vegetation.

At first, Kyle had no idea where their airship was going to land; there didn't seem to be any even ground anywhere in the valley. They flew to the doors of the city and then, to his surprise, up over them, and hovered across the land beyond. Here the ground was flatter, and swept clean of obstruction by the cold and the wind. The airship touched down on a misshapen patch of land that may or may not have been a real airdock. They heard the engines switch off, and before they knew it the ramp had been lowered and the airship's passengers were shuffling down it. They gathered up their belongings and followed.

The path that led from the airdock to the doors of Rhann was ill defined and treacherous. It wound between outcroppings of rock that formed the lip of the valley, and zigzagged down the valley's wall. Some parts of the path were fenced off, but for the most part these were old, rickety structures made with wood and rope. Kyle wasn't normally afraid of heights, but looking down into the valley below made his stomach churn. He kept one hand on the cliff face beside him and slowed his pace.

Finally the path swung around, and came to an end directly in front of the doors of Rhann. They were even grander up close. The dark blue stone was weathered, but looked incredibly solid, and each door bore numerous carvings that Kyle couldn't quite make out or understand. From here he could see that the doors were completely closed, though each bore a tiny rectangular entrance near its edge. They were six feet tall by four feet across; large enough for a human to pass through, but positively minute compared to the doors themselves.

Nihs dismounted from Lugh and led the others inside. Lugh had to hunker down to fit through the entrance, though Kyle had an easier time of it. He felt the smooth blue surface of the door to his left as he passed through; it was at least ten feet thick. He expected to come out on the other side of the door, but instead they ran into a steep incline, almost a wall of stone, into which had been carved a ladder of sorts. Nihs had already disappeared up it by the time Kyle reached it, and Lugh had craned his neck to see where it led.

"Damn," he said. "They don't make it easy for you, do they?"

He grabbed the ladder and started to climb. Kyle waited for a few moments, and then followed. The rungs were cut deep into the rock, and offered a good grip, but he still felt uneasy. The passage was incredibly narrow, and must have been at least partially natural, as it twisted, grew and shrank as Kyle climbed.

He heard running water up in the distance, and the rock beneath his fingers became slightly damp. All of a sudden, he emerged into a large cave lit by a multitude of lights of different colors. Still the ladder continued upwards, though now it was made of wood instead of stone. Kyle didn't dare look around while he was climbing; he focused on following Lugh instead.

The ladder went up and up for at least fifty feet more, until finally it came to a wooden platform that clung to the side of the cave. Kyle, shaking, stepped onto the platform and looked around.

The cave was actually a huge tunnel that disappeared deeper into the mountains. There was water below, flowing gently forward but mostly held still by the doors of Rhann. On either side of the river were huge rambling structures made of wood. Thick beams fastened to the cave's walls and floor supported platforms, walkways, ladders, and even houses, some with multiple floors. Ropes and bridges stretched across the river and joined the two sides of the cave together. There was no central source of illumination, but thousands of lanterns filled the air with multicolored light.

A sigh of wonder went through their group as they all gathered on the platform. The chamber was nowhere near as impressive as the Buorish capital, but there was an intricacy here that Kyle had never seen before even in Deriahm's homeland. The longer he looked, the more details emerged. Absolutely no space in the cave had been wasted; the floor, walls, and even ceiling of the cave were covered with wooden structures, and every outcropping of rock had been hollowed out or tunneled through, used as a house or pathway. The Kol must have had no sense of personal space or property: houses grew out of other houses or sat across walkways, and goods were stored outside under small shelters wherever they would fit. Almost everything in the cave was either built of wood, hewn from stone, or fashioned from stained glass.

"Welcome to Proks," Nihs said, his tone sardonic. He jumped onto one of the wooden beams that kept their platform in place. "Watch your step. We Kol are strong climbers, and we tend not to think about the needs of the other races. Many parts of the city are not…outsider-friendly."

"I'll keep that in mind," Lugh said, stepping carefully to the lip of their platform and peering over the edge. "Nice place you've got here," he added. "Can't believe it's taken me this long to see where you came from!"

"I didn't come from here," Nihs said. "This is western Proks. My family is from eastern Proks."

"Aren't they the same place?"

"Barely. The two cities—"

Nihs was silenced by a voice that cut through the quiet of the cave. It emerged from a stone passageway connected to their platform by a small bridge.

"*Nizu!*" Kyle heard, and then a stream of sounds that he couldn't hope to understand. The voice was higher than Nihs' and was very animated.

Nihs jumped down from his post and peered into the gloom.

"*Nellazan!*" he called back, and continued to speak in what Kyle could only assume was Kollic.

Another Kol came leaping down the passage. She dashed across the wooden bridge and ran up to Nihs, grabbing both of his raised hands in hers. The two Kol touched their foreheads together, and their ears unfolded and wound around each other. Both of them were smiling, and chatting away rapidly in Kollic.

They broke apart, and Nihs turned to face the others. "Everyone," he said, "this is my older sister, Nella."

"Pleased to meet you," Nella said with a small bow. When she wasn't speaking in Kollic, her voice was slower and calmer, but also somewhat stilted, as if she wasn't used to the language. She was about the same height as Nihs, but was much thinner, and her skin was smooth and a darker green. Her eyes were amber and almond-shaped.

"Pleasure's all ours," Lugh said. "So you're the one Nihs spends all his time talking to?"

Nella smiled. "We are always…" she said a word in Kollic, then shook her head. "That is to say, close, even when we are far apart. When I heard he was coming back to Proks, I had to come to meet him." She put her hands on Nihs' shoulders. "There is someone else who has come with me," she said.

"Really? Who?"

Nella just smiled, took Nihs' hand, and led them into the tunnel she'd come down. The bridge she'd run across was short, but it swayed perilously under Kyle's feet as he stepped onto it. They climbed inside the tunnel and followed its gentle curve to the right.

There was another Kol waiting there. As soon as she saw Nihs, she squealed in joy and dashed toward him. Judging by her size and the pitch of her voice, she was younger than both Nihs and Nella. She sprang into Nihs' arms, jabbering away in Kollic. At first Nihs looked astonished, but then he smiled and started to laugh, fending off her affection.

"My other sister," he said, by way of an explanation. "The youngest. Kisi Ken Dal Proks. *Kisiren…*" and he continued in Kollic, prying her arms from around his waist.

"She is meant to be studying right now," Nella said, "but she insisted on coming with me."

"She did?" Suddenly Nihs sounded worried. He looked down at his sister, who was vibrating with excitement. "You shouldn't have done that, *Kisiren*," he said.

"It's all right!" Kisi said. "I'm still way ahead of everyone else!"

"It doesn't matter. Your schooling should come first. Go back before you're missed." Nihs directed his gaze at Nella. "Why did you let her come with you?"

Nella's expression was sad. She said something in Kollic, to which Nihs snapped a reply. Nella answered calmly. She walked forward put her hands on his shoulders, touching her forehead to his as she had done before.

Nihs sighed.

"All right," he said finally. "You can come with us until we reach the hall of colors. But then you need to get back to your work, do you understand?"

Kisi had been following the conversation with a muted look on her face, but now her energy came back. She laughed and skipped ahead of the others as they started to make their way to the back of the cave. Nihs and Nella came after her, while everyone else followed behind, trying not to hit their heads on the low ceiling.

Nihs and Nella talked almost constantly as they walked. They kept very close together, holding hands with their foreheads almost touching.

"So that's Nella," Lugh whispered to Kyle. "Nihs talks about her all the time. I'm pretty sure he's in love."

Kyle was shocked. "She's his sister!"

"They're not actually related. It's a thing the Kol do. When you get really close to someone in another family, you start calling them your sister or father or whatever. "

"Oh, that makes more sense. What about Kisi?"

"She really is his sister. Can't remember how many brothers and sisters Nihs actually has. I think there's five of them in all? You'll have to ask him, I can never keep the little bastards straight."

Kyle wasn't in the mood to ask Nihs about his family, especially since he couldn't tell if the 'little bastards' part of Lugh's description had been a term of endearment or something less benign. He chose instead to watch the caves around them, at least when he wasn't watching his feet.

The cave narrowed up ahead, and the buildings below them grew closer and closer together until they finally merged, forming a single platform that blocked the cave floor below from view. They walked along the tops of the buildings until the cave opened up again. Now, patches of solid, flat ground showed between the wooden boards. A river flowed across the chamber, though it was small and possibly even temporary.

There were a number of buildings here, some of them built directly on the ground and some of them on stilts. There were also more locals, and the appearance of Kyle's group among them caused a few stares.

"Oh, look!" Meya said in wonder, touching Kyle's arm.

There was a huge mushroom attached to the side of the chamber. It was at least fifty feet across and glowed with a hypnotizing bioluminescence. Water trickled down from above, running off the cap of the mushroom and forming a waterfall before adding to a small pool beneath it.

Nihs smiled. "You haven't seen anything yet. Wait until we get to the hall of colors. It's the main section of western Proks."

There were multiple paths leading out of this chamber. Kyle and the others followed Nihs and Nella through another stone passage, trusting that they knew where they were going. It was only when the ceiling lowered that Kyle started to feel claustrophobic; having to bend down to fit through certain passages was uncomfortable in more than just body. Lugh, who was a foot taller than him and who had much broader shoulders, had even more trouble.

They walked, climbed, and even crawled through the next hour or so. Deriahm had been right about Proks being a huge, sprawling city, and it didn't take long for Kyle to become completely lost. At any given moment he couldn't tell if they were still inside the city, or had wandered into some completely unknown area. Some passages led up, others led down, still others turned sharply or suddenly widened into inhabited chambers. Some caves were partially flooded, and some were covered in luminescent mushrooms. The walls of a few chambers glittered like gemstones, while others were plain but lit by the Kol's lanterns.

Finally they came to what Nihs had called the hall of colors. It was astonishing. They stopped to take in the sight, and even Deriahm, who was normally happy to keep to himself at the back of the group, came forward to admire it.

It was significantly larger than any of the caves they had encountered thus far. The far walls weren't even visible from where the party stood, and the entirety of this huge space was filled with mushrooms. They were all different sizes, and some of them were different shapes, though for the most part they were akin to the flat, luminescent types they had seen before. As with the cave behind the doors of Rhann, every available space here was built on. Many houses were perched on top of the mushrooms, with wooden bridges creating a network between them. Some sat under the wide caps, or were carved into the mushrooms themselves. Even the cave's stone walls had been hollowed out and turned into dwelling places.

It was clear why this place was called the hall of colors. Most of the mushrooms glowed with a soft blue light, though some of them were green, red, or even yellow. This combined with the Kol's own lanterns meant that the entire cave was a kaleidoscope of color. It was incredibly bright for being underground.

"All right, Kisi," Nihs said, "we've reached the hall. Now get back to your work."

"But I want to go with you!" Kisi wailed.

"Listen to your older brother, *Kisiren*," Nella said. "Run along. You can meet up with us again once you've finished for the day."

Kisi pouted, but didn't protest further. She ran off, and within seconds Kyle had lost sight of her in the confusion of the cave.

Nihs sighed, folding his arms. "It's a good thing she's so brilliant, or her behavior wouldn't be tolerated. I only hope she doesn't get into too much trouble."

"She had to come to see you," Nella said. She added another word in Kollic.

Nihs grunted. "As long as my father doesn't find out. He's angry enough about her without having me thrown into the mix."

"Does *Darizot* know you are in the city?"

"I haven't told him, though he may have gotten wind of it. I suppose it's inevitable that he will find out, though I'd prefer this visit to be as discreet as possible."

"Why is that? You are being very mysterious, *Nizu.*"

"I couldn't tell you with Kisi around. And I'd rather not talk out in the open, either. *Nellazan*, could you ask Jire and Rehs if we can stay with them while we're in the city? We'll draw less attention there."

Nella looked confused, but she said, "Of course. I will ask."

Kyle wasn't used to seeing anyone but Nihs enter the overhead, so it struck him as a little odd at first when Nella did so. They stood around, waiting for her to reemerge. Kyle had questions for Nihs, but his friend had folded his arms and was staring into the distance, clearly distracted. Kyle decided it could wait.

Nella's eyes opened. She folded her ears back against her head and stood up.

"They would be pleased to have us," she said.

"Excellent," said Nihs. "Let's not waste another minute."

"*Jiresi* and *Rezu* are family of mine who live in the city," Nella told them, as they walked. "I believe that staying with them will be easier than staying with Nihs' family. They are used to company, and outsiders."

"A lot of things sound easier than staying with Nihs' family, from what I've heard," Lugh said. Nella didn't answer, though her expression spoke volumes.

They walked down the length of the hall of colors for a short while before turning off and once again entering the caves. Walking on top of the mushrooms was a strange experience. Kyle had expected them to be soft, but they were as hard as stone. If he crouched down and chipped away at one, he could end up with a bit of phosphorescence under his fingernail, though overall the mushrooms were very resilient.

The caves beyond the hall were not so much tunnels as they were clusters of connected chambers. Spongework caves, Deriahm called them. He touched the side of the chamber with a gloved hand.

"The composition of these caves is fascinating," he said. "Here, one can see the history of the earth laid bare before us. This place has not changed since the world was in its infancy; nowhere on the island of Buoria can you see stone as old as this. These caves had already been housing the Kol for centuries when our homeland began to emerge from the sea."

"Didn't know you were so into rocks," Lugh said.

"On Buoria there is precious little else. We have no trees or plants whose shapes we can memorize. Instead, our attention is turned to the earth itself."

It was clear that many Kol lived here. There was a decent amount of foot traffic in the caves, and some of the passages were clearly thresholds, blocked off by colorful wooden or cloth barriers. Still, no one recognized Nihs or Nella, and the gazes their group attracted ranged from welcoming to unfriendly.

At the end of one passage was a human-sized entranceway covered by an ornate red curtain. Nella came up to it and called out something in Kollic, then brushed it aside and stepped in. Nihs followed her and the rest of them came after.

Beyond the curtain was a round chamber that might have accommodated fifteen people. Kyle could see another four rooms attached to this one, though this was clearly the main area of the house.

The décor Kyle could only describe as 'cozy'. The same ballistic approach that the Kol took to their architecture apparently applied to their decorating as well. On the floor were no fewer than a half-dozen rugs, all of different colors and textures. Cushions, presumably for sitting, were strewn about. Containers made of stone, wood and wicker were clustered in the corners of the room. More supplies hung from the ceiling, and there were even a few shelves made from cave mushrooms.

Against the wall to their left was what must have been the house's kitchen. A large device that gave off the blue glow of Ephicers was probably a type of oven, and the stone counter-top around it was the only raised surface in the room.

No one seemed to be home, until a stout Kol came waddling out of one of the side rooms and caught sight of them. He was male, older and more thickset than Nihs, dressed in a brown suit trimmed with gold. A pair of thick, square glasses was perched on his nose. His face lit up when he saw Nella, and he ran over to greet her, arms outstretched. After sharing a few words with her, he shook Nihs' hand as well. Kyle saw Nella gesture towards him and the others; the new Kol's gaze panned to the side and then up and up and up to meet Kyle's own.

"Well!" he said, taking off his glasses and cleaning them on his shirt. "It's been some time since we've had such…large visitors. Come in! I must know all of your names. Sit! Sit!

"I am Jire Sott Dal Proks. My partner Rehs is out getting groceries at the moment. We've housed outsiders before, you see, and we know what fantastic amounts of food you require. Most other Kol in the city have no such familiarity!"

"We're in luck, then," Lugh said, grinning, "I can really eat."

Jire was more pleased about this than anything; he was obviously enjoying the opportunity to harbor such rare, exotic creatures. His speech was much faster and more natural than Nella's; he must have spent more time practicing it.

He offered them all fortified cider, which Lugh was quick to accept. Kyle, in keeping with his habit of trying everything at least once, did as well. Once they had all settled down on the cushioned floor, they moved on to introductions. Kyle was deliberately vague when it came to his turn, as he didn't yet know if they were planning on trusting Jire with his secret.

Rehs arrived soon after, carrying huge bundles of supplies with her—at least, bundles that were huge for a Kol. She had to make multiple trips to bring it all in; that was, until Deriahm offered to help, and carried it all the rest of the way as a single armload. She greeted Nella, Jire and Nihs warmly, and then it was time for introductions all over again. Once she had gone around and shook everybody's hand, she took charge of the kitchen while Jire entertained.

Kyle leaned back against the cave wall. He was feeling much more comfortable than before. The atmosphere inside Jire and Rehs' home was warm and welcoming, nothing like the neutrality bordering on hostility he'd sensed in other parts of the city.

As they talked, Rehs brought in dishes of food from the kitchen in a steady stream. At first, Kyle was worried despite Jire's confidence that there wouldn't be enough, but Rehs was clearly prepared. Kollic food was surprisingly hearty, if almost entirely lacking in meat. Most of the dishes contained mushrooms in some capacity, and other strange vegetables and greens. Kyle was ravenous in any case, and so had nothing but appreciation for Rehs' cooking. The others clearly felt the same; the only two exceptions were Deriahm, who never ate regular food, and Meya, who didn't seem to have much of an appetite.

After they had eaten, and were sitting around the table enjoying their second round of cider, the subject of Nihs' return to the city came up once again. Both Jire and Rehs had asked the question before in passing, and now Nella was urging him to answer.

"What is it, *Nizu*, that you could not tell me with *Kisiren* around? You are not here to become a sage, are you?"

This prompted excitement from Jire and Rehs, but Nihs shook his head.

"No, no, it's nothing like that. I can tell you now, but I want to keep this as confidential as possible. There is a matter about which I want to consult the elders, but it may be hard to explain." He sighed, and looked at Kyle. "Why don't you start with the boat?"

How many times now had Kyle told his story? To Lugh and Nihs, to Meya and Phundasa, to the students Oklade and Yuma, and finally to the Buorish court. Now it was time to tell it again, only it had gotten much longer over the past several days. He covered everything up to their arrival in Proks, with the others filling in the details he missed or couldn't have known.

Truth be told, he enjoyed telling the story—at least most of it. Jire and Rehs' reactions were certainly amusing. Their shock and excitement was almost comically pronounced, and only hampered by a slight dash of skepticism. Nella's approach was more level-headed. She asked a number of probing questions and then examined Kyle's memory.

"I am amazed," she said after she had done this, taking her hands from his forehead. "All seems in harmony, and yet…" she struggled to find the right words, and then gave up and started speaking in Kollic. Nihs replied in kind, and the two of them shared a few words. Finally Nella said,

"So this is why you wish to meet with the elders. But do you really think they will be able to help?"

"Possibly," Nihs said, "though to be honest I'm more concerned that they will refuse to. Kyle has an unusual soul, but he was cursed by the assassins who were after us. He can't draw his soul sword, and you saw for yourself what happens when you try to read his memory. I'm afraid that we may not have enough proof."

Nella nodded gravely. "To meet with the elders, you need the approval of the council, and Kyle cannot come with you to the council chambers."

"I know. I'll have to try persuading them some other way."

Nella didn't seem pleased by this prospect, but for the moment she directed her attention back to Kyle. "It is amazing," she repeated. "If it is true that you have come from another world, then so much that we thought we knew is wrong. Your arrival here will not be celebrated by all."

"Tell me about it," said Kyle.

"I would like to sense your aura," Nella said then. "It may help us understand."

"That's right!" Nihs said. "You can sense auras! We haven't had anyone do it yet, and not since Kyle was cursed, either. I'd like to see as well." He stepped over and took Nella's hand.

"Do I need to do anything?" Kyle said.

"Only do not move," Nella said. She reached out an arm towards Kyle. Her eyes glazed over, and then glowed violet, while Nihs' own fluttered shut. Magic rose up around Nella, and she started to shake. Then the energy faded, and the tension went out of her body.

"Interesting," Nihs said.

"What is it?" Kyle asked.

"I sense great power in your soul," Nella said, "but it is dampened by an angry black fog that clings to your heart."

"Your soul and your soul sword are one and the same," Nihs added. "The curse is eating away at both. Right now your soul doesn't appear much different from the average Lorian's. I think we would have seen something very different if the curse wasn't dulling its power."

Kyle instinctively clutched his chest. The curse was always in the back of mind, but it was only when the subject came up that he truly sensed its presence.

"Any new ideas of what to do about it?" he asked.

"We cannot help you," Nella said, "but we are not the wisest nor the most powerful Kol in the city. The aid you seek may still be found here."

"*If* those wise and powerful Kol will agree to help him, that is," Nihs said, his voice mired in skepticism. "Which brings us back to the issue of how to handle this."

"*Nizu*," Nella said, "do you truly intend to address the council yourself?"

"I don't see that I have much choice."

"If you could prove to someone that Kyle's story is true, they may speak in your stead. You can't bring Kyle into the council chambers, but you can show him to those in the city."

"And who could I bring him to?" Nihs asked. "Who in the city do I know is trustworthy, and reputable enough to make an impression on the council?"

"Your father—"

Nihs looked as though he'd swallowed a lemon. "My father will be harder to convince than the council in its entirety. And he would never address the council in my name, even *if* he were absolutely sure that I was telling the truth. He would never take the risk, not for me."

"You cannot know that for certain."

"I'm not willing to find out."

"Then you are as stubborn as he!" Nella snapped.

"I suppose it runs in the family, then!" Nihs retorted.

Nella opened her mouth to bite back, but Rehs spoke something in Kollic, cutting her off. Both Nihs and Nella settled down as she talked, eventually replying to her in subdued voices. Jire joined the conversation and the four of them talked for some time. Kyle and the others had no choice but to sit back and wait for them to finish. Lugh shrugged and helped himself to more cider.

Eventually Nihs said, "The rest can wait until morning. It's late, and there's nothing to be gained from sitting around here talking about what may or may not be."

"You are right," Nella said. "Let us rest for tonight."

Jire and Rehs' home consisted of a small cluster of caves sectioned off from the rest of the network. Each cave was its own room, kept separate from the others by curtains or panes of colored glass. When Kyle saw what a Kollic bed looked like, he immediately understood why Nihs was always making nests out of pillows wherever they rested. Each bed was a mound of cushions piled under a cloth canopy. Initially, these were too small for the likes of Kyle and the others, but Jire and Rehs brought in extra pillows and blankets and helped them expand each bed into something useable.

Kyle settled down, unsure of how he would take to this strange arrangement. It was surprisingly comfortable, and the soft light coming from the glass lamp in his room was just dim enough to be soothing. It wasn't long before he drifted off to sleep.

Kyle dreamed, but not as before.

His dreams—in Loria, at least—had always been clear and consistent, but now things were different. Scenes from Earth mingled with more recent memories, and Kyle skipped forwards and backwards in time. Now he was in college, walking to the convenience store; now he was on the bridge of the *Ayger*, standing next to the inky ghost of Phundasa. Now he was a young child, sitting in English class surrounded by goblins; now he was standing on a black plain, facing a pale, slender figure.

Something in his mind jangled. This dream was not like the others. He blinked, and tried to focus on the man in front of him. He realized who it was just as the man began to speak.

"Have you made it to Proks?" Todd Wilder asked him. "I think I can sense you, but I can't be sure."

Kyle tried to answer, but no sound came from his mouth when he opened it.

"You can talk," Todd said, "don't convince yourself you can't. You need to answer me."

Kyle struggled to reply. "Yeah. I made it."

"Excellent. Listen carefully. Find a Kol whom you trust. Tell them to enter the overhead and ask where they can find brightfish this time of year. It's a code—a Kol by the same of Salo will answer. He can bring you to me. Do you understand?"

"Yes," Kyle said. He wanted to say more, but couldn't muster the energy.

"Good. I can't keep you here much longer. I look forward to meeting you soon. Oh, but one more thing. Tell no one else that you are here. The more who know of you, the more perilous your life becomes—and there are few in this world who are worth telling."

With that, Todd's frame flickered and disappeared, and the black plain dissolved into smoke. Kyle's vision faded, and he started to fall through the darkness.

His eyes snapped open, and he found himself back in Jire and Rehs' home.

For a moment, he sat in stunned silence, surrounded by his pile of cushions. Then he sprang to his feet and ran off to find Nihs.

He found everyone gathered in the main chamber, seated for breakfast. He scanned the group and located Nihs, sitting between Jire and Nella.

"How's it going?" Lugh said, twisting around in his seat. "You're finally up!"

"Yeah," Kyle answered, distracted. He was desperately trying to hold on to the details of his dream. "Uh, listen, Nihs—I had another dream last night."

Nihs' attention was instantly his. The Kol jumped up from the table and came around it to face him. "You mean you spoke with Rosshku again?"

"Yeah. He asked me if I'd made it to city and I said yes. Then he gave me instructions to meet him."

"Yes? What were they?"

"He said to find a Kol that I trusted and to get them to go on the overhead and ask where they could find brightfish. He said a Kol named Salo should answer, and that he could lead us to Todd."

"Really?" Nihs said. "So this man has Kol working for him, whoever he really is."

"He sounds pretty determined to meet you," Lugh added.

By this time, breakfast was entirely forgotten, and everyone had gathered around to listen. Nihs climbed up onto Lugh's shoulder and Nella did the same with Meya.

"So the question is," Nihs said, "what do we do? Before you woke, we were discussing meeting with the council. Do we put off contacting Salo until we've heard the council's verdict?"

"That reminds me," Kyle said, "Todd told me not let anyone else know that I was here. He said there weren't many people worth telling."

Nihs harrumphed. "Well! He's certainly sure enough of himself. He must think that no one but he can help you."

"If he's really that sure of himself, maybe he's right," Meya said. "Either way, I think it would be worth our while to meet with him."

"I agree," Lugh said. "Whether or not this guy is really Rosshku doesn't matter. I want to find out who he is and what he's after."

"Telling the council of Kyle is as much of a risk as meeting this man," Nella pointed out. "Others may come to know about him if we do. And we never were sure if they would be able to help us."

Nihs cupped his cheek. "So we forget about the council—the reason we came to Proks in the first place—and put our trust in the man claiming to be Rosshku?"

"The decision is yours to make," Nella said to Kyle. "It is your fate we are writing."

Kyle had already made up his mind. "Let's meet with Todd—Rosshku," he said. He wanted to add more, to justify his choice, but really, all he had was a feeling that it was the better one.

Nihs gave him a searching look, and sighed. "All right, then, we'll do things your way. Let me go on the overhead and see about these brightfish."

It wasn't long before Nihs' eyes opened once more, and his ears curled themselves into spirals at the sides of his face. Everyone immediately gathered around him for questioning.

"I've met Salo," he said. "He answered as soon as I asked about brightfish, and said he was a fisherman who could take me to where they swam. He wants to meet in Eirzed hall."

"So far so good," Lugh said.

"What's Eirzed hall?" Meya asked.

"One of the old stone halls in eastern Proks. There's nothing in it, but it's a passageway to many other parts of the caves."

"Did he wish to meet you right at once?" Nella asked.

"He said whenever I was ready, but I got the impression that sooner was better."

"Let's not waste any time, then," Lugh said. "Who's coming along?"

"As many of us as possible should go," Meya said. "In case we do run into something bad."

"We'll stay here," Jire said, putting his arm around Rehs. "Someone should stay in the house and it may as well be us. We're no fighters, I'm afraid."

"I wish to come with you," Nella said.

Nihs nodded. "Let's get going, then."

They thanked Jire and Rehs for their hospitality and made their way back to the hall of colors. It was busier at this time of day—whatever time this was—and their group attracted a number of stares from the city folk. A few people hailed Nella in Kollic as they walked, to which she always replied in kind.

They walked down the length of the hall, stepping from mushroom cap to mushroom cap. At the far end of the chamber was a narrow fissure bridged by planks of wood. They squeezed through, and emerged into another cave, this one devoid of plant life. A thin stone bridge stretched across the chamber, and Kyle could hear water running below.

"Watch your step," Nihs said. Kyle didn't need telling twice. The bridge was barely six feet wide, and the cave floor below was lost in the gloom.

It didn't take long for Kyle to become lost once again. Proks truly had no rhyme or reason; the Kol simply built wherever the caves would allow, and no two sections of the city looked the same. Nearly every cave they chanced upon had multiple entrances and exits, some of which were unreachable, or too small for someone of the likes of Kyle to enter. Some areas were lit by glass lamps or showed signs of habitation, but others may well have been miles away from the city, and Kyle would never have been able to tell.

Finally, they reached Eirzed hall. It was a huge cave with an incredibly high ceiling, and was more manufactured than other parts of the city. The floor was quite flat, and the stone columns, which lined the hall, were carved into some semblance of order. There were a number of Kol here, but the space was so vast that the hall still felt deserted.

"Here we are," Nihs said. "Salo should be around here somewhere."

Kyle felt the tension within the group increase. He touched the hilt of his sword at his hip for reassurance. Seeing the others check their weapons, he realized that while he, Meya and Lugh were all using the arms given to them by King Azanhein, Nihs still wasn't wearing his red sagecloak.

They found Salo at the far end of the hall, leaning up against one of the stone pillars. Somehow, Kyle recognized him the moment he saw him.

Though he was male, his physique was more like Nella's than Nihs'—he was slender, and was the tallest Kol Kyle had seen yet. The green of his skin was tinged with yellow, which gave him a swarthy appearance. His ears weren't folded at the sides of his head like the other Kol; instead, they ran down his back like two extremely large strands of hair.

When the group caught his eye, he got up from the wall and beckoned them over.

"Salo Rai Dal Proks?" Nihs asked.

Salo nodded, and extended his hand.

"And you must be Nihs." His eyes scanned the group. "With quite a lot of friends, I notice."

"Will that be a problem?" Nihs asked.

"Most likely not, provided the Buor there doesn't sink my boat. But let's not stand around talking. Follow me."

Salo's demeanor was kind, but it was clear that he wasn't comfortable talking where they were, so they followed him down a passage that led away from the hall. Nihs kept pace with him as he walked.

"Did I hear you correctly?" he asked. "We're actually going on a boat? I thought the brightfish were just a cover."

"Yes and no. I actually am a fisherman, as it happens. But brightfish have nothing to do with it—the best way to get to where we're going is by boat."

"Is it inside the city?"

"No, it's on the surface. Close enough to be reached from Proks, but not so close that others will stumble upon it. I'll tell you more once we're farther away."

Kyle didn't care much for the idea of following Salo through the dark tunnels to some unknown destination, but he still couldn't see anything worrisome about the situation. Salo certainly seemed harmless, and his reluctance to share details was reasonable enough given the circumstances.

This section of Proks was slightly different than what Kyle had seen before. Stonework was more common here, replacing the ramshackle wooden construction that was prevalent in western Proks. Bridges and passages were more likely to be naturally occurring, which meant their route was even less intuitive than before. Salo, however, walked with a confidence that suggested he'd made this trip many times before.

Eventually they came to a long stone slide. Its mouth was marked with a glowing lamp, but its ultimate destination was impossible to discern in the gloom.

"We're almost at the lake," Salo said. "We're going down this way. You big ones watch your heads." And with that, he sat on the lip of the slide, pushed himself off and zoomed down into the darkness.

Lugh put his foot on the edge of the slide and leaned over it.

"Great," he said, "this should be fun. I'll go first. If I get stuck I'll need you guys to come down after and dislodge me." He unhooked his weapon from his back and sat down, holding it in his lap. He pushed off with his hands as Salo had done.

"Here goes nothing!" he called out as he started to gain speed. A moment later, he was gone.

Nihs went after him, then Nella and Meya. Kyle went next, leaving Deriahm for last—the *irushai* insisted this be so, saying that he would have to figure out a way of using the slide in his heavy and distinctly non-slippery armor.

Kyle sat down and pushed off. The ride began slowly enough, but then the chute got steeper, and Kyle started to pick up speed. The chute curved to the left, carried on for some time, and then dropped off steeply. Kyle sucked in his breath and flattened his back against the floor; the ceiling was so low that even sitting down he would have hit his head.

By now, the chute was incredibly steep. It twisted to the right, becoming shallower. Suddenly, it was over, and Kyle surprised himself by landing on his feet when the chute ejected him several feet off the ground.

He staggered upright and got his bearings. The others were gathered nearby; Lugh was sitting on the ground, and Meya was healing a cut on his temple. He grimaced at Kyle when he saw him approach.

"Bumped my head," he said, pointing to the cut. "Damn Kol. How was I supposed to get through that in one piece?"

"You need to be more careful," Meya said. "I don't think you can afford much more damage to this area."

Lugh laughed out loud, and Kyle found himself laughing as well.

Deriahm came down not too long after, having padded his back with his cloak and the contents of his travel pack. He came out of the chute feet first, with his arms crossed over his chest, and landed smartly on two feet. Lugh glared at him but said nothing.

"Are we all here?" Salo asked. "Good. Follow me."

He took off at an angle to the mouth of the chute. Kyle and the others followed, trying to get a sense of the new space they were in. To their left was a solid stone wall, but to their right Kyle sensed a large empty space. It was only after his eyes became attuned to the darkness that he could make out the smooth black mass that blanketed the right side of the chamber.

It's a lake, he realized.

Salo led them around the edge of the lake, until they reached a small dock attached to an equally small storehouse. The lights were off and the building looked abandoned, but Salo walked in as if it belonged to him and took some equipment from inside.

At the end of the dock was an oddly-shaped boat. It had a wooden frame lined with golden tigoreh, and instead of a motor had a number of fins extending out from behind.

It must have been a large boat by Kol standards, since it was just big enough to fit all of them inside. The crystal-clear water of the lake rippled as they embarked. Once they were all on board, Salo untethered the boat from its dock and jumped in himself. He switched it on, and the boat hummed into life, a faint light coming from its tigoreh fins. It slid gently away from the dock and set out over the lake. Kyle could see absolutely nothing ahead of him, but Salo apparently knew where they were going.

Their guide relaxed once they were out over the lake, satisfied that no one would be listening in.

"We've got a ways to go," he said. "There are three more lakes between where we are and where we're going."

"Where exactly *is* it we're going?" Nihs asked.

"There's an exit to the surface to the east of here. I found it by accident once while I was fishing. My employer decided to settle down in a valley nearby, since no other Kol knows about it, as far as I'm aware."

"Your employer?" Nihs said, unable to keep the skepticism out of his voice.

Salo smiled thinly. "What would you like me to tell you, *Nizu?* You know who he claims to be. And yes, that is who he is—but you won't believe that until you've met him. So I'll let you decide for yourself."

This obviously rankled. "You mean to tell me," Nihs said, "that Rosshku the Archmage lives still, that he's hiding not too far from Proks—and that you're the only one who knows about it?"

"Of course. He doesn't want his existence to be widely known. And the reason he chose me as his spokesperson is that I was convenient. I have access to his hiding place, but more importantly, I have no reputation to uphold in the city. A more influential or respectable Kol wouldn't have been able to keep the secret nearly as well."

Nella said something softly in Kollic, and this garnered a few replies, but soon the conversation died down again. Not for the first time Kyle wished he knew what had been said.

The boat glided smoothly across the lake, and passed under a stone archway. The next cave was larger, and a tiny bit of light shone down upon it from above. Craning his neck, Kyle thought he saw the fissure that was the source of the light.

It was completely silent out over the lake; the effect was both calming and eerie. Salo's boat barely made any noise, and the others had all fallen silent, perhaps as a result of the quietness of the environment.

Once they had crossed over the second lake, Salo made a left turn and squeezed the boat through a tunnel narrow enough for Kyle to reach out and touch the cave wall on either side. The water here was flowing, if very gently.

They emerged into a small cavern with no fewer than six exits. Water rushed in and out of these exits at various speeds. It was quite loud, and the current was surprisingly strong.

Sal pointed across the chamber. "That's where we're headed," he said. "Be careful now, I might scrape against the walls a tad. I'd appreciate it if you could keep me away from them."

He revved the boat's motor and set off at a good speed, trying to beat the influence of the current. The boat wobbled, pitched to the right, and would have crunched against the cavern wall if Lugh hadn't reached an arm out to steady it. Salo, his brow furrowed with concentration, wove the boat into the exit and then immediately turned left through a passage Kyle hadn't seen.

This was incredibly narrow, and made worse by the fact that the wall on their left bulged outward above the water, forcing them all to the right side of the boat as they passed by it. Salo's boat scraped both sides of the passageway and once got completely stuck; they had to shift around inside the boat and push against the cave walls to get it moving again. Once they were through, the passage widened, at least enough so that they weren't in danger of getting wedged in place.

Salo let out a relieved sigh. "I was worried about that part," he admitted. "I've never done it with so much weight in the boat. We're almost there now."

Kyle let his eyes and mind wander as they continued on their way. He couldn't believe that all of this was under the mountains of Eastia. It was no wonder that no one else had found this place; he never would have been comfortable exploring these maze-like caves on his own. Though he realized that the Kol probably never really worried about getting lost—after all, they could always rely on the overhead for help.

The cave grew brighter and brighter as they moved forward. The air became moist, and greenery clung to the ceiling and flourished in the water around them. The boat came to a gentle slope that rose out of the water and led upward through a moss-covered passageway. Salo drove his boat up onto the shore, and they disembarked.

Lugh stretched, his hands brushing against the vines that dangled from the ceiling.

"Phew! What a ride. Couldn't Rosshku have picked a better spot to hide out?"

Salo grinned. "This way," he said, running up the passage. "Be careful, your eyes will take a moment to adjust to the sun."

The passage had a low ceiling, but was wide, and its slope was gentle. The amount of greenery on the floor and ceiling increased along with the light from the sun as they walked. Finally they emerged into daylight, and Kyle gasped, squinting and shielding his eyes with a hand.

They were in a secluded valley surrounded on all sides by low mountains. It was lush with green and gold vegetation, and the air was surprisingly warm under the sun. Nestled in one of the crooks of the valley was a large silver airship. Kyle stopped to stare at it as did the others; it was one of the last things he'd expected to see here.

"That is Rosshku's airship," Salo said. "In Kollic, it is called *Aresa Bign.*"

"The moving mind," Nihs said in wonder. "Rosshku has an airship? I never would have imagined."

Kyle had to agree. It was difficult to reconcile the idea of an ancient sage with that of a modern airship. By now he was burning with curiosity and a desire to meet this mysterious figure.

They followed Salo up through the valley and toward the *Aresa Bign.* It was a beautiful airship; the rich quality of its silver polish made Kyle think of white gold, and its execution was simple but graceful. It was about the same size as the *Ayger*, but its shape was fuller, reminding Kyle more of a whale than a bird.

He looked over at Lugh and saw an expression on his friend's face that could only be described as lust.

"Saints forgive me," he said, "but if there were ever an airship that could replace the *Ayger*…"

"I hope you're not thinking of stealing the Archmage's ship," Meya said. "Something tells me that wouldn't end very well."

The *Aresa's* ramp was already lowered as they approached. The ship had clearly been docked here for some time.

Salo paused as they were about to embark.

"I'm sure I don't need to tell you this, but you're about to enter the presence of Archmage Rosshku. Please be courteous, and don't poke around his ship without his permission. He has a huge collection of books and many of them are extremely rare." Salo's demeanor had changed; he had become calmer and more humble the closer they came to the *Aresa.*

"Books, huh?" Lugh said. "You need to be warning Nihs, not me."

"Rosshku is said to be one of the first great minds of magical study," Deriahm said. "Is it possible that many of these books he wrote himself?"

"Yes, that's correct," Salo said. "Now, shall we enter? The Archmage already knows we are here. I would prefer not to keep him waiting."

There was a tangible change in the atmosphere as soon as they boarded the *Aresa Bign.* Everything felt welcoming and calm, and a deep serenity permeated the air. Whatever doubts Kyle had about the imminent meeting with Rosshku faded away. He felt safe, refreshed, and clear-headed, and the longer he stayed inside the *Aresa* the stronger the feeling became.

He looked at his companions and could tell they were feeling the same.

"What's going on?" he asked. His voice came out quieter than he had intended.

"This must be Rosshku's aura," Nihs replied. "It's saturated the entire ship."

Salo nodded. "I've boarded the *Aresa* a dozen times and I'm still getting used to it. Come this way."

Walking on to the *Aresa* was more like entering a library than an airship. Books filled every available space, in such volumes that it was impossible to make out anything else about the room they were in. Shelves extended from floor to ceiling, each one completely crammed with books of every shape, size, and age. Any space not occupied by books was taken up by potted plants, intricate tigoreh devices, desks covered in writing materials, and other curios that must have come from all corners of the world.

Kyle felt as though he had stepped into Rosshku's mind by boarding his airship. Though there were many places where disorganization had won out, none of Rosshku's possessions gave the impression of being neglected or forgotten. In fact, Kyle could sense a sort of energy emanating from the bookshelves, as if the airship and everything within it was alive.

As Kyle watched, a book slid out from its shelf of its own accord and drifted serenely down the hallway and up the stairs. Another book floated across its path a few seconds later, and slotted itself into a narrow space near the ceiling.

"Is Todd doing that?" Kyle asked quietly.

"Yes," Salo answered. "The library is an extension of his mind, and his mind is constantly changing and improving. Remember, don't touch anything."

Salo led them up the same set of stairs that the book had taken, and they emerged on the ship's bridge. There were books here, too, though they were kept to the back of the room to allow space near the front window. The ship's wheel was mounted in the center of a huge desk that followed the curve of the hull. The desk was covered in books, papers, writing materials, and a myriad of tools and trinkets.

There was a man seated at the desk, with his back to the party. The book that had flown upstairs before them was floating at his side, open, along with two others. The man was glancing up at them as he wrote in another book with a delicate glass pen. He continued to work for a moment after they came in, then stood and turned to face them. The three books snapped shut, but they remained floating, their covers facing the party as if keeping an eye on them.

Kyle instantly saw the similarity between this man and the one who had spoken to him in his dreams. Rosshku was tall and slight, his hair was completely white, and he had the faintest hint of a beard. There were differences as well. The Todd in his dreams had had glassy blue eyes, but this man had eyes that were deep violet. This Rosshku was also older, though there was something about his face that tricked the eye. At first glance, he looked as though he might be thirty or forty, but a moment later it seemed reasonable to think he could be seventy or eighty. Kyle wondered if it was possible for a face to accumulate so many wrinkles that it began to give the impression of smoothness once again. Rosshku wore a plain but elegant suit in muted colors, and his expression was welcoming.

As before in Azanhein's throne room, Kyle felt his senses shift and distort in Rosshku's presence. This, more than anything else, proved that he was genuine—at least, genuinely powerful. While Azanhein's aura had blurred Kyle's mind and made him feel the weight of the Buorish king's power, Rosshku's was serene, friendly and wise. When the Archmage smiled in greeting, Kyle felt as if he'd known him his entire life, and his fears and concerns melted away.

Salo approached and bowed deeply. "I have brought the ones you sought, *Solrusien Rosshku!*"

"You have my thanks, Salo," Rosshku said. "May you leave us for the time being? We have quite a lot to talk about."

"Of course, great Archmage." Salo rose to his feet and promptly left.

Rosshku smiled. "I've given up on telling him to refer to me without titles. I think he relishes the opportunity for ceremony. Welcome, all of you. I am Archmage Rosshku. I have a number of other names, but I find that the more I collect, the more I come to miss the one I was given the day I was born. So, please—call me Todd. What are your names?"

"I'm Lugh," Lugh said. "This is Kyle and Meya. Short one's Nihs, the other short one's Nella, and that's Deriahm."

"A pleasure to meet you," Todd said. "There's much I have to tell you, but I'm sure you have your own questions to ask. I'll answer them as best I can."

Where to start? Kyle thought.

"I have a question," Nihs said. His voice was trembling, but he strode forward and looked up at the Archmage. "Are you really the person that the old legends speak of? Are you the same Rosshku who was said to be alive seven hundred years ago? The one who established some of our earliest magical laws?"

"I am, though the races' knowledge of me has been corrupted over the years. I don't know what you've heard about me, Nihs, but I can tell you that some of it is true, and some of it is not. It is true that many of your laws of magic are derived from discoveries that I once made. There was a time that I lived and worked openly with your ancestors; that time, as you can see, has passed."

Nihs was unable to keep himself from talking further. "If that's true," he said, his voice stuck between disbelief and awe, "why have you hidden yourself away from the world for so long? Where have you been, what have you been doing? And why are you coming to us now?"

Todd smiled. "Simple questions with complicated answers. To answer your second question, I've been around the world a hundred times since my disappearance. As for what I've been doing, 'studying' would likely be the best way to describe what's kept me occupied for all that time.

"The answers to your first and third questions are linked. As a Kol, you feel a close connection to the earth and the balance of nature, don't you?"

Nihs looked surprised. "Well…yes. I suppose so."

"There's no need to be humble. The Kol have always taken pride in their attunement to the forces that control this world. After all, your society is built around magic, and you can't study magic without becoming swept up in it."

Todd stepped over to a bookshelf near his desk and traced a finger down the spine of one of the books. Kyle would have sworn that it trembled slightly at his touch. "I've dedicated my life to the study of magic, and my life has been a long one. I've gained quite a bit of power over the course of my studies, and this means that I share a link with the earth that runs deeper than most. That's why I spend most of my time observing the world, rather than acting on it. If I were to exercise my power, I could very well change the nature of the world itself, and the course of racial history. Interference is a dangerous path to tread, so I distance myself from the conflicts of the world." He looked at Deriahm. "I believe the Buors have taken a similar stance in the past."

Deriahm was surprised that Todd had singled him out, but he cleared his throat and said, "That is true, *Solrusien.* They believe it is often preferable to allow history to run its course, than to force Buorish values and judgments upon others."

Todd nodded. "Does that answer your question, Nihs?"

Nihs looked down at the floor. "I suppose so," he said. "But that still leaves why you chose to reveal yourself to us now."

"The reason is simple. A little less than a month ago, I sensed an imbalance in the forces of nature; an incredibly vast power where none had existed before. Even when my mind was unfocused, I could feel it moving around the world, every one of its footfalls an earthquake that changed the makeup of the earth."

"Me," Kyle said sullenly.

Todd gave a faint smile. "Yes, Kyle, it was your presence that I sensed. At first, I wasn't sure what it was you were. But now that you're standing before me, I have no doubts. You're a traveler from another world, are you not?"

"That's right," Kyle said. His heart was pounding, as it always did when he felt he was close to getting answers. "So you know about people like me?"

"In theory, yes. Certain magical conjecture speaks of beings known as 'vagrants'...creatures that travel between worlds."

"Vagrants, you say?" Nihs said. "So there's a word for what Kyle is. But do these beings exist only in theory?"

"It's difficult to say. I myself have never encountered one before now, and there's no way of knowing how many others there have been in the past."

Kyle's heart sank. If Todd himself had never met a vagrant before, how was he going to help them? There were other questions on his mind, but right now he had to know one thing. "Todd," he said, "can you help me? I mean—is it possible for me to go back to my own world? Can you do that?"

Todd looked at him gravely. "I can't," he said, "but I know someone who can."

It was later. At first, Todd had refused to talk more about getting Kyle back home. Before he did, he wanted to know everything there was to know about Kyle's situation. They talked for hours under the influence of his aura of lucidity. They told the Archmage of Kyle's life before Loria, of his arrival on the planet, and of his first days there. They talked about Reno and the goblin mine, where his soul sword had first appeared. Then they spoke of Buoria, and the monster that had arisen from Kyle's phone. Finally they spoke of the assassins, Lian and Lacaster, who had sealed his soul sword away in trying to capture him.

Todd listened to all of this in attentive silence. Books were constantly floating around him, and every once in a while he would glance at one as it opened in front of him. This had been going on ever since they'd entered Todd's company, and Kyle was starting to think that it never stopped.

"I see you've experienced for yourselves the fate of the vagrant in this world," he said when they were done. "Despite your best efforts, Kyle, you influence the world around you with every action you take. A simple mistake like losing your phone led to the birth of a monster. And the people of Loria aren't without guilt, either. Power is captivating, and your soul is incredibly powerful. You've been in Loria for such a short amount of time, and already you've brought out the worst of some its inhabitants."

"But it's not Kyle's fault these things are happening!" Meya said.

"Of course not. But the problem remains. Whether Kyle's power is used for good or evil, it's still power—unnatural, unfathomable power. Loria trembles under his influence, and if someone were to capture Kyle or cause him to turn his power against it, it could easily be destroyed."

Kyle shivered. He was reminded once again of King Azanhein's parting words, and wondered just how much the king had understood. But something wasn't quite adding up in his mind.

"I don't understand," he said. "A couple different people have said how much power I have, but I don't seem to have that much power at all.

Even if my soul sword can cut through anything, it's still just one sword. As far as I know I can't do anything else."

"You haven't yet discovered your true potential," Todd said gravely. "But once you do, the only thing left to limit you will be the boundaries of your own mind."

"What exactly do you mean by that?" Nihs asked. "Just how powerful *could* Kyle become?"

"He is from a universe that follows the same rules as that of our creator," Todd said. "He's as powerful here as a manifestation of our world's creator would be. One particle of his soul contains as much energy as the rest of the universe combined."

Silence greeted his words. "He's more powerful than the universe?" Nihs said, in a small voice.

"He has the potential to be. This potential can be limited; raw magical capacity doesn't necessarily translate into power. But even at a fraction of his full strength Kyle would be a force to be reckoned with."

"Maybe it's a good thing I was cursed, then," Kyle said. "If it keeps me from drawing my soul sword, maybe it'll keep me from becoming too dangerous, too."

He could tell from Todd's expression that the Archmage did not agree. "Your curse is extremely worrisome," he said. "I don't know how a Lorian managed to create something that can limit your power. I suspect there is something deeper at work here."

"You think whoever cursed him is a vagrant, too?" Meya said.

"Not necessarily. But whoever it was has access to knowledge that he or she should not have. In any case, I would like to perform some tests on you, Kyle. I wish to better understand the nature of your soul, and of your curse."

The Archmage read his memories and sensed his aura as Nella had done, and then carried on with a number of other tests Kyle did not recognize. All while he worked, books flew to and fro, opening up for the Archmage to read and then floating back to their shelves. Some of them lingered even when their work was done, as if watching Todd's progress. Kyle was somewhat intimidated by his bizarre audience.

When he was done, Todd said, "The curse has put your soul in conflict with itself. It's clever—quite possibly the only way of limiting your power. I may be able to break it, but it will be difficult, and painful. Would you like me to try?"

"Please," Kyle said.

Todd nodded, and made a beckoning movement with his hand. A large, red volume flew in front of him, and he held out his hand, causing it to flip open. He glanced at it for a moment, and the pages stirred.

"Brace yourself," he said.

A wind stirred inside the airship, and the room filled with the sound of rustling paper. It was as if the books were all murmuring in response to Todd's power. He extended his free arm, and his eyes glowed violet. Light built up, and pain started to grow in Kyle's chest. The wind, the light and the pain grew together in intensity until Kyle sank to all fours, blind and deaf. The force of Todd's power was overwhelming. He could feel it washing over him, engulfing his being and drilling into him, seeking the source of the curse. The angry presence at his core flared up even as the magic attacked it, until the pain became all-encompassing.

Finally it was over. Kyle remained on all fours, panting, trying not to throw up, until Lugh and Meya ran to his side. They helped him to his feet, and Meya conjured a soft light that soothed the pain in his chest.

"The curse is tenacious," Todd said, as the red book in front of him closed with a *snap*. "Make no mistake, your enemy is a dangerous one."

"You couldn't break it?" Nihs said, dismayed.

"Not completely, no. But I have weakened it. It should be safe to draw your soul sword now."

"That's great!" Lugh said. "That sword's been the difference between life and death before."

Once Kyle felt steady enough on his feet, he raised his arm and focused. His soul sword grew out of his hand, hissing and shooting sparks. It looked the same as it always had, except for a barely perceptible black fog that curled around his hand. It hurt; stabs of pain shot through his arm and his closed fist throbbed. But it was his soul sword, and he could draw it again. It was an immense relief.

The others sighed in wonder, and even Todd looked impressed. "Excellent," he said. "I'm sorry I can't restore it fully. As it is, the curse will weaken you as long as the sword's drawn. Only use it when you absolutely have to."

Kyle absorbed the sword back into his palm. "I'll remember that," he promised.

"I hadn't counted on you having some of your powers sealed," Todd said. "The road ahead would have been difficult enough at your full strength. All of you will need to be as prepared as possible for what is to come."

This made them pause. "What do you mean?" Kyle asked.

Todd took a moment to answer. He leaned on his desk, looking out of the *Aresa*'s picture window. He said, in a faraway voice, "As far as I'm aware, there's only one other being in this world who has a greater understanding of magic than I do. A very long time ago, this man was my mentor. His name is Archsage Vohrusien."

"'Son of the void'?" Nihs translated what Kyle could only assume was a Kollic name. "I've never heard that name before."

"You wouldn't have. My name has been forgotten by history, but my tutor's name was never known to begin with. He lives a life of deep isolation, imprisoned by an ancient magical seal. He can't leave his dwelling place, nor has he any desire to."

"Where is this dwelling place?" Meya asked.

"He lives in a black tower on the continent of Westia. You would know its location as the impact site of the meteor that struck the planet over a thousand years ago."

"No," Nihs said quietly. A noticeable shiver went through the others in the group.

Kyle was confused. "I don't get it," he said, "what's so bad about that?"

"The impact site of the great meteor is the most dangerous place in the world," Nihs said, his voice subdued. "The area is saturated in wild magic, and is swarming with powerful monsters."

"Some people say that the meteor is what brought monsters to the world," Lugh explained. "I don't know if I believe it, but either way the impact site's one nasty place. You have to be insane or insanely powerful to go there. So how are *we* supposed to do it?" he asked Todd.

"I'll provide whatever help I can," Todd said, "but even so, yes, it will be difficult—the most difficult journey of your lives thus far, I'm sure. But if you want to have any hope of returning Kyle to his home world and restoring balance to ours, you don't have a choice."

Silence greeted his words. Kyle could tell that his companions were deep in thought. It was the first time he'd seen Lugh react to a proposal with anything but confidence.

"It's late," Todd said, glancing out the window. "You all have an important decision to make, and I'm sure you'll want to discuss things in private. You can stay here for the time being; Salo will show you to your rooms. I'd offer you something to eat, but I have nothing—I have no need for food. My aura will grant you the same ability, at least for a few days. We can continue in the morning. By then, I need to know which of you will be going with Kyle to the end of his journey."

Salo appeared a moment later, as if summoned. He led them to the back of the *Aresa*, where there were a number of unoccupied rooms they could stay in.

"Rosshku wishes to see me," he said, once he was done showing them around. "I'll be back later if you need me." He scampered off.

Unlike the *Ayger's* rooms, which had been designed for single occupants, each of their rooms on the *Aresa* had at least two beds each. They were clearly never used, since they were as full of books and knickknacks as the rest of the ship.

They gathered in Kyle and Nihs' room to meet, as had become their tradition.

"Well, would you imagine that," Lugh said, stretching. "It turns out Rosshku was real after all."

"We've all been treated to an amazing honor," Nihs said quietly. "We've met a living piece of our world's history. If only I had time to speak with him more."

"I am sure the opportunity will come," Deriahm said. "But for the time being, there is a more pressing matter that demands our attention. *Solrusien*'s final mandate was that we decide who will be making the journey to Westia. I believe that this matter should be settled before all else."

"You've got a point," Lugh said, tapping at his stone eye patch. "Well, I'm in."

"Lugh, you don't—" Kyle said.

"Hey," Lugh said, jabbing a finger at him. "Don't you start with that again, you hear? I'm seeing this through to the end."

"Me too," Meya said. "We still haven't found the one who sent the twins after you. Until we do, Das' real murderer is at large. Besides," she added, with a hint of her old humor, "you need me. You won't survive Westia without a healer."

"I'm coming too," Nihs said. "I think that should be obvious. We're on the cusp of some amazing things here. I wouldn't miss what's coming next for the world."

"My journey has been a short one so far," Deriahm said, looking at the ground. "I am inexperienced, and am painfully aware of the difficulty of the mission that Rosshku is suggesting. However, I also believe that he would not set a goal upon us that he thought impossible to achieve. With his guidance, I am sure we will return safely from Westia."

That left Nella. She dipped her head and said, "I am sorry, *Nizu*. I cannot come with you. I am not an adventurer, and I have responsibilities in the city I cannot abandon."

"That's all right, Nella," Nihs said, touching his forehead to hers. "I wouldn't expect you to. Besides, I need at least one person outside of my family mentoring Kisi while I'm gone. Otherwise she might turn out like them."

Nella laughed, and the others laughed with her. Lugh caught Kyle's gaze from across the room.

"Well, Kyle?" he said, spreading his arms. "What do you think? Look like a good team to take with you to meet an ancient wizard at the end of the world?"

At first, Kyle couldn't figure out why Lugh had said this. But then, as the others turned their attention to him, he realized what his friend had done. Lugh had subtly elected him as the leader of their group. Before, Lugh and the others had always been leading Kyle to his new destination. But the journey to Westia would be his, and his friends would be following him. He felt his heart swell.

"Couldn't have asked for a better one," he said. "But I don't have much of a choice anyway, do I? You'll follow me whether I want you to or not."

"That's right, so get used to it." Lugh scratched his chin. "Westia, huh? Never been there. Heard it's cold as hell once you move inland."

"The continent is in the dead of winter right now," Nella said. "You are going to need some very warm clothes."

"Not to mention provisions," Nihs said. "There are no settlements inside the impact site, which means we'll be making the trek with whatever we can bring along."

"It is true that the impact site is barren and uninhabited," Deriahm said, "though the local Orcs have a number of encampments scattered most everywhere else on the continent. They are said to be somewhat xenophobic, but I am sure they will be willing to lend us assistance in the areas leading up to the crater."

"We also haven't seen what kind of help Todd is willing to lend," Nihs said. "Who knows what kind of aid the Archmage has in store for us."

"We'll figure it out," Meya said firmly. "One way or another, we'll get to that tower. We've gotten through everything else so far."

"Damn right," Lugh said.

In the past—or even a few days ago—Kyle might not have believed this. But right now, oddly enough, he did. For the first time since he'd arrived on Loria, he knew exactly where he had to go and what he had to do. Get to Westia, reach the impact site, meet with Archsage Vohrusien. It wouldn't be easy, but Kyle wasn't worried. The confidence his companions had in him was infectious, and he found himself reciprocating their faith.

Whatever this world threw at them, they would face it together. And they would win.

End of Book 2